Rufus
The Lost Years

In 1840 the demand for beaver was gone, leaving the mountain men searching for another way to survive.

James Oliver Virmala

Edition 1

Cover Photo By James Oliver Virmala

"Lower Falls from Artist Point
Yellowstone"

DEDICATION

This book is dedicated to the volunteers who spend hours doing for others and ask for little more than a thank you in return. The satisfaction from doing good is their greatest reward.

CONTENTS

BOOKS BY THE AUTHOR

Oli's Gold Book One
Search For Oli's Gold Book Two
Return To Oli's Gold Book Three
To Be A Mountain Man
Trouble On The Kansas Plains
Frontier Justice
Return Of The Mountain Man
The Tall Man
The Prospector
The Green Valley
Twilight Of The Mountain Man
The Mother Lode
Quest Of The Mountain Man
Journey's End
Rufus Pike
Rufus And The Pup
The Winding Trail Home
Rufus The Lost Years
The Kankakee Kid
Bogus Island
Tyler Tomas The Brothers' War
War of 1812 The Choice

CHAPTER ONE

Thunder crashed and the rain poured down over the confluence of Green River and Horse Creek. It was 1840 and the mountain men and several braves from surrounding tribes had gathered for the final Rocky Mountain Rendezvous.

The weather did not dampen the spirits of the hard-drinking and playing attendees. One of them was a buckskin-clad man with shoulder-length, light brown hair and a winter beard with some streaks of gray showing. His name was Rufus Pike. He was of medium height and had a gravelly voice and an infectious laugh.

The 34 year-old mountain man sat under a spreading oak with a bottle of whiskey. His only regret was that the inclement weather had stopped the card game he had been in when he was sure that things were just about to go his way. He had been coming to the rendezvous since the first one in 1825.

This rendezvous was put together by Andrew Drips, Jim Bridger and Henry Fraeb. They had left

Westport with more supplies and whiskey than the year before, even though the yield of beaver pelts had continually decreased each of the past several years. Many of the trappers were now going to Fort Hall, Fort Crockett, or Fort Robidoux to trade, paying lower prices for their supplies. What they didn't get were the festivities that the rendezvous provided, and that was something Rufus would not miss.

Rufus saw a lanky figure running toward him, splashing in the puddles with every step. He recognized the tall, dark-haired man as his trapping partner, Caleb Weeks. Caleb's father had been a tall Englishman and his mother a Mexican beauty. He carried characteristics of both. In 1836 the mountain man had rescued the young man, on the open prairie after his father had been killed by Cheyenne and mother had died from a lingering illness.

"It looks to be clearing in the west," Caleb called to him.

"I sure hope the hell it does," Rufus replied. "The caravan is fixing to leave in two days and I got whiskey money left, not to mention there's a sweet woman I promised to visit tonight."

"I got most of our stuff packed and ready under the tarp, and then the rain come," the young man told his friend.

"You been a good trapping partner, Pup" the mountain man told him. "If you change your mind about going to your uncle's in Santa Fe, you are welcome to join me in Franklin. Maybe we could find something else to hunt and trap next winter."

Pup was a nickname Rufus had given Caleb. His name in the Bible meant "the trusted one," or "faithful dog." He had told Caleb he called him that because when they met, the young man was just a pup. Caleb remembered how hard Rufus had tried to get rid of him back in 1836, and now he was offering another winter together.

Taking the bottle from Rufus, the young man took a swig and handed it back. "It's time for me to settle down and start a family," Caleb told him. "That won't happen here in the mountains."

"Hell, in the next two days I can get you a wife from one of the tribes. She can travel with us and take care of our camp," the mountain man offered.

The young man just smiled and shook his head no. While he loved the carefree life of living in the mountains, he felt an emptiness and hoped it could be filled in Santa Fe.

The rain was beginning to slacken and the two men sat without speaking under the oak, each in their own thoughts. There was little doubt that while Caleb's went to Santa Fe, Rufus' thoughts didn't go any farther than this evening and the woman he was to meet.

* * *

Two days later the two men had their last breakfast together, and after a quick wave Rufus rode east along the Sweetwater River. Thanks to Caleb hanging on to his supply money, the mountain man would be in good shape this coming winter. Rufus had little control with his spending when there was whiskey, women, or cards available. When he mixed the latter two with whiskey, he was an easy mark.

Rufus did not mind losing his money as long as it wasn't plain that he had been cheated. The mountain man always figured there was a way to make more either working with a pack train, guiding hunters from the east, or even scouting for the army. He didn't much care for manual labor unless it was to build a shack for winter or cut firewood for cooking, and he sure as hell wasn't going to go buffalo hunting. He had done so in his youth, but no more.

His first stop would be Fort William on the Laramie River. He needed supplies for the remaining trip to Franklin, Missouri. In Franklin he had a good friend living there who had trapped with him for 12 years. Walter Gray had taught Rufus the finer points of catching beaver.

The two of them had been coming back from a rendezvous when they'd been attacked by Blackfoot. Walter had ended up with a broken leg and had been scalped. While he had survived the attack, his days of trapping were over. Walter had purchased a livery in Franklin and Rufus would go back and see him each summer. Rufus often said that it was because supplies were cheaper there, but the truth was Walter was the closest thing to family that the mountain man had.

Rufus was riding a grulla and leading a brown mustang with his packs. He had had his Hawken rifle converted to percussion caps two years ago and carried it across the saddle in front of him. He would meet up with the caravan from the rendezvous at Fort William and travel with it most of the way east. They had to stop at Fort William and get rid of some of the unsold supplies that were left due to the smaller rendezvous crowd.

The first evening he waded the horses across the fifth crossing of the Sweetwater River and made camp. The spot offered good cover from anyone looking for trouble and had plenty of wood for a fire. After pulling the gear off the horses, he picketed them on some lush grass and went to collect sticks and some bigger branches for his fire.

"The darn pup could have come with me," he complained. "He could have had coffee on while I got the horses taken care of."

Each year Caleb had gone with him as far as Fort William and then they would partner up again when Rufus came back from Franklin. The mountain man would make a few dollars helping out the caravan on its trip east, mostly hunting for meat and providing an extra rifle for protection.

The mountain man also carried two Kentucky flintlock pistols, which provided extra firepower in a close-up fight. One of the pistols was always carried in his broad belt next to his short axe, while the other was kept loaded and ready in his saddle bag. He had been a bit envious when Caleb had returned the first year with a Colt Paterson that held five rounds. He never did admit it to the young man, and he did appreciate having the extra firepower along.

The trip from the South Pass to the fort would take around 10 days. Rufus could make it in less but didn't feel the need to push his horses. His meal that night was simple. He had shot a rabbit earlier in the day, roasted it over his fire and made a fine supper. Rufus put a portion aside for his breakfast. He had bought coffee and tobacco at the rendezvous and he enjoyed them both after eating.

The night was still, with only the sounds of the river flowing through the rock-strewn bed. It was almost too quiet. Rufus had dowsed his fire before dark and sat listening. Either a storm was coming or there was something prowling around. He wanted to spit but didn't want to alert anything of his presence. Soundlessly, the mountain man moved back into the boulders behind his camp.

There was a splash! Rufus held his breath and looked up-river. Then he heard muttering. "You damn clumsy bastard. Can't you watch your damn step?"

Relief swept through Rufus. It wasn't Indians and surely wasn't a wolf or mountain lion. What the hell a white man would be doing stumbling in the dark, Rufus did not know. The mountain man remained quiet and watched for the man, or men, to appear.

The complaining continued. "You smelled the damn meat cooking. There got to be a camp around here someplace."

Then, in the dim light of a quarter-moon, Rufus saw the shape of the man. He was bent over and had a walking stick. If he continued, the man would walk right into Rufus' camp. "Stop where you are!" the mountain man commanded.

The poor bastard almost jumped out of his skin as he stumbled back and tripped. Again, there was the sound of splashing and he landed on his backside in the river. "For God's sake!" the man exclaimed. "You damn near made me mess myself."

"Well it would have all worked out," Rufus replied. "You are already in the river and could have washed up."

The mountain man watched as the man crawled out of the river. Using his walking stick, he stood up. "Was that your cooking I smelled?"

"If it smelled like a rabbit roasting, it was mine," Rufus said.

"Rabbit," the man said. "I sure do like rabbit."

In the moonlight, Rufus saw an old, bent, white-haired man with a beard and moustache that was in need of trimming. He wasn't over five feet-tall and his clothes hung loose on his skinny frame.

"My name's Rufus Pike," the mountain man told him. "I'm headed for Fort William."

"I heard of you," the man said. "They say you're a mean cuss. My name's Rollie"

"Well, Rollie, I guess I don't have to shoot you. I got a bit of rabbit left and some coffee that might still have some warmth in it," Rufus said. "Put down your pack and I'll get it for you."

Sliding his knapsack off his back, Rollie stomped his feet to shake some of the water from his wool pants. "You ain't set up much of a camp," the man pointed out. "You ain't even got a fire going."

"Don't need a fire after dark," Rufus replied. "It just brings in bad company."

"There you go," Rollie said. "That's the meanness they talk about."

Laughing, the mountain man replied, "The meanness they talk about is when I loosen someone's teeth or break a nose. Not having a fire after dark is just common sense."

"So you say," the man replied. "Now about that rabbit."

Rufus brought over the last of the rabbit and his coffee pot. He heard Rollie's clothes squish when he sat down. Setting them down near the man, Rufus turned his head and spat.

"That kind of thing don't make food very appetizing," Rollie complained.

The mountain man felt a bit of a burn, but chose not to respond his guest. To get away from the man, Rufus went to check on his horses. Behind him he could hear Rollie muttering as he tore at the rabbit. Maybe he thinks I ate too much or roasted it too long, the mountain man thought.

While at the rendezvous, Rufus had seen the old man. The man probably looked older than his years. He tended to hang around the supply tents and didn't seem to participate in any of the festivities. He usually came and left with the caravan. What he was doing wandering around the plains alone Rufus did not know. Also, it appeared he did not have a horse.

After taking his time with the animals, Rufus went back near the little man. "You cook good rabbit," Rollie told him.

"How did you come to be alone out here?" the mountain man asked.

"Damn whiskey," Rollie spat out the words. "I got drunk and when I come to my senses, the damn caravan was gone."

"I take it you were supposed to go with them," Rufus said.

"I usually stick with them and help out enough for my meals and such," Rollie replied. "I ride on one of the carts and help out with taking care of the mules. I found me a cache of whiskey that some trapper probably lost and figured to have a nip. Well, you know the rest."

The old man's story explained why he was afoot. In the dark the short, old man did not look like much. Rufus wanted to get an early start, so he told Rollie to pick a spot to sleep and then went to his own blankets. Sleep was slow to come.

Curiosity about the old man kept Rufus' mind working. A man alone without horses and apparently without a rifle, out on the plains, made little sense. There had been no talk of having lost his rifle and, evidently, he depended on the carts for transportation. The sounds of his guest muttering as he got out of his wet clothing and worked toward going to sleep didn't help. And then there was the lingering thought: *Could he be trusted?*

The next morning the sun was breaking the eastern horizon when Rufus opened his eyes. Not 10 feet away was Rollie, and the sight did not change the mountain man's opinion one bit. The old man lay in stained long johns, half in and out of his blanket, his clothing scattered about, the rabbit bones laying in the vicinity of where he'd eaten, and the coffee pot on its side still filled with grounds.

Rufus liked to keep a tidy camp. Even when he was blind drunk he would wake and find things in their place. Sitting up, the mountain man cleared his throat and coughed. Rollie didn't move and continued to snore softly.

Angered by his disheveled guest, Rufus pulled on his boots and got up to put some coffee on. Picking the pot up, he looked inside. "The grounds are good enough for another pot."

Banging and clunking things while swearing, the mountain man got the fire going and put on the coffee pot. Rollie never opened his eyes or moved. Only the sound of his ragged breathing told Rufus that the man wasn't dead. Resisting the temptation to give the man a kick, the mountain man checked on his horses. After watering them and putting them on fresh grass, he dug into his pack for something for breakfast.

The slices of side meat hadn't snapped but a couple of times in the blackened frying pan when Rollie sat up. "Is that side meat I smell in that pan? I sure do like it with biscuits."

"If you expect to eat any of this, you best get that damn mess around you cleaned up," Rufus growled.

Snorting, the feisty old man began to collect his things. Rufus heard him mutter, "I was told he was mean."

While moving the side meat around in the pan, Rufus snapped, "You damn right I can be mean. Shortly I will be riding out of here with or without you. It makes no difference to me."

Grumbling, the old man went around behind the rocks to relieve himself. The mountain man would have made some frying pan bread along with the side meat, but he was out of flour until he got to Fort William.

Rufus stared at the pile of soiled clothing while he cleaned up after breakfast and started to put the gear onto the horses. Rollie remained sitting near the fire and staring into his cup. "Damn weak coffee. You must have gotten some bad beans," he complained.

The mountain man chose not to comment and finished getting the horses ready. Rollie hadn't done anything about getting dressed and still sat in his long johns. With everything ready he looked at the old man and shook his head. "Well, I will be seeing you at the fort."

"What? Hey, wait a minute," Rollie exclaimed. "You ain't leaving me here. You got two horses and you're going to let me walk?"

"I sure as hell intend to," Rufus said, his gravelly voice sounding stern. "I told you I was leaving early and you just sat on your behind while I got my stuff together. Like I said, I'll see you at the fort."

As Rufus swung up into the saddle, the old man stumbled to his feet and began to pull on his damp and soiled clothing. "Give me just a bit," he said. "I'm almost dressed."

Watching the helpless man, Rufus knew he couldn't just ride away, but he wanted to make a point that if Rollie was going to slow him down, he just might leave him. Surprisingly fast, the feisty man was dressed and holding his knapsack.

"You ride on the mustang," Rufus told him.

"It ain't got no saddle," Rollie complained. "How can I sit on a horse without a saddle?"

"Uncomfortably," Rufus replied. "If you noticed, I arranged the packs so you'll be able to sit between the sides of the sawbuck and it will give you something to hang on to."

Swinging back off the grulla, the mountain man led the mustang next to some boulders. "Climb up on there," he instructed the old man.

Rollie's clothing had a sour smell, and when he settled onto the packs Rufus hoped that they wouldn't transfer the odor to his gear. "You all set there?" the mountain man asked.

"Hand me the lead rope," Rollie replied.

As Rufus took the lead away from the fifth crossing he could hear the old man muttering. Tearing a chew off the tobacco twist, the mountain man rolled it in his cheek and pulled down his hat brim to shade his eyes. It was only nine days to the fort and then he'd be rid of his unwelcome guest.

11

Doing his best to ignore his guest during the trip, on the third day Rufus rode right past the ice slough, an area that was covered with marsh grasses and tufted marsh plants that create an insulating layer. Beneath the plants there was winter ice that would last into the summer.

After passing the area Rufus could hear Rollie complaining that they didn't stop and enjoy some of the frozen crystals. For the first time since the mountain man had gained the riding companion he smiled. His goal was to get Rollie to the fort as quickly as possible.

When they reached a narrowing of the Sweetwater Valley they would cross the river three times in less than two miles. They met a half-dozen carts being pulled by oxen coming west while at one of the crossings and had to pull over and wait.

Digging a piece of jerky out of his saddle bag, Rufus stood holding the grulla. "You ain't got some extra by chance?" Rollie asked.

"You been eating my supplies for the past two days," the mountain man said. "Ain't you got anything to eat in that damn knapsack?"

In a complaining voice, the man replied, "All my supplies were in the caravan carts."

"You mean, all the caravan supplies which you'd eat went with them," Rufus told him as he dug out some jerky for the man.

The two men watched for a half-hour as the carts slowly traversed the narrow valley. Neither realized that in the future this same area would be a bottleneck for the many wagon trains that would be heading for Oregon or California, and could delay travelers for up to a week.

Rollie had slid off the mustang and finished chewing the jerky. Both men drank from the river before the carts got too close and churned up the water.

"You wouldn't have an extra chaw in them saddle bags? I got a bad tooth and it seems to help," the old man asked.

Cutting a chunk off a twist with his Green River knife, Rufus handed it to the man. "Should be enough for a couple of chews on that chunk."

The mountain man turned away, shaking his head as his guest stuffed the whole thing through the moustache covering his mouth. One advantage was that with a mouthful of tobacco, Rollie wouldn't be able to talk. As the last cart went by, the two men waved to the driver walking alongside.

When they reached Independence Rock they were still five days from the fort. After the stern warning the first morning, Rollie was quick to get ready each day after that. Rufus also learned that if he told the old man to do something, he would do so without much complaint. If he didn't mention anything to Rollie and expected him to take the initiative, the old man would just sit idle and wait for things to come to him.

That evening Rollie took his walking stick and went to read the names carved into the large domed rock. Rufus decided that they needed to spend a day to rest the horses. The supplies he had carried were all but depleted with two of them eating from them. He had seen some pronghorn south of the rock and figured to get some fresh meat.

He had the fire going and the coffee water on when Rollie came walking back from reading the names. Rufus was sure he saw tears in the man's eyes. "I'll boil us some beans for supper. Why don't you go and see if you can find some greens and wild onions to add to the pot?"

"They were young men," Rollie said. "Too young to die."

Without waiting for Rufus to reply the old man headed out to find something to add to the bean pot. Rufus frowned, wondering what he'd meant by the statement. That night the two men sat around the fire drinking the last of Rufus' coffee and chewing the last of the tobacco. Rollie kept staring at the dome rock.

"You know some men whose names are on the rock?" Rufus asked.

"Four friends," Rollie said. "We was on our way to trap the Wind River. It was in '31. Just west of here we come upon some Lakota. They seemed friendly enough, had women and children with them. Tucker was our leader. He was a couple of years older than the rest of us."

The man quit talking for a bit. Rufus spat and then took a sip of his coffee. It had gotten cold by then. The mountain man wanted to ask about the four friends, but it appeared Rollie had said all he was going to on the subject.

Then he cleared his throat. "Tucker liked the ladies," Rollie said. "Most often they liked him. We camped near the Lakota and even shared a meal with them. That night it happened." Again, there was a long pause.

"Tucker took a fancy to one of their women. We were already in our blankets when he went to find her. She didn't want nothing to do with him. I guess he was holding her and trying to convince her that she should and then we was woke by some shouting and screaming. I saw some of the braves come at him." Again, the man took a minute.

"He started fighting with the braves, and then some others come after us. There were trees not far from where we were sleeping and we tried to get to them and set up some kind of fight. We had our rifles loaded and tried to stop them but they come too fast. Something hit me and things went dark."

"It was late morning when I come to. It was quiet except for birds. I remember the birds singing like nothing had happened. At first I thought it had been a bad dream, but it wasn't. I was lying in a wash in the trees. Blood was all over the side of my head. I looked over the edge of the wash and the Lakota were gone. There in front of me were two of the friends. All bloody and scalped." There was another pause.

"You don't have to tell me no more," Rufus said. "I've heard this kind of story before."

"I never told no one," Rollie said. "Seeing their names on the rock made me want to tell the story. I ain't saying the Lakota were wrong. Tucker should have just gone to sleep like the rest of us. I buried them, and then with my hatchet I come back here and carved their names in the rock. I didn't go trapping no more. With only the hatchet and my knife, I walked back east. The hit on my head made it harder for me to think so I learned to let others think for me."

It explained a lot to Rufus why Rollie was the way he was. It could have been the loss of his friends or more than likely the hit on the head that caused him to need someone to do the thinking for him. They were less than a week from the fort. The mountain man would let the man know what needed done each day and deliver him clean and presentable to the caravan. After that, he would go visit Walter in Franklin.

CHAPTER TWO

It was mid-July when Rufus and Rollie saw the log fort with the blockhouse over the front gate showing a cannon to keep the peace. In 1840 Fort Williams was owned by the American Fur Company. It was 150 feet-square palisades with several small dwellings abutting to them. The fort also had some businesses within, including a trading post which served as a tavern. Wagons would bring supplies in from the east and then return filled high with buffalo hides, beaver pelts, and other furs such as wolf and bear.

As Rufus wove his way through the Cheyanne teepees scattered around the front of the fort he could see the deterioration of the fort built in 1834. There had been talk of a new fort being built. Rollie was dressed in worn but clean clothes and the two of them had been living on beans and fish with one instance of a pronghorn. They had passed several herds of buffalo, and even though Rollie had begged Rufus to shoot one, the mountain man refused, not wanting to take the time to process even a little of the meat.

Rufus was looking forward to two things. One was handing the old man over to the caravan, and the second, which was just as important, was to sit down in Louie's trading post with a bottle of whiskey. Louie worked with the American Fur Company buying furs and selling supplies on their behalf. The need for protection had prevented Louie from building his own business outside the fort. He did have plans of eventually doing so.

The carts from the rendezvous were loaded and parked outside the fort. Several men were stationed around them to protect the beaver pelts. Those carts that had carried supplies back from the rendezvous had already been emptied and were being loaded with buffalo hides to bring back to Westport. Rollie recognized the men guarding the carts and waved wildly to them.

Rufus felt relieved. Even though he had gotten used to having Rollie around, it would be good having one less thing to worry about. Handing the man over to the caravan took only a short time. No explanation was given as to why they'd left him and it appeared that none was expected by Rollie.

The feisty old man appeared to be busy and Rufus was impatient, so no long goodbyes were done. The mountain man nodded to the men guarding the carts and continued into the fort. Every time Rufus arrived, memories came back of the time that he'd brought Walter in need of medical help. Having no need for a sawbones himself, the mountain man wasn't even sure if the same doc was still at the fort. What he did know was that the trading post and whiskey was here and open.

Louie was a stocky man with slight graying in his thick, dark hair. He had a short beard which gave him a grizzled look. He was dickering on some supplies when Rufus walked in. The smells of the leather, rope, spices, and tobacco were quite pleasing to the mountain man. Walking up to the plank bar, Rufus waited for the owner to finish his business.

Once done, Louie headed back toward the bar. A smile broke out on his face. "I see you survived another year, Pike."

"That I did," Rufus replied. "After rendezvous I have a couple of dollars left to buy some whiskey."

"Did you like the whiskey at the rendezvous?" the grizzled owner asked.

"It depended on the cut," Rufus told him. "Some had a bit too much water."

"Well I bought some of the leftover stock and I make a proper cut," Louie told him, bringing a pint bottle and a glass to the mountain man.

After watching Rufus take his first drink, Louie said, "You come here every year, yet you trade your pelts at the rendezvous. I can make you a better deal."

"Maybe so," Rufus said, "but it wouldn't be the same. There is something about being close to the mountains and enjoying friends around you while you waste all your money."

Laughing, Louie replied, "I can't argue with that."

The whiskey burned nicely in his throat. The trading post had several customers digging through the shelves and stacks of goods. Some Rufus recognized, while others were probably from the east with plans of going after buffalo.

Louie came back to check if the mountain man needed another bottle. "You're drinking kind of slow today," the grizzled man said, noticing that the bottle was still quite full.

"I'm thinking too much," Rufus said. "Things are changing too fast out here. Buffalo hunters replacing trappers, buildings setting where there used to be open prairie."

"Some of those buildings are mine," Louie said. To the west of the fort I'm building the Buffalo Hide Saloon, and not far from it will be a place with rooms, sort of a boarding house."

"What are you doing here if you got all that going on outside the fort?" Rufus asked.

"Protecting my interest," Louie replied. "Word is this old fort is going to be tore down and they plan to build a bigger one just to the west. Then there is Lupton, who's building a fort to the north that should be finished next year that will be called Fort Platte. Damn competition right on our doorstep."

"It will bring more folk in the area," Rufus said. While he didn't say it, he did think that it would provide better prices. While they might still be too high, he thought about having more than one company at the rendezvous. It always helped.

"One of the caravan drivers came in and told me you brought Rollie in with you," Louie said.

Nodding, Rufus replied, "Found him wandering along the Sweetwater. He looked like he needed help." The mountain man didn't say what he originally thought of the disheveled old man.

"He had a run of bad luck," the owner told him. "His hunting party was killed by Lakota and he was the only survivor. Got his noggin rung pretty bad and has problems thinking. He managed to find his way back east and hangs around the businesses in Westport running errands for handouts, sleeping in alleys or barns, and always manages to join the caravan to the Rockies. It guarantees him four to five months of steady eating."

"With the end of the rendezvous that will be the end of his five months of steady eating," Rufus pointed out.

Agreeing, Louie said, "There will still be caravans coming west with supplies. Maybe he'll come out with them. What you did was good bringing him in. When the caravan didn't find him before it left, they figured he'd went off with some trappers."

Slipping the rest of the bottle into his possible bag, Rufus began to collect up some things he'd need for the trip to Franklin. He would stay with the caravan for protection until the split of the North and South Platte Rivers, and then strike out on his own. The caravan would make 20 to 25 miles a day. On his own he would make something over 30 a day.

Rufus left the trading post with two large bags of supplies. Stopping near the mustang, he began to store them away for travel. He noticed Rollie coming out of the doc's office. He was holding his jaw and spitting blood.

"Did you get the bad tooth pulled?" the mountain man called to him, noticing that the doc had trimmed the moustache to see in his mouth.

"Damn sawbones nearly broke my jaw getting it out," the feisty old man complained.

21

Laughing, Rufus told him, "You could have had old Doc Freeman. I hear this new man Ward is a real doctor and dentist."

"At least Freeman would have gotten me drunk first," Rollie muttered.

Reaching into his possible bag, Rufus pulled out the partial pint. "Here you go, Rollie. This will help the pain."

Giving the mountain man a crooked smile, the old man grabbed the pint. "I thank you for this."

Quickly the old, hunch-shouldered man headed for the caravan camp, his walking stick in one hand and the pint in the other.

Louie had a small livery in the fort, and Rufus decided to store his gear with the animals there. After that he'd check with the leader of the caravan and see if they needed another man. If they didn't he'd just tag along with them.

* * *

Two days later Rufus left the fort with the caravan. He had the task of hunting for meat, which meant that he'd range out ahead and bring down whatever was available, skin it and have it ready when the caravan caught up. There were over 40 men to keep fed.

Rufus was glad to be out ahead of the caravan. Several carts were loaded with smelly buffalo hides and his goal was to keep away from them. Rollie had no problem. He proudly sat on top of a cart loaded with hides and was as happy as could be.

Three days from the fort, they spent the night at Chimney Rock. The towering spire had been seen a full day before they arrived at its base. Rufus had shot and skinned a young bull buffalo. By the time the caravan arrived the meat was waiting, wrapped in the hide and with the tongue saved for the leaders of the caravan. The mountain man had already made a meal out of the liver and had some still warm in his frying pan as they pulled up.

Rollie caught the smell of the fried meat, quickly climbed off the cart and came to get a share. "I could smell it a mile back," he announced as he plucked a chunk out of the pan with his fingers.

From the time Rufus had first seen the short, bent old man until now the mountain man's opinion of Rollie had changed. His first thought had been of a grouchy and sloppy man who was only interested in his own needs. Slowly Rufus had realized that the blow on Rollie's head had left him a child in a man's body. He liked to do things to please people but could become easily confused, which brought out the grouchiness.

That night Rufus made his camp a short distance and upwind from the carts. The evening was warm and there was no need of a fire. He heard someone coming. The muttering coming from the person let him know it was Rollie.

"No damn coffee. No damn tobacco," he said, talking to himself.

"Can I help you, Rollie?" Rufus asked.

"You got no fire," the old man said. "They got a fire but no coffee."

"I got tobacco," the mountain man told him. Reaching into his possible bag, he cut off a small chunk and handed it to the man. Sticking it into his mouth, Rollie sat next to Rufus.

"It don't smell here," the old man said.

"That's why I chose to sleep away from the carts," Rufus told him.

Without another word the man got up and headed back towards the carts. The mountain man watched him and shook his head. Rollie was a strange one.

Putting down his ground cloth and spreading his blanket, Rufus made ready to get some sleep. As he pulled off his boots he heard his muttering friend coming back. As the mountain man turned there was the sound of the knapsack being dropped.

"We will need a fire in the morning," Rollie said as he got his bed ready.

Pulling his blankets around himself, Rufus replied, "We'll make a fire in the morning."

After that, Rollie joined Rufus for a chew each night. If there was coffee left from supper, the man would drink it and always complained that it wasn't hot. He did put a dent in the mountain man's supplies, but the company he provided was a fair trade.

When the caravan reached the confluence of the North and South Platte rivers, Rufus spent the last night with them. Rollie came over and seemed agitated. "They told me you were going. You got a fire."

Rufus kept his fire going and had a hot pot of coffee waiting. He also had a small bag with small chunks of tobacco. "That's right, Rollie. Come morning I will be riding out. I will make much better time alone than staying with the caravan."

"Am I going with you?" the man asked.

"They need you to help with the mules," Rufus told him. "I have some hot coffee for us tonight."

"No chew?" Rollie asked.

Holding up the bag, Rufus told him, keeping his gravelly voice earnest, "I have put many chunks of tobacco in this bag. It is for you, but you can only chew one piece each evening."

Reaching for the bag, the man replied, "I can do that." Looking in, he took out a piece and stuck it into his mouth.

The two of them sat in silence with the coffee and chew for some time. Then Rollie spoke. "You will get to Westport before us."

"I won't be stopping in Westport," the mountain man told Rollie. "I'm headed for Franklin. I have an old friend that I want to see."

"I'm an old friend," Rollie replied.

Fighting the urge to laugh, Rufus replied, "You are right. You're old and you are my friend. That makes you an old friend."

* * *

Rollie was busy helping harness the mules the next day when Rufus rode away. There had been no long goodbyes that morning. The old man had finished his breakfast and had hurried away to start collecting the mules. Rufus smiled and thought, *You take care, old friend.*

The day was hot and sticky, with heavy cloud cover. The mountain man wished it would start raining to cool things off. He was under three weeks from Franklin. When he turned south at the Missouri River he would be halfway there. The wait each night for the caravan to catch up had given his horses plenty of time to graze, and they were in good shape.

The first day away from the caravan Rufus rode about 40 miles. Despite the sticky day, it felt good to be away from the slow progress of the caravan. The mountain man was short on tobacco and side meat, so he figured to have more meals of cold flour and have only one chew in the evening.

As it got dark there was lightning flashing toward the south. Rufus kept the horses close to his camp in case the storm broke and they became scared of the loud crashes of thunder. He was sure there would be rain before morning, so he covered himself and his gear with the tarp. He didn't want to take time to rig and unrig the fly tarp.

The mountain man was up before daylight. The wind had picked up and he figured he was better off continuing on rather than sitting and waiting for the storm to hit. Rufus thought if he found some kind of rock formation, he'd hunker down and sit out the storm.

While putting the gear onto the horses they tended to prance nervously. "Settle down, damn you," he said in a soft voice. He feared that it would be a whale of a storm and the horses knew it.

Daylight took its time due to the heavy cloud cover. The wind whipped around the mountain man and his horses as they moved through the gloom. Rufus thought about the gulch he had passed late yesterday. It would have been perfect for sitting out the storm, but there was no way he was going to turn around and try to reach it.

Then came the hail pelting down on them. The bruising ice chunks bounced off the ground around them and he expected the grulla and mustang to bolt at any time. The river was just over a mile from them so, turning the horses toward it, Rufus hoped he could find any type of cover. Through the gloom it looked like the prairie was alive with movement. Then Rufus felt a flash of fear run through him. There were buffalo coming toward them, stampeded by the thunder and hail!

The buffalo were coming from the east and the only chance of escaping the herd was to ride hard toward the north. Spurring the grulla, he brought it to a gallop toward the river. The mustang was slow to react and almost pulled the lead rope out of Rufus' hand. The mountain man squinted against the stinging rain and hail coming down on them, not daring to look in the direction of the buffalo. The rumbling of the herd, accented by cracks of thunder, made it feel like they were right on top of them.

Then came an unexplainable roar and the wind struck the rider and his animals. Rufus lost his grip on the lead rope and almost went off the grulla as it stumbled and then regained its footing. Finally, they reached the river and he saw a tree, something to get behind. Then they went over the bank. The grulla lost its footing and Rufus threw himself clear of the animal as it went down. Dust and dirt flew around the mountain man, making it impossible to see. He hugged the ground and prayed.

Then the severe wind was gone and there was only the sound of his heart pounding and the buffalo charging by above the river bank. In all of Rufus' 34 years, he had never felt so close to death and so helpless to do anything about it.

The mountain man slowly sat up, brushing the dirt and prairie grass off his face and wet buckskins. Not a hundred feet from where he was he saw the twisted and uprooted willow tree that had been his objective as he reached the bank. On the ground around him were hail stones. Exhausted and nearly in shock, Rufus pick up a piece and put it into his mouth.

The sound of the buffalo above the bank began to ebb as they moved away to the west. "Damn, that was close!" he exclaimed. He looked around for his horses. Neither was in sight. He felt near his broad belt. He still had the Kentucky Flintlock pistol, his short axe, and knife. The possible bag and powder horn had swung around on his back but appeared to be intact. Then he noticed his hat was gone.

Rufus attempted to get to his feet and almost went down again. He had twisted an ankle when he'd hit the ground going off the grulla. "I sure as hell don't need this," he muttered. As it was the mountain man realized that he might be walking to Franklin. There was a chance that the mustang was swept away with the buffalo and the damn storm might have driven the grulla off.

Getting to his feet, Rufus tested the ankle. It hurt, but he was able to put some weight on it. He managed to get to the top of the river bank. The heavy cloud cover still threatened more rain or worse. He gasped as he looked around. Across the prairie to the east were over a dozen buffalo lying injured or dead. He realized that it had been a tornado and it had traveled right through the wooly beasts.

Rufus thought of Caleb and the mule. No matter where it was, Caleb would whistle and it would come. It was too bad he hadn't taught the grulla or mustang to do so. He could give a whistle and then . . . then again, Rufus realized that they both might have been killed in the storm.

In the gloom he looked for any sign of the mustang above on the prairie. He half-expected to see it lying with the buffalo. He remembered that the grulla had gone down. It could have very easily broken a leg in the fall. If it had survived the fall it had to be somewhere along the river.

Turning, he looked up and down the river. Then, on a small, brush-covered island halfway across, he saw it. The grulla had ended up in the river and had managed to get to safety. From this distance Rufus couldn't tell if it was injured or not. It just stood among the brush with its head down.

Limping, Rufus made it down the river bank and to the water. He stood calling to the animal, but it did not react. He even tried whistling and got no response. "Damn the luck," he complained as he stripped the belt, possible bag, and buckskins off. "I survived a killing storm and will probably drown going after an injured horse."

Rufus tried stepping on the ankle without the boot on. It hurt worse and he decided to keep them on along with the belt and the knife. If the grulla was injured he might have to put the horse out of its misery, and that could be done with a quick cut of the knife.

The mountain man entered the river with only his boots and long johns on. This time of year the water was low, which was an advantage. The muddy, sulfur-smelling water flowed around him as he waded out. Only a few yards from the shore, he stepped on a submerged log and almost went down, pain shooting through the ankle.

Halfway to the island the water was chest-deep. He lost sight of the horse hidden in the brush. He worried that it might have seen him as something coming at it and it might have gone off to the other side of the island, heading for the far shore. He shook his head and said, "The horse would recognize me."

Finally, he reached the island without having to swim. Rufus began to speak softly to the horse. It had been through a severe storm and could easily be spooked. Climbing out of the river, the mountain man stood with water running off his soaked long johns. The grulla's head came up and it looked at him.

"That was one hell of a storm wasn't it?" he said keeping his voice low. "I come to take you off this island."

The horse snorted and stepped away from him. While it was not what Rufus wanted to happen, it did give him hope that the animal wasn't injured. Standing 20 feet from the animal, the mountain man continued to talk softly. It didn't matter what he was saying, but the sound of his voice seemed to settle the grulla.

After several minutes of the two standing on the island, the horse finally decided that Rufus wasn't a danger and pushed through the brush toward him. "We got to go back and look for the mustang. Don't worry about the water, it ain't too deep. You might not have noticed that with the storm all around you."

Rufus continued to say whatever came to mind as the horse held out its head and he took the reins. Carefully the two of them waded back across the stretch of water. About halfway across, the mountain man hung onto the saddle horn for support due to the ankle. Once on the bank, Rufus tied the grulla to a sapling and loosened the cinch.

He stood letting the water drip off as he again looked up and down the river for any sight of the other horse. The grulla began to pull at the grass nearby, letting Rufus know that it was no longer thinking about the storm. He limped around the river bank and collected kindling to build a small fire. Most of his supplies were on the mustang, but he did have the coffee pot and some beans on the grulla.

While the long johns dried some, he sat naked and ate some hard bread with coffee. Rufus was half hoping that making coffee and the grulla grazing might bring the other horse back to the familiar sounds. Fearful that the animal was lost, Rufus dressed in the buckskins and put the wet boots back on.

With what he had packed on the horse, he limped away from the river and tightened the grulla's cinch. Climbing into the saddle, he looked around. Two of the buffalo had gotten to their feet and were slowly walking away. Three other animals were still down, too injured to get up. Rufus wished that the Hawken hadn't gotten wet in the river. It would not be right to leave the animals suffering. He pulled the Kentucky Flintlock pistol from his belt and got the second one from his saddle bag.

An hour later Rufus rode toward the east with a couple of buffalo tongues. The two pistols with their .50 caliber balls had had sufficient impact to kill the injured buffalo at close range. He had looked around for the other horse but saw nothing of it or any of the packs that might have been torn off by the storm.

The clouds broke in the afternoon and the sun came out. It was still hot and sticky. His damp clothing chafed as he moved with the rhythm of the horse. Rufus was without many supplies and no dry clothing to change into. Those were in the packs on the mustang. He realized that he could sit and wait for the caravan to catch up to him and continue east with them. Shaking his head, he wasn't ready to use that option. He would continue on. Once he reached the Missouri River there were some places where he could get a few supplies and a hat.

CHAPTER THREE

It was mid-August when Rufus reached Franklin. In 1827 much of the town had been washed away by the flooding Missouri River. What was now New Franklin was rebuilt on higher ground. The livery that Walter Gray had purchased had been rebuilt away from the river by a long-time friend named Sal.

When Walter had broken his leg and lost his scalp, Rufus had taken him to Fort William, where an old army medic named Freeman had been able to heal him well enough to travel back to Franklin. At Walter's request, Rufus had gone back to the mountains, trapping.

Walter had stayed with Sal and his wife Tiny in Franklin. While Walter wasn't in any condition to go back into the mountains and wade in icy ponds, he was well enough to help Sal around the livery. It wasn't long before Sal's health had forced him to retire and using savings from trapping, Walter had bought the livery. He also got a small house not far from the livery, and had hired a housekeeper to come in and take care of laundry, cleaning, and making his supper.

Each year Rufus had come back from a season of trapping to spend a few weeks with Walter in Franklin. While Walter would try and get him to stay at his house, Rufus insisted on sleeping in the tack room. After a night of drinking and card playing the mountain man didn't want to come staggering into his friend's house. Also, if Rufus met a lady he wouldn't need a place to stay for the night.

Riding through the streets of Franklin, Rufus felt as close to home as any place. Each year Walter would try and convince him to stay and work with him at the livery. Each year the mountain man would decline the offer. Rufus knew this year would be tough, because there was no trapping to go back to and Walter was aware of this.

As he rode toward the wide bay doors of the livery, Rufus noticed that a lean-to had been added to one side of the building. *Business must be good,* the mountain man thought. He stopped at the watering trough in front of the livery and let the tired grulla drink.

From inside the livery he heard, "I thought I smelled a nasty mountain man."

Walter Gray came walking out of the bay doors with a big smile on his face. "I just put on a pot of coffee. Bring the horse in out of the sun and have a cup."

Rufus led the horse into the building and looked around. "You done some cleaning in here."

"I had me a part-time man for the winter and he liked to keep busy," Walter said. "This spring we built the lean-to. It has all the comforts of home."

"I hope the tack room is still available," Rufus said. "It kind of has the feel of home in it."

Walter was pouring their coffee and a frown crossed his face. "The lean-to is for you. I figured without beaver trapping you might want to spend a little more time in Franklin."

"There is a whole lot of things a man can go after other than beaver," Rufus replied. "I been thinking of going after wolf and bear. I hear they are plentiful in the Yellowstone."

Changing the subject, Walter asked him, "Where is your trapping partner? I expected the pup to be with you."

Taking the cup from his friend, Rufus tasted the hot brew. "You do make good coffee. Caleb went back to Santa Fe. He plans to work on his uncle's ranch."

"He's a smart man," Walter replied. "He is building a future. Probably have a wife in no time."

Giving his friend a sideways glance, Rufus asked, "Are you saying I am not a smart man?"

"I ain't saying nothing of the kind," his friend told him. "I just said Caleb is smart."

Finishing the coffee, Rufus tossed out the dregs. "I best take care of the grulla. It is in bad need of some grain."

"You're missing the mustang," Walter said. "Did you lose it to one of the tribes or playing poker?"

"I lost it to a damn big storm," Rufus told him. "Had a tornado in the Nebraska territory and it took the horse, my supplies, and my hat."

"Damn shame to lose a hat," Walter said.

Reaching into his possible bag, the mountain man said, "By the way, you best keep this for me. After replacing my supplies and hat, I ain't got much left for celebrating here in Franklin."

Taking the money, his friend replied, "That's a shame. The saloons will suffer from it."

Stripping the gear, the horse was put into a stall with hay and grain. Rufus picked up his saddle bags and blanket roll. "Follow me," Walter said.

"I know where the tack room is," Rufus replied.

"I filled it with the junk that was laying around in here," Walter replied. "You'll have to stay in the lean-to."

Snorting, Rufus followed his friend. "You put me out of my home."

The lean-to was well-constructed and was one large room with a table, chairs, a stove on one side, and a bunk along one wall. There was a dry sink with a basin and bucket for cleaning up, food prep, or doing dishes.

Rufus looked around the structure. "This is a damn nice place. I will spend all my time worrying that I might spill or break something."

"That's why I didn't put a nice pitcher and bowl in here for you to clean up. I also put a mirror above the sink so you could look at who's hungover each morning."

While Rufus played down what he saw, the truth was he was very impressed. He was fully aware that Walter had built this hoping he'd stay. There was no way he wanted to hurt his friend, but the last thing Rufus wanted was to stay in Franklin and help out in the livery.

Right after a quick supper with Walter, Rufus headed for the Frontier House. The original saloon had been washed away with the flood and the owner took a few years to rebuild. The new building looked much like the original and that suited Rufus just fine. After a few drinks and some cards, Rufus would then go to Tillies, where he had a special friend.

The night was not a disappointment for the card sharks, saloon keepers, or the gal named Cheri at Tillies. Rufus spent like there was no tomorrow. He didn't have a chance to sleep in the new lean-to that night. It was mid-morning when the mountain man came dragging into the livery. Walter was busy cleaning the stalls.

"Coffee is on," he called to his hungover friend.

Rufus' stomach churned and his head pounded. "I think that the Frontier House is putting something bad in them drinks."

"I believe they call it alcohol," Walter replied. "You got any money left?"

"I put some in my boot," Rufus said. "I checked this morning and it was still there."

Walter looked at the buckskin-clad friend. "You really need to put on some different clothes."

"I lost everything with the horse," the mountain man told him.

"I still got the clothes you left here a couple of years ago," Walter reminded him.

"Weren't they some worn?" Rufus asked.

"They might be worn, but they will look a hell of a lot better than what you got on," his friend said.

Getting himself another cup of coffee, Rufus returned to his chair. "Maybe a haircut and bath might be a good idea. The gal last night kind of suggested it."

After a breakfast of biscuits, Rufus headed down the street with a bundle of his old clothes. He had the new hat tilted back on his head. The barber looked him over as he walked into the shop. "Looks like you need about everything," the man said.

"Just a little trim and a bath will do just fine," the mountain man replied.

"You want me to burn the old buckskins?" the owner asked.

"I kind of hope to get another winter out of them," Rufus told him.

It began with a haircut and trimming of the beard. A large pile of hair collected around the wooden barber chair. Taking out the straight razor, the barber began to strop it. "I'll clean up the neck for you."

Dabbing on the barber soap, the owner's expert hands quickly removed the neck hair. "You got quite the scar on one side."

"It was from my youth," Rufus replied, not explaining how he'd been shot in New Orleans while dealing faro.

Sliding into the metal tub, the mountain man wished it was a little warmer. He took his time scrubbing off the months of trail dust. As he climbed out his skin was tingling from the lye soap. Walter had handed Rufus the bundle of clothing. Unrolling it, the mountain man found not only the worn wool pants and shirt, but also new long johns and wool socks.

Once dressed, the mountain man stepped out of the back room and paid the barber. "You want me to launder the old long johns?"

"Naw," Rufus said as he collected his buckskins. "You can just burn them."

After cleaning up, Rufus felt quite good. He felt the breeze blowing over his shaved neck. Instinctively his hand went to the scar on the right side. His thoughts went back to the night as a young man dealing faro in a saloon. When he'd called one of the players a cheater the patron had pulled a gun and shot at him. He in turn had put a ball into the man's stomach. The man's brother controlled the wharf and a reward was put out for the young man.

If it hadn't been for a Creole woman who was a voodoo queen he would have probably been found dead and hanging from a post on the wharf. She was able to smuggle him out of New Orleans and had given him a new name and an amulet to protect him. Later Rufus gave the amulet to Walter after he had been scalped.

The memories of New Orleans were not bad memories. While there his name had been Tom Wallingford. He had grown up in the saloons and brothels where his father had played piano or dealt faro. His mother had died when he was six and the care for the youngster fell on the ladies working in the places. One of his mentors was a Creole named Damas, the owner of a livery.

By the age of 15 he'd been working for tips hawking customers and taking care of the front porch of a saloon and brothel named La Maison. From the constant calling to prospective customers his voice had taken on a gravelly sound. Schooling had never been an option for the young man. He learned numbers because money and cards were part of his life. Other than that, he learned to write his first name and this he would carve on posts and boards to mark his territory.

When his father had gotten sick with consumption, he had been let go from the La Maison and the young man found a place for his father to live near the waterfront. That was also when he'd met the two Creole women, Camille and her daughter Gabrielle. It turned out Camille was a voodoo queen and feared by those around the waterfront.

It was after his father died that the young man had run into trouble dealing faro on the waterfront. With the help of Damas and Camille the young man, at the age of 17, left New Orleans by steamboat with a new name, Rufus Pike. Once in St. Louis he'd tried buffalo hunting and did not like it. Then Rufus went trapping, which he loved. He and Walter had met at the 1825 rendezvous and partnered up until Walter had been injured in 1833.

The slap of a board onto a pile brought Rufus out of daydreaming. Franklin was growing and the boards would be used on a new building. He turned up the alley leading to the livery and found Walter sitting in a chair near the bay door.

Looking up, his friend said, "Have you seen Rufus Pike in your wanderings? He's dressed in dirty buckskins and had straggly, long hair. You couldn't miss him if you saw him."

"That's a hell of a welcome when I spent good money getting cleaned up," the mountain man said, pretending to be hurt.

"You look almost civilized," Walter acknowledged. "I hope you feel like working, because I got a load of hay coming in."

During his brief visits to Franklin, Rufus would always help Walter with the livery as long as it didn't get in the way of his night life. Walter was several years older than Rufus and had grown up in the world of accounting. Somewhere along the line his friend had gone into trapping for a living and had put enough money away to purchase the livery.

One thing Rufus could depend on was lectures about putting something away for the future, and a list of chores or projects that Walter had lined up for his visits. The mountain man would grumble and complain while doing them, but in truth he enjoyed spending time with his friend and was glad he could help.

Stripped down to his long john top, Rufus helped his friend unload the hay. The mountain man pitched it into the loft from the load while Walter tossed it back into a pile. Rufus remembered doing the same thing with Damas in his youth. He didn't mind the dust and loved the smell of fresh-cut hay.

With their work done for the day, Rufus joined Walter at the man's small house. It was built on high ground and had a great view of the Missouri River from the front porch. Walter had some cider from some early apples and they sat sipping the sweet beverage.

"Should let this age a while," the mountain man said. "A couple of glasses would then make us forget the work we did."

"I am partial to hard cider myself," Walter replied. "This is the first from the mill down the street and while it is a bit tart, it tastes too good to wait."

The door opened behind them. A stocky, gray-haired lady came out. "I'll be leaving now, Mr. Gray. There is chicken soup on the stove and some fresh bread in the box."

"Thank you, Mrs. Tuttle," Walter replied. "I do like your chicken soup."

Rufus nodded to the woman and in return received a hard stare. Carrying a few items that she was going to wash for Walter, Mrs. Tuttle hurried down the street.

"Ain't she a widow now?" the mountain man asked his friend.

"Her husband died two years ago," Walter told him.

"I figured you would have done some courting and be married to her by now," Rufus said kiddingly. "You know she can clean and she is a good cook. Yes, sir. I fear you're moving too slow."

Snorting and shaking his head, Walter said, "I agree she is a fine housekeeper and she can cook, but she tends to be a little pushy. In no time I would be dressing formal for supper and going to church two, three times a week."

"Going to church ain't a bad thing," Rufus told him. "It's akin to sitting on a mountain ledge and taking in a beautiful view."

"Did I mention she doesn't much like you?" his friend asked.

"I have noticed a coldness when we meet," the mountain man replied.

"Coldness, hell," Walter said, laughing. "She would take her broom and chase you out of the county if she was mistress of my place."

Being a little short of money, Rufus spent the next two days hanging around the livery helping with things and sitting on Walter's porch. The two of them relived many adventures they'd had over the years and talked of many of the trappers that they knew. On the third night Rufus was cleaned up to go into town when Walter came out to the porch.

Smiling, Rufus said, "I got some money that needs spending."

"I told you about a man that worked for me over the winter," Walter said. "He was without a horse and we kind of did some trading. Some for his work and some for trading."

Seeing the serious look on his friend's face, Rufus asked, "Did you get something that is illegal or stolen?"

Giving his friend a sideways grin, Walter replied, "That I will never know. You have helped folks over the years. When building the livery after the flood, you missed a fall's trapping. Most important, you come all the way back here every year when it would make more sense for you to stay west and resupply at Fort William."

"You were right there with me when we missed the fall's trapping and I hate to tell you, but it is that little gal, Cheri, at Tillies that brings me back here every year," Rufus said, chuckling.

"I'm sure it is," Walter said. "That explains why you hurry back out of town each year without a glance back at Tillies."

Feeling awkward talking about things he had done for others, Rufus looked up the street. "I best be going before I have to fight some bruiser that gets to her first."

"Please sit for a minute," Walter requested. "I got something I need to talk to you about."

Not liking the serious look on his friend's face and wanting to put any conversation off for another time, Rufus said, "I am going to spend some time at Tillies. Tomorrow, or maybe the next day, we'll talk."

The mountain man put on his hat and headed up the street. There was a worry in the back of his mind. The way Walter was talking there was a chance that he might be sick. The nagging thought remained with Rufus and his night of pleasure was pretty much ruined. After a few drinks and some conversation with Cheri, the mountain man bid everyone goodbye and headed back.

Avoiding the small house, Rufus went directly to the livery. There was lantern burning low just inside the bay door. Walter often left some of the afternoon's coffee on the pot belly stove. Finding enough for a cupful, Rufus filled one and carried the lamp and coffee over to the lean-to.

Rufus sat at the small table, setting the lantern down. It almost tipped over due to something that had been left on the table. "What the hell . . ."

There on the table lay a Colt Paterson .36 caliber revolver. Rufus looked at it and furled his brow. He saw that the Colt looked like the one that Caleb had had when he'd come back from Santa Fe. Picking it up, Rufus hefted the revolver. It had some kind of lever under the barrel that Caleb's did not have. Other than that, it was the same.

The mountain man had shot Caleb's revolver a few times, but still preferred his own Kentucky flintlocks. They required much less care than the Colt and Rufus was able to fix almost anything that happened to them.

The coffee was bitter and less than satisfying. Rufus continued to sip the brew as he looked over the revolver. There was nothing else on the table. Not even a note, which would have done little good for the mountain man. Then, Walter would know that. The

Colt appeared to be unloaded, with empty chambers and no caps on the nipples. Rufus toyed with the lever and wondered what its function was. As far as he could tell it just got into the way.

With the coffee finished, the mountain man removed his boots and put them near the cot. He then placed his shirt and pants onto a nearby chair. The lantern and Colt remained on the table next to the cup. As he lay down, Rufus kept thinking about the revolver and Walter's strange behavior.

After what seemed like a long time of tossing and turning, the mountain man laughed. "You best not have done all this just to get me to come back early tonight."

The next morning Walter was hard at work in the livery when Rufus walked in the bay door. He looked at the mountain man and said, "Someone stole the lantern and a cup last night."

"I got them right here," Rufus said, holding them up.

"You're looking better than I expected this morning," Walter told him. "The coffee should be done. Pour a couple of cups. I'm just about finished here."

Hanging the lantern onto its peg, Rufus went to the potbelly stove and filled a couple of cups. Setting one onto Walter's chair, he then sat down and tasted the coffee. "Much better than last night," he muttered.

Walter picked up his cup and sat heavily onto the chair. "I'm too damn old to keep running this place alone," he said, giving a sideways glance at the mountain man. "Sure would be nice if I had some help."

"I saw the Colt," Rufus said, choosing to ignore the bid for help.

"What did you think?" Walter asked.

"Looks a lot like Caleb's revolver," the mountain man replied. "They take a lot of fussing with."

"It's a good thing you have lots of spare time sitting around your fire in the mountains to do that fussing," Walter told him.

Looking at his friend, Rufus asked, "You didn't go and buy that for me? You know I got two Kentucky flintlocks."

"I didn't buy it for you . . ."

"Is that what you wanted to talk about?" Rufus asked, interrupting. "Hell. I thought you were dying."

"Once again," Walter said, "I didn't buy the Colt. I traded for it, and I ain't dying."

Finishing the first cup of coffee, Rufus got up and refilled his. "You want some more?"

Walter held his cup up while the mountain man poured. Waiting until Rufus sat back down, the livery owner continued. "You remember the man I told you about that worked the winter? I got it from him. The man said he won it in a poker game and then had to kill the man who lost it when he tried to take it back."

"It will be a good weapon for you, Walter," the mountain man replied.

"I want you to have it," his friend said.

"I got no need," Rufus told him, "I got two flintlocks that are fine for what I need."

"They're slow to load and you got only one shot each," Walter pointed out. "You gave me this amulet that was given to you for protection and now I want to give you this revolver to do the same for you."

"I'll buy it from you then," Rufus suggested, wanting to end the discussion.

"You don't have enough extra money to buy the Colt," Walter told him. "I had an old horse and the man needed a way out of town. He traded the revolver for the horse. I got almost nothing in it."

"I got my supply money," Rufus said.

"How about you work for me this winter and I'll throw in your food and the Colt, and a pack horse?" Walter proposed. "You can spend your supply money at Tillies and come spring you can head back to the mountains."

Desperate to end the conversation, Rufus replied, "I'll take the damn Colt and leave in a couple of weeks."

Smiling, Walter asked, "Did you notice the lever under the barrel?"

"I did," Rufus said. "It don't seem to have a use except to get in the way."

"It is for loading the Colt," his friend told him. "That way you don't have to remove the cylinder.

Rufus wanted to make a cocky reply in the worst way, but said, "That's a good thing."

As it turned out, Walter had also gotten some .36 caliber balls, some caps, and tools for maintaining the Colt. The two men rode out to the prairie and fired the revolver. Rufus was pleased at its ease of shooting and having four shots without reloading. The Colt was a little difficult to clean, but as it turned out not much more so than the flintlock.

The next week went by quickly and Rufus began to make ready for leaving. He bought some of the supplies and put off getting the side meat until just before leaving. Walter wanted to give the mountain man a pack horse, but Rufus was determined to take some money out of his old age savings to pay for it.

The two men were in a heated discussion about the horse when the sheriff came riding up. "Do I have to break the two of you up?" he asked.

Shaking his head, Walter said, "No. I'm just having a bit of trouble with this bullheaded . . ."

"Now, no name calling," the sheriff said, grinning.

"What can I do for you?" Walter asked.

"I had a man come into town this morning looking for Rufus," the sheriff replied.

The mountain man felt the hair on the back of his neck stand up. "Did the bastard have a New Orleans accent?"

"No. He didn't have much to say except asking for you," the sheriff replied. "He said he had your horse."

"Horse?" Rufus asked. "Was this person a bent-over old man that tends to be grouchy?"

"That kind of describes him," the sheriff agreed. "When I asked him to wait in the jail, he seemed pretty upset. He was muttering and complaining a lot."

Looking at his friend, Rufus said, "I may not be needing a packhorse."

Following the sheriff to the jail, the mountain man saw the mustang with the pack saddle and packs standing at the rail. "You can go and let Rollie out. He was just bringing me back my horse."

As the man came out of the jail he saw Rufus. "I found your horse. It was near the dead buffalo. Your hat was near the river. When I saw the horse, I told everyone it was yours. Why did you leave your horse behind?"

Thanking the sheriff, Rufus told him, "I'll take care of him."

Then to Rollie he said, "I was in a big storm and it scared the horse and it ran away."

"You have a new hat," the old friend noticed. "Can I keep your old one? It fits my head."

"You can keep the hat," Rufus told him. Then he asked, "Did any of the others come with you?"

"We got back to Westport and I told them I knew where you were only I didn't know where Franklin was," the old friend said. Holding up a piece of paper, Rollie continued. "They drew me a map and I followed it."

Taking the mustang's lead rope, the two walked toward the livery. "Did you lead the horse or ride on the packs?"

"I rode on the packs. They were uncomfortable," Rollie told him.

Walter was standing in front of the livery and watched the two of them as they talked back and forth. "Looks like you found a friend," Walter said.

"I am an old friend," Rollie said. "Rufus said I am old and I am a friend. That makes me an old friend."

Before leading the mustang into the livery, Rufus motioned Walter aside. "His name is Rollie and he got hit in the head during an Indian attack." Then the mountain man added, "He found the horse after I lost it in the storm. After that he was on a mission bringing it back to me."

As he brought the horse into the livery to strip the packs and give it some hay and grain, he heard

Walter introducing himself to Rollie. When asked where he'd met Rufus, the old friend started with, "He gave me some rabbit. I was wet."

That evening, when Rollie was watching Mrs. Tuttle finishing supper, Walter asked, "Does he have a place to stay or are you going to take him hunting? I didn't notice anything but a knife to hunt or defend himself."

"I believe God watches over those that need it," Rufus said. "Rollie has no home. He lives in Westport on handouts. He sleeps wherever he can find a place."

Walter sat for a bit, deep in thought. Then he asked, "Do you think he would stay with me and help out in the livery?"

The request came as a surprise to Rufus. He was sorry that he hadn't thought of it. Rollie needed a place to stay and someone to keep him fed and warm in the winter.

"He might," Rufus replied. "You would have to tell him things you need done and possibly every time. I know he is good with animals."

"When you leave, do you think he will try and follow after you?" Walter asked.

"I think if I told him not to he'd stay," the mountain man replied. "You would have to watch him for a bit."

For the next week, Walter had Rollie help him around the livery. Much of what was needed doing was done well by his old friend. An extra cot was put into the lean-to and Rollie was asked to stay there when Rufus went into town if not visiting with Walter.

When the day came for Rufus to leave, the three of them stood in front of the livery. "I have to go and do some hunting and I want you to stay here and help Walter. He is an old friend of mine," the mountain man told Rollie.

Looking Walter up and down, Rollie replied, "He is old, and he is your friend. Like me, he is your old friend."

Nodding, Rufus continued, "You understand that you can't follow me."

"I will stay here and help your old friend," Rollie said, stepping closer to Walter.

Rufus had the gear and supplies on his horses and climbing into the saddle, he promised, "I will be back next summer."

The mountain man watched as Rollie headed into the livery saying, "I need to feed the horses."

Waving to Walter, Rufus rode away from the livery. This departure seemed different than others. Usually the mountain man looked forward to getting back to the mountains and getting his traps into the water. Most often he had someone he was partnering up with, but this year he would be all alone. His first stop would be at Fort William, and then . . . he wasn't sure.

CHAPTER FOUR

It was mid-September when Rufus crossed the Laramie River and rode up to Fort William. Several teepees were erected in front of the log fort. With times being peaceful, the gate stood open. He would spend a week or so at the fort before continuing west. He needed to purchase some buckskins and replace a few supplies.

In his broad belt, Rufus had the Colt Paterson, a short axe, and his Green River knife. While he had doubted it, he quickly grew to like the revolver. He had shot most of his meals on the way out with the Colt. He still had one of the flintlocks in his saddlebag, while the other he had given to Walter. It would be handy in case he had to put down an animal.

Pulling up in front of the fort, Rufus tilted back his flat-brimmed leather hat. His light brown hair had already grown down below his ears and his beard had taken on a scraggly look. On the back of the saddle he had his rain gear, along with a wool coat tied to the blanket roll. The Hawken was in the saddle scabbard.

Rolling the chew in his cheek, the mountain man spat and headed into the fort. His first stop would be at Louie's for a whiskey. Louie offered rye whiskey that came out with the caravans. It was aged in barrels and had an amber color. For those who wanted a cheap drink, he also had the whiskey sold at the rendezvous or to the tribes, which was cut with water and clear in color. What Rufus drank depended on the time of year and how much money he had left.

Tying the horses at the rail, Rufus walked into the trading post. He noticed a strange face behind the bar. Leaning against the plank top, the mountain man ordered a bottle of the good stuff. The bartender had slicked-back, dark hair and a full moustache.

Giving the man a coin for the bottle, Rufus asked, "Did Louie take the day off?"

"He's at the Buffalo Hide today," the man said. "I work in here most days now."

"If you see him, tell him Rufus was in," the mountain man said.

"I heard talk of you," the man replied. "My name's Hube, or Herbert. I'll let him know."

The trading post had a different feel to it. Louie had told him that he planned to sell, but that hadn't happened yet. Somehow it felt . . . different. What Rufus did not realize was that he himself was different. Usually he was rushing to the mountains to start trapping. Even now he was weeks late getting to them.

Rufus left with the bottle. Sticking it into his saddle bag, he looked around the fort. Many of the men he would normally see were missing. Then again, he reminded himself that it was later in the year. He decided to take care of the horses first. At the livery they would get some grain. While he hadn't pushed them, he had been on the trail for a little over three weeks.

Leading the horses into Louie's livery, Rufus heard someone in the back. "I got a couple of horses in bad need of grain and grooming," he called.

"Give me a minute to finish here," the man called back.

The voice was familiar and the mountain man was anxious to see a face he knew. From the back came a white-haired man, and it was a face he knew. "Hello, Johnson," Rufus said.

"You're late getting to the mountains, Rufus," the smoky-eyed man pointed out. Johnson had a look of dislike on his whisker-covered face.

"No reason to rush," Rufus said. "I won't be after beaver, so let the damn ponds freeze."

"Folks still going after beaver," Johnson replied. "Just because the rendezvous are gone doesn't mean you can't sell pelts at the fort."

"A man would be working for almost nothing," the mountain man told him.

"Maybe so," Johnson agreed, "but it would keep you in beans."

Back in '24 Rufus and Johnson had partnered up to trap with William Ashley as company trappers. You were required to sign a contract for one to three years. The two men spent that winter learning the finer points of trapping beaver and then enjoyed the first rendezvous in July of '25.

At the rendezvous the smoky-eyed man learned that Rufus had only signed up for one year with the company while he had signed up for three. Ever since then the smoky-eyed man had had a dislike for the mountain man.

Johnson felt he'd taken Rufus under his wing, helping him make some money hunting buffalo and then joining Ashley and Henry as a company trapper. With Rufus being younger than him, the smoky-eyed man had sort of considered himself the leader of the two of them. He had felt betrayed when Rufus had gone trapping with Walter the next year.

It didn't help that as years went by Rufus was just a little better at everything than Johnson. After getting out of his contract with the company, Johnson had taken up horse trading, which he was much more suited for, buying and selling stock, and often setting up his own livery. While Rufus didn't much like the smoky-eyed man, he did like the way he took care of horses.

"I expected that you would still be at Bents Fort," Rufus said.

"Like you, I go back and forth," the smoky-eyed man replied. "I move stock wherever there is the best market."

"These horses have come a long way, and after some grain they could use some grooming," the mountain man told him.

"Two bits each for the hay and grain, another two bits for the grooming," Johnson told him.

"Can you also check their hooves?" Rufus asked. The smoky-eyed man just nodded and took the reins and lead rope.

After Johnson went back with the horses, Rufus put his gear near the tack room. He thought about pulling the bottle out of the saddle bag and then figured he'd better not. That he would save for later.

Walking through the fort, the mountain man realized that he had gotten a lift seeing a familiar face, even if it was Johnson.

Rufus met with some Cheyenne outside the fort and made a deal on a set of buckskins. He also wanted calf-high moccasins. To the north he could see construction of an adobe fort. He figured that must be Fort Platte. He wondered when they would start on the replacement of Fort William.

Looking to the west, he could see several buildings that made up sort of a spread-out town. He headed for one of the larger buildings, which he figured was the Buffalo Hide Saloon. Stopping at the front door, he looked around. It had sort of a nicer appearance and not the rough-cut look of most buildings on the frontier.

Stepping inside, it was like walking into a different world. Chandeliers lit up the room, and to the right side there was an ornate bar and behind it was Louie. Seeing Rufus come in, the grizzled man waved him over.

"What can I get you?" Louie asked.

"By the looks of it, I can't afford anything in here." Rufus told him.

"Don't let the looks worry you," Louie said. "The prices are reasonable. I had all the fancy stuff shipped in for my sister Lucy. She won't come out unless I build something nice."

Soon Rufus had a rye sitting in front of him. The amber liquid had a smoother taste than he was used to. He wondered if Louie had cut it with too much water. After a couple of drinks, Rufus knew that it hadn't been cut because he started to feel warm all over.

After the drinks, Rufus had a meal at a table set with nice silverware and plates. He was almost afraid to cut the steak he had on the fragile-looking plate. Mashed potatoes and some type of green vegetable was served with the steak. There was also fresh bread and butter. The mountain man had buttermilk and coffee with his meal.

The coffee could have been a little stronger, but overall it was one of the best meals he'd eaten out on the plains. The price of the meal and a couple of drinks cost as much as a night of drinking and one spent with Cheri at Tillies. Rufus had to admit he was satisfied and wouldn't have a hangover the next day.

Going back to the livery, Rufus saw Johnson sitting outside. Walking over, Rufus took a seat next to him. "Did you buy into Louie's place?"

"No," Johnson said. "I drove the horses to him, and his hostler had just been injured by a mule. He asked if I could handle things for a while."

"Word is they are going to tear this place down soon," the mountain man said.

"That's what they say," the smoky-eyed man replied. "Louie was smart when he built his places. Most folks used the fort palisade walls for their back and when the fort comes down, so will their buildings. Louie's are free-standing, so with the fort gone he'll just have a better view."

The two men sat in silence for some time. Rufus wondered what kept Johnson out on the frontier. With his talent for trading horse flesh, he could do just fine in St. Louis or any of the cities. The mountain man knew why he himself stayed in the west. There was a man with vengeance on his mind who still had men traveling up and down the Mississippi looking for a man with a bullet scar on his neck. So far they hadn't made the connection between Tom Wallingford and Rufus Pike.

"I best go find a place to sleep," Rufus told him.

"You're a friend of Louie and have your horses in the livery," Johnson said. "You can sleep in the loft."

"That's good of you to offer," the mountain man told the smoky-eyed man.

"It's not my policy," Johnson replied. "It's Louie's."

With a place to sleep settled, Rufus went over to the trading post. Hube came over with a bottle of the good stuff. "You best get me one of the cheap bottles," the mountain man said.

"Louie wouldn't like it if I served you the cut liquor," the bartender told him. "It'll be the same price for the good stuff."

Thanking the bartender, Rufus watched him pour the drink. Taking the glass, he sipped the amber liquid. It was good, but the mountain man worried that he might take a liking to it and wouldn't be happy going back to the cut liquor.

With the drink in his hand, Rufus turned to face the room. Three men were playing cards and on the other end of the bar were a couple of men working on getting drunk. Just beyond the area of the bar were the shelves of goods for sale. Rufus had already gotten the extra clothing and most of his supplies in Franklin.

Suddenly, four buffalo hunters burst in, talking loudly and wanting whiskey. Instinctively, Rufus' hand went to the Colt in his belt. To give them room, the mountain man moved to the far end of the bar. As they settled in next to Rufus the smell of rotting hides filled the area.

Hube brought the men a bottle and four glasses. "That will be two dollars," he said.

"Damn high price for water and a splash of whiskey," the huskiest of the group said, laughing.

The bartender ignored the comment and took the money. Rufus should have just moved away from the men. They'd just gotten in from hunting on the plains and were looking to unwind. The ripe smell and their loudness were getting on his nerves.

With no place to move further on the bar, Rufus tried to concentrate on his whiskey. The four men made short work of the bottle and ordered another. Hube brought a second and waited for their money. "That last one tasted like one-dollar whiskey," the big man said.

Without smiling, the bartender replied, "Two."

The man swore and slapped a coin down on the bar. "At the rendezvous you would be paying $4 for that bottle," Rufus told the man.

The four men looked at him. "Did you hear that, Jake?" one of the confederates asked the big man. "He must be one of them rich trappers."

The big man turned to Rufus, "You saying we should be paying more for our whiskey?"

Rufus felt the heat rising in his body. "I just said the $2 is a good price."

"The damn swamp rat here thinks it's a good price," another of the men chortled.

Now he had been insulted, and since leaving Franklin Rufus had been carrying a feeling of being lost. That feeling now turned to anger. The big man walked around his friends and pulled himself up to full height. He stood maybe an inch or two above Rufus and had another hundred pounds on him.

Rufus pulled the Colt and the man froze, asking, "You afraid to back up your talk?"

"Hube, come over here," Rufus said.

The bartender came over and saw the drawn Colt. "What the hell, Rufus. We don't want no killing in here."

Without taking his eyes off the big man, Rufus held the revolver toward Hube. "I want you to keep this Colt on his three compadres and if they try and help Jake here, I would like you to shoot them. Now me and Jake are going outside so we don't mess up Louie's place."

With a look of relief, the bartender took the Colt and kept it aimed in the direction of the three other hunters. The men playing cards, overhearing the fighting talk, headed outside to watch. Rufus placed his knife on the bar when the man swung.

At this time, Rufus wasn't near drunk enough to be an easy mark. He managed to dodge, taking a glancing blow off the side of his cheek. At the same time, he brought his right up, hitting the man in the stomach and then followed with a left to the man's jaw.

Surprised at the quickness of his opponent, the big man stumbled back a couple of steps. With a roar he came back, attempting to crush Rufus against the bar. The mountain man was able to side step enough to avoid the full impact of the charge but was knocked into the wall at the end of the bar.

Figuring he had Rufus trapped between the bar and the wall, Jake lowered his head and charged for the second time. The mountain man had had enough time to brace himself and he stepped away from the bar as he swung, landing a punch on the man's ear. Jakes momentum carried him into the wall head-first.

By this time the other three men had been motioned back by the Colt-carrying bartender. Stunned, Jake turned, in an animal rage, looking for Rufus with wild eyes. The mountain man threw his next punch, breaking the big man's nose and spraying blood across the bar.

Clinging to the bar, trying to clear his head, the big man saw Rufus' knife. He grabbed it and, waving the knife, went after Rufus. Grabbing the knife-wielding arm by the wrist, Rufus let the man's momentum bring Jake past him as the mountain man stuck a leg out to trip the hunter.

The big man hit the floor with a crash with Rufus on top of him. The mountain man had twisted the arm and he put the knife under the man's throat. "Are we done here, or do I have to shove this blade to the hilt and end your miserable life?" he hissed. To make a point he pressed the tip into Jake's throat, breaking the skin.

He heard one of the other buffalo hunters holler to Hube, "Make him stop. He is going to kill Jake."

The big man was beaten and bruised, but not ready to die. "I'm done," he said, feeling blood run down the side of his neck.

"You finished beating on him?" Hube asked.

Taking the knife out of the big man's hand, Rufus replied, "I believe so."

The mountain man stood up, using the bar to steady himself and said to the bartender, "I'll buy the next bottle for these men."

His friends helped the big man up. One of the men turned to Rufus. "I appreciate you not killing Jake. He's married to my sister, and if I let him die I'd have hell to pay."

Another of the men thanked Rufus for the bottle. The card players came back into the trading post, disappointed that they had missed the fight by going outside. Rufus rubbed the bruise on his cheek and his hand came back bloody. The first punch from the big man had split the skin.

It was two hours later and dark outside when Rufus left the trading post. By that time he and the buffalo hunters were good friends. The mountain man staggered toward the livery. The feeling Rufus had had since he'd left Franklin was gone. He was looking forward to reaching the mountains and doing some hunting.

The sound of groaning the next morning alerted Johnson that Rufus was awake. "If you ain't too sick, come on down for coffee," he called to the man in the loft.

Rufus sat up and hurt all over. The eye above the bruised cheek had swollen partly shut and his beard was stiff with blood. The hangover was worse than the beaten body as his head pounded and his stomach churned. His jaw hurt when he smiled. It had been a good night.

Climbing down from the loft, the mountain man steadied himself at the bottom. Johnson looked at him. "You look like hell and what is that smell?"

"Had a disagreement with some buffalo hunters and some of the smell rubbed off on me," Rufus said. Then he added, "But I won."

Disappointed, the smoky-eyed man replied, "I imagine you did."

Johnson had some porridge on the potbelly stove to go with the coffee. It should have been a treat for the mountain man with the honey in it, but Rufus ate it kind of slow, letting his upset stomach get used to the breakfast.

"Where are you heading for?" Johnson asked.

"There's a place near the Yellowstone that was never worth going to because it only had a few beavers. Being that it is late in the season, I figure to trap a few for pelts and meat."

"You coming back here to winter?" the smoky-eyed man asked.

"I think I will build me a nice little shack and winter in the mountains," Rufus told him. Truth was, he didn't have much money to spend at the fort. It would have to be a dry winter.

"Well, I won't miss seeing you," Johnson replied.

Something in his voice made Rufus not quite believe him. Just maybe Johnson was sorry to hear he wouldn't be coming back for the winter.

* * *

The last of the leaves were falling from the trees as Rufus rode into the mountain valley. He was just south of the Teton mountains. A stream ran through the valley and had a couple of dams and several beaver lodges. There was an abundance of pine, balsam, and poplar for building the shanty. The valley was protected by the mountains from the most severe storms.

Setting up his fly tarp near the stream, he stored his packs under it. He then led the horses a short distance away and picketed them on the knee-high, brown grass. "This will be our home this winter," he told the animals. "Plenty of grass and enough beavers to keep me busy until the ponds freeze over."

Since leaving the fort, Rufus had found himself talking to the horses more. With no prospect of another voice around him, he figured he'd have to listen to his own. With the animals taken care of, the mountain man put together a fire and set his soup pot heating so he could boil the traps he had taken with him.

Rufus had already chosen a spot to build his winter shelter. To the north there was a slope with tall pine. The first year he had come trapping the company had them build shanties for the winter. They had been simple structures with wide doorways on the south side and fire pits near them for heat and cooking. Either canvas or buffalo hides were hung to close the openings when storms blew in. The mountain man had a buffalo hide gotten from the hunters.

Putting a little oil into the steaming pot, he put in some of the traps. Rufus then walked towards the nearest pond to pick out spots to set the traps. Finding several places, he then went into some small poplar and cut stakes for securing the traps and baiting them. Arriving back at the fire with the stakes, Rufus was pleased to find the pot boiling. Fishing the traps from the water, he lay them on a windfall to cool and then put a couple more into the water.

It was late afternoon when Rufus left the camp leading both horses. He had the pack saddle on the mustang with the traps hanging from it. Rufus had decided to take both animals and water them while he was setting the traps.

"Sure wish I had Caleb here to set these traps," he said, chuckling as he remembered the young man complaining of having to set the first traps.

It was starting to get dark when the mountain man returned to the camp, with his buckskins wet to the knees. The fire was down to coals, so he broke up some branches onto them before filling his coffee pot from the stream. Placing the coffee water to heat, he sat onto the windfall. Looking around the valley, he thought about the coming winter.

In all his years of trapping, he had only spent a couple by himself. If it hadn't been for finding Caleb stranded on the prairie, he would have probably continued trapping alone. The kid was only 15 then and had been determined to go trapping with Rufus. While the mountain man had had his doubts about taking the young man, it had worked out very well and had continued until the past year.

What Rufus figured he would miss the most on the long winter nights was when the young man would read his books to Rufus. The mountain man hadn't any books with him because he could not read. He had grown up on the move with his father dragging him from one saloon or brothel after another, so the possibility of any schooling had been out of the question. Rufus had picked up working with numbers, reading cards, and counting money.

After drinking some coffee and chewing jerky for his supper, Rufus spread out his blankets under the tarp. He had the Colt within easy reach under the saddle and the Hawken next to his blanket. The night sounds gave him no cause for alarm. Soon the mountain man was asleep.

The sounds of the horses snorting woke him just before daylight. There was a near full moon that bathed the valley in a pale light. Rufus took the Colt from under the saddle and quietly turned to look for anything that might have disturbed the horses. He caught a glimpse of something, maybe a wolf, trotting away from the camp.

"You bastard. You best be just passing through," he whispered, "or I'll be stretching a wolf skin."

By the stars, Rufus knew it was near morning, so he pulled on his boots and started putting a fire together. As he worked on heating water for his breakfast, the mountain man worried a bit about the wolf. It could be in the area hunting beaver, or his animals might have attracted them.

While the water heated, he rummaged through the poplar branches he'd brought back. Selecting some about the right length and thickness, Rufus began to make some hoops for the beaver pelts. The morning was frigid and the wool shirt over his long johns left him feeling the chill. He experienced a stiffness in his joints as he moved around.

Rufus was only 34 years-old, but to look at him one would think he was older due to his rugged, weathered face from too many years in the outdoors. Sleeping on the ground most of the time had also taken its toll. In return the lifestyle had given him strength and stamina.

He felt restless, anxious to go and check the traps. He dug out the frying pan and some side meat and began making some for his breakfast. Even the meat seemed to cook more slowly this morning.

"Damn!" he scolded himself. "This ain't your first morning of trapping. Settle your damn self down. Them beaver will be there when you finish eating."

It brought to mind the first morning Caleb had set traps and how the young man had begged to hurry and check the traps. A smile spread across the mountain man's face as he thought about his young partner.

Then Rufus froze. Something had moved near the pines. He had just caught the slight change in the shadows from the corner of his eye. Slowly pulling the Hawken across his lap, he sat watching. He could feel eyes on him.

"Just do as much as a heavy breath and I'll put a ball right through your middle," he threatened in a raspy voice.

Suddenly his attention went back to the frying pan and he smelled his breakfast burning. Pulling the pan off the fire, Rufus felt the sting of the hot handle. Most of the grease spilt onto the coals, flaring up into black smoke and flames.

Shaking his burnt fingers, he swore, "You damn fool. Way to scare away whatever the hell is near the pines."

The mountain man also knew that rather than a wild animal, it could be some Blackfoot, Shoshone, Bannock, or Cheyenne watching his camp. Of the tribes, he got along with all but the Shoshone and Bannock. Even they should be more to the west this time of year.

Quickly eating the burnt meat and dabbing some hard bread into what was left of the grease, he finished his meal. He hadn't gotten any coffee into the pot, so he just drank the heated water. Following his own rules, he cleaned up the dishes in the stream before going to check on the traps.

Again, he led the two horses, not wanting to leave one alone in case a wolf should come after it, or a brave would make a prize of it. There were two prime beavers in the traps. After resetting the traps, moving one, and adding castor to the bait sticks, Rufus headed back to his camp. The two beavers were between 30 and 40 pounds and would make a fine start for his catch.

It was two more days before Rufus began building his shanty. He swung the axe with a woodsman's expertise. Large chunks flew as he cut the notches, felling the trees. He used the mustang to skid the limbed pines to the building site. He had moved his camp near the site even though the stream ran several hundred feet away. The shanty would be on a high spot and safe from the spring floods.

Each morning, after checking the traps, Rufus would skin any beaver he caught and then go to work on his winter quarters. He had flattened two sides of the logs so they would fit closer together. Lots of small cracks were left and would allow the winter winds to blow in, but once the snow was deep enough he'd shovel it up against the windward side to seal them.

The shanty appeared much larger than one man would need, but Rufus planned to bring the stock inside during severe snowstorms. It would protect the horses and offer him the warmth from their bodies. The downside would be he'd have their droppings to clean.

The leeward side of the shanty was a couple of feet higher than the windward side to allow a slope to the balsam pole roof he was going to build. Half of the roof area would be covered by his fly tarp to keep the rain and snow off his sleeping area and packs. The rest of it would be covered with balsam boughs and a few poles to hold them in place.

After two weeks of work, the shanty was complete. Rufus had put a low wall beyond the fire pit to deflect heat toward the shanty opening. While skinning and fleshing his morning catch, he looked at the building. The mountain man was pleased with the crude shanty. It would make a fine winter quarters.

After removing the pelts and meat, Rufus had been hauling the beaver carcasses about a half-mile from the shanty. He noticed that the wolf, or a coyote, had visited the remains and would tear them apart and often drag some away. The few tracks around the carcasses told him that whatever was coming was a lone animal. A plan started to form in his mind. It was almost time for another full moon. Rufus would find a place to watch for the animal to come and bag himself a nice wolf skin, or maybe a coyote.

With the shanty complete and his traps in place, he now had two more things to do before the snow flew. Rufus needed fire wood and some meat to hold him over during the winter months. It was freezing most nights, but the days were still too warm to hang a haunch or two. It was time to make wood.

The beavers had cut several poplars down near the ponds, so Rufus began to skid them near the shanty. Three items he had brought from Fort William were the axe, a shovel, and a buck saw. It had been necessary to cut the doorway and now would be good for cutting firewood. The chores needed for survival were good for the mountain man. They kept him busy and prevented him thinking about being alone.

Three days of cold rain gave him a chance to spend time in the shanty. One night he brought the two horses in to see how they all fit. Their steaming bodies did keep the building warm, almost too warm for the time of year. Another month or two and they would do a fine job of keeping the edge off the cold. With the horses inside it was close quarters, but would work out.

The rain took whatever leaves that were left off the trees and it was now stick season with the naked limbs of the poplar and maple. The dark, rich green of the balsam and pine gave a cozy look to the valley. The moon was full and it was time to do some wolf hunting. With the sun just above the mountains, Rufus headed out with the Hawken to watch the carcass pile.

He had just settled in when he caught movement in the trees. "Well," he said, "you are either brave or damn hungry. I just tossed the morning catch on the pile."

With a chew in his cheek and the rifle ready to bring up, Rufus anticipated the wolf coming to the carcasses. Again, he saw movement. There was something in the balsams and it was being careful about coming out. The mountain man held still and watched. A bit of excitement ran through him that every hunter feels when they know game is close.

Then, in the dim light of the setting sun, he saw the animal come out. Disappointed, he realized it was large but not a wolf. He watched as the animal approached the carcasses and sunk its teeth into one and dragged it a short distance. It then lay down and began to tear chunks off the beaver.

Two things became readily apparent. It was neither a wolf nor a coyote. It was some kind of white, long-haired dog! *What the hell is a dog doing out here alone?* Rufus wondered.

There was no value in a dog skin and if he wasn't going to eat it, it was not worth killing. For the next hour the mountain man watched as the dog tore at the carcass. He could see it was a male. It had probably been with one of the tribes and somehow gotten left behind.

The moon was going behind some clouds when Rufus finally stood up, scaring the animal away. "I'll keep you fed until the ponds ice over," he called to the fleeing animal.

CHAPTER FIVE

Large snowflakes were falling as Rufus rode away from the shanty in search of winter meat. The ponds had started to have ice forming along the edge and he had pretty much trapped the area, leaving enough beavers to restock the pond for future seasons.

For the last few weeks he had been leaving scraps of meat closer and closer to the shanty. The dog would wait until dark and come and get them. Several times Rufus had been able to sit near the shanty and watch the animal work its way to the meat before grabbing it and running off. The mountain man would talk softly to the white animal as it came, hoping to make it aware that he wasn't a danger.

To the northeast, Rufus had heard elk bugling and hoped to find an area where they grazed or bedded down. It was late in the rutting season, so soon the herd would wander to lower elevations for the winter. The ground under the trees was covered with pungent-smelling gold leaves. The grulla kept up a good pace, appearing anxious to be going beyond the valley.

Rufus had the mustang's lead rope tied to the back of the saddle.

His Hawken was balanced across the front of his saddle and the Colt was in his broad belt. Rufus had seen holsters at the fort, but wearing buckskins and a broad belt left no way of carrying it on his hip. The revolver, weighing almost three pounds and being nearly 14 inches-long, had to sit at a slant in the broad belt. The mountain man preferred it that way. It made the Colt easy to draw.

Climbing out of the valley, Rufus entered the pines. The smell of the poplar leaves was replaced with that of evergreens. He was following a winding trail made by deer, elk, or buffalo as they traversed from valley to valley in search of grazing. At noon he stopped to rest the horses with the view of a long valley cut by a rapidly flowing river. Along the valley there were several swampy areas with dense growths of cedar trees. He hoped to find elk or deer in these areas.

As Rufus chewed on some jerky, something following his trail caught his eye. Smiling, he recognized the dog. "Are you worried about missing a meal?" he called out.

It had disappeared into the trees. "With luck we'll both have meat for the winter," he said to himself.

By nightfall Rufus had ridden well into the valley and chose to spend the night in a growth of spruce trees. In late afternoon he had heard the bugling of bull elk farther down the valley. With luck he'd come across a herd sometime tomorrow.

Using a large spruce for cover, Rufus set up a quick camp. The horses were picketed a short distance away and had been watered. Over a small fire, the mountain man boiled some cold flour and made coffee. What was left of the cold flour would make an easy breakfast. As he ate the thickened mixture, Rufus listened to the night sounds. There were owls, wolves, and the grazing horses.

Rufus slept in his clothing with a blanket covering him. He lay thinking of how he'd process the meat. Making some into jerky was a possibility. The sun was just breaking over the eastern hills when he woke.

Lying with his eyes closed and enjoying the warmth of his blanket, the mountain man listened for the horses. Then he realized that not far from him he could hear breathing, or more like panting. Without moving, he opened his eyes and looked around. Whatever it was, it was slightly behind him. Sliding his arm under the saddle, he gripped the Colt and drew it near his chest.

His hat, which he slept with to cover his head and face, had fallen away during the night. With the Colt ready, Rufus slowly craned his neck to look in the direction of the breathing. Then he stopped! Not 30 feet away lay the shaggy white dog, its whiskers cover with frost from the steam of its breath. It had evidently been out for a morning hunt and was still panting from the excursion.

Softly, Rufus said, "Nice to see you're still around."

The sound of his gravelly voice startled the dog and it bounded away into the trees. "You don't have to be that way," he called to the dog. "I am about to get some nice, fresh meat."

There was no sign of the animal as Rufus had his breakfast and broke down the camp. With the gear on the horses, he took one more look around. "I'll be going now," he called, not knowing if the dog had even stayed around.

About another mile down the valley, Rufus was coming over a rise when he saw a small herd of female elk. For a while the mountain man had been hearing a male bugling in search of the females. Sliding out of the saddle, Rufus led the horses, using some trees for cover. The wind was in his face, so he wasn't worried about them catching his scent.

When he was about 300 yards from the elk he saw movement across the valley. It was a bull elk. Its head was stretched out and its horns laid back as it searched for the smell of a receptive female. Then there was movement further down the valley. Another male had appeared. The two males immediately turned toward each other.

"Looks like we have a fight coming," he said to the grulla.

Within view of Rufus the battle for the females began. The two males locked horns and began testing each other's strength. As the challenges became more aggressive, clods of dirt began to fly and two angry bulls pushed one another back and forth, trying to gain dominance.

While all of this was going on, Rufus had picked out the female he wanted to bag. They had continued to graze, ignoring the fighting suitors. "I hate to break up this fun," he said as he brought the Hawken to his shoulder, "but a man has got to eat."

Lining his sights on a large female, Rufus pulled the rifle to full cock. He pulled the set trigger and then touched off the hair trigger. The Hawken recoiled, sending smoke and fire out the barrel as the ball streaked across the valley.

For a second nothing happened, and then as one the female elk leaped into action. The sound of the shot echoed in the valley while the determined bulls kept on fighting. Rufus watched as one of the females began to lag and then went down. By this time the two bulls had either realized that the females were leaving them, or the sound of the rifle had sunk into the fevered brains. They took off in the direction of the females, still making swipes at one another.

After reloading the rifle, Rufus climbed onto the grulla and led the mustang toward the downed elk. Having eaten beaver meat or jerky for over a month, the mountain man was looking forward to the elk meat and the liver. Swinging off the horse next to the elk, Rufus tapped the downed animal with the Hawken barrel. He could see that he'd hit the elk just behind the shoulder.

Leaning the rifle against a boulder, the mountain man pulled out his Green River knife. Working quickly with the knife, he cut open the elk and removed the guts. When he removed the liver, he laid it onto the boulder. "Makes a man look forward to an early supper," Rufus said, smiling.

Something moving in the trees caught his attention. He looked up, expecting to see the white dog. It was not the dog, but the silver outlines of two wolves. Wiping the knife on the elk hindquarter, he watched them move. There was a good chance that these wolves spent time on the plains following the buffalo hunters. The sound of the rifle was like a supper bell to them.

The mountain man had put the Colt into a saddlebag to prevent it from getting bloody while cutting up the elk. He now went and retrieved it. He noticed that the horses were staring at the trees nervously. Rufus talked softly to the animals as he moved them, putting the kill between them and the woods. He tied the reins and lead rope to a small poplar. It wouldn't prevent the horses from breaking loose if the wolves came out of the woods to claim the kill, but it would prevent them from trying to put more distance from the wolves prior to any aggressive behavior.

While keeping an eye on the wolves, which kept disappearing into the trees and then reappearing, Rufus hurried to finish cutting up the elk. He removed much of hide for use during the winter. He then began to load the choice cuts and hind quarters onto the mustang. Rufus had had plans of starting a fire after cutting the animal up and frying the liver, but the close proximity of the wolves changed them.

Once the elk was loaded, he casually picked up the Hawken while keeping his eyes on one of the wolves. His intention was to shoot one for the skin. The wolves had evidently been shot at before, because he'd hardly moved the rifle and they were gone. Rufus slid the Hawken into the scabbard and then, as an afterthought, he went back to the elk and removed part of the shoulder and some ribs.

Climbing onto the grulla, he adjusted the Colt and headed back towards his camp. No doubt after he was out of sight the wolves would be back fighting over the remains of the elk. He felt some regret, because he figured the dog would have liked to have made a meal before following Rufus back to camp.

The mountain man stopped just before going over the foothills to his valley and made camp. His mind had been on the elk liver since starting back.

Rufus doubted that the wolves would follow him. They had several days of good eating at the elk. He stopped at the head of the stream that would eventually flow past his shanty. There was some grass for the horses and the spot was sheltered by a growth of pine.

Remaining alert to the actions of the horse and the sounds around him, Rufus put together a fire. While he wasn't worried about the wolves he'd seen, there could always be more, or even bears that could catch the smell of the fresh meat. As he waited for the fire to get hot enough for frying the liver, Rufus took the shoulder and ribs. Walking about 30 paces from his camp, he set them down.

Looking around he said, "This is for you, dog. I don't expect you were willing to fight the wolves for your share."

His words echoed off the hills with no sight of the white, shaggy dog. Returning to the fire, Rufus took out some side meat and sliced a couple of pieces into the blackened frying pan. As they began to snap, he went and filled his coffee pot and set it near the flames to heat. Slicing the liver, he laid the slabs into the frying pan. The smell of the frying side meat and liver made his mouth water with anticipation.

While eating his meal with his knife out of the frying pan, Rufus caught sight of the large, shaggy animal sitting a short distance from the elk pieces he'd left. "It's yours, dog," he called to it.

Taking its time, the dog walked toward the ribs and shoulder. It appeared to be favoring a back leg. Sniffing the elk, the dog began to lick the ribs. Rufus could see that it already had some blood on its muzzle. He moved to get more coffee and the dog's head came up. Its tail, which was normally down, went up over its back and then it growled. "Don't be like that," Rufus told the dog in his gravelly voice. "You got yours and I had mine."

The mountain man noticed that the dog had just given a warning and did not try and drag the meal farther away. As the sun went down, Rufus could hear the animal gnawing on the bones. In the distance the sounds of the wolves howling drifted into the camp. The horses remained calm, cropping the grass.

The next morning Rufus was up early. He didn't like to leave the shanty vacant for any length of time. He had extra supplies and the beaver pelts stored in it, and the smells could tempt a predator. With the gear on the horses and the elk meat on the mustang, he was ready to go. The white dog remained near the elk ribs and shoulder. He noticed that it was licking the injured back leg. In the morning light he had seen some blood on the leg as well as its neck.

"You got into it with the wolves and got some licks in, didn't you?" he told the dog. "I'm just sorry that I didn't get a ball into one of them. I think you could have taken the rest of that elk fighting them one on one."

He was about to ride out when he heard the dog whine. Looking back, Rufus saw it standing on three legs looking at him. "Last night you were growling and snarling at me," he told the white animal. "Now you're whining like you don't want me to go."

A feeling of dread came over the mountain man. There was a good chance the dog was injured more than he'd thought. It wouldn't be right to leave it to suffer. Climbing off the grulla, Rufus looped the reins around a low bush. He adjusted the Colt in his belt. Then he took a few steps toward the dog.

It continued to stand on three legs staring at him, but now the tail was over its back. Rufus put out a hand and took a few more steps. The dog tried to move away, but ended up falling into a sitting position. It then laid down and looked up at the mountain man, its lip quivering off its teeth.

"Is it your intension to attack me?" Rufus asked. "You are in pretty damn bad shape to try and do that."

It was a standoff. The dog lay growling softly, and Rufus stood watching the animal and trying to determine how bad the injuries were. "How about I get you some water and we can talk about this."

Heading back toward the horses to get something to carry water, he heard the dog whine. Ignoring the animal, he dug into his pack and fished out the frying pan. Walking over to the stream, he filled it with water and then walked back toward the dog. As the mountain man got closer, the dog again let out a warning growl.

"I got some water here for you," Rufus said. "If you snap at me and make me spill it, I ain't going to fetch another."

Rufus could now see the injured leg. The wolf had managed to sink its teeth into the lower thigh, leaving bloody streaks on the dog's leg. The mountain man knew that there might be tendon damage. In that case he'd have no choice but to put the dog down.

Standing a short distance from the animal, Rufus waited until the warning growls ceased. He set the pan down and slowly slid it toward the dog. He could see that the animal's eyes were on the pan and not him. Rufus also saw that one of the small triangular ears was split and bloody. He left it about two feet from the animal. The water, along with the smell of side meat and liver in the pan, should tempt the dog enough to move.

Rufus walked back to the horses and watched the dog. It had been in a fight with the wolves and survived. The mountain man had a new respect for the animal. The dog had pulled itself closer to the pan and was lapping some water. Rufus had to be heading back to the shanty and the dog was beginning to be a problem. He was only a half-day from the shanty and was beginning to think he'd give the dog a couple of hours. If it wasn't back on its feet, he'd have to save it from a slow and lingering death.

Leading the horse back to his campsite, Rufus pulled the pack off the mustang and sat on a windfall. Reaching into his possible bag, he took out a twist of tobacco and tore off a chew. For the next hour he sat watching the shaggy, white dog. It remained lying down and reached over every once in a while, to lick the back leg.

The mountain man was half dozing when there as a snarl and he looked. The dog was on its feet, tail over its back, facing a wolf not ten paces away from it. Without thinking, Rufus drew the Colt and sighted on the wolf and fired twice. The wolf wheeled, yelping, and ran for the trees. The dog attempted to take chase, but stopped after a short distance, its neck hair on end and its back leg shaking.

When Rufus had fired the wolf was just 50 paces away, which was well within the range of the Colt Paterson. The impact of the .36 caliber ball would be enough to cause serious damage to the wolf if the shot was well-placed. Whether that was the case, Rufus did not know. All he knew was that the wolf was focused on the injured dog and had paid little attention to anything else. One other thing he knew was that he was not going to shoot the dog. It had too much heart.

Sticking the Colt into his broad belt, Rufus got the Hawken from the scabbard and went to find out how badly he'd hit the wolf. He walked right past the dog and it didn't appear to notice him as it stared in the direction of the retreating wolf. Rufus saw blood on the leaves. He had hit the animal.

The wolf had taken a beeline for the trees and the mountain man found several drops of blood as he followed the animal. A short distance into the trees, he caught sight of the gray fur of the wolf. It had fallen and rolled into a ball against a pine. It lay with its head against the ground and growled threateningly at Rufus. Drawing the Colt from his belt, Rufus put a killing shot into its head.

Grabbing the back legs of the wolf, Rufus dragged it out of the trees and left it near the growling dog. "You saw it first," he said. "I'll get the horses while you figure what you're going to do with it."

Walking toward the horses, Rufus could hear the dog following behind him. He grabbed the packs and placed them onto the mustang, then turned to get the elk hindquarters. The dog was sniffing the hide and then moved away when Rufus approached. "That meat will get us through the winter," he told the animal as he got hold of a hind quarter and lifted it onto the horse.

It was a long trip back to the shanty. Rufus had tied the wolf over the grulla's saddle and he walked, leading the horses all the way over the foothills to the valley. The dog stayed a short distance behind, favoring the back leg. Rufus talked to the dog about trapping, building the shanty, the weather, and anything else that came to mind.

It was dark when they reached the shanty. Rufus was thankful that nothing had gotten into the furs or supplies. He had plans of building a closure out of balsam logs to put in front of the building when he had to leave, but that had not been done yet.

The air was cold and it smelled like snow was coming. Rufus was stripped down to his long john top, having been too warm with the buckskin shirt during the hike. The dog lay a short distance from the shanty and watched him as he got the fire going.

"After we eat the rest of the liver, I got to hang the meat high enough so wolves or bears won't be able to reach it," he told the dog. It ignored him and licked the wounded leg.

* * *

The mistrust between them was gone. While the dog was on the mend, Rufus would share some of his meal with it. Evidently the leg was more bruised than cut by the wolf attack. Once the bruising had healed the dog would disappear during the day and hunt for its own food. They had been having light snowfalls, which mostly melted off if the day was sunny.

In late December they had their first heavy snow. By this time, the dog would remain outside the shanty, near the horses. When Rufus had the horses close to the shanty it would venture into the structure and lie on some balsam branches that the mountain man had stacked just inside the doorway.

The snow had stopped and Rufus sat in the shanty, wearing his warm wool clothing, looking out the opening. The night had brought a foot of frozen white stuff. The dog had moved near him, offering some warmth, or maybe it was receiving some. The snow was thick on the horses' backs and melting down their sides. Rufus pulled on his calf-high moccasins and ventured outside.

The firewood was cut and stacked along the high side of the shanty. Rufus knocked the snow off some smaller sticks and then kicked the snow out of the firepit. He had some dry pine needles for tinder and soon had the fire going. Packing snow into the coffee pot, he put it next to the flames. He looked back and saw that the dog had remained in the shanty.

"You going to spend all day lazing around?" he asked it. "You should be out hunting a rabbit or grouse by now." The dog ignored him and laid back down.

Smiling, the mountain man got out the frying pan and some side meat. "It'll be a fine day for making frying pan bread," he told the dog.

It felt good having the animal around to talk to. While it seemed to ignore him, Rufus was sure it listened to everything he said. Rufus spoke some Cheyenne and Crow, so he tried talking to the dog in those languages in case it had once been with one of the tribes. He received the same lack of interest from the animal.

The mountain man had dragged a good-sized log from a windfall to the front of the shanty and had flattened one side to make sitting on it more comfortable. As the side meat sizzled in the blackened pan, he sat on the log and looked around the valley. The snowfall had made it a winter wonderland.

"You don't find beauty like this in the south," he told the dog. "A man's got to come up here into the mountains to see this."

The dog got up and lifted its leg, relieving itself on the edge of the shanty doorway. Then as it trotted away, Rufus called after it. "You could have gotten a little further from the damn shanty before pissin'."

With his breakfast cooked, Rufus sat on the log with the pan of bread, side meat and a steaming cup of coffee. Long ago he realized that he didn't much like eating alone. He looked wistfully at the tracks the dog had made as it headed out in search of its meal. With nobody to talk to, the mountain man wolfed down the meal and gulped down the quickly cooling coffee.

Using the snow to clean his frying pan, he then placed it on top of his packs before going to take care of the horses. He had a brief concern when he saw other tracks in the snow around the horses. It quickly went away when he realized that the dog must have come out during the night.

Most of the snow had slid off their backs, so a few swipes removed what was left. "You're going to have to dig for your meal today," he told them as he led the animals out to graze.

Kicking snow away to pound in the pickets, he thought about what was to come. Soon the ground would be too frozen to pound a picket in and he'd have to sit out near the animals while they were wandering and grazing. Rufus had put up some hay behind the shanty for stormy weather when he'd have to keep the animals inside.

He still had some of the elk left, but with the change in the weather, Rufus figured he'd best see if he could spot a mule deer or even an elk that had come down from the higher elevations. For any of the smaller game the mountain man would be competing with the lynxes, bobcats, and coyotes. The area also had big cats, and possibly some bears that hadn't denned up yet.

After letting the horses graze for a couple of hours, Rufus brought them to the shanty and put on the saddles. On the mustang he placed a few things in a pack that would be needed if a storm came in before they returned.

Turning the grulla toward the west, Rufus rode down the valley. Breathing the crisp air and watching the snow fly from the horse's hooves breaking through put the mountain man into a good mood. About five miles west, the valley opened to the south with some marshy areas. He would also take this opportunity to gauge the beaver activity and see if it would be worth moving there in the spring to finish his trapping.

The two horses walked through the new snow with ease. The night had been mostly calm and there was very little drifting. With the leaves gone from the trees, it made spotting game much simpler. Then again, the game had the same advantage, so it made getting close more difficult.

The sky remained covered with thin, high clouds and a cold breeze came over the mountain and across the valley. Rufus left the Hawken in the scabbard and had the Colt under the wool coat. He wasn't hunting for anything that would bound away quickly, so he was able to keep his gloves on when gripping the cold metal of the rifle.

He came to the widening of the valley without spotting any movement on the ridges of the tree-covered foothills around him. While he hadn't expected to see anything, he had hoped that luck would be with him and he'd get a shot at a mule deer.

Swinging off the grulla near an open stream, Rufus let the animals drink while he pulled the canteen from under his coat. It was filled with the morning's leftover coffee and he took a sip of the cold, bitter brew. It was better than water, but not much.

As the horses pawed the ground, looking for forage, Rufus slowly looked around the hills and valley. Squinting against the glare of the snow, he could see some dark figures moving well down the valley. By the size he guessed that they were elk.

Climbing back onto the grulla, Rufus looked again for the elk. It appeared that they were moving further down to the west as they forged on the brown grass. He could take advantage of the valley widening to the south, circle around the elk and intercept them. Cutting across the valley floor to the south, the mountain man began his quest for the elk.

He came to an area where the stream cut across the valley and into the marsh. With the snow cover masking the wetland, Rufus had to be careful not to guide the horses into the swamp's muddy bottom. Cattails protruding up from the wet areas guided Rufus around the marsh. In the distance he could see willow trees growing near the edge.

Looking toward the west, Rufus could no longer see the elk. The ground in the center of the valley had risen, hiding the hunter and also the game. The mountain man was debating whether he should ride to higher ground and relocate the elk when an aggressive grunt was heard, causing the grulla to react.

Looking toward the swamp, Rufus' eyes grew large. Not 50 paces ahead of them was a bull moose challenging their passing! The large, lanky, big-nosed animal swung its horns and grunted again, repeating the challenge. Rufus knew that time was short. He had intruded on the bull eating the aquatic plants in the open water, and at any moment it could charge and injure his horse, not to mention himself.

The moose would be as good as an elk, Rufus thought. Pulling a glove off with his teeth, the mountain man reached down and pulled the Hawken from its scabbard. As the glove fell to the ground, he brought the rifle to his shoulder and pulled it to full cock. The moose grunted again and came at them! The grulla began to move, trying to get away from the bull.

"Damn!" Rufus shouted as he jumped from the horse, sliding onto his rear. Still in control of the Hawken, the mountain man rolled to his stomach, his knees on the marsh ice, and lined the sights on the charging moose.

The bull was focused on the horses and only 25 feet away when Rufus fired at the exposed shoulder. The .54 caliber ball struck the moose, breaking the shoulder and causing it to fall toward the mountain man. Flailing and kicking, the animal wasn't ten feet from Rufus. Rolling away, he felt the mushy ice give way as his knees sunk into the frigid water.

The sight of the huge hooves on the spindly legs and the webbed antlers only feet away from him was a terrifying sight for Rufus. Dropping the rifle, he tore at his wool coat to get to the Colt. The .36 caliber balls would do little to stop the wounded animal, but bogged down in the swamp the mountain man had few options.

Pulling out the Colt, he aimed and fired three shots into the bull. The moose laid there taking ragged breaths. The mountain man held the revolver level, sighting on the moose, his heart pounding until the animal finally lay still. Rufus gave it another minute before he finally climbed out of the swamp, water dripping from his soaked wool pants.

Picking the Hawken from the snow, he blew off the action and looked at the moose. Poking it with the barrel got no response. "You got me in a hell of a mess," Rufus told the bull.

Looking up, he saw the two horses an eighth of a mile into the valley, looking back at him. The cold was penetrating his legs and he began to shiver. Rufus leaned his legs against the moose, hoping to get some warmth from it. Even though he had never taught the animals to respond to a whistle, the mountain man did his best to try and get the horses to come.

They didn't move. There were no trees near Rufus and the willows were a couple hundred paces up the marsh. He yelled, "Hey, damn you! Come here! I got grain for you."

The mountain man gave up, realizing he either had to walk to the willows, taking a chance he would end up on more weak ice, or try and chase down the horses. One other thing he was aware of was that rather quickly the moose would start to freeze, making getting the hide off difficult.

Rufus started walking toward the horses, his pant legs had already frozen and his legs were aching with the cold. He stuck his bare hand into the front of the wool coat to protect it from the cold. "I should have looked for the damn glove," he muttered.

Suddenly, he caught sight of something white going after the horses! Blinking to clear his eyes, Rufus realized that it was the damn shaggy dog! Standing in disbelief, the mountain man saw the dog round up the two horses and drive them towards him. "You were trained to herd," Rufus breathed.

The mustang briefly tried to challenge the dog, then turned and followed the grulla. As soon as the dog had the horses near him, it quit chasing them and sat with its tongue hanging out. Rufus grabbed the reins of the grulla and then steadied himself against the horse. The mustang was only a few feet away, carrying a lifesaving pack.

In the pack were dry britches and wool socks. It was only a matter of minutes before Rufus changed into the clothes and benefited from their warmth. "You watch the horses," he told the dog as he turned to attend to the moose.

Other than the long, skinny legs, big hooves and nose, the moose was very much like a big deer or elk. After gutting the bull he tossed the kidneys to the dog. It lay chewing on them as the mountain man worked. With quick motions, Rufus removed the parts of the animal that he wanted to keep.

It was dark when Rufus arrived back at the shanty. He hadn't taken time to eat since breakfast, so the first thing he did before even unpacking the horses was get the fire going. He lay the moose liver nearby to be cooked for his supper.

As he pulled the gear off the animals and hung the meat in the pines near the shanty, Rufus thought about how close he'd been to freezing. Years back, when the mountain man was in his first year of trapping, he'd been hunting with a man named Harold, who had gone through the ice. If it hadn't been for Rufus being with him he would not have survived, even if he'd been able to get out of the river.

He thought about how important it was to be with a partner. Looking over at the dog, Rufus said, "I guess you are my partner on this trip."

The short winter days, followed by long nights, blended one into another as the mountain man went through the moves needed to survive the winter. Rufus found that the dog would watch the horses while they wandered and grazed, freeing up the mountain man.

Tending the fire, making meals out of shorter and shorter supplies, and telling the dog stories were pretty much Rufus' life for the coming months. He regretted not going back to Fort William for the winter. He could have hunted for meat to make a few dollars to keep him in whiskey.

Some afternoons he found himself repeating stories that Caleb had read to him from the books. The dog would listen while chewing on a bone that had the meat boiled off. The mountain man was thankful for one thing. He had lots of wood and often had a good-sized fire going.

In February the valley had its first blizzard. Rufus saw it coming over the mountains and quickly brought the horses next to the shanty. The wind was picking up and the blowing snow obscured the valley to the west.

Piling additional wood onto the fire, he put the bean pot and coffee pot to heat. Rufus led the horses into the shanty and lowered the buffalo hide that was rolled up above the doorway. He secured it on one side as the wind tore at him. Rufus looked around but did not see the dog.

Ducking into the shanty, he grabbed a bag of rice. Heading back for the fire, Rufus poured some into the bean pot and then sat upwind from it to help block the storm. He could feel the blowing snow getting into every loose part of his clothing.

While he was less than ten feet from the shanty, soon he could hardly see it. Rufus had no idea whether or not the rice had had enough time to cook, but it no longer mattered. Soon he wouldn't be able to even see the pot, much less the shanty. It was time to get under cover.

The wind howled and tore at him as he carried the sloshing pot of rice toward the shanty. The untied side of the buffalo hide was whipping in the storm. Rufus ducked under it and gained the safety of the shanty. It was almost dark inside and he felt his way between the wall and the mustang as he worked his way to the back.

There wasn't much more than three feet between the horse's heads and the back wall. He had hay piled in the area that he used to sleep on. It would be the feed for the horses during the storm. Rufus could feel snow hitting his face as it blew between the logs. The shanty wasn't weather-tight, but it would help.

Going back to the opening, Rufus hollered for the dog. His words were torn away by the wind and he knew it wouldn't be able to hear him. He was unable to see the fire out front. No doubt the wind had blown it out. Grabbing the buffalo hide, he pulled down on the loose end. A gust almost jerked the mountain man out of the shanty. Holding tight, he managed to tie it down.

He sat near the opening, breathing hard, wondering about the dog. The sound of the storm around the shanty was deafening. An awful feeling of sadness swept through Rufus as he realized that he'd probably never see the shaggy animal again. The rest of the winter he would be truly alone.

Rufus crawled to the back of the shanty sat on the hay. Pulling his gloves off, he felt for the pot of rice. In a short time, most of the heat was gone from the pot. He lay on the hay, thinking that he'd better eat some of the rice before it froze. Exhausted from fighting the storm, he dozed.

Snorting by the horses brought him back awake. Then he heard something. Then it came again. It was a growl. The dog had managed to get in under the buffalo hide. "Don't be scaring the horses," he warned the animal. "The damn animals will kick this place apart and we'll all be back in the storm."

For the next two days, the horses, the large, shaggy dog, and Rufus huddled in the crude shanty, which defied the storm as it battered the structure. The horses ate most of the hay, leaving the mountain man lying on the frozen ground. The rice had been crunchy and soon froze. Rufus had managed to drink the water from the pot before this happened. His coffee pot was still somewhere near the fire, hopefully still full of frozen water to prevent the wind from blowing it away.

At no time did they have enough light to be able to tell if it was day or night. The horses would lick at the snow that was blowing into the shanty, but it did little to help stave their thirst. Rufus would feel around and take some of the drifting snow and eat it. The saving grace from all of this was that with the two horses in the shanty, the temperature remained bearable. The dog remained close to Rufus and kept the horses at bay.

Up until the storm, the white dog had not let Rufus get close enough to touch it. In the cramped quarters the mountain man's hand had rested on its back. Rufus felt the animal stiffen, but it did not move. He could feel the coarse outer hair, and then his fingers felt the soft, thick under-fur. The big, shaggy animal was designed to handle winter weather in the mountains.

In spite of the storm, the dog would leave the shelter and venture outside the shanty. How far the animal went Rufus didn't know. Maybe it was just to relieve itself, or eat some snow to quench its thirst. After some hours it would return and lay near Rufus again. The mountain man had resorted to relieving himself against the short wall of the shanty. If he had tried to do so at the buffalo hide the wind would have blown it back onto him.

It was dark when the wind died. The mountain man had no idea how many days they had been hunkered down in the shanty. Hungry and thirsty, they sat in the gloom of the shanty and waited for any sign of daylight. Abandoning the blanket that he had kept around him during the storm, Rufus went outside of the buffalo hide.

A light wind was still blowing and clouds still filled the sky, preventing him from seeing the stars and determining what time it was. It appeared that the snow had blown from the front of the shanty, so Rufus decided to build a small fire. He could then use the bean pot to warm some water.

Turning to the side of the shanty with the wood pile, the mountain man took a couple of steps and then walked right into a drift that was higher than his head. Stumbling and falling against the drift, he rolled back and sat near the buffalo hide.

"Damn darkness. Damn snow," the mountain man grumbled. "Where the hell is the sun? A man could freeze or starve just a few feet from his wood."

Feeling the chill of the cold night, Rufus went back into the shanty. Without the high wind, the two horses made the inside quite comfortable and soon Rufus was sitting near the back wall with his coat off. He dug a handful of rice from the pack, and after sucking on some he would chew the hard kernels. They did little to stave off his hunger, but it kept his mind off his conditions.

It was light outside and the shaggy dog was back when Rufus opened his eyes. Somehow in his misery he'd fallen asleep. He now felt a bit of a chill and pulled the blanket around his shoulders. He stared at the light coming around the buffalo hide. Relief went through his body as he realized that the darkness was gone.

With the blanket still draped over him, Rufus got up and moved toward the light. The dog went out ahead of him. Pushing past the buffalo hide, the mountain man was blinded. The brightness hurt his eyes and he closed them tightly. Then, squinting, he looked around. Rufus fully expected to see a wall of snow all the way around the shanty.

To his surprise, the only drift was on the wood pile side of the shanty. Much of the valley in front of the shanty was blown nearly clear of snow. Stems of grass stuck out of the remaining snow. The windfall he used to sit on and the fire pit were covered with a small drift. He looked around for the dog. It was gone. Again, the frigid morning air chilled Rufus. He went back into the shanty.

The pungent smell of the interior hit him. Just a few minutes in the fresh air had cleared his senses. Running his hand over the mustang's thick, hair-covered back, he said, "I best get you two out of these cramped quarters."

The warmth they put off was immediately felt, and Rufus figured that the horses would have to wait until he got a fire going. Pulling on his coat and taking the short shovel he carried, the mountain man again went into the brightness of the outdoors to shovel a path to the wood pile and clear the snow from the firepit.

It was an hour before Rufus had enough snow removed to start his fire. He did not find the coffee pot. With snow melting in the bean pot, the mountain man opened the buffalo hide closure. A good amount of manure was piled behind the two horses. Rufus began to shovel the partially frozen piles from behind the animals.

As soon as the snow melted in the bean pot, Rufus drank some and then continued to melt more to give to the horses. Later today, the mountain man planned to lead the horse along the stream and find a place to chop a hole in the ice so they could have a proper drink.

CHAPTER SIX

By the end of February, Rufus was back to making wood. His horses looked gaunt from a diet of sparse grass or any other edible vegetation, or by chewing on the tender ends of the poplar branches. While the animals searched for food, the shaggy, white dog remained close to them.

Rufus led the horses to the farthest pond and dragged back two poplars felled by the beavers. He no longer rode the horses, preferring to do everything possible to conserve their strength. One other benefit was that the mountain man was kept warmer by walking.

Arriving back at the shanty, Rufus stripped the gear off the animals and let them wander into the valley. The dog followed them and would then lie and watch them while they foraged. The mountain man had often said that wood would warm a man twice: Once when he cut and chopped it, and again when it was burnt.

After he limbed the two trees and tossed some of the branches onto the fire, Rufus took the buck saw and started to cut them into blocks. He no longer piled the split wood next to the shanty. It made little sense because the wood would be burnt in the next few days. While it was sunny, the air was still frigid. In another month the winds would change and more temperate air would flow in, starting the thaw.

The mountain man was almost out of meat. He now wished that he'd have kept the complete elk and moose. He'd left a lot of bones that could have been used for broth. Now, as Rufus used the meat, he would save the bones and then break them to get at the marrow. After boiling them, there was little left for the dog.

The second week of March a pack of wolves came into the valley with intentions of making a meal of one of the horses. Rufus was coming up from the stream with a pot of water when he saw the black and gray wolves racing across the snow crust toward the stock.

All he had with him was the Colt. Dropping the pot, Rufus ran for the Hawken in the shanty. Grabbing the rifle, he ducked out from under the buffalo hide and looked toward the horses. The white, shaggy dog was in full fight mode. It tore into the pack of wolves, its tail curled up across its back and its teeth bared.

The dog surprised the wolves and their pursuit was broken momentarily. The horses began to run away as the dog fought the wolves to keep the pack from getting to them. Two of the wolves got past the dog and Rufus kneeled down with the Hawken. With the pursuing wolves only 150 paces from him, he pulled the rifle to full cock and lined up on the lead wolf.

The roar of the Hawken echoed in the valley and the ball struck the wolf just behind the rib cage. The .54 caliber ball tore through the animal's body, sending it yowling and rolling in the snow.

Without hesitating, Rufus reloaded the rifle. The sound of the shot had broken the attack and the wolves scattered across the valley, with the dog in pursuit of the nearest one he'd been fighting. With the Hawken loaded, the mountain man drew down on two wolves running side by side across in front of him. They were now about 300 paces away.

Again, fire belched from the barrel as a ball was sent after the retreating wolves. One of the wolves broke its stride and almost went down before it continued, now lagging behind the other wolf. Grabbing the ramrod, Rufus reloaded the Hawken. By now the wolves were disappearing into the far foothills.

Looking around, Rufus saw that he'd killed the one and knew he'd wounded another. "The bastards will be making a meal out of the one I wounded," he snarled.

He saw that the horses had stopped about a quarter-mile away. The thankful mountain man watched as the shaggy dog trotted across the valley to continue protecting the stock. Being short of meat, Rufus walked over to the dead wolf and dragged it back to the shanty. He'd get a buck for its skin and a few meals from its carcass.

That night, when he brought the horses in, he looked at the white dog. There was plenty of evidence of the fight. Its fur had plenty of blood on it, all of which was not from the dog. "You did a hell of a job breaking off the attack," Rufus told the animal. "Where you came from, I do not know, but I sure as hell owe you."

After roasting one of the back legs of the wolf, Rufus cut slivers of the meat and tossed them to the shaggy animal. Between the bites of meat the white dog licked its wounds, appearing to have completely put the incident out of its mind.

Why and how the dog had learned to protect his horses would remain a mystery to the mountain man. All he knew was that he was thankful it had found him.

* * *

The temperatures in mid-April were getting into the high 40s and Rufus was starting to break camp. The snow had melted on some of the sunny hillsides and he and the dog would take the horses there to graze. The valley he was in had worked out for the fall trapping and wintering, but he'd have to find another if he hoped to trap any more beaver.

The wolves had appeared in the valley one more time about a week later to look over the horses. As it happened Rufus was with the dog and horses when he saw them trotting towards them. The dog stood at the ready, its tail over its back. Not wanting to endanger the shaggy animal, the mountain man had lined up on the wolves while they were still a quarter-mile away. He shot once, and whether or not he scored a hit he didn't know, but the pack scattered and wasn't seen again.

His meat was gone and he was living on rice and beans. Each day the dog would disappear for a couple of hours and go hunting. More than once Rufus heard the shrill screams of a rabbit as the shaggy dog closed in on it. The mountain man knew that unlike a fox or a lynx, the white dog would kill the rabbit quickly and not play with it.

Deciding that it was time to go, the mountain man built a balsam pole closure for the front of the shanty. Rufus rode south through the valley on his way to the Wind River range. The shaggy dog continued to follow him, straying off every so often to hunt for a meal. The first afternoon out, Rufus came upon some mule deer grazing on one of the hillsides.

Looking forward to something other than beans and rice, the mountain man swung down from the grulla and walked a short distance ahead of the horses. Cocking the Hawken, he sighted on one of the younger mule deer. The rifle recoiled against his shoulder and he was rewarded with the animal dropping and sliding a short distance down the hill. The rest of the herd bounded away.

Rather than continuing on, Rufus stopped for the day and let the horses graze. The shaggy dog watched them, knowing it would have a meal coming shortly. The mule deer had little fat after the long winter. The mountain man saved all he could as he cut up the animal. It had been a long time since Rufus had had fresh meat, and his mouth watered as he fried the liver in the blackened frying pan.

Two days were spent at the hillside as Rufus dried some of the meat for future use. The low moisture of the mountain air worked in his favor for making jerky. A smoky fire was used to help the process along. Quite satisfied with eating meat again,

Rufus figured that what remained would last him until he trapped some beaver.

It was the first of May before Rufus found some ponds to trap. The grass was starting to come up, providing better grazing for the horses. They were still thin, and as their winter hair started to shed the ribs and hip bones were more exposed.

There were three ponds and about eight lodges. After trapping these out, Rufus planned to head for Fort Hall. It was much closer than Fort Laramie and there he could sell his catch.

The frigid May nights kept a rim of ice around the ponds. Rufus would clear a section of the bank and set a trap, hoping to attract beavers to an area with easy access in and out of the pond. By this time most of the beavers' food stored in the bottom of the pond had been eaten. The willow and aspen trees nearby would make a tempting meal.

The first few days the rodents successfully avoided the traps. By that time Rufus had a better idea of where they were entering and exiting the ponds. Sloshing through the cold water, the mountain man reset the traps. The next morning, he was rewarded with two large beavers.

Looking at the shaggy dog, he said, "Now we eat some tasty beaver meat."

The dog lay near the horses, panting and staring toward the foothills. While Rufus hung the beavers onto the mustang, he scolded the dog. "You lay there ignoring me about the offer of some beaver. I bet if I ate it up and didn't offer you any, you would pay a little more attention to what I say."

That night, with his stomach full of fresh meat, Rufus turned in early. He had hardly gotten to sleep when the sound of the horses woke him. They were stomping and snorting. The mountain man also heard growling from the white dog.

Wearing only his long johns and wool socks, Rufus came out from under the fly tarp with the Colt in his hand. There was only a sliver of a moon, so it was difficult to make out what was happening. Then the horses moved and Rufus saw the shaggy dog in a battle with three wolves.

The mountain man brought up the Colt, but hesitated to shoot for fear of hitting the dog. When it lunged at a wolf heading for the stock, Rufus had a clear shot at the other two. He fired three shots, wounding both of the wolves. Ki-yi-ing, the animals disappeared into the trees. Saving the fourth shot, Rufus looked at the white dog. The shaggy animal had the last wolf down and had clamped its jaws onto its throat.

"If you kill it, I'll skin the damn thing in the morning," Rufus told the dog.

Walking across the frost-covered ground, the mountain man was beginning to feel the night chill. He felt relief inside as he thought about his good fortune finding the dog. Never before did he have anything that would guard his camp as well as the white, shaggy dog.

By mid-June Rufus had the ponds trapped out and he tallied up his year's catch. He had 42 beaver pelts, three wolf skins, the buffalo hide, and two lynxes. Rufus hoped to get at least $100 at Fort Hall. He might have gotten more at Fort William, but that was over twice the distance to travel.

At the last rendezvous most of the trappers talked of quitting the ponds and finding other ways to make a living. Rufus had been warned that he might be walking in the cold ponds for nothing. Word was that the prime beaver pelts wouldn't fetch more than $1.50 a pound.

Rufus was confident that the pelts would retain some value. While they had less demand for felt, there was still the demand in the coat and parchment industries. He tied the packs onto the mustang as he readied to leave.

The white dog had gone hunting shortly after Rufus had got up. Looking around, he noticed that it had not gotten back. He remembered that the dog had followed him in the past. The mountain man left expecting to see the dog by the time he set up camp.

The trip to Fort Hall would take about five days. It had been months since Rufus had run out of coffee and tobacco. He looked forward to having both as well as some whiskey. The mountain man was going to make an effort to cut down on his drinking and to stay away from cards. With the price of beaver down, he worked too hard for the money he got. Then there were the women. There was the one at the fort that he'd gotten quite cozy with. He hoped that she was still there.

As Rufus rode south and west towards the fort, he passed several streams with ponds. They often had a lodge or two on them. Making a note of the locations, the mountain man began to make plans for future trapping spots. Rufus loved the mountains and had no intention of doing anything else than trapping. As long as he could make a few dollars each year to stay in supplies, the mountain man would never leave them.

The trail was good and Rufus made about 40 miles the first day. He had kept glancing back but hadn't seen the white dog. As he set up camp, Rufus began to worry that he might have gone too many miles and that the dog might not be able to catch up. With this thought, the mountain man decided to put up the fly tarp and give the horses an extra day to graze. He had been brushing them daily and had managed to get much of the winter coat off.

Having not seen anything to shoot for his supper, Rufus boiled the last of his beans for his meal. Other than some salt, and a few wild onions, he had nothing to put in them. The mountain man had never found the coffee pot after the blizzard, so he put some water into his pannikin and heated it next to the fire. Once it got hot, he'd put some wild flowers into it to steep.

After eating the poorly flavored beans Rufus sat with his pannikin and sipped the mountain flower tea. He listened and watched in the gathering dusk for the white dog. It made no sense to him that it hadn't caught up yet. The mountain man even began to consider going back in case it had lost his trail. Rufus knew that it made no sense that the dog couldn't have been able to track him. He had made a trail so obvious that even an easterner could have followed it.

The next morning Rufus ate the rest of the beans and drank cold water. He moved the horses to fresh grazing and then walked back up the trail with his Hawken. He had told the grulla that he was going to look for some fresh meat, but in truth he was walking back in the direction that the dog would come from.

The mountain man was so intent on the trail that he all but missed seeing some pronghorn grazing on the north side of the valley. He was already by them when one of the bucks jumped playfully. The flash of its white belly caught Rufus' attention, thinking it was the shaggy dog. Stopping, the mountain man turned quickly.

While Rufus should have been pleased to see potential meals, his heart sank. It wasn't the white dog. Lifting the Hawken, he put the sights on the playful buck and touched off the hair trigger. The lethal ball reached the buck seconds before the sound of the rifle. The stricken buck leaped into the air. The sound of the rifle sent the remaining herd bounding away before the buck collapsed to the ground.

The buck lay on the valley floor, ready to be skinned, but Rufus remained still, watching up the valley. He hoped that the sound of the shot would bring the white dog toward him, hoping for a meal. For ten minutes Rufus stood watching and listening. Nothing. Disappointed, the mountain man walked toward the downed pronghorn.

Once gutted, the buck weight about 60 pounds. Rufus put it over his shoulders and started back to his camp. Behind him he dragged a piece of the innards. He was making a trail that even a blind coyote could follow. A gloom had settled on the mountain man. Had anyone ever told him he could feel this way about a dog there would have been a fight, because he'd have called them crazy.

Once the pronghorn was skinned, Rufus fried up the liver. It was the first fresh meat he'd had since catching the last beaver. All that was left in his packs was a little rice and a handful of jerky. The pronghorn would prevent him from running out of food before getting to Fort Hall.

The next day, Rufus had the packs and gear on the horses. He was now angry with himself. Since realizing the dog was gone, the mountain man had done everything possible to make his passing noticeable. Had there been braves looking to steal a couple of horses, he had left a blatant trail for them to follow. Rufus had even abandoned the animals while going hunting. There were wolves, bears, and big cats that were partial to horse meat.

After shooting the pronghorn, Rufus had left a scent trail right to his camp, plus he'd tossed the unusable parts of the buck just a stone's throw away from where he was sleeping. Only a damn fool would do that. To survive in the wild country, a man has to be on guard all the time. He needs to pass through an area leaving as little sign as possible. Over a dog, Rufus had ignored all of the rules.

Riding away with his jaw set and a glare in his eyes, the mountain man continued toward Fort Hall, following all the rules of survival, aware of his surroundings and looking ahead, not back.

* * *

Fort Hall was run by the Hudson's Bay Company. It was located in the Snake River valley, about 150 paces from the river. The original fort built by Nathaniel Wyeth and his men had measured 80 feet by 80 feet and consisted of two buildings and some corrals enclosed within the log palisades. In 1836 Wyeth had been forced to sell to the British company.

The Hudson's Bay Company had continued to expand the fort, and emigrants had built farms around the outside, growing crops to sell. This was encouraged by the company to help cut the costs of supplies. The mountain man had visited the fort many times and found supplies to be reasonable and the whiskey satisfying.

The day was hot when Rufus rode up to the gates leading the mustang. The mountain man stopped in front of the building that handled the trading of furs. He had two 30-pound packs of beaver pelts on the horse. During better times, Rufus and his partner would have packs totaling 240 pounds on their horses.

The mountain man noticed a difference of attitude in the fort since the demise of the rendezvous system. There was little competition, with this being the closest place to trade furs. Being an American didn't gain him any favors. What the mountain man had going for him was his history in the trapping industry, and most knew that his pelts would be prime.

Rufus spent two hours haggling over the price of his furs. Finally, his desire for whiskey overtook the want for higher prices and he settled on $78 for the beaver and $50 for the other furs. The upside of the fort was that prices for goods were much more reasonable than at the rendezvous. Once he had the money, Rufus went across the room and was able to purchase tobacco, coffee, and pints of whiskey, side meat, and a new coffee pot.

With his horses taken care of in the fort and the fly tarp set up under a tree near the river, Rufus opened the first pint. The liquor burned his throat on the way down and quickly spread warmth through his body.

With nobody to listen, Rufus complained, "I got almost as much for the damn buffalo hide, and a few lynx and wolf skins, as I got for all the damn beaver pelts."

While he pondered if it was worth going after beaver, the mountain man watched activities in front of the fort. There were some wagons, pack animals, several braves who appeared to be Shoshone, and a small encampment of covered wagons that Rufus guessed were missionaries.

Figuring he had better stop drinking after the first pint was gone, Rufus roasted and crushed some coffee beans and put on a pot. Then, in the heated frying pan, he sliced some side meat. Blowing the dust from his pannikin, he looked forward to a strong, hot cup of coffee. The side meat fried quickly and Rufus began to spear strips with his Green River knife.

He was feeling pretty good after downing the pint and stared at the heating coffee pot. "Some times a good thing can take a long time," he declared.

Needing something to wash down the side meat, the mountain man opened the second pint. Again, it hit the spot. He leaned back against the tree and continued to watch the activities at the fort. Rufus had hoped that he'd see a familiar face, but so far he'd had no luck. Before he knew it, he was sipping the last of the second pint.

"Damn good thing that I didn't buy three bottles," he said, staring at the empty.

He could see that the coffee was boiling over. Rufus attempted to get up and found that the whiskey had affected his coordination. Sitting back heavily against the tree, the mountain man began to laugh at himself. "You ain't going to let two little bottles put you down, are you?"

Seeing the blackened frying pan lying next to the fire, Rufus shook his head. "Nobody likes a messy camp."

Crawling over to the fire, he grabbed the frying pan and continued crawling to the river. Kneeling next to the water, Rufus grabbed a handful of sand and began to rub it into the pan. He fell forward into the river and caught himself elbow deep in the water. Again, he laughed at himself.

Rinsing the frying pan as best he could in his condition, Rufus crawled back to the fly tarp and tossed it onto his packs. The coffee forgotten, he looked over at the open gate. "I bet I can stand up and walk up this hill to the fort," he said, challenging himself.

"If I can," Rufus continued. "What will I get for it?"

Again, he laughed and slapped his knee. "It's got to be worth at least another bottle!" the mountain man exclaimed.

Using the tree to stand up. Rufus took a deep breath and headed for the fort. Those sitting around the fire in the missionary camp watched the inebriated man stagger up the hill. "It is a shame what men do to themselves," a stern-faced woman named Eunice said.

"It's the mountains," her husband, Golan, replied. "It lets the devil get in them."

Rufus was unaware his progress was being watched as he finally reached the fort gate. Pleased with himself, he headed for the trading post. Had the mountain man known that the owner, Finn, cut his whiskey much less than the rendezvous, he might have paced himself.

The owner looked at him and smiled. "Back

so soon? Stick around, a card game should start in a bit."

CHAPTER SEVEN

A wedge tent stood alone a few feet from the covered wagons as the cold drizzle saturated the countryside. A candle provided dim light for the figures crouching around a still form inside. Not far from the tent a man collected stones next to a campfire fighting to stay lit.

"We should have left him lay where he fell, Grace," a stern female voice inside the tent said.

"Mama," a young woman said, "it wouldn't have been right to leave him."

Then the male voice said, "I got some more warm rocks."

"Help your father change them," the stern woman said. "For two days our sleep was disturbed by this character walking or crawling back to his camp singing and yowling at the dark. Tonight, all was quiet until you went out for nature's call."

"It was a good thing I did," Grace said. "There in the lightning I saw him. The rain was soaking him and he looked like a sodden mass."

"Mother, she is right," the man said, getting up from changing the rocks. "By morning he would have been dead."

"And the devil would have had another lost soul to deal with," the woman snapped.

Her sharp words broke through the liquored brain of the mountain man. Rufus was hurting all over. He couldn't stop shaking and had no idea where he was. Opening his eyes, he saw canvas above him. There was warmth around him and it almost felt like he was submerged in a warm bath. He heard the rain hitting onto the canvas and the sound of someone nearby.

Suddenly, a face of an angel moved over Rufus. She saw that his eyes were open. "I'm Gracie," she said. "We found you out in the rain."

The mountain man tried to move. "Don't," she said. "We put warmed rocks around you. You were lying in the cold rain for some time."

The angel of mercy went away and then the stern-faced woman was near him. "I got some broth heating on the fire. It'll be ready for you soon. Thanks to you we burnt two day's wood warming your hide."

All Rufus could think was, *Get me out of here!*

As he tried to sit up, his stomach lurched and his head pounded. Unable to get up, he fell back, the world spinning around him. For a moment Rufus was sure he was going to vomit, and he tried to roll onto his side. He felt a hand on his shoulder and a kind voice said, "Let me help you."

Evidently his stomach had been emptied while he had been outside, because all he got were dry, painful heaves. As she helped him lie back, Grace put something under his head. Looking down, the mountain man noticed that his wool clothing was wet and he could see that his legs were steaming from the heated rocks.

Gusts of wind brought waves of rain into the tent as well as the cold night air. Someone pulled the front of the wedge tent closed. Rufus tried to put together the events in his memory. He had bought two bottles and drank them. Then he'd gone back to the fort for more whiskey. He had gone to play cards. That was pretty much the last thing he remembered.

Golan came back into the tent. "I got you some dry clothing. I'm a bit heavier than you, so they should go on okay." He then helped Rufus sit up.

"Let me get something warm into him first," Eunice said.

Taking the cup from her, Rufus sipped the liquid, spilling some down his beard and onto the wet wool shirt. He found it hard to swallow due to his throat being sore. His stomach didn't want to take in anything and he handed the warm cup back to the woman.

"Thank you," Rufus said, his voice sounding hoarse. "Give me a minute and I'll try some more."

The two females left the tent and Golan moved the rocks away from Rufus. "You will find Eunice a bit harsh, but she is a caring woman."

Still under the influence of the whiskey, Rufus was clumsy in the confines of the 6 x 8 wedge tent. He slowly began to remove his wet clothing. Golan had also brought him some dry long johns. When he removed the last of his clothing, the minister noticed several bruises on the mountain man.

"Looks like you been in quite the fight," he said, handing the dry clothing to Rufus.

"I don't remember any fight, but the inside of my mouth is some cut up and I ache all over, so I just might have been," the mountain man mumbled.

Once he was dressed, a look of concern came over Rufus. "You didn't see my possible bag by chance?"

"It's right here," Golan told him. "We took it off when we carried you over."

Relieved, Rufus took the bag and tried to laugh. "Most everything worth anything is in this bag. I'd hate to lose in my first night here."

Furling his brow, Golan replied, "You been here three days. You ain't had a sober day yet, but it has been three."

Confused, the mountain man said, "You sure it's been three days?"

"I sure am," the minister said. "Each night you woke us with your yahooing on the way back to your camp. Come morning you'd head back to the fort. That is, except last night. Grace saw you lying on the hill to your camp."

Accepting what the minister said, Rufus was surprised. He had gone on many a drunk during rendezvous and had maybe forgotten a night before, but not the days before. An actual feeling of concern came over him. In past years he had met a few men who could stay drunk for days on end, but he didn't want to be one of them.

"I appreciate you and your family bringing me in out of the rain," the mountain man said, feeling kind of humbled.

"We're all God's children," Golan told him. "No doubt he brought Grace out of the wagon to find you."

The next morning the rain had ended, but it brought Rufus more bad news. The river was up and it had flooded his camp, washing some of his gear away. The fly tarp had collapsed, only to be saved by the pegs holding the low side of it to the ground.

Still feeling the effects of the hangover, he dragged the remaining items higher onto the bank. One of his food packs, his blankets, the bean pot and frying pan were gone. The coffee pot had been near the fire, just above the fly tarp, and it had been saved. His saddle bags and saddle were soaked. After a quick check under the saddle, he had no idea where the Colt or even Hawken was. The Kentucky flintlock pistol was wet from being in the saddle bag.

Rufus spread things out onto the river bank to dry. The weight of the saddle had prevented the ground cloth from washing away. A pack with a bag of beans, his extra wool clothing, and the stained buckskins had been saved by the weight of the beans.

Feeling sick inside due to the whiskey and the loss of several items, Rufus slowly sorted things. He had checked in his possible bag and found that and most of the money he'd gotten for the furs was gone.

With things slowly drying, the mountain man sat near his cold fire, feeling ill from the three-day drunk. The full realization of all he had lost hadn't fully hit him yet. As soon as he felt a little better, Rufus planned to go to the fort and inquire about his revolver and rifle. He prayed that he hadn't gambled them away.

He heard footsteps coming up behind him. Turning, he saw Golan. The man was carrying a pot of coffee. "If your cup wasn't washed away, I got some hot coffee here," Golan said.

His pannikin was sitting next to him with the coffee pot. Dumping the water from it, he held it up and watched as Golan poured the hot, brown liquid into his cup. "Thank you," the mountain man said as he tasted the bitter brew.

"The ladies washed your wet clothing," Golan said as he poured himself coffee. "I'll bring them down when they're dry."

"I guess I didn't make a very good first impression on you folks," Rufus said, his gravelly voice sounding more normal.

"Eunice was some let down, but that's because her father was a drinker and it made her younger years difficult," the man told him. "I myself don't pay much mind to first impressions. It takes more than a moment to gauge a man's character."

Not wanting to end up getting a whole sermon, Rufus finished the coffee. "You make good coffee," he said. "Now I best go back to the fort and see about my horses."

Looking a bit skeptical, the minister got up. "You are welcome to join us for supper. It looks like most of your supplies were ruined by the water."

Thanking the man again, Rufus walked up the hill to the fort, feeling true concern over what he might find. "I ain't never lost my damn rifle before," he muttered.

The door to Finn's stood wide-open. The owner was busy sweeping the place out, and on the ground in front was some broken furniture. As Rufus walked in, the man looked up at him. "Am I glad to see you," the owner said. "You were in no shape to leave in the storm, but after the fight you were determined to go back to your camp. I went out to look for you this morning and saw your camp was mostly washed away and figured you had drown."

Not wanting to admit how bad off he'd been the night before, Rufus told him, "I spent the night with the missionaries."

Smiling, Finn said, "They're good, giving folks. You here for a drink? You had a bit left in the last bottle."

The mountain man almost told him yes, but then the realization of the lost days came back. "Not today," Rufus said. "I got to get my stuff dried out and sorted."

"I got your Hawken and Colt and hat behind the bar for you," Finn said. "I also got the $50 you gave me to hold if you need any money."

Relief flooded over the mountain man. Even as drunk as he'd been, he had still had the good sense to take care of things. Rufus noticed that the table in the corner was gone, no doubt the busted one outside.

Finn saw him look at the corner. "The man shouldn't have been cheating you. If I'd have known that he wasn't straight I wouldn't have let him play here. Even drunk, you thrashed him good, and at first light I saw him hightailing it east."

"I will need a few things," Rufus said.

After getting some basic items and his guns, the mountain man got his money and settled up. He declined the drink Finn offered him and went to check on his horses. The old hostler saw him coming and shook his head.

"I ain't never been on a three-day drunk and here you are, looking like you just come from church," the old man told him.

"That's because these clothes were loaned to me by a preacher while mine dry," Rufus told him. "I'll be needing the horses today."

Leaving the fort with the animals, Rufus walked down to what was left of his camp. He set up his fly tarp a little higher from the river and collected everything that had dried and put them into it.

Feeling much better than he'd felt earlier, Rufus left the horses picketed and walked down the river to look for any of his gear that might be nearby. His hat was tilted on his head to keep it away from sore spots. He carried his Hawken in the crook of his arm and had the Colt in his waist band.

Only a couple of hundred feet down the river he was rewarded by finding a blanket snagged to some brush. He rinsed the sand and dirt off it and draped it onto some bushes to dry. *One less thing to buy*, he thought.

Rufus had hoped to find the pack of supplies that had washed away, but after walking about two miles down the river he hadn't found any more of his gear. He had just started back toward the fort when six pronghorns came running over the hill. It was apparent that they weren't running from something but rather were coming to water.

Hunkering down in the brush, the mountain man watched them stop at the river. They drank and played near the water. When they came out of the bushes near the river and began grazing, Rufus brought the Hawken to full cock and sighted on a large buck.

The sound of the shot echoed along the Snake River as five of the pronghorns disappeared back over the hill. Rufus walked up to the downed animal and pulled his Green River knife. After gutting it, he built a small fire and broiled the liver.

It was late afternoon when Rufus returned to his camp, carrying the blanket and with the prong horn buck over his shoulders. After dropping off the blanket, he went straight to the missionary's wagons and presented Golan with the buck. "This is to thank you for taking care of me last night," the mountain man told him. "I'll go clean up and be back for supper."

As he left, Rufus noticed the glare from Eunice and the smile from Grace. By this time, he was feeling good about himself. He had returned a favor and had a blanket to sleep under for the night. The mountain man found that his spare clothing had dried and he changed into them so he could return Golan's.

Eunice was a good cook and put on a fine meal, which included some of the venison in a thick stew. It was served with freshly baked cornbread and a dessert made with wild strawberries. Rufus met the other two families. Allen and Mary were headed for Willamette Valley to farm and had a 10 year-old son named Tony. There were Robert and Emma, who planned to join Golan and Eunice at Waiilatpu with the Whitmans to do missionary work. Another thing Rufus learned was that Grace was 19 and planned to teach until she met someone to farm with.

While Rufus was not totally comfortable in the presence of the well-groomed group, who all seemed to have their lives planned out, it was nice to spend a sober night and converse with folks. Throughout the evening several questions were asked about the trail west to Oregon and if their covered wagons could make the trip.

When the ladies started cleaning up before dessert the young boy sat near Rufus. "Are you a real mountain man?" he asked.

"That I am," Rufus told him. "I have been trapping in the mountains since before you were born."

"Do you kill Indians and grizzly bears?" the boy asked.

Realizing that the young man had only heard things about mountain men that was written in the east, Rufus chose his words carefully. "It is true that some of the tribes and mountain men have gotten into fights, but most of the time we prefer to stay friends with the Indians. They provide us with buckskins, some of our food, and even some of the beaver pelts we sell."

Some of the things that were done when seeking comfort or a bride, Rufus chose to avoid talking about. Young Tony continued to ask questions about the mountains and hunting until his mother sent him to get more wood for the fire.

When he'd gone Mary smiled at Rufus. "Our son had wanted to be a mountain man since he was old enough to walk. One of my uncles had spent time in the mountains and filled his head with stories."

"I hope your son is happy in Oregon," Rufus told her, "because the day of the mountain man is pretty much gone. There are those of us that still travel the high country trying to make due, but it can be a lonely, lean living."

"Is that why you spent days unwinding at the fort when you came down from those high places?" Mary asked.

Chuckling, Rufus replied, "Maybe so."

It was late when Rufus got back to his camp. After the dessert and coffee, the group of adults continued to talk around the fire while Tony fell asleep in his mother's lap. By the time he left, Rufus was feeling pretty comfortable and had to admit it had been a nice change from drinking whiskey.

Rufus was up early and started packing. It took a bit of work to get his morning coffee on when he found the last brew burnt to the bottom of the pot. Eunice had given him a couple of biscuits to take back and he ate them with the coffee.

With his packs ready and the fly tarp struck, Rufus was ready to saddle the horses. He was pleased to see how much they'd filled out with the grain at the fort. He planned to pick some up before leaving the area. His attention was caught by the three men walking toward his camp.

The mountain man rolled his chew into his cheek and spat towards the fire. Golan led the group. "Just emptied the last of my coffee," he called to them, smiling.

"We have come with a proposition," Golan told him. "We are heading for Oregon and are waiting for others that will be here in about a month. The three of us discussed it and would like to pay you to guide us from here."

The request caught Rufus off guard and his jaw dropped. "Guide you to Oregon?" he asked.

Rufus was aware that many of the mountain men had become guides. Even Joseph Meek and Doc Newell had guided some families and folks west last year. Word was they reached Fort Nez Percès near the Columbia River by wagon.

The trip with covered wagons pulled by oxen would take a month and a half. The return trip on horseback from the Walla Walla River to Fort Hall would take just under three weeks. Some years back, Rufus and Walter had made that trip when trapping well west on the Snake River. They had decided to winter along the Walla Walla River and purchased spring supplies from the Hudson Bay Company.

"My intentions are to go east for the summer and then return to this area in the fall and hunt or trap till spring," Rufus told them.

"We were told by the men in the fort that we should abandon our wagons and get pack animals to make the trip," Golan told him. "We think with the proper guide we can make it with the wagons."

Then Allen piped up, "We think you are the right guide."

Robert added his voice in agreement.

"I thank you men for your confidence, but in a minute I plan to put saddles on these horses and ride east," the mountain man said. "I have an old friend in Franklin, Missouri that is expecting me. As it is, I will be late."

In desperation, Golan doubled what they had planned to offer Rufus. "We will pay you $100 at the start of the trip and another $50 when we arrive in Oregon."

The other two men's eyes went wide when they heard Golan's offer. Then, after a second or two of surprise, they both agreed.

The offer stopped Rufus from what he was doing. Setting the saddle down, he turned to the men. "That is a lot of money you are offering for less than two month's work. You have three wagons and there

are many things that could go wrong during the trip."
Taking a second to make sure Tony was out of earshot,
he added, "We could be easy picking for the Bannock,
Shoshone, or even the Cayuses once you arrive at the
Fort Nez Percès. You would be safer with a larger
group. I would wait the month."

Rufus continued readying the horses as the
three men turned and walked back toward their camp.
The mountain man had an uneasy feeling inside. He
realized that he was rethinking his objection and was
working through the challenges of the trip in his mind.

Right now, the Indian trouble was at a low.
The missionaries weren't asking him to take them all
the way through the Cascades or down the Columbia
River. The worst that could happen as far as using the
wagons was that they'd have to abandon them and use
the oxen to pack their stuff the rest of the way.

The mountain man shook his head. He needed
a drink to clear his mind. He wasn't thinking straight.
He looked up the hill at the fort and thought, *Maybe a
bottle to go.*

Then he saw Grace and Tony coming his way.
The young boy waved wildly as the got closer. "We
come to say goodbye," he shouted.

Grace blushed at the boy's enthusiasm. As
they approached, the young woman said, "My father
told me you were leaving and Tony couldn't let that
happen without coming over."

"Can I look at your horses? Do you have
buckskins?" the boy asked, almost breathless with
excitement.

"You can touch the horses," Rufus said, "but
go slowly so you don't scare them."

"My father is going to the fort to try and find someone else to guide us," she told the mountain man.

Rufus caught his breath when she told him. He had hoped that they had decided to wait until the other wagons arrived. Also, Rufus couldn't think of anyone at the fort he could even recommend. Most of the experienced trappers had all gone west or back east.

"I was hoping that he would wait for the others," the mountain man told her. "There is safety in larger numbers."

"We heard that there was little trouble with the Indians right now," Grace said.

"It is other troubles that could happen," he said, not wanting to expand on them.

She smiled and called Tony over. "We should be getting back to the camp. Stop by before you go."

"I will," he promised.

The mountain man took his time packing his gear. He still needed to stop in the fort and get a frying pan and a bean pot. He had waited, hoping to find them along the banks of the river. While he worked, he kept glancing at the missionaries' covered wagons. It appeared that the men had gone to the fort with inquiries.

With the horses ready, Rufus led them toward the fort. He had an empty feeling inside, almost like he'd let a friend down. It was Grace who had spotted him and probably saved his life. His turning down guiding them affected the young woman as much as the rest of the party.

Tying the horses in front of the trading post, Rufus walked inside. The only light for the dim interior was a dusty window and the open door. He saw Finn hanging stuff on the back wall. "I will need a couple of things for cooking and some side meat," Rufus called to him.

"I still got that bottle for you," the owner said as he opened a trapdoor to get the side meat from the cellar.

Standing by the counter with the pot and pan, Rufus waited for Finn to emerge from the cellar. "I got some buckskins from the Shoshone, if you'd like to try some on," the owner said as he came toward Rufus.

"I best wait on them," the mountain man replied. While paying for the items, he asked, "Have the missionaries found someone to guide them?"

"I saw them talking to a couple of locals, but haven't heard if any accepted the job," Finn replied. "I know I wouldn't take wagons west. We recommend they leave them here and use pack animals."

The mountain man was aware that the Hudson Bay Company did everything possible to discourage emigration to the Oregon Territory. The task of walking and leading pack animals for five to six hundred miles would give many people second thoughts.

Guilt was weighing heavily on Rufus. "Give me the rest of the bottle," he said.

It only had a couple of gulps left in it, so the mountain man removed the cork and drank them down. The liquor still hurt his tender throat. "I best be going," he told Finn. "See you next trip."

The July sun was bright, causing Rufus to squint coming out of the trading post. He took the lead rope of the mustang and then climbed onto the grulla. Slowly he rode out of the fort. Near the front gate was a string of mules with packs being readied to go east. No doubt his furs were on one of them.

He wished there had been some freight wagons. They would move faster and he could have traveled east with them. Remembering he'd promised to say goodbye to Grace and the others before he left, he rode the hundred yards to their camp. The men were in a deep discussion at the fire and the women were hanging wash near the wagons.

Tony was helping his mother and the first to spot him. He ran to meet Rufus. The mountain man held a hand down and hoisted the lad into the saddle in front of him. Beaming from ear to ear, the young man rode with Rufus into the camp.

Lowering the boy to the ground, Rufus swung down from the grulla. The three men stood up and looked at him. None seemed too happy. Finally, Golan came over. "I see you are ready to go."

"Pretty much," Rufus replied.

"Well, may God be with you," the man said. Rufus watched as the others from the camp came to wish him well.

As the others circled around him, Rufus looked at the group. "Would I be in charge of the trip if I were to guide you?"

There was confusion in the three men and they whispered among themselves. Finally, Golan said, "As far as decisions on the trail, yes, you would. As far as serving the lord, that would remain with us."

"Do you all have rifles and know how to use them?" the mountain man asked.

Again, the men seemed confused. Then Golan replied, "We have two flintlocks, a long rifle and a Harper 1803. We can learn to shoot."

"You'll need no less than four more rifles, and everyone, including the women, will have to be able to load and shoot," Rufus told them.

Without hesitation, Golan replied, "We will do that."

Suddenly, Eunice asked in her harsh voice, "Have you been drinking?"

"God, I hope so," Rufus replied. "What we are about to do is something a sober man would question."

Without asking if the same terms of payment applied, Rufus had another urgent mission. He saw Grace walking with an empty basket. The mountain man motioned her over.

"Is there something you need?" she asked.

"I need you to write a letter for me," Rufus replied.

Thirty minutes later the mountain man hurried to the pack train with a letter for Walter Gray explaining that he wouldn't be coming to Franklin this year.

* * *

The three wagons with canvas stretched over wooden bows had been well-equipped for the trip from St. Louis. They were not the heavy Canastota type, but rather sturdy farm wagons. They had extra wheels to share and tongues. The boxes had already been sealed with bees wax or tar for the crossing of the Sweetwater River. Each had been pulled by six oxen. Four more would need to be purchased for the trip. The only one with a horse was Allen.

Rufus was tasked with getting the men four more rifles. He had seen some at the trading post and hoped they were in working order. The owner was sitting next to the counter enjoying some vegetables from his garden.

"I figured you'd be headed for the Green River crossing by now," Finn told him.

"Things changed since I left here," Rufus told him. "I need some rifles."

A surprised look came across Finn's face. "Something wrong with your Hawken?"

Grinning at the owner, Rufus shook his head no. "The missionaries have a musket and an older Kentucky flintlock. They will need four more."

"They going on a crusade?" the owner asked.

Rufus had no idea what a crusade was, but he told the man no anyway.

The owner went behind the counter and selected muskets from some leaning in the corner. On the wall he had Hawkens, Bakers, and Kentucky rifles. Rufus saw that the ones Finn was getting were older and normally traded with the tribes.

"Let me see the ones off the wall," Rufus told him.

A look of disappointment went across the owner's face. Evidently, he had hoped to get rid of some of the rougher stock.

"The ones you're asking about are fine rifles and will cost a lot more." Finn cautioned him.

"Four of them are flintlocks and appear to have had a lot of use," Rufus pointed out. "If the works aren't loose and the barrels aren't worn or bent, we should be able to make a deal on them."

Three of the long rifles were .48 caliber. They had seen lots of shooting and there was some wear in the barrels. Rufus figured that would affect accuracy, but make it easier for the missionaries to load. He found the .625 caliber Baker in the same condition. Overall the mountain man thought that the rifles would be satisfactory.

After a lengthy period of dickering which even brought the muskets back into play, a deal was made on the long rifles and the Baker. Extra lead, powder, linen for patches, and molds were bought as well as powder horns. The total cost was $60. Hoping to extend the deal, Finn offered two of the muskets for another $7, which Rufus declined. He figured it would only add weight to the trip and offer little firepower.

Golan was skeptical when Rufus sent him back to pay and pick up the rifles. "Are you sure we'll need that many?" he asked.

"Let's hope we won't," Rufus replied, "but if we do, the women will be loading one while we are firing the other."

"You have only one rifle," the man pointed out.

"Yes," Rufus replied, "and I have a Colt that can carry five rounds, and also a Kentucky pistol."

"About the money," Golan said, looking down at the ground. "Rifles and the supplies are making us kind of short."

"So, you don't have the $150?" Rufus asked.

"We got a promise from Whitman's Mission of money to cover the trip," Golan told him. "It will be more than enough to settle up in Fort Nez Percès."

"You got $50?" the mountain man asked.

"We do," the man replied.

"You pay me $50 now and another $50 when we get to Fort Nez Percès," Rufus said.

For a moment, what Rufus said didn't sink in and Golan looked confused. Then his eyes brightened. "Fifty, you said?"

"You best get it to me before I change my mind," the mountain man replied. Rufus had a few things he still needed to get.

It had never been about the money, but rather the danger and difficulty of the trip that had made Rufus hesitant. Not that he feared either one, but the families he would be traveling with hadn't been tested in the harsh west.

The missionaries were anxious to continue their trip west and worked from dawn to dusk lubricating axles, fitting oxen to yokes, purchasing supplies, and evaluating what was being carried in the wagons. Golan made sure that all the heaviest items were packed in the bottom of the wagons. The wagons tended to tip easily if not packed correctly. There was also the weight of the extra wheels and tongues stored under the wagon box, which helped lower the center of gravity.

Rufus also helped them choose what should be kept for the trip and what should be discarded. Some of the wagons had unnecessary furniture. The mountain man pointed out that every additional pound used up the strength of their oxen. Some of the areas they would be going would have little water and poor grazing. To lose an ox for wanting a dresser made little sense.

It was decided that Rufus' packs would be put into Robert's wagon. Much of what the mountain man needed was in his saddle bags and tied to the back of his saddle. He would be eating whatever the travelers with him cooked.

Several residents of the fort stood outside and watched the missionaries prepare for the trip. Some would call out, warning about trying to take wagons over the impassable trail west. Rufus told his group to ignore them. The mountain man had already warned them that they would come up against obstacles that appeared to block their way, but they would have to take the time to fill the washes, cut the trees, or move the rocks to make the way clear.

CHAPTER EIGHT

It was July 12, 1841, when the three covered wagons headed west from Fort Hall. The day before there had been a long sermon and lots of praying for the success of their trip. Golan had forewarned Rufus that during the trip Sundays would still be observed for worship.

The additional oxen were tied to the back of two of the wagons, and Rufus' mustang was tied to the back of the lead wagon with Allen's horse. Rufus' stomach was tight, feeling the weight of being responsible for the lives of the missionaries.

Young Tony was in a state of blissful happiness. He had been helping his mother put the last of the breakfast items into the wagon when Rufus rode up. The mountain man had on a new pair of buckskins and his flat-brimmed leather hat. In the broad belt around his waist was his Kentucky pistol, a short axe, and the Green River knife in its sheath. The possible bag hung over his shoulder with the powder horn tied to it. Rufus looked every bit the mountain man.

Rufus had chosen to keep the Colt in his saddle bag to prevent the weather or dust from fouling it. It had four chambers loaded and was within easy reach. The Kentucky pistol would work well for shooting a rabbit, or other small animals. The Hawken would be across the saddle or in his scabbard when he needed his hands to be free.

The mountain man had informed the men that there would be firing of the rifles each morning to make them familiar with loading and sighting on a target. The women were also involved with loading and cleaning the rifles. An offer was made to let them fire the rifles if they wanted to. None took him up on it. Should they be needed for defense, Rufus didn't want any of the party to be unsure about using the rifles.

Much of the pressure of anticipating the trip disappeared from Rufus as the wagons rolled away from the fort. The first 180 miles would be on the south side of the river. Once they reached the Three Island Crossing, the south side would become too difficult to continue on, so they would be making the dangerous crossing to the north side.

Rufus was pleased to see how disciplined the group was. Normally the first day of a wagon train would be filled with false starts and problems with the wagons, stock, and keeping the group spaced and in line. Those driving these three wagons had learned much during the long trip from St. Louis to Fort Hall. With everyone and the animals being fresh, and a good trail, they traveled nearly 20 miles the first day.

The day ended with the wagons parked in a triangle and a common fire in the middle. The mood of the group was high from finally being back on the trail. Rufus had shot two rabbits and they were added to the evening's fare.

On the second day the wagon train stopped early in the afternoon at the American Falls. So far the trip had gone well, with the men and women taking turns driving the oxen. Tony did his part watching for kindling and tossing it into a canvas that had been slung under one of the wagons. Much of the trail from Fort Hall to Fort Nez Percès would have adequate wood, but searching for kindling gave those walking beside the rough-riding wagons something to do.

Rufus carried his Hawken across his saddle and had ranged out in front of the wagons, looking for the best route through the ridges and washes. From a distance much of the trail along the south side of the Snake River looked good, but as the unseen obstacles became apparent they needed to be avoided or dealt with.

The wagons went through a granite gap that was just wide enough for a single wagon. The granite cliffs rose on both sides, making it a perfect place to attack the wagons. Rufus rode through and then waited on the other side with his Hawken ready. He also had the Colt in his broad belt.

In the future this gap would be called the Gates of Death due to the emigrants' fear of being attacked in it. As the wagons continued down the south side of the Snake River, the land became more arid and collecting fuel for the evening fire became more difficult.

The party camped at the Raft and Snake River confluence on the fourth night. In the future this would be known at the Parting of The Ways, when those going to California would follow the Raft River and those on the way to Oregon would continue along the Snake River.

With the foothills and mountains rising on the south side, they travelled on a shelf that was bordered to the north by the river gorge. The water had cut into the rock over thousands of years as the river flowed west. The steep sides made it harder to get water for the animals and cooking.

About a week after crossing the Raft River, the wagons reached the Salmon River Creek. The group became alarmed as they saw the smoke and viewed the tops of teepees ahead of them. Rufus assured them that the Shoshones or Bannocks at the creek would be friendly. They fished for salmon and dried them to trade for goods.

The covered wagons were parked near the Salmon River and the travelers could hear the water rushing over the falls as it cascaded towards the Snake River. Golan and Rufus met with the Shoshones and traded goods from the wagons for both dried and fresh salmon. Despite Rufus' assurances that the missionaries were safe from attack, the men still kept their rifles loaded and ready.

Leaving the Salmon River, the wagons continued along the south side of the Snake River. They now encountered rolling hills. Many had winding streams cutting through them or were tree-covered. Hours were spent breaking down the stream banks for crossing, or cutting the evergreens to allow room for the wagons. If others had found an easier way, Rufus did not know of it. Trails through the trees were obvious, but they'd been made by wildlife and then followed by the pack animals.

Finally, a grass-covered slope from the hills to the river appeared to offer relief in getting to the water. But as Rufus rode down ahead of the wagons driving the extra animals, he knew that they had reached one of the more severe challenges of the trip: The Three Island Crossing.

Everyone walked down the slope while the men driving the oxen struggled as the wagons tended to slide sideways. The oxen wanted to turn directly down the slope which would have left the animals and wagons in a heap at the bottom. Mary had tied a rope to the back of their wagon. She and Tony were on the slope above the wagon pulling for all they were worth attempting to help keep the wagon from sliding sideways.

Laughing and talking with relief as the last wagon made it to the flat near the river, the travelers looked across the wide Snake River. While Rufus had warned them about the crossing, they could see the three islands in the river that would make the wide river much easier to cross. The current at the river's edge didn't appear to be too bad.

Two days were spent on the south side preparing the wagons. The boxes had to be resealed, and again the travelers had to evaluate whether all the items in the wagons were needed. Then it was time to make the crossing. The next morning some packs and the extra oxen would be taken across, followed by the wagons crossing in the afternoon. Rufus didn't want to keep the travelers on the south bank worrying about the river any longer than necessary.

Allen and Rufus chose to drive the extra oxen across the river ahead of the wagons. Extra rope was taken with them as well as some of the supplies were packed onto the oxen. While Rufus didn't talk about it, he wanted to make sure some supplies were on the far side in case some or all of the wagons didn't make it.

Rufus drove the oxen into the river just below the first island with Allen following, leading the mustang. Even though they would be crossing against the current, the water was shallowest at this point. Reaching the first island, which was the longest of the three, was easily accomplished. Rope was left there to be used if needed during the wagon crossing. This would be repeated on the next two islands.

After locating the best place to cross, which was on the upstream end of the island, some debris and rocks had to be moved for the wagons. The oxen grazed while the men worked. Rufus and Allen crossed to the second island. Again, the horses and oxen were able to reach the river bottom.

Rufus continued to the third island at the upstream end. Even though the animals were able to reach the bottom, the current tore at the cattle and horses, pushing them down river before landing.

The mountain man was aware that the final crossing would be the most difficult. It had the swiftest water and was the deepest. Each year, during the spring thaw, the flooding would change the river bottom, creating deeper holes in some areas and filling others.

The growth on the islands made it impossible to see the wagons back at the camp. Rufus did notice that some of the travelers had climbed the grassy slope so they could watch the men's progress.

"This is the widest crossing and the current is the strongest," Rufus told Allen. "As we get near the far side, we have to watch for the best area to get the cattle and horses out of the river. If we lose an ox, don't go after it. We'll just have to hope it gets ashore downstream."

Allen acknowledged what Rufus was saying, his face showing the fear he felt. The fear was from thoughts of his wife having to cross in the wagon. The oxen readily entered the water, seeing the safety of the riverbank on the far side. The mustang entered, carrying its packs right behind the oxen. The two men kept their horses on the downstream side of the animals as they shouted encouragement and waved their hats.

Suddenly, Rufus saw one of the oxen disappear under water as it went into a hole in the river bottom. Thrashing in the water, it came up. The mountain man saw that its pack had slipped around under its belly. Realizing that the ox couldn't swim with the pack under it, Rufus ignored his own instructions and tried to get his swimming horse closer, hoping to cut the strap holding the pack.

Then the oxen rolled in the water, its legs flailing above the water as it fought to get upright. Helpless to give aid to the animal, Rufus continued across the river. The remaining oxen and the mustang reached the far side, slipping and stumbling they climbed out of the river onto the bank. Rufus and Allen followed them and sat on their horses, water running off the animals and men as they caught their breath.

Looking down the river, Rufus saw the drowned oxen floating on its side in the middle of the river. The two men pushed the oxen a short distance from the river near some good grazing. "With luck they won't wander too far with all this grass to chew on," Rufus said.

Stripping the packs off the oxen and leaving only the pack saddle on the mustang, Rufus tied the horse near the shore before he and Allen headed back across the river. Arriving back at the camp, the mountain man was pleased to see that Golan had the wagons ready to cross. Rufus noticed that the canvas tops were rolled up part-way, making getting out of the wagon easier in the case of tipping. Nothing was said about the lost ox.

With the water being low enough to reach the bottom, the first two crossings were made only using a rope tied to the lead oxen to help Rufus guide them to the islands. Two wagons were kept on the second island while the lead wagon crossed to the third. The mountain man had made a note of where the deep hole was so it could be avoided. Hopefully he wasn't moving to an area with an even worse washout.

Allen's wagon was the first to go across the third crossing. Rufus crossed with Tony sitting in the front of his saddle. The mountain man trailed ropes tied to the oxen. Once across, he lifted Tony off, got the mustang and tied the rope to it and his grulla.

Directing the young boy to stand clear, Rufus said, "Whatever happens, don't worry. I'll get your folks across." The mountain man hoped the boy didn't have visions of the drowned ox floating in the river.

Once the slack was taken up, Allen climbed into his wagon with Mary. He stationed himself at the front with a long rod in his hand. On Rufus' signal, both riders in the wagon shouted to get the oxen started across.

Water churned around the wagon, the white canvas top swaying back and forth as the oxen entered the final crossing. Rufus kept the ropes tight, his heart pounding in his chest. The horns of the struggling oxen clacked against each other. The mountain man kept tension on the rope as the oxen and wagon made slow progress across. The current began to swing the wagon downstream as it began to float. Then the oxen were swimming, their eyes large and heads up as they fought to stay above water.

Finally, the oxen found the bottom again and continued pulling the wagon tongue, which was now at a right angle to the wagon. The wagon jerked to the side as it touched bottom and Allen shouted "Whoa!" to the animals. They continued to pull and the wagon bumped sideways.

Leaping from the wagon into waist-deep water, Allen fought the water, pulling himself with anything he could grab on the bovines, until he reached the lead oxen. "Whoa!" he shouted again.

As if by miracle, the oxen stopped, snorting and shaking their heads. With a firm grip on the lead rope, Allen commanded, "Gee!" The oxen moved to the right along the river, straightening the tongue. Then in a lower voice he said, "Haw," and the lead oxen started a slow turn to the left and up onto the riverbank.

Allen hadn't noticed when Mary had climbed out of the wagon and came alongside the oxen closest to the wagon, the current sweeping her dress back. She was also giving low commands to the oxen. Rufus could see that the wagon was wobbling as it was pulled through the water. He was sure that there had been damage to one of the front wheels.

Soaking wet, Allen and Mary walked onto the bank alongside their oxen, the water running off them and Mary's dress plastered to her body. Rufus looked away and rode around the back of the wagon. Spokes from the left front wheel were broken. With luck the axle would be undamaged.

Slowly the wagon was moved to make room for the other wagons. Mary shook her dress loose and told Rufus, "Tony and I'll watch things here. You an Allen go after the other wagons."

She got the mustang and bent over to pick up the ropes. Allen had taken the other ends of the rope and rode into the river, hauling them back to the third island. Rufus followed on the grulla. "You can pull the oxen and wagon from the shore," the mountain man said, "and I'll tie a rope to the back of the wagon and try and keep it from drifting downriver."

The plan was made for bringing the other two wagons across. Tying the rope to the back of the wagon did not prevent them from swinging some, but it kept the angle to the oxen acceptable for being pulled onto the north river bank.

It was late afternoon when the last wagon was across. Camp was set up and everyone got into dry clothing. Golan and Allen got to work replacing the broken wheel. Not having the tools needed to repair it, the wheel was discarded. Robert and Emma's wagon was the last to cross. The two of them sat near their wagon in prayers, thanking God for a safe crossing.

Rufus, back in his wool shirt and pants, rode out of the camp to see if he could find any game. He needed to get his mind right. He kept seeing Mary's shapely body with the wet dress clinging to it, and then when she bent down to pick up the ropes he had turned away quickly, fearing that Allen would see him staring. Up until now, wearing the loose-fitting gingham dress, the mountain man hadn't noticed her figure.

As he rode, looking for something to shoot, he thought about the other women. Emma was a little plump and had a rosy face from hours in the sun. Eunice had sharp features, which matched her personality. She had softened some since he had taken on guiding them, but seldom showed Rufus a smile. Gracie was young and all sweetness, too young for the mountain man to take notice of her.

Rufus got along well with all of the men and respected their abilities on the trail. They looked to Golan for guidance and Golan looked to Rufus. The mountain man was very satisfied with the arrangement. Yet there was . . . Mary. He'd have to keep away from her.

Then he saw movement ahead. It was a good-sized mule deer. Sliding out of the saddle, he raised the Hawken. Fire and smoke shot from the barrel as he touched off the hair trigger. Struck by the .54 caliber ball behind the shoulder, the deer jumped to escape and then collapsed.

The ride away from camp was good for the mountain man. It went a long way to clearing his mind. He had determined that the stress of the Three Island Crossing had got him thinking crazy thoughts. They were less than two weeks from Fort Boise and he knew someone there to spend time with.

Riding into camp with the mule deer across the back of the grulla, Rufus waved as Tony noticed him and came running. With the boy on front and the deer on the back, the mountain man rode into camp like a conquering hero. That night they ate well. Golan had a barrel that could be used to salt down the extra meat for future use. Tomorrow was Sunday, so extra soup was made so there needn't be cooking. Rufus could expect a long sermon.

* * *

The Three Island Crossing shortened the route to Fort Boise, their next supply opportunity. The pack lost on the drowned ox wouldn't leave them short of food in the near future, but would have to be replaced at the fort. The first leg of this route would be short on water and firewood, with sparse grazing. They would have sage and greasewood to fuel their cookfire.

With a day's rest and the water barrels on the sides of their wagons full, they left the Snake River with mountains on the far horizon. The wagons would be traveling for two weeks in a wide basin between two mountain ranges. The Boise River would offer them some water and other isolated streams and potholes. Dry creeks and river beds would crisscross the basin.

The group was relieved to be out of the foothills and dense trees they'd encountered on the south side of the Snake River. They were down to two spare oxen. After the crossing it was discovered that another ox had been injured. The animal was able to keep up with the slow pace of the wagons, but couldn't handle the work in the yoke.

Mary had presented Rufus with the dried buckskins and his other clothing washed. "Tony insisted that I get these to you so you would look like a mountain man," she told him. As she handed him the clothes, her hand brushed his. Rufus jerked back, almost dropping the items. Laughing, she headed back to her family.

Moods were good for the first three days, and then the unchanging terrain began to wear on the travelers as they trudged on with sameness around them, seeming to get no closer to the distant mountains. Time was lost filling in dried washes cut by spring floods and going out of their way for water.

During the evening fires Tony would drag Rufus over to sit with his parents. Mary would always look up and give him a quick smile. The mountain man would always give his attention to the young boy or find things to discuss with Allen.

Rufus was sure that the thoughts in his head concerning Mary were just that. It had been a while since he'd been with a woman, and there in front of him was a happy couple and their child. These were things that the mountain man did not have, things that on the lonely winter nights he would wish for.

While they were a small party, Rufus managed to stay busy away from the group, especially from Mary. Young Tony would follow him around and ask him to come and visit with his mom and dad. Enjoying the young lad, Rufus didn't want to be stern with the boy and send him away, so he always found a reason to do something away from the wagons with the oxen or horses.

In the evenings Rufus would ride either the grulla or mustang and check the trail ahead. He'd always carry the Hawken at the ready for trouble or game. He liked the freedom away from the wagons. It was uncomplicated with just the wild country around him. One evening he found the spot where he and Walter had camped. It wasn't that far from the wagons. He decided to spend a little time away from them.

Standing near the few fragments of the fire, he looked around. For the last two days they had been using water from the barrels. Rufus remembered that they had gone northeast from the camp and had found a valley with water. He sat as the sun went behind the mountains, recalling the route.

Getting up, the mountain man gave the mustang a little water from his canteen and took a drink himself. Patting the shoulder of the horse, he said, "We best be getting back before we're missed."

Climbing into the saddle, he headed back toward the wagons. Glancing at the stars, Rufus realized that he'd let time slip by. He figured that he could justify it by letting them know he knew of some water.

The greasewood fire had burnt down when he rode into camp. Golan and Robert came to meet him. "You missed supper," Golan told him. "We were worried."

"I am sorry I was gone so long," Rufus apologized. "I did find water about a day's travel to the northeast."

"That will work," Golan said. "Tomorrow is Saturday and we can spend the lord's day near blessed water."

"That's just what I was thinking," the mountain man replied, realizing it was a little white lie.

A candle was burning in a lantern near the wagons. As the three of them walked within the wagons, the others rushed over. Mary reached them first. In the lantern light, Rufus saw tears in her eyes. "I thought you were lost," she said.

Allen followed up behind her. "I told you he was okay." Then to Rufus he said, "She gets this way sometimes. She worries too much."

Using the lame excuse, the mountain man said, "I found water."

He then saw the stern face of Eunice. "I saved you some supper. The fire's out, but the stew should still be warm." Then he heard her mumble as she walked away, "Just like a man, making us worry over nothing."

Sitting on a crate by the cold fire, Rufus ate the stew. It was quite good. Eunice had made it with the last of the salted mule deer. It also had some root vegetables that she had brought from Missouri.

Tony was already sleeping, and all but Allen and Mary had turned in. The three of them sat around the cold fire, speaking little as Rufus ate the stew. Finally, the mountain man asked, "Did Eunice make this?"

"Yes. Mary made the biscuits," Allen told him.

"They go really well with the stew," Rufus told her.

"I think the bottoms got a little burnt," she said in the dark, her voice still sounding heavy.

"They are just the way I like them," Rufus lied. They certainly had been a *little* burnt. "I am sorry that I was out so late."

"I tried to explain to Mary that you have to go out ahead and find the best trail," Allen said, "but she was sure something bad had happened. She wanted me to saddle up and go find you."

Trying to lighten the conversation, Rufus chuckled and said, "Then in the dark you might have gotten lost and they'd be looking for us both in the morning."

"You shouldn't kid about things like that," Mary said with a sniffle.

"You are right," Rufus replied. "I can't say it won't happen again, but if I expect to be gone later, I will let everyone know and also let you know what direction I plan to go."

"It would be helpful," Allen told him. "When Tony went to bed, he told his mother not to worry because you were a mountain man."

The three of them laughed, lightening the mood.

The next morning most of the water in the barrels was used for the animals. What was left would be enough for the group, and a little for supper if necessary. The animals would have to wait until they got to water. Rufus wondered what Golan would do if they didn't reach the valley tomorrow. Would he make everyone sit and wait through Sunday to continue?

Rufus was saddling the grulla when Mary came over with Tony. She was smiling like nothing had happened the night before. "Tony has a request," she said. "Can you let him ride with you for a while this morning?"

"I don't think that should be a problem," Rufus said, taking the boy and setting him into the saddle.

"He sure does like you," Mary said, looking at her boy, her eyes shining. "He wants to be a mountain man someday."

While the boy hugged the horse's neck, Rufus said, a bit seriously, "I would discourage that plan. He should farm with you and your husband. It has a future, but the day of the mountain man has gone by."

"Yet you continue to do it," she said. Patting his shoulder, she walked away.

As Rufus climbed onto the grulla behind the boy, he could still feel her hand on his shoulder. Handing the reins to the boy, he said, "You can take us out of here."

With the assistance of Rufus' heels, Tony got the grulla going, the mountain man showing him how to control the animal. Mary stood near the wagon, beaming at the sight. Allen walked up alongside her. "He's good for the boy," he said. "He'll miss Rufus when we get to Oregon."

"Yes. Yes, he will," Mary said, turning to put the last of the items into the wagon.

It was late afternoon when they reached the valley. Rufus had switched to the mustang during the noon break. The water was about a mile up the valley and the mountain man hoped that it was still there. They were all but out of water.

The shimmering pond came into view and Rufus heard cheers behind him. Eunice was driving the oxen of their wagon and Golan ran ahead to be

149

with Rufus. "Your knowledge of the trail is worth every penny we are paying you," he said.

The group and the animals enjoyed a cool drink of mountain spring-fed pond before starting to set up camp. The travelers would spend at least three days at the pond to observe the sabbath, rest, bathe, and do wash.

The valley also had the best grass they'd seen since the crossing. The horses were picketed and the oxen were allowed to wander to graze. Most of the day the injured ox had lagged behind. Rather than getting better, the leg was getting to be more of a problem. If they spent a week or two in the valley the leg would probably heal just find. On the trail it was not going to.

After the wagons were set and tents were put up, Golan came over to Rufus, who was brushing the horses. "What do you think we should do about the ox?"

"We could leave it in the valley and as long as a varmint didn't get it, it would do just fine," the mountain man told him.

"It's a bit on the skinny side, but I say we should butcher it," Golan replied. "We could use any meat the bovine has."

"I'll do that tomorrow," Rufus told him.

"Tomorrow!" Golan said. "That's the lord's day. There'll be no working on the lord's day."

The next morning, the group ate biscuits made the night before for breakfast and drank cool water from the pond. A lengthy sermon was given by Golan which gave the God the credit of leading them to this water using one if his flock, Rufus. The mountain man listened and wondered. It was being at the old camping site that reminded him of the valley. What was it that had led him to the old site?

Riding was okay on the sabbath as long as it wasn't done for the purpose of work. After the services were over, Rufus went and saddled the grulla. He and Walter had never gone into the valley to explore it. Now would be a perfect time to do it to get away from the group, and Mary.

The mountain man was tightening the cinch when Allen walked up to him. "If I was to saddle my horse, would you take Tony for a ride?"

The request surprised him. "I might be gone for a while," Rufus told him. "Maybe until late afternoon."

"That's what I told Mary," Allen said, "but she was sure if the boy was with you, he'd be okay."

"How about if we put the saddle on the mustang," the mountain man suggested. "That way if she got worried, you could ride your horse out to find us. We'll be in the valley so you wouldn't miss us."

"Robert has a saddle," Allen said. "I will get his."

The man hurried away, calling to Mary as he went by the wagon. Before he could return with the saddle, Mary and Tony came over, the boy's face showing excitement. "Mama says you are going to let me go riding with you."

Allen returned with the saddle. Rufus put it onto the mustang and adjusted the stirrups for the boy. "This horse is used to following me," Rufus told the boy in a kidding voice. "I don't want you to go galloping past me."

"I won't," the boy said as his father lifted him into the saddle. Allen handed the reins to his son. "I want you to do everything that Mr. Pike tells you."

"Who's Mr. Pike?" the boy asked.

"That's my last name," Rufus told him, "but if it is okay with your father you can call me Rufus."

Walking back beside Mary, Allen said, "It is okay with me."

Mary rushed up and hugged the boy. "Now you be good for . . . Rufus."

The few lessons that the mountain man had given the boy had been well-learned. Along with the mustang being used to following the grulla and the guidance of the boy, the two of them rode into the valley.

Rufus adjusted the Kentucky pistol and short axe in his broad belt and led the way around the pond. Once they headed past the water, the mountain man let the boy come alongside and he pointed out things to Tony. They were the type of things a person needed to know if they were coming back alone.

It was a habit that Rufus had learned when he'd first came into the mountains. An old timer named Otis had taught him to look for points of reference to keep his sense of direction and guide him if he should ever come back.

The mountain man didn't have to make much conversation. Tony talked a mile a minute about every thing they saw. He asked endless questions, which Rufus patiently answered. The answer would always be followed by a "Why?"

The valley went for several miles and they passed a couple of smaller ponds. One of the ponds was filled by a small waterfall. Rufus spotted a rabbit and pulled up. The mustang stopped beside him. "If I shoot the rabbit," he whispered, "we can cook and eat it."

"Can I shoot?" the boy asked.

"No," Rufus said. He then took out the Kentucky pistol. "Hang on to the saddle horn.," he told the boy.

The shot echoed in the narrow valley as the rabbit kicked its last. Swinging out of the saddle, Rufus helped the boy down. "Now," he said. "If we do this, I don't want you telling anyone back at the wagons. It would make Mr. . . . ah, Golan angry, because he doesn't believe in cooking on Sunday."

"I won't tell," Tony said, still whispering.

The rabbit was quickly cleaned and skinned. Rufus had a fire going, and using some green sticks he speared the rabbit and put it over the fire to broil. Tony continued to go around picking up sticks to add to the fire.

While waiting for the rabbit to get done, the boy sat next to Rufus, in deep thought. "Could you be my daddy?" Tony asked.

"Be what?" the mountain man asked, sure he had misheard.

"Mamma likes you and I like you," the boy said. "So, if you like mamma, you could be my daddy."

Unsure what to tell the boy, Rufus wondered if the lad had seen him looking at his mother. "Don't you like your daddy?" he asked.

"Yes," the boy said. "He is very good to me. He let me ride with you today."

"I can't be your daddy," Rufus said, unsure of where to go from there. "Your daddy would miss you."

"Maybe if you talked to him, he'd let you be my daddy too," Tony suggested.

Struggling with his thoughts for a minute, Rufus finally said, "Do you know what a friend is?"

"Yes, I do," Tony said. "I had two friends in Missouri."

"I can't be your daddy, but I can be your friend," Rufus told him.

"But friends go away," the boy told him. "If you were my daddy, you won't go away."

"A real friend never goes away," Rufus said. "As long as you remember the good times you had, they are still your friend."

The mountain man then began to tell the boy about Walter. As they ate the rabbit, he was still telling the story. The bad parts wouldn't have helped his objective, so he left them out. By the time they were washing their hands from eating the rabbit, Rufus was pretty sure he had convinced the boy that to have a friend was even better than a daddy.

As the two of them rode back toward the wagons, Rufus made the boy repeat the important things. "We don't talk about the rabbit," Tony said, "and a friend is better, but daddies are more important."

Finally riding into the camp the sleepy boy could hardly hang onto the saddle horn. Rufus had a lead rope on the mustang. Mary came hurrying over. "Did you have a good time, Tony?" she asked.

Suddenly the boy was wide awake. She lifted him off the horse and asked him, "Did Rufus teach you anything?"

He looked up at his mother. "Don't talk about the rabbit, and a daddy is important but a friend is better."

A look of confusion crossed her face. "Okay," she said, then looking at Rufus, she told him, "It sounds like you two had a full day."

Blushing, the mountain man quickly began pulling the gear off the horses. Allen had been talking to Golan when he saw his wife and son walking towards the wagon. "I see you made it back," he called to Tony.

"He did," Mary said. "Go help Rufus with the horses."

The next morning the injured ox was butchered and the meat was salted and packed. The liver and tongue were cooked for supper. Rufus worried all through the day that Tony would say something in the group. Not so much about the rabbit, but the daddy-friend thing. Other than the slip-up with his mother, the young man was mum on the conversation.

CHAPTER NINE

The wagons pulled out of the valley and continued on the trail. After two days the wagons crested an overlook known as Bonneville Point. The travelers stopped and audible gasps could be heard. After days of traveling in the arid basin, there ahead of them was a valley with a tree-lined river. The Boise River flowed through and the name Boise was credited to Captain Bonneville's French guide, who called it "Les bois," the woods, and also to French trappers who called it, "La rivière boisèe", or the wooded river. The overlook had come to be known as Bonneville Point after the American captain.

The Boise River Valley offered the travelers water and plenty of wood from the cottonwoods along the river. They were now only four or five days from Fort Boise. Rufus surely had a friend as Tony followed him everywhere in the camp. The mountain man tried to avoid Mary, who had been taking every opportunity to come and talk when the boy was with him.

The wagons only went about 10 miles each day, giving the oxen time to graze. With plenty of wood, large fires were built every evening. Rufus took the opportunity in the evenings to go hunting. He saw plenty of evidence of old beaver activity. Most of the rodents had been caught by the French-Canadian trappers.

Fort Boise was built to compete with Fort Hall when it was owned by the American, Nathaniel Wyeth. Both forts supported the fur trapping industry, and then later the emigration to Oregon. Rufus had been to the fort on three occasions with Walter Gray. The last time he'd met an Owyhee woman who had come from the Sandwich Islands. He had promised her that he would return, even though he had doubted it at the time.

The fort was on the north side of the Snake River and below the confluence with the Boise River. The sight of the adobe walls of the fort brought joy to the travelers after they'd spent just over a month on the trail seeing little civilization. Their supplies were running low and the wagons needed repair. It was decided that the party would spend a week at the fort. For that week, Rufus would be free to do whatever he wanted.

Rufus helped the travelers park their wagons just up from the fort near the river. While Fort Boise offered a degree of protection, he still reminded the men to keep their rifles clean and loaded. Satisfied that he had done everything he could, the mountain man got his packs from Robert's and Emma's wagon and put them onto the mustang. He needed to go through them before purchasing any supplies. He even considered leaving most of the gear here to pick up on his way back to Fort Hall.

Golan went with the mountain man to purchase some supplies. He was surprised when he saw all the Owyhees. At first he thought one of the tribes had taken over the fort, but Rufus let him know he needn't worry. The Owyhees were from somewhere in the Pacific and wouldn't hurt him.

The two men went into the trading post first. Rufus busied himself looking through things he could use trapping. He watched as Golan chose items that Eunice had sent him after. He also picked up things he could use doing minor repairs to his wagon.

With his bag of goods, Golan turned to Rufus. "Do you want me to wait?" he asked.

"I'm still looking," Rufus said.

"Don't get too much," Golan advised him. "Prices are kind of high."

Nodding, the mountain man said, "They are about the same as Fort Hall."

Looking impatient, the missionary finally said, "I got to get back. Can we expect you for supper?"

Rufus rubbed his hand down his beard. "I'll be staying here the next few days, but don't worry. I'll be back and ready to go when you are."

Snorting, Golan replied, "You're looking in the wrong area. The whiskey is toward the back." With that the man headed out of the trading post.

Under his beard, Rufus was blushing. "Ain't nothing wrong with a man wanting a drink," he mumbled.

The mountain man's hair hung to his shoulders and his beard was down on his chest. It was time to get a trim. The woman he'd met here did a fair job of cutting hair. With the missionary gone, Rufus walked over to the back and leaned against the plank bar.

"Give me a bottle," he told the owner.

For the next hour, Rufus loitered near the bar, finally sitting at one of the tables. "You want something to eat?" the owner, Pika, asked.

With the whiskey burning his stomach, the mountain man figured it might be a good idea. "I'll have whatever you have."

"Stew it is," the owner said.

As he was eating the stew and chewing on some coarse bread, he saw a familiar face come in. It was Lani, the Owyhee woman he knew. She was carrying things from her garden to sell. Sitting in his buckskins and all haired over, Rufus looked like any number of trappers who traveled through the fort. He brushed the drops of stew and bread crumbs from his beard.

"Is that you, Lani?" he called over.

Recognizing the gravelly voice, she smiled and asked, "Would that be you, Rufus under all the scraggly hair?"

Pushing the bowl away, he smiled under the whiskers. "It is."

After dickering a bit with Pika over the vegetables, she took the money the owner gave her and then walked over to the table. "My brother tells me I shouldn't come to the back of the post. Bad men sit there."

"I agree," Rufus told her. "That is why I am back here to protect you."

She looked into his bowl and pushed it back to him. "You haven't finished eating. A man must eat to keep his strength up."

Taking the spoon, Rufus shoveled a heaping spoonful into his mouth. While he chewed she said, "It is good stew. My vegetables are in it."

With the meal finished, the mountain man poured himself another drink. He didn't offer one to Lani because he knew she didn't drink. Rufus remembered when he had been walking south of the fort and had first seen her in her garden weeding. She had a crude fence around it to keep out animals. One side was damaged. He had offered to fix it, and after that they had visited and he had admired her garden. After another visit, she had invited him into her log home. It was built into a hill, with a root cellar in the back. Another building near it had a corral for horses or mules.

Many enjoyable nights had been spent in the cabin. She lived there with her brother, who was gone most of the time leading pack trains to Fort Hall or to Fort Nez Percès, transporting supplies or furs. Rufus knew that if her brother was home, Lani would not invite him in.

Finishing his drink, the mountain man looked at the bottle and put the cork back in. "I can save this for later."

"I have some early potatoes to dig," she told him.

"Is your brother helping you?" Rufus asked.

"He is at Fort Hall," she said. "You should have passed him."

"We crossed at Three Island Crossing," he told her. "I believe he takes the south side of the Snake River."

"He does," she replied. "I expect him back in four or five days."

Rufus knew that the pack trains would travel 25 to 30 miles a day, which would make the trip from Fort Hall to Fort Boise in less than two weeks. "I could use a haircut," Rufus told her.

"Potatoes first, and then a haircut," she told him.

The potatoes were dug and cleaned in record time, and soon Rufus was sitting in the cabin having his hair sheared. In front of the cabin was a caldron with water heating for his bath. Lani liked things clean.

The next four nights went quickly, with the soft, warm body of Lani in his arms. She would tell him stories of what life was like on the Sandwich Islands, of the ocean trip across the Pacific and life at Fort Vancouver before coming to Fort Boise. It had been her brother's work that had caused her to leave Fort Vancouver.

"Rufus, you must get up," Lani called to him. "You promised to help me with the fishing before you go back to the missionaries."

Getting up in the bed, he sat naked. She came in with clean clothes for him. "The night breeze dried them," she said.

"Would you like to come back to bed before I get dressed?" the mountain man asked.

"Yes, I would," she said, a twinkle in her eye, "but I am not. We need to check the nets."

Groaning, the mountain man swung his legs out of the bed and began to dress. In the evenings Lani would put gill nets in the river and then whatever fish she caught would be sold fresh to the trading post, or dried to sell later.

The mountain man looked across the cabin. On the counter sat the whiskey bottle that he'd brought from the trading post. When he was with the woman, he was always too busy to take time to drink. Before he had his coffee, the two of them were near the river, pulling the net and removing the catch. She had promised him fried fish before he headed back to the wagons.

Lani would not take any money from Rufus. She told him she was not that kind of woman. She laid with him because she liked him, and only because she liked him. He always noticed she did not say love. Instead, Rufus would purchase some coffee, rice, beans, and salt and sugar from the trading post to replace the items he'd eaten while visiting.

Walking back to the wagons leading the horses, Rufus was wearing his wool shirt and pants. On the mustang he carried a couple of bags. His other packs were safely stored at Lani's. Tony came running when he saw the mountain man.

"You were gone a long time," he squealed. Then he stopped dead in his tracks. "Your beard and hair are really short."

Smiling at the young lad, Rufus said, "Every once in a while I have to get them cut so I don't trip over my own beard."

Laughing, the boy said, "You can't trip over a beard."

It was quite a change. Rufus' hair was cut mid-ear, and the beard had been shortened and shaped. "Can I ride?" the boy asked.

Picking Tony up, Rufus hoisted him into the saddle on the grulla. "Sit still, because I haven't tightened the cinch," the mountain man cautioned him.

Mary was standing near their wagon, watching him come. She wasn't smiling. As he approached she asked, "Did you have a good time?"

"Yes, I did," Rufus replied. "I even got a haircut."

"Your packs are missing," she said, looking at the mustang.

Trying to keep things casual, Rufus told her, "I left them at the fort. I won't be needing the traps and stuff, and figured I could pick them up on the way back."

Her brow furled. "So you won't be staying in Oregon?"

"I just signed on to bring the wagons to Fort Nez Percès. After that I am heading back east." Then he asked, "Did I do something wrong?"

Suddenly, she gave him a strained smile, "No, you didn't do a thing wrong. I guess I just worried a bit when you weren't coming back for supper."

"I did tell Golan that I'd be gone a few days," Rufus told her.

Laughing, she said, "I'm sorry to be this way. You certainly deserve a few days away from all this." Lifting the boy off the horse, she said, "Tony has been asking about you every day. I am glad you are back."

Walking into camp, Gracie was near the fire. She saw him coming and called over, "I got some corn bread here that needs testing." She then cut a piece of the warm bread and handed it to the mountain man.

It was warm, moist, and sweet. "It is perfect," he told her.

"It was really quiet when you were gone," she said. "You missed church yesterday. Daddy had a good sermon on the evils of drinking. Some folks from the fort came."

Grinning at her, he said, "I am truly sorry I missed that one. Where is your dad?"

"I see him now," she said, pointing.

Golan was coming from the makeshift privy after nature's call. The missionary looked at Rufus and said, "I expected to see you in worse shape, but here you are all cleaned up."

"I met someone whose brother runs pack animals between here and Fort Nez Percès," the mountain man told him. "He should be back today or tomorrow and I hope to talk to him about the trail to the fort."

"You been on it before, right?" Golan asked.

"I have, but things change from year to year, so he may have suggestions that will make the trip easier," Rufus told the man.

Nodding, the missionary asked, "Have any luck hunting?"

"Got a bag of fresh fish on the mustang," the mountain man told him.

"That will be good," Golan said. "Give them to Eunice to clean. They'll make a good supper."

Unable to avoid giving a little dig into the man, Rufus said, "I heard you gave a good sermon yesterday. Sorry I missed it."

Giving the mountain man a hard look, Golan replied, "Now that you are back, maybe I'll give it again."

Smiling, Rufus went to give the bag of fish to Eunice. In the other bag were a few supplies and the partial bottle of whiskey.

* * *

Rufus had a chance to talk to Lani's brother before they left. The man had several good suggestions about the trail. He also suggested a place where they could cross the Snake River before cutting northeast avoiding the worst of the Blue Ridge Mountains. They were about two and a half weeks from Fort Nez Percès. Her brother knew of a trail that had been cut for wagons partway to the fort. He did caution Rufus that they might have to abandon the wagons after that.

The three wagons led by Rufus left Fort Boise in mid-August. Lani's brother caught up with them at the crossing. At this time of year the river was at its lowest, but the wagons still had to deal with the steep river banks. The four men using shovels and axes quickly improved the entry as the pack train crossed and disappeared on the other side.

Then Rufus and Allen drove the extra oxen and the mustang across and did a little digging on the exit side. By early afternoon, the wagons were headed northeast, leaving the Snake River behind. In another 200 miles or so, they would arrive at the confluence where the Snake River flowed into the Columbia River.

It was difficult to make the 12 miles a day with all the delays improving the road. Washes had to be filled and ways around ridges had to be found. Soon they would encounter nearly impassable forests. The party remained confident because other wagons had found a way through, but they had hardly left a mark of their route. Every couple of days they would pass, or be passed by, pack trains hauling stuff between the forts. Questions were asked by the missionaries and suggestions were made by the pack train leaders. Also, there were warnings about big cats and grizzlies.

Even though it was the peak of summer, it was cool in the evenings. Rufus tended to sleep under the stars most nights, but with the wind on the colder nights he'd stake down his fly tarp for protection. He'd been hearing things that he didn't like, making his sleep restless. Somewhere in the dark there was a bear.

"I heard something last night," Allen told Rufus. "Sounded like a pig, but out here I think it was a bear."

Trying not to alarm the man, Rufus told him, "That's why we have to stay alert and keep the oxen and horses close."

For all the mountain man knew, the bear was just passing by, testing their scent and moving on, not being comfortable with the smell of man. Then a couple of nights would go by before he'd again hear grunting or the tear of bark as it raked its claws down a tree. The thin mountain air would carry sound for miles, so Rufus had no idea how far away the grizzly might be.

The wagons had left the arid plains with waist-high sage brush behind and now had sparse grass and lines of trees along streams or rivers. Their stock was getting thinner, and they feared that oxen losses were in the near future. Both the plains and the forests had offered little grazing. A week into the trip, they came to a mountain lake with thick bunchgrass in the valley and trees in the foothills. They decided to spend two days to let the oxen graze.

Rufus was readying his Hawken when Golan came up with the other two men. "Are you going hunting or getting ready to leave us?" Robert kidded.

"If I was to leave, you'd have one less mouth to feed," the mountain man kidded back.

"You figure we got another two weeks to Fort Nez Percès?" Golan asked.

"A good two weeks by wagon," Rufus replied. "If you leave the wagons, you got maybe a week from here."

"We got things we need in the wagons," Golan said. "A couple of days of grazing should help the oxen."

"From here on the grass will be mostly sparse, with few areas of plenty," the mountain man told them. "We can't afford the time to hunt for grass, so soon we will start losing oxen. At some point we'll only have enough to pack what we need and we'll be forced to leave the wagons."

Golan's face got really serious. "We will draw straws and choose which wagon is left behind first as the oxen fall."

Allen and Robert gave him a shocked look. Until now it had just been talk of losing oxen. Choosing which wagon would get left first and then second made the probability very real. Both nodded in agreement.

"You do what you got to do," Rufus said. "In the meantime, keep your rifles loaded and watch your stock."

"You think Indians will come and steal them?" Allen asked.

"I wouldn't worry about the Indians," Rufus said. "They got better game to kill. We got grizzlies and big cats around here, and they will scatter and kill the oxen just for sport."

"Our rifles will be ready for whatever comes," Golan promised.

"I will be gone overnight," Rufus told them. "I'll be scouting a trail, and maybe I'll get lucky and get an elk. We been hearing a bear at night. Could be I'll get my sights on it. Depending what I find, it may even be another day. You decide whether you want to wait an extra day." Then, pointing to the northwest, he said, "If you go, head straight toward that highest peak and then watch for a way through the mountain."

"You sound like you ain't coming back," Robert said.

Feeling a bit of frustration, Rufus told him, "When a man rides out into this wilderness, he never knows what might happen. Hopefully nothing will happen, but if it does, you need to know how to get out of here."

"Rufus is right," Golan said. "The lord hasn't abandoned us and he will be back. I suggest you all keep praying while you're watching the oxen."

Mary met him as he was getting the grulla. "Don't go alone, Rufus. Take Allen with you. I can drive the oxen if we need to leave before you get back. We can't lose you."

He saw the tears in her eyes. "I will only be gone one night, Mary. You and Tony need Allen to stay here." As he climbed onto the grulla, the look she gave him made Rufus unsure that that was completely true.

The mountain man was glad to get away from the wagons. The hardships of this trip would make any group of people give up hope. He needed to do two things: First, find a trail that would prevent them from having to leave the wagons or do any backtracking.

With a horse a man would just ride around a mountain if one got in the way. With wagons that wasn't so easy.

The second thing was the grizzly. They had one following them, and before long it would get brave enough to attack the camp. The bear needed killing.

His plan was to ride out a half-day and scout the trail. Then Rufus was going to circle around, see if he could spot the bear, and if possible kill it. He just hoped that its appetite for oxen held off for a couple more days.

By mid-afternoon the mountain man was feeling good about the trail. Other than some washes, they would make good time in the next couple of days. It was time to circle around the east side through the tree-covered foothills. He had a bear to deal with. By late afternoon Rufus was a couple of miles east of the camp. He could hear someone chopping wood and so could the bear.

By the sounds the mountain man had heard the past couple of nights, the grizzly was less than a mile behind them. Killing an ox and leaving it for the bear would have done little good. As thin as the cattle were the bear would eat what it could and then be after another in no more than a day.

Rufus found a spot in the trees to sit and listen. He was less than three miles southeast of the camp. As he sat, the mountain man heard the normal night noises: Owls calling to each other, wolves howling in the distance, a fox yipping as it hunted rodents. Suddenly, there was a screech of a fisher. While it was chilling, it was not a threat to the missionaries or their cattle.

It was near midnight when Rufus heard the grunting of the bear. It was a little further south of the wagons than he was. Come morning, he would move closer to the clearing where the camp was and watch. The Hawken had an effective range of 400 yards and a maximum range of 800. Often it took more than one shot to bring the big bastards down.

After dozing against a cottonwood tree, Rufus woke just before sunrise. The grulla had spent the night with the cinch loosened on the saddle. The mountain man led the horse through the trees, slowly closing the distance between himself and the clearing.

Stopping within the trees, Rufus could see the white canvas tops of the wagons. They were about a quarter-mile across the opening. Tying the horse to a sapling, Rufus settled down to wait. He listened more than watched for the bear. The horse would smell the bear before the mountain man, so he depended on it to alert him.

The day went by without a sound or smell of the bear. Rufus chewed on some jerky and drank water for his meal. He was fighting the urge to doze when the grulla snorted. Rufus remained motionless and searched for any movement in the trees. Then the smell hit him, carried by the breeze from the west. The bear was not far away.

Rufus saw that the horse was staring through the trees toward the northwest. The mountain man began to move. Soundlessly, he crept toward the edge of the trees. Using some brambles for cover, he scanned the valley surrounding the wagons. A breeze stirred the grass and he could smell the bear. He saw the movement of the oxen as they grazed, unaware of any danger. All was quiet in the camp. He knew that the bear was near, so it had to be somewhere in the trees watching the oxen.

There was the rustling of the trees, movement of the grass, some eagles gliding on the wind above. The mountain man searched the wooded foothill for a glimpse of the behemoth. Then a cold flash went through Rufus. The open area surrounding the wagons had depressions that could easily hide the bear.

He rose to look over the brambles. All was quiet. Then he saw it come. The bear appeared as if by magic, charging at top speed toward the oxen! The golden fur on its back rippled as it ran. Rufus brought the rifle to his shoulder. In just seconds the bear would be between him and the wagons, preventing Rufus from firing.

Swinging the rifle, he got the sights on the bear and touched off the Hawken. The rifle recoiled against his shoulder, sending the lead ball at the animal as the sound of the shot bounced through the valley. The charging bear seemed to miss a step, and then continued its charge.

Things became a blur as Rufus frantically reloaded the Hawken. The bear was closing in on the oxen! The shot had started to scatter them. Unheard by the mountain man were the shouts from the wagons. The bear was only 50 feet from the nearest ox when Rufus brought the rifle back to his shoulder.

Then came shots from the wagons. Their rifles discharged as one at the grizzly. As the mountain man attempted to get the bear back in his sights, it collapsed and rolled once before sliding to a stop. With his eyes on the bear, Rufus brought the Hawken back to half-cock. He watched as three men ran from the wagons toward the grizzly.

Rufus rushed to the grulla and was shortly galloping across the bunchgrass toward the bear and

171

the men. Allen was poking the grizzly with the barrel of his Baker. The mountain man pulled the grulla up and leaped from the saddle.

"I hope you men reloaded those rifles," Rufus said. "If not, keep away from that bear."

Robert was at the height of excitement. "We got it! We shot the bear!"

"You did at that," Rufus replied.

"We heard you fire," Golan said. "The bear would have killed an ox if you hadn't shot first."

"I thought you were scouting the trail," Allen said as he loaded his rifle.

"I rode the trail to the pass through the Blue Mountains," Rufus told him. "It will need a little work, but we should be at the pass in two days. After that, I decided to find this damn bear and get it off our trail."

"You should have told us you were after the bear," Robert said. "We could have hunted it with you."

"If we were all after the grizzly we'd never gotten sight of it. We would have made too much noise to get close, and we would have been leaving the women and oxen unguarded."

Smiling, Golan told him, "Eunice fired one of the shots at the bear."

It was time to quit admiring their kill and skin the bear. Someone also had to go after the scattered oxen. Rufus pulled his Green River knife and made the first cut. There wasn't a big enough tree close to the camp to use for skinning, so the mountain man commenced doing it on the ground. Golan and Allen went after the oxen.

With Robert's help, Rufus got the skin removed from the grizzly, along with the paws and head. With the skin spread on the bunchgrass, the mountain man rolled the carcass back and forth. His shot into the right side had hit a little high behind the shoulder. A killing shot, but the bear would have run for a while. On the other side, there were four bullet holes. They went from the front of the shoulder to the back hip. The one just behind the left shoulder had been the one that brought it down.

"I think that one is mine," Robert said. "I shot this Kentucky rifle and it has a smaller ball."

"Golan shot the Harper 1803, and its ball is about the same size," Rufus said. "You can cut the grizzly up and find the ball if you want to see if it's yours, but I figure you all did a hell of a good job hitting the running bear."

The mountain man could see that Robert would like to go back to the wagons claiming the killing shot. Rufus had competed many times at the rendezvous and it did feel good to have bragging rights. But there was no way Rufus was going to cut into the bear for the man. They'd take a few choice cuts for the cook pot and leave the rest to be scavenged by the birds up in the sky and other varmints prowling the area.

With the oxen rounded up, the other men came back to the kill. "Damn," Allen said, "skinned it looks like a man lying there."

Golan looked over the bear. "I'll be," he said. "We all hit the bear. Eunice will be tickled."

Looking at the man, Robert said, "She had the other long rifle. Could have been her shot that hit behind the shoulder."

Rufus knew that Robert said that to make points with Golan, who was the lead missionary. All the mountain man knew was that his wasn't the killing shot, but then the bear had been running and he was a quarter-mile away. Inside he was feeling pretty good.

Not much meat was taken from the grizzly. Golan salted down some of the roasts and the back straps. Fat was collected to be used to lubricate the wagon axles. Rufus negotiated getting the hide as the remainder of his pay for guiding the wagons.

The next morning one of the oxen wasn't able to get up. It had probably been injured during the bear attack. They now had only one spare ox and some of the hardest part of the trail left ahead of them as they went through Blue Mountain pass. Again, only a little of the butchered animal was taken with them. As the wagons left the mountain lake, they left plenty for the varmints in the area to eat.

The trail leading to the pass was plagued with exposed basalt and other igneous rock jutting up from the ground, making the travel punishing on the wagons. One back wheel had to be replaced at the end of the first day and a broken axle delayed them the second day.

Again, Rufus rode ahead, hoping to find a better trail, but none was had. In his heart, he felt it was time to abandon the wagons, but Golan was determined to continue. The mountain man knew that going up over the pass would be tough on the oxen, but once over the top, the steep descent with the wagons could be the end of more than one of them.

It was dark when Rufus got back to the wagons. Gracie saw him walking toward the fire. "Mother boiled up some of the bear. Let me know when you're ready and I'll make you a plate."

"Give me a minute to take care of the horse," he told her.

Picketing the grulla near the mustang, Rufus headed back past Allen's and Mary's wagon. She stepped out of the dark. "How does the trail ahead look?"

"I wouldn't take a wagon over it," the mountain man said in his gravelly voice.

"Allen is worried about our oxen," she told him. "We had trouble keeping up today."

Rufus stopped and almost told her that the wagons wouldn't make it over the mountains, but changed him mind. It made no sense to worry her. When the oxen fell, it would be soon enough.

She didn't follow him when he went to the fire. Gracie handed Rufus a plate heaped with potatoes and bear meat. "It was the last of mother's potatoes. She was afraid of losing them."

The mountain man figured that it was a miracle that she even had any left since their trip had started in St. Louis. The potatoes were very good, while the bear was a little chewy. The meat gave the stew a taste that Rufus was familiar with from prior kills. It wasn't bad, but it wasn't like elk.

Golan asked him, "How is the trail ahead?"

"Based on what I saw ahead, we can figure it was good road up to now," Rufus told him.

"That bad," the missionary replied.

The next morning Rufus was getting the mustang ready and he saw Golan and Robert moving things into Golan's wagon. A few items were set aside to be put into Allen's wagon.

Walking over, the mountain man said, "I see you've made a decision."

Golan turned from placing a bag into the back of the wagon. "We have. Robert and Emma will leave their wagon and their oxen will be used to help pull the other two wagons."

After emptying the wagon of all necessary items, an axle, front wheel, and back wheel were removed to replace those from under the remaining two wagons. The white canvas top was also taken, leaving the abandoned wagon with its skeletal bows remaining on the side of the trail.

The moving of contents and stripping the wagon had taken most of the morning. Rufus had ridden part-way looking for the best route. He came back following a pack train from Fort Nez Percès. No new information was gotten from the leader. He just shook his head when he saw the wagons.

The trail to the summit was a series of valleys and inclines, but none as severe as some earlier ones on the trail. The trail itself was punishing, with basalt ridges, gorges, and the occasional tree that had to be removed to widen the trail for the wagons. The extra oxen were kept in their yokes and driven behind the two wagons.

The trail up to the summit was just over 10 miles. The party managed to make only four miles before Rufus recommended they stop for the night. There was an area that was somewhat level where the wagons could be parked, and there was water. They were at an elevation of just over 3,000 feet, and in the coming day they would climb another 1,000 feet to the summit.

Rufus had finished the ride to the top and surveyed the far side. After the summit, the trail would drop the 2,000 feet into a valley in just six or seven miles. A series of sharp turns zigzagging back and forth would be required.

Returning to camp, he told Golan, "We need to cut a couple of logs to lock the back wheels of the wagons. On the steepest areas that will be the only way to slow them."

The next morning they found another ox lying dead. Not wanting an extra ounce to carry to the summit, it was left untouched where it lay. They now had nine tired teams of oxen. It was decided to put five teams, or 10 oxen, on Golan's wagon, which was the heaviest, and four teams on Allen's.

With the braking logs tied to the back of the wagons, the party continued toward the summit the next morning, climbing the last thousand feet. Several times they had stops to work on the trail. Only enough improvement was done in each case to continue on.

It was late afternoon when the wagons finally reached the summit. The party stood staring out on the panoramic view below. In the distance they could see the blue line of the Cascade Mountain Range. They were now less than a week from their goal. Their stomachs got tight as they peered down the steep slope in front of them. Miles below they saw a pack train slowly climbing toward the summit.

After supper was over, the group sat and watched the brilliant reds of the sunset in the western sky. Tony sat near Rufus and talked a mile a minute while the mountain man chewed his tobacco and worried about the descent they would face tomorrow.

CHAPTER TEN

It was Sunday morning as the group slowly woke. A haze hung over the valley below. Rufus had lost track of the days and felt frustration when Golan started setting up for his sermon. As he walked to take care of the horses, he suddenly felt ashamed. The group was about to descend on a steep, winding trail and it was possible that not all would survive. Some time in prayer would be a good thing.

The day passed slowly as Rufus sat around with nothing to do. No benefit would be gained by looking at the long, steep slope ahead, and he sure as hell wasn't going to go back along the trail they'd just passed. Golan had given a good sermon that morning. Not too much brimstone and plenty of hope for the future in Oregon.

While he was moving the horses onto new grass he heard someone come up behind him. The steps were not of the young boy who'd spent a lot of time following him. They were others that he recognized. Without turning he said, "It's a fine morning, Mary."

"Oh. You saw me coming," she said.

Turning, he noticed that she was carrying something wrapped in a cloth. "I made cornbread last night and thought you might like some. It's a long way to supper."

Taking the package, Rufus smiled and said, "Thank you. I saw you at the fire last night. I figured you were making something for your boy."

Turning to the west, she looked up at the sky. "Wasn't it a glorious sunset last night?"

"Yes, it was," Rufus replied. "But I don't think you came here to talk about the sunset."

Turning back and looking down at her hands, she told him, "Allen and I were talking. When we get to Fort Nez Percès, we will rest a couple of days and then head for the Willamette Valley. We decided that he would build a raft and take our stuff down the Colorado River. He wanted to talk to you about taking Tony and me along with the oxen over the Cascades, through the pass near Mount Hood."

"I been that-a-way, and it is not a short trip," Rufus told her. "You're talking about 100 miles with an awful bump in it going past Mount Hood."

Moving close to Rufus, she whispered, "Don't tell him I said anything. The river is dangerous, and he is fearful of our boy drowning in some of the rapids." Then Mary turned and walked back towards the wagons.

"Damn," he mumbled. "I didn't say I would do it."

While Golan frowned on it, Rufus got out the brush and began grooming the horses. He had once told the missionary that it made him feel closer to God. The man did not buy it, but the mountain man had continued with the horses. He could feel the bones under the hide and knew that the horses had suffered during the trip. Rufus had carried some grain from Fort Hall and then gotten some more at Fort Boise, but it hadn't been enough.

"Can I help?" a young voice called to Rufus. Turning, he smiled at Tony. "I'll let you brush near the belly, but don't get under the horses."

Giving the brush to the youngster, Rufus dug a chew out of his possible bag. That was another thing the missionary didn't like. Biting some off the tobacco twist, he stuck it back into the bag. The mountain man knew damn well that Mary had sent the boy out to help change his mind. Rufus knew good and well that the trip down the Columbia River was dangerous. With lots of small rapids that were easy to go through, there were three mean ones that could smash a raft to pieces.

That night, while eating a cold supper, Rufus expected Allen to come over and talk to him about taking his family over the pass. Allen played with his boy and talked with others at the camp, but he never mentioned a thing to the mountain man. Rufus hoped that they'd changed their minds.

The next morning, after a hot breakfast and a few prayers, the oxen were hitched to the wagons. The logs would be dragged all the way down the slope except, when necessary, they'd be tied to the back wheels to lock them up. They would go back and forth down the slope, making one hairpin turn after another. Most of the time the wagons would be leaning dangerously to one side, and something as small as an anthill under the upside wheel could tip the wagon.

The women and the young boy would be walking, more or less straight towards the bottom while the wagons went back and forth. Robert and Rufus walked above the wagons, leading the mustang and grulla with a rope tied from the saddle horn to the wagons' high sides to help prevent tipping.

Each turn was harrowing as the long teams of oxen had to be turned 180 degrees at each end with shouts of "Haw" and "Gee" ringing out. The long tongues of the wagons would be strained to near the breaking point as the front wheels slid and shuddered, threatening to snap their spokes. After each turn shouts of "Whoa" brought the teams to a stop, while Rufus and Robert switched their ropes to the other side.

By midday the men were exhausted from walking on the side hill and struggling through the repeated turns. Rufus realized that they had not gotten halfway down the 6-mile hill. Regardless of how long the trip down took, there would be no stopping until the wagons were on the flat below.

At one point, Eunice and Mary tried to take over driving the oxen so their husbands could rest, but the men refused to let them. At any one of the turns, the steepness of the hill could cause the oxen to slip and panic and head straight down the hill, with tragic results.

After a quick break for some water and biscuits, the men continued the slow progress down the hill. A pack train came behind them from Fort Hall, and the three men driving the mules offered the men a couple of bottles of whiskey to celebrate once they got down. A stern no from Golan sent them on their way. Rufus continued with the grulla, keeping tension on the rope, but he was steaming. The damn whiskey would have tasted mighty good at the end of a long day.

Again, there was a beautiful sunset in the west, but the men on the hill took no notice of it. They had another hour of zigzagging before they reached the bottom. At one point they were temped to head straight down where the slope had less steepness for a short distance, but fear of the teams getting away from them prevented it.

Below, the men could see a fire going and the women and Tony standing around it, watching their progress. They had carried some supplies with them, so the men could expect a meal when they reached the bottom. It had been full dark by the time they got to the bottom, which had made each traverse that much more difficult. After sixteen hours, the wagons pulled up to the fire.

The moon came up over the summit, and looking up Rufus could see the top. What would have taken him by horseback less than two hours had taken a full day, but it was now behind them and Fort Nez Percès was just five days' travel away. They would have to spend a couple of days resting the animals at the bottom, but now Rufus could almost count the hours before he would be pouring the first whiskey.

* * *

Fort Nez Percès was built in 1818 by the North-West Company of Montreal, Canada and was taken over in 1821 by the Hudson's Bay Company. The fort was built with double thickness palisades, and had towers with water tanks on the four corners to fight fires started during an attack. It also had two small cannons for protection. Storage buildings and quarters for occupants were built within the wall, along with corrals for large numbers of horses. The logs to build the fort had been floated down the river from as far as 100 miles away due to lack of timber at the location.

The two wagons slowly rolled up to the front of the fort. Everything that could have offered cover had been cleared for a good distance. In its heyday the fort had been a key location during the fur trade period. They were still an important location supplying goods to Fort Boise and Fort Hall.

Rufus felt he'd done his job, and he bade farewell to the missionaries and Allen's family. Young Tony seemed the most upset by the mountain man leaving. Mary just stood back, staring at Rufus, saying nothing.

Leading his horses into the fort with the bearskin on the mustang, Rufus headed for the trading post. Things were busy in the fort with tradesmen and visitors doing business. One of the Hudson's Bay employees came up and looked at the grizzly skin.

"It's a find one you got there," the man said. "I saw you come in with them folks in the wagons. So did Leaf at the trading post. He don't like seeing wagons and emigrants, so don't expect him to offer you much for the skin."

"It's salted down," Rufus told the man. "If Leaf's got a problem with my bear, I'll haul it back east with me."

"I see you got the head and paws," the man replied. "If a company man brought that in, Leaf would give him, maybe, £20 or a bit more."

The mountain man knew that each pound was worth $5. Thanking the man, Rufus headed for the trading post. Leaf was standing near the door with his arms folded. He had thick, red hair and a neatly trimmed beard and moustache. Rufus tied his horses to the hitching rail.

"I see what you got there," Leaf said, with a thick brogue. "I ain't much call for them."

In his gravelly voice, Rufus asked, "You ain't got a need for skins?"

Nodding toward the gate, the man said, "Them easterners. I saw you come in with them."

"They're bringing religion to the Indians," Rufus told him. "I am glad to be rid of them. Finn from Fort Hall asked me to watch over them and I must have been drunk, because I said yes."

Snorting, the red-headed man said, "£10 for the skin. It smells a bit rotten to me."

"Rotten, hell!" Rufus exclaimed. "The damn hide ain't hardly cooled since it was shot. I'll take it back over the mountain and see what Fort William offers me. Louie's whiskey ain't watered down, either."

Anger showed on the owner's face as it got red. "You saying my whiskey ain't what it should be?"

"It's what I was told," Rufus replied. "Too bad I won't get to try it, but Louie's got the best I've tasted."

"The hell you say," Leaf spat out. "His whiskey wouldn't be good enough for the Owyhee working for me."

Turning to leave, the mountain man said, "I best be heading east for some good whiskey."

"Spread the damn hide out and let me see what you got," the owner snapped, not wanting to lose the profit on the hide.

It was a large bear, and was impressive as the mountain man slowly spread it out, placing the head and paws in their proper places.

"The hide's got good color," Leaf said, walking around it. Squatting, he looked at the left side. "How many shots did it take to bring it down?"

"I had a few friends helping me weigh it down with lead," Rufus told him.

Shaking his head, Leaf said, "That's a lot of buttonholes in the hide."

Rufus began to fold the bear skin back up. The owner again stood with his arms folded. He watched as the mountain man readied the hide to take it with him.

"£18," Leaf told him.

Rufus stopped what he was doing. "£22 and you got it."

Again the red creeped into the owner's cheeks. It appeared that neither was willing to budge. As the mountain man finished readying the hide to put onto the mustang, Leaf said, "I'll let you taste my whiskey. Then you can decide if you want to haul it over the mountain."

The two men walked into the trading post, the familiar smells filling Rufus' nostrils. The mountain man always felt excitement when he was surrounded by the leather goods, metal traps, beans and coffee, tobacco, and shelves filled with notions and spices.

To the left was a plank counter with bottles of rum and whiskey lining the back wall. The bottles were filled with an amber brew which was not often seen in the west. Most whiskey was shipped from the east. unaged, in small barrels, was clear and nearly 200 proof. Then it was watered down to whatever proof those drinking would bear.

The whiskey was good. Leaf leaned over the plank counter with his face close to Rufus. "Good, ain't it?"

The mountain man tossed down another shot and felt the whiskey warm his belly. "It will do after a long trip over the mountains."

"Hell, it will do anywhere," Leaf said. "£19 and no more."

Taking another drink, figuring that while they were dickering it was on the owner, Rufus said, "$100 in gold or silver and a couple of bottles of the whiskey."

The owner growled as he paced back and forth behind the counter. "Them are big claws on that grizzly."

Rufus quickly poured himself another drink, knowing the dickering was almost done. The mountain man was feeling pretty good as he walked out of the trading post. He'd gotten a fair price for the bear skin and drank most of a pint of whisky. Leaf sent two **Owyhees working for him to haul in the bear.**

Leading the horses to the livery, Rufus instructed the hostler to give the animals plenty of grain and hay. The mountain man had $100 and two bottles in his possible bag that needed his attention.

Walking back out of the fort with his bedroll slung across his back, the Hawken cradled in his right arm, the Colt and short axe in his broad belt, Rufus felt that it was a good day. He had delivered the wagons, the pressure was off, and in the next couple of days he'd be heading back to Fort Boise and the warmth of Lani.

Allen waved Rufus over. "Eunice made a johnnycake to go with the soup. Join us for supper."

Young Tony was thrilled to see the mountain man walking towards the camp. "Did you sell the bear?" he asked.

"Sold it and got a good price," Rufus said, smiling.

Eunice passed him and replied, "Paid you in whiskey I see."

Defending the mountain man, Grace followed her mother saying, "Mr. Pike just took us safely from Fort Hall. He deserves to have a drink."

Her mother continued to scold her daughter at such a thought, but Rufus didn't care as he sat down. He was feeling good and Tony was plying him with dozens of questions about the fort and where he was going.

Mary came over and motioned Allen. "Have you asked him?"

"I was about to," her husband said. "You take Tony for a walk."

Rufus heard what they'd said, and he anticipated what was coming. He already knew what his answer would be. *No.*

Allen came over and asked, "Can you take a walk with me?"

Hell, Rufus thought. Everyone wanted to walk. He was feeling mellow and just wanted to sit. Sliding the bedroll off his back, Rufus slowly got up. "A walk wouldn't hurt me," he told the man.

Just out of earshot of the missionaries, Allen said, "Mary and I will be heading for The Dalles in a couple of days. There I will get a raft to take our things down the Columbia River."

"I wish you and your family well," Rufus said. "I hear there is plenty of farm land in Willamette Valley."

"I worry about the river," Allen said. "There are some pretty rough rapids to go over."

"Get yourself a good guide and it shouldn't be a problem," Rufus suggested.

"Mary and the boy can't swim, and she is already having bad dreams about going down river," the man confided in him.

The two men were a distance from the wagons and Rufus asked, "Would you like a taste of whiskey?"

A fearful look came to Allen's face as he glanced back toward the wagons. "I guess it would be okay."

Rufus pulled a pint out of his possible bag and handed it to Allen. The man removed the cork and took a swallow. In turn, the mountain man drank. "Hate to say it, but the Brits make good whiskey."

"Yes. Yes, they do," Allen replied, wanting to get back to his conversation. "Like I said, Mary is fearful and I think Tony is worried."

"The boy would find it an adventure," Rufus told him. 'It would be something he'd talk about the rest of his life."

"Rufus," the man said, stopping to face him. Rufus held up the bottle and Allen shook his head. "I would like to pay you to bring Mary and Tony with the oxen over the pass near Mount Hood. Lord willing, I'd be on the other side waiting for you."

Fulling intending to give the man a resounding no, Rufus turned as Tony came running up to him. "You and daddy taking a walk too?" he asked.

Mary called him back, "Your father and Mr. Pike are talking. Let's go back to the wagon. I need to clean you up for supper."

As she passed Rufus she mouthed the word, "Please."

"You best have another drink with me, because I am about to say something stupid," Rufus told the man as he held out the bottle.

After taking a drink, Rufus asked, "What happens if you don't show up on the other end? Like you are telling me, it is a dangerous trip on the river."

They turned to walk back to the wagons. Allen took a while to answer. "Mary will have money to buy the farm, and if needed she will find someone to help her."

Rufus walked in silence. *If needed,* he thought. *You mean, if I didn't stay.*

The johnnycake was good and the bean soup thick and tasty. The mountain man couldn't complain about the food during their trip. Eunice had a knack to make almost anything taste good. While Rufus hadn't said yes to Allen, he had implied it.

When Tony came up to him all excited and told him, "Mama said you are going to take us the rest of the way!" Rufus knew it was decided.

Suddenly the supper wasn't settling as well in his stomach. It was the end of August. The trip he'd agreed to was 100 miles to The Dalles and another 100 to Willamette Valley. It would be almost a month before he'd be back at **Fort Nez Percès.**

When the hell am I going to have a chance to do any trapping or hunting? he wondered.

Rufus made it clear to Allen that he'd need a few days before making the trip. The man was happy with that because his oxen needed rest and the wagon needed minor repairs. The first leg of the trip would be across the Columbia Plateau to The Dalles, and then over the Cacades to Willamette Valley. The plateau was basalt rock, with a fertile top layer which grew grass, greasewood, and sage brush. With the oxen pulling the wagon they should make almost 15 miles a day. After that, with the help of some native boys, the oxen would be driven over the Cascade pass while he, Mary and Tony could ride horses.

After promising to be back in three days and wishing the missionaries a safe trip to Whitman Mission, Rufus headed back to the fort, carrying his bed roll. His intention had been to sleep near the wagons. Now he needed to be away from them and have a few drinks.

The hostler was sitting outside the livery enjoying the evening air. Rufus took a bench beside him. "Do you feel like a drink?" the mountain man asked.

Through the course of the evening, the two pints were finished and Rufus climbed into the loft for a blissful night's sleep.

* * *

Three days later, with a heavy head and an upset stomach, Rufus rode out of the fort, leading the mustang to the lone wagon. Allen had the oxen hitched to the wagon and was ready to go. As usual

Tony was glad to see the mountain man. He ran to meet him and Rufus lifted the boy onto the saddle.

The wedge tent had been taken down and stowed in the wagon. The fire was out and everything at their camp was ready to go. It was evident that they had been waiting for Rufus to appear. "I knew you would come," Tony told the mountain man, giving him a hug.

Allen shouted, "Get up!" The oxen took a strain on the wagon and slowly headed to the west. Mary came from the other side of the wagon, riding their horse. She sat straddling the animal as a man would rather than sidesaddle.

Coming alongside, she looked at the mountain man and decided not to make conversation. Three days of drinking doesn't make a man very appealing. It didn't appear to affect the young boy as he kept up a constant chatter, pointing out everything to Rufus.

The trip to The Dalles went well. The oxen were rested, had been fed well, and the trail was broken in by years of traffic back and forth. There was one noticeable change. Mary wasn't the cook that Eunice was. The meals lacked the taste that Rufus had enjoyed. Biscuits ranged from slightly underdone to a little burnt. With the horses to ride, all three took turns driving the oxen.

The Dalles was a French term meaning "sluice," or "slabs," referring to the water running over the long basalt slabs, resulting in the rapids. At this point steep cliffs went to the Columbia River and wagons couldn't go any further.

The Indians had traded fish, berries and other items at this location for 1,000 years, and Lewis and Clark had camped near it in October of 1805. While there were several tribes in the Oregon area, Allen would be negotiating for a raft with the Cayuse, Chinook, or Wasco tribes.

The wheels would be removed from the wagon and the box lashed to the raft. Portages would be required over more than one falls or rapids. Once they arrived at Oregon City, the wagon would be reassembled and offloaded. If the raft was to get away and miss one of the portages, those on board would be facing almost certain death as they went over the roaring rapids.

Allen's timing was good. He was able to procure a raft for the day after arriving at The Dalles. The trip down the Columbia would cost him almost as much as Rufus had gotten for the bear skin. Three young boys from the Chinook tribe were hired to drive the oxen over the Mount Hood pass.

The next morning, Allen and Mary stood near the roaring Celilo Falls as he held her close. After a moment together, Mary came and climbed onto her horse. She looked at Rufus and said, "He will be alright. Let's go."

Tony waved wildly as he shouted goodbye to his father.

The pass by Mount Hood was long, much of it steep, with thick tree cover. The three young natives carried switches and shouted at the six oxen as they drove them toward the paths leading into the tree-covered slopes. Tony sat in front of Rufus and a pack on the mustang carried the supplies, including the wedge tent that they could use for the nights.

The 100-mile trip over the pass could be accomplished in five days. It was early September and the days were warm. The nights would be cool, with the trees preventing the chilling winds from reaching them.

The first night, Mary was busy taking care of her son. Rufus got the fire going and sliced side meat into the frying pan. Seeing him, Mary called, "I can make supper."

Smiling at her, the mountain man said, "I thought I'd make you a mountain man's meal tonight."

Finishing with the boy, she walked over and sat next to Rufus. Watching as he put bread dough into the pan, she said, "I can't say it looks good, but it does smell good."

"I roasted some beans, if you'd like to crush them for coffee," Rufus told her.

"You don't have a grinder?" she asked.

"No, I don't," he replied. "I'll show you how I do it after I flip the bread."

The beans were cooling on a flat stone. Rufus took another rock and crushed the beans. He then scraped them into his hand with his knife and dumped them into the boiling coffee pot water. After giving them a quick stir with the blade, he poked at the side meat and bread in the pan.

"It's done," he told her.

Mary got some plates and called to Tony, who was playing a short distance away. "Come and get a mountain man's supper."

What it lacked in appeal was made up in taste. Mary laughed as she picked the side meat up with her fingers and put it into her mouth. "This is not an acceptable way to eat."

"You're right," Rufus told her. "We shouldn't be eating off plates. We should be spearing our meal with our knives right out of the pan." Her laughter could be heard echoing through the trees.

Before they got going the next morning, the native boys started the oxen up the slope and they quickly disappeared into the trees. Only their shouts at the cattle gave any evidence that they were ahead of them. Rufus knew it was unlikely they could keep up with the oxen.

With the weather being fair, the group had been sleeping with only the trees for protection. On the third night, Mary asked Rufus to set up the wedge tent. They were camped near a stream coming from the hills.

Water had been heated in the bean pot for bathing. "Tony is beginning to look like a wild one digging in the dirt," she told Rufus.

As the sun went down the night air became cooler from climbing toward the pass. Rufus cut extra wood to keep the fire burning in front of the tent. It would offer some warmth into the night. With an arm load, he walked toward the fire.

Having finished washing, the young boy came out of the tent, naked and full of energy. Rufus heard his mother warn him about getting dirty. Smiling, the mountain man brought the wood to the fire and dropped it within easy reach. He looked up at the tent and froze.

The young boy had left the front open and inside the tent Mary stood naked from the waist up, bathing. The fire reflected on her satiny skin and round breasts as she washed. Rufus turned quickly away, almost falling as he moved away from the opening. In his haste to move away, the mountain man did not see the look, with a hint of a smile, that Mary gave him.

The rest of the evening, Rufus stayed very busy grooming the horses and any other chores he could think of that would keep him away from Mary and the boy. The darkness offered him some seclusion. Extra wood was put onto the fire and it was time to sleep. Mary took the boy's hand and led him into the tent.

Turning to Rufus she said, "Thank you for putting up the tent. We really needed to get cleaned up."

Blushing again with the memory, Rufus said, "No problem. I best get some sleep. We got an early morning."

The next morning continued to be awkward. Mary made a porridge in the very pot she had heated water to bathe in and slowly stirred it as the mixture thickened. Rufus could only find so many things to do away from the fire and finally had to join them for breakfast.

"I don't hear the boys with the oxen anymore," she said. She sat eating slowly and deliberately, licking every morsel from the spoon.

Shoveling the porridge into his mouth, Rufus replied, "They will be at Oregon City a full day ahead of us."

Mary helped Rufus take down the wedge tent. As they were folding it before rolling, she stood on the very spot he'd seen her the night before. Again, the mountain man had to look away. Rufus had never felt anything that relieved him more than when they rode away from the campsite.

On the fourth day, the party crested the mountain pass and stared at the steep descent. The boys with the cattle were long gone. To their right, Mount Hood towered above them. In front were deeply cut trails made by horses sliding on their haunches down the steep slope as they descended. Keeping the young boy out of the way of the animals, they were led down, often in an uncontrolled slide.

After an exhausting trip over the pass, the party arrived in Oregon City. The boys were holding the oxen near the landing. After the oxen were taken care of, the young native boys received their pay and were off. "We got lucky," Rufus said.

"We did?" Mary asked him.

"The boys we hired did a good job. I have heard stories of people hiring Indians to drive their cattle over the pass and never seeing the stock again," he told her.

"Have you heard stories about the rafts?" she asked.

"No," he said, "I've heard none about the rafts." Truth was Rufus had, but it would have done little good to share them with her.

After putting the horses into a livery, they made inquiries about any rafts arriving from upriver. None had come recently. Sitting near the river with Tony sleeping in her arms, Mary said, "What will I do if he doesn't make it?"

"It is too soon to worry," Rufus told her. "They might have run into trouble at some of the portages."

As she looked down at her son and gently brushed his hair with her fingers, Mary asked, "Will you stay with me if he doesn't make it? I would make you a good wife. We could build a farm together."

Rufus gave her a look of wonder. They didn't even know if Allen was in trouble and she was already making plans to replace him. "It is not something that should be talked about right now," he told her. "Allen will be coming in soon."

"You're going to leave me and Tony here alone," she whispered, tears running down her cheeks.

Inside, Rufus felt anger. As soon as Allen stepped off the raft, he was going to hightail it back over the pass and put all of this behind him. "Nobody is leaving you," Rufus said in a voice that was much gentler than he felt. "Your husband will be along shortly."

The young boy turned restlessly in her lap and looked up. "Mommy. Why are you crying?"

"She is worried about your father," the mountain man told the boy. "She thought he'd be here by now."

Hugging his mother's neck, Tony said, "Don't worry, mommy. We got Rufus to help us."

Trapped! Trapped! That was the only word going through Rufus' mind. How could this happen? There was no way he was going to stay here in Oregon and farm. Maybe it was time to start praying, praying that the raft bumped up against the shore right now.

The sunset was beautiful in the west. Rufus didn't notice it. His mind was filled with worry. They found an inn to stay at. It had only one room left, so the mountain man let Mary and the boy have it. She offered to let him sleep on the floor near the bed, but he declined. He would sleep beside the building under the stars. Rufus sat on a bench at the front with a chew in his cheek and his bedroll beside him. He had himself a quandary. It would be simple to get out of. He could go get his horses and be long gone in the morning. Hell. He could even pay for her room before he left.

A sound beside him made him look up. Mary was standing in the moonlight. "Tony is sleeping. The trip over the pass really tired him."

Moving his bedroll, the mountain man made room for her to sit. "Thank you," she said. "I was afraid you would be gone. I didn't want to wonder all night and had to come and find out."

Rufus decided that honesty was needed. "I have had thoughts about leaving."

"Yet, you are still here," Mary replied. "I have money I can give you. Just stay for a while until I know. You can help me tell Tony."

Snap! The trap was sprung. There was no way he could leave before knowing if Allen made it. After that, could he leave her and the boy and live with himself. "No money," he said rather sternly. Then softening his voice, Rufus said, "I will stay until we know, but then I must head back east. I . . . I can't stay in Oregon."

She leaned and lay her head on his chest. "I can make you . . . happy," she whispered in a faltering voice.

The mountain man sat there on the bench. He couldn't push her away. She felt warm and helpless and instinctively he put his arm around her. Rufus nodded off a bit that night, and come morning he was still on the bench holding a woman who was begging him to stay.

Aching from being in one position too long, Rufus tried to move. Mary woke and sat up. "I'm sorry," she said. "I must have fallen asleep."

Rufus could feel the dampness of her tears on his shirt. "You should check on the boy," he said softly.

She stood and looked at him. The mountain man told her, "I am not going anywhere until we know."

Getting up slowly, Rufus went to the back of the building and found the little house. He had been having to go for some time. Washing up at a hand pump near the side of the building, Rufus went back to the bench.

Then Mary came to the door. "Come in," she said. "I've paid for our breakfast."

All the mountain man wanted was to be back on the pass and cooking side meat in his blackened frying pan. He followed Mary back into the building. There was a long table on the right side of the room with two benches. There was the smell of pancakes frying from the kitchen.

Tony was sitting at the table, all smiles. "Sit near me, Rufus," he said.

Taking a seat next to the boy, the mountain man asked, "Did you sleep well?"

"I must have," he replied. "When I woke up it was daylight and mommy was gone. But I stayed right in the bed until she came back."

"You're a good boy," Rufus said. Then the pancakes came and it was time to eat.

The meal was good and the coffee was strong. Mary sat across from them, smiling every time the boy said something to Rufus. "You quit bothering Mr. Pike and eat your pancakes," she said, scolding him gently.

"Is daddy coming today?" he asked her.

"We hope so," she said, choking up, her eyes filling with tears.

"Mommy gets sad when I ask about daddy," he whispered to Rufus.

"You don't have to ask," the mountain man whispered back. "Your daddy will be here soon."

Gathering their things, the three of them walked back to the river. Inquiries of whether a raft had come in got replies of, "Not this morning."

At midmorning everyone near the shore craned their necks, looking upriver. Before Mary could get to the river, a canoe pulled up to the shore. A buckskin-clad trapper climbed out and pulled it out of the water.

One of the men near the river asked the trapper, "Did you see a raft on your way down? The woman and her boy are waiting for one."

"I saw a couple of canoes, but no rafts," the man said. "I left The Dalles four days ago and shot all the rapids. They might have been in a portage, but I weren't looking around in that rough water."

Hearing his words, Mary felt weak and Rufus had to hold her to prevent her falling. "Let's find a place for you to sit," he told her.

After finding a place for Mary, Rufus wanted to talk to the trapper. The trapper had found a man who had coffee and was filling his cup. He looked up at the mountain man and asked, "Something I can help you with?"

Nodding, Rufus said, "The woman and boy over there are waiting for her husband. He left The Dalles six days ago on a raft. You say you didn't see one on your way."

"I paddled from dawn to dusk," the trapper said. "I wasn't looking around and there are plenty of places a raft could tuck in for a portage. Could be I passed one and didn't see it."

It was near supper time and Tony was becoming difficult from waiting. Mary's face was streaked with tears. "I have to take him back to the inn," she said.

"I'll wait here for awhile and then be along," Rufus told her.

Sitting beneath a cottonwood, the mountain man watched her walk with the boy. Mary was a good-looking woman. Many lonely men would be rooting for her husband to never show up. They would settle down and live a happy life. But he did not want to farm and did not want to stay in Oregon. Rufus liked the mountains and the life he had hunting and trapping. While it had gotten a little lonely after Caleb went back to Santa Fe, it still offered the freedom he wanted.

It was dark when Rufus reached the inn. A candle was burning inside. Stepping in, he saw a plate on the long table with a cloth over it. A voice startled him. It was the lady who ran the inn. "She asked me to leave something out for you."

It was a cold plate of cheese, meat and bread. A dish of butter was in the middle of the table. "I have some coffee left from supper, if you'd like a cup," she said.

"I would," Rufus replied, "and thank you."

As he ate, he had the feeling that it was sort of like a wake, where someone was gone and everyone felt bad. Rufus ate, expecting Mary to come down at any time. The food was surprisingly good and he was hungry. The mountain man realized he hadn't eaten since this morning.

After the meal, and with a tepid cup of coffee, Rufus went out on the bench to have a chew. The moon had come up and was hiding some of the stars. There were lamps burning down towards the water. He could hear a piano and joyful voices from a brightly lit building not far from the inn. The thought of some whiskey went through his mind. Then he thought better of it.

He was beginning to doze when footsteps woke him. He expected to see Mary. It was a short man with a slouch hat and a white beard that reflected the moon light. "Do you know where the lady is"? he asked. "A raft just come in. I don't know if it is the one she's been waiting for or not."

Rufus' first impulse was to go wake Mary. Then he thought about the disappointment she'd feel if it wasn't Allen. "Thank you," he told the man. "I'll go down and see if it's the one she was looking for."

The walk to the river seemed to take forever. Rufus could see that the raft had a wagon box on it. He became hopeful as he got closer. Then he saw Allen standing on the shore. "You had us worried," the mountain man called out.

Mary's husband turned and smiled. "You made it over the pass. I was afraid you would have trouble," Allen said.

CHAPTER ELEVEN

It was the beginning of October when Rufus got back to Fort Nez Percès. The mountain man was thankful that things had worked out for Allen and Mary. He was able to ride out the hero, standing by her until her husband returned. As it turned out, the raft had run into problems and spent a couple of days in a cove making repairs.

When he went with Allen back to the inn and Mary was woken, she ran and threw her arms around her husband. As they held each other close, Mary looked over Allen's shoulder and the sad look in her eyes would haunt him for the rest of his life.

Leaf greeted the mountain man with a smile when he entered the trading post. "You deliver your lady?" he asked.

"The whole family has probably gotten a farm by now," Rufus told him.

"I figured you might run off with her. Ain't many as pretty as her out this way," the owner said, laughing.

"She was a pretty one, but in love with her husband and boy," he told the owner.

The owner said, "Sure has been busy around here," as he poured a whiskey for Rufus. "Had an American named Wilkes. He come up the Columbia by ship. I guess he lost one on a sandbar."

As Rufus swallowed the whiskey, he replied, "It's a damn rough river to navigate. In my youth I marked the depth for a steamboat on the Mississippi. That river was much easier to travel than the damn Columbia."

"Up in Canada we had some rivers that would bring the hair on your neck to standing," Leaf said.

Taking another drink, Rufus asked, "Where are the folks out front of the fort going?"

"That's the Sinclair party. They have over twenty families from the Red River area," the owner told him. "Hudson's Bay Company brought them in to compete with all the damn Americans coming over the mountains. This way we can show you that this is British territory."

"You can keep it as far as I am concerned," Rufus told him. "It's too damn far west for me."

Laughing, Leaf told him, "When you get back over the mountains, make sure you tell folks that."

"Have another bottle?" the owner asked the mountain man.

"This will have to do," Rufus told him. "I'm heading up the big hill come morning."

That afternoon, the mountain man took what was left of the bottle and some additional supplies and headed for the bottom of the hill. He planned to work his way up enough to see a fine sunset.

The next morning Rufus continued up the big hill. It was a hell of a lot easier by horseback than with wagons. A pack train was not far behind him, promising company during the trip to Fort Boise. Looking out on the plateau, Rufus could see Mount Hood rising above the Cascades. Another he could see was Mount Adams.

The pack train caught up to Rufus as he reached the summit. During introductions, the mountain man saw smoke coming from the north. "What the hell," Rufus said. "Looks like a big grass fire."

The leader of the pack train was named Leon, and he looked and shook his head. "Damn big fire. Hope it ain't the fort." Rufus and the men with the pack train left the summit, unaware that it was indeed Fort Nez Percès.

The pack train and Rufus reached Fort Boise without incident. The weather was cool and most of the leaves were off the trees. The mountain man liked the pungent smell of the leaves. His plans were to see Lani for a couple of days and get his packs before heading for Fort Hall. There he would stay until spring trapping.

The winter at Fort Hall went slow. Rufus had arranged quarters with some company men. It was the American against the British all winter. While the kidding didn't develop into violence, it did get old for the mountain man. Rufus drank his share of whiskey and lost some money at cards. He'd given Finn money to hold for him so he'd have enough for supplies.

Nothing had ever looked as good as the spring thaw. The mountain man purchased his supplies and was off to seek ponds to trap before the ice had melted from them. Even though the price of beaver was down, it was still money to be made as far as Rufus was concerned. While trapping he could do some hunting. In the back of his mind he hoped he would find the white dog again.

* * *

Trapping had been fair, and by the end of June Rufus had 37 beaver pelts to bring to Fort John on the Laramie River. He also had a number of wolf, lynx, fox, fisher, mink, and muskrat pelts, plus a young grizzly. Over the winter word had reached him about the fire at Fort Nez Percès. Rufus was thankful that he had left rather than keeping the horses in their corrals while enjoying Leaf's whiskey.

Louie's trading post was in the process of closing. Fort John had been built by the American Fur Company to replace the deteriorated Fort William. It was a larger fort built with adobe bricks. The new fort offered better protection from thievery or attacks. It was named after John Sarpy, a partner in the company.

After a couple of drinks with the grizzled owner of the trading post, Rufus asked, "Do you buy furs or do I have to go to the new fort?"

"I still buy them," Louie said, "but to be honest, they pay a little more."

"Hell," the mountain man said. "Money isn't everything. We've been friends for a long time. I'll sell mine right here." Rufus liked Louie and the man's whiskey.

It was early July, and the time of year brought the rendezvous to mind for the mountain man. He missed the other trappers, the drinking, the games, and the general camaraderie. The Sioux had teepees erected outside the fort walls. Rufus planned to purchase new buckskins from them. He had been wearing wool shirts and britches since discarding his old ones at Fort Boise. They had gotten wet too many times, had gotten stiff and were very stained.

After spending time visiting Louie, Rufus put his horse up in Louie's livery. The mountain man then walked to Fort John to look it over. He walked under one of the bastions built on the front corner of the fort. The main entrance had two closures. When the outer one was open, the inner one could remain closed. There was a small opening in the inner door where business could be discussed when unsure of the visitor.

On this day, both of the gates were open to allow freight wagons to enter. A couple of armed sentries were stationed outside the main entrance. These sentries could easily be mistaken for trappers lounging at the entrance. Rufus recognized a man named Chess, and the two of them visited while the wagons rolled in.

A wagon following the freighters was filled with buffalo hides. It stopped for a couple of minutes near Rufus. The rotten smell hit the mountain man and he snorted, "Damn buffalo hunters."

"Lots of the trappers have gone over to buffalo hunting," Chess told him. "With the beaver gone there aren't too many jobs that require them skills. Shooting and skinning fits right into a trapper."

"But the damn smell," Rufus complained.

"A trapper can get $2 for a skunk," Chess said. "Most trappers won't pass them up, and once you got them in your packs the smell stays with you the rest of the season. After a while you don't notice it. It's the same with buffalo hides."

It made sense to Rufus, but it didn't change his way of thinking. The wagons were inside the fort and it was time to close the gates. The mountain man went in, promising his friend that they'd have a drink or two before Rufus headed east to Franklin.

Structures were built along the back and right walls of the fort. All of their doors and windows opened into the fort. Some of them had kitchen gardens in the front. Coming out from the back wall toward the center was a building that housed the trading post and offices for handling the purchase of pelts and hides. To the right were the offices of the American Fur Company. An American flag flew proudly over the fort.

Rufus quickly noticed that while this fort was built to protect valuable furs, it was also built for defense should one of the tribes decide to attack. Memories of Bent's Fort near Santa Fe came to mind as he looked around.

The mountain man found his way to the saloon located next to the trading post. Four men sat at a table playing cards. There was a faro table toward the back that was sitting idle. Walking up to the bar, Rufus was impressed. The closely-fitted planks were smooth, and some kind of oil was rubbed into it to give it a little shine from the reflected light of the lamps hung around the room. He gently leaned the Hawken against the wood.

Hube was the manager and bartender of the saloon. He came up to Rufus and asked, "What'll you have?"

"Whiskey," the mountain man replied. Soon a bottle and glass were placed in front of him and Rufus poured himself a drink. The whiskey was better than that served at rendezvous.

"Did you bring in your furs?" Hube asked.

"I did," Rufus replied. "I traded with Louie."

"You could have gotten more in the fort," the manager told him.

"That's what Louie told me," the mountain man said. "He'll probably sell them here at the fort and make a couple of dollars."

Shaking his head, Hube went down the bar and busied himself stocking. Everything around Rufus looked new and was in good repair. He chuckled to himself. After a couple of seasons of trappers, the place would have a whole new broken-in look.

The stop at the fort would be short for Rufus. His plan had been to sell his furs and then join a freighter to travel back east. It would take the wagons that came in a day or two to offload supplies and reload with furs to take back to St. Louis, and Rufus hoped to be going with them. He could hire on as an extra rifle and hunt meat for them.

After a few drinks, Rufus found the leader of the freight wagons and made arrangements for his trip east. He then picked up some supplies he'd need at the new trading post. The mountain man was impressed with the items they stocked. It had lots of things that could be used by the emigrants coming west.

The sun was low in the west when Rufus left the fort with an extra pint in his possible bag. He saw some Sioux women near their cook fire. The mountain man decided to check with them about buckskins.

Again, it worked out well and they could have some for him by morning and do any adjusting that same day.

The next morning, Rufus woke up looking at the vent opening at the top of a teepee. Memories of the evening before flooded back into his mind. Turning, he looked at the sweet and warm Sioux woman next to him.

* * *

The trip east with the freighters went smoothly. Rufus was surprised at the number of wagons they passed heading west. Most were families carrying everything they owned in the covered wagons being pulled by oxen or mules. Most of them talked of free land in Oregon. A few were headed to California.

Some of the freight wagons were filled with buffalo hides, and Rufus tried his best to stay upwind of them. The 10 freight wagons were pulled by teams of six mules each and traveled 25 or more miles a day. Grain was carried for the teams to keep their energy up. Wranglers drove extra mules to be used if an animal was injured.

The teamsters and guards slept under the wagons at night. The mules were kept close with night guards taking four-hour shifts. Rufus would ride the grulla or mustang during his watch, slowly circling the mules.

Rain or shine the freight wagons bumped along the trail east. After long pulls uphill the mules were given a breather, and men would check the stock and the wagons. Rufus would leave early and range out ahead of the wagons to hunt for meat. Often the fare was buffalo or deer.

One day, the mountain man dropped a female buffalo and was about to start skinning. Out from a swale rode four Arapaho braves. Rufus stood looking at the braves, his loaded Hawken within easy reach, the Colt in his broad belt.

One of the braves signed that they wanted the buffalo for their village. Rufus noticed that the two other braves were looking at his horse standing nearby. Making a sign of friendship, Rufus nodded and backed away from the downed animal. Slowly he took the rifle by the barrel and went to his horse.

An Arapaho started his horse to block Rufus' exit. Casually, the mountain man turned his horse so that the Hawken across the saddle lined up with the brave. A command from one of the other Arapaho stopped the brave from cutting him off.

With his nerves on edge, the mountain man turned his horse and rode away from the buffalo. Between the Colt and rifle, he could have put up a decent fight and probably won. But what Rufus didn't know was how many additional braves were just within the swale.

That night the teamsters ate beans with side meat. Extra guards were put on to watch the mules. Rufus thought over the meeting with the braves and had to believe that they were there just for the meat. They were probably a hunting party and had heard his shot. He may even have been able to negotiate sharing the buffalo, but getting away from the braves with his horse and scalp felt like a fair trade to the mountain man.

About a week out of St. Louis, Rufus left the freight wagons and headed for Franklin, Missouri. It had been almost two years since the mountain man had seen his friend Walter. Rufus was looking forward to bring his friend up to date on things in the west and talk over the old days.

CHAPTER TWELVE

It was the middle of August 1842 when Rufus rode down the dusty street of Franklin on his way to the livery. The mountain man knew he was a month late getting to see his friend. It was almost the time he should be leaving to go trapping, but Rufus had made his mind up that he wasn't going to do the fall trapping. He would head back to Fort John toward the end of September and winter there. Come next spring he would head out to trap.

Rufus figured that it would be a nice surprise for Walter. He would also be surprising his friend with the $200 left from leading the wagon train, trapping, and working with the freighters. The livery bay doors were wide open, letting the breeze and noonday sun into the building.

There was movement inside. Smiling, Rufus called, "Is that you, Walter?"

Using the fork to lean on, out of the livery walked Rollie. "I'm not Walter, but I remember you. You have been gone a long time," his old friend said.

"It's been two years," Rufus replied. "Where's Walter?"

"Rufus! I remember your name now," Rollie said. "I am your old friend."

Swinging off the grulla, the mountain man led his horses into the livery. It was a relief to get out of the hot, sun-baked street and into the cooler, dim interior of the livery. His old friend followed him in. Again, Rufus asked, "Where is Walter?"

"He went home to rest and asked me to feed the animals," Rollie replied. "Do you want me to feed your horses?"

Remembering that the old friend needed directions, Rufus replied, "Finish feeding the others first while I get the gear off my horses. Then you can feed mine."

Surprised that Walter would leave Rollie and go home to rest, the mountain man wondered why. Was age finally catching up to him? Once the horses were in stalls and his gear was near the tack room, Rufus turned to his old friend. "Did Walter ask you to do anything else while he was resting?"

"Yes," Rollie replied. "Clean the stalls."

Smiling, the mountain man replied, "You best do that, then."

Following Rufus out of the livery, his old friend said, "You put your stuff near the tack room. Ain't no room in there. You can stay in my house."

The lean-to, while small, would be big enough for the two of them, but Rufus would prefer to be in a place where he could come back drunk and not bother anyone. "We can do that later," Rufus told him. "Now get your chores done. I'm going to see Walter."

Walter's small house was a short walk from the livery. Rufus climbed the rise to it and looked back at the Missouri River. The view gave his friend a glimpse of freedom that they had both enjoyed in the west.

Stepping onto the front porch, Rufus knocked on the door. He heard some quicks footsteps and the door was pulled open. The angry face of Mrs. Tuttle confronted him. She had her finger to her lips and shushed him. "Walter is resting," she whispered.

"I'll wait out here until he gets up," Rufus said. "Is there any coffee?"

"Just sit here," she said. "I'll get you some." Then the door closed in his face.

Sitting on the bench, Rufus looked out at the river. His brow was furled as he began to worry. He wondered if something could be wrong with his friend. Two years ago, Walter had hired a man to help him over the winter. That was the man he'd gotten the Colt from.

After the coffee and something to eat, it was almost an hour before Rufus heard the sound of movement in the house. Then the door opened and Walter stepped out with a big smile on his face. "I knew it was you by the look on Rosie's face."

"She told me to wait out here," Rufus said. "She can't be too mad at me. She brought me biscuits and a good cup of coffee."

"That's because she didn't see you spitting your tobacco off the porch," his friend said when he noticed some that had missed the edge of the boards.

Standing to shake hands, Rufus said, "That's dregs from the coffee."

After a few pleasantries back and forth, Rufus asked, "You ain't been sick, have you? I found Rollie taking care of business at the livery and Mrs. Tuttle barred me from coming in so you could rest. Only a sick man needs that kind of stuff."

"I did get your letter," Walter told him. "Mighty pretty writing. This Grace said the Lord led her to you and saved you when you lay drunk in the cold rain. She said you were taking them to Oregon."

"The hell you say," Rufus growled. "All I told her to write was that I wouldn't be back last year and I would see you this year."

Grinning, Walter said, "It was a very revealing letter. She was saving you from the evils of drink."

"Damn," the mountain man replied. "I thought she was writing awful long for what I asked her to do."

Laughing at the frustrated mountain man, Walter said, "We best go and see how Rollie is doing."

As they walked to the livery Rufus told his friend about the new fort and the trip to Franklin. Walter was very interested in Rufus' trip to Oregon. He recalled the trip he and the mountain man had taken in the '30s while trapping the Snake River. Walter was surprised a wagon could make it.

Rollie had finished his chores and was sitting in front of the lean-to. "I got our house nice and clean for you," he told Rufus.

"You still have two cots in the lean-to?" the mountain man asked.

"I have two cots and I keep yours made every day for when you come back," Rollie said.

It was decided. It would be the lean-to, not the tack room.

After a couple of days of catching up, going to the bank, giving Walter money to hold, and dodging

Mrs. Tuttle, Rufus was ready to visit the Frontier House. Walter shook his head and told his friend, "When you get that out of your system, I got some things that need done."

Telly gave Rufus a grand welcome and set him up with a bottle and a glass. The mountain man took a big swallow and enjoyed the familiar feeling it gave him. He looked around the saloon. It was a little worse for wear since he'd left, but it still had the smells and the feel that he looked forward to.

"I been gone too long," Rufus told him. "Your place is the second-best thing in Franklin."

Frowning, Telly asked, "Is Tillies first?"

Shaking his head, Rufus replied, "No. That would be third. Walter is first."

Rufus was finishing his second drink when Telly came by and said, "Had a fellow looking for you last spring."

"For me?" the mountain man asked. "Was he a trapper?"

"No, not a trapper," the owner replied. "Good-looking fellow, clean cut and all."

"Sorry I missed him," Rufus said, pouring his third drink.

"I told him you hadn't been around for a year and were out west someplace," Telly replied. "He hung around for a couple of days and then was gone."

Choosing to stay away from Tillies that night, Rufus staggered back to the lean-to. Stumbling through the door and knocking over a chair, the mountain man finally steadied himself against the table.

"You need help getting into bed?" Rollie asked from out of the darkness.

"I guess I'm all right," Rufus laughed. "I can just fall into it."

The next morning the mountain man woke hung over, to the smell of breakfast. Rollie had side meat and eggs cooking. Seeing Rufus stir, he said, "Walter let me raise chickens. We got eggs and I got the coffee made."

Sitting at the table with his head hanging, the mountain man sipped the coffee, trying to settle his stomach. He knew that he had to eat the breakfast so as not to disappoint Rollie. With the meal finished, Rufus watched his old friend hurry around the lean-to, doing dishes and straightening up.

Then he turned to Rufus and smiled. "See how nice I keep the house?"

"Very nice," the mountain man replied in his gravelly voice. It was now time to see what Walter needed done.

The mountain man pitched in to help Walter extend one of the corrals. He also had some boards to build three more stalls. As they worked, Walter would sit and rest every so often. "I ain't got the wind I used to have," his old friend said. "I'd have never made it the last two years without Rollie."

"Maybe it is time to sell the livery and retire," Rufus suggested. "You have enough saved to live comfortably."

"How do you know what I have saved?" Walter asked.

"You make me save some each year," the mountain man reminded him. "I know you got a hell of a lot more than I got."

"That money is for my old age," his friend told him.

The next few days kept them busy on the stalls. Rollie would watch Walter cut the boards to length and then cheer when the excess fell off. Rufus liked the smell of fresh-cut wood. It reminded him of cutting and fitting the logs for a shanty.

The mountain man had let Walter know that he'd be spending the winter in Franklin. A look of relief passed on his friend's face. "Good, I won't have to be worried about you," Walter said.

By the time the leaves fell and the first snow came, the two old friends had fallen into a routine. Time was spent each morning talking about old times and trying to decide what needed to be done. Then they had something to eat at noon. Some work was accomplished in the afternoon before taking time to plan the next day's project.

Once or twice a week, Rufus would go into town and have a few drinks. Walter kept him on a strict budget, which the mountain man didn't mind at all. At his friends request, Rufus stayed away from cards.

One crisp morning, Walter came limping into the livery. Rufus had the coffee on and was on his second cup. Rollie was feeding the horses. "We should go out and do some hunting," Walter told his friend.

"Are you sure you're up to a couple of nights on the prairie?" Rufus asked.

"Hell," Walter said, "I was sleeping in snow banks when you were still in high britches."

It was settled. The next morning the two men rode out, leaving Rollie in charge. Business was slow at the livery and Walter made sure that his helper knew exactly what to do. The two men were each leading a pack horse. Walter suggested following the Missouri

River north. There were some cedar swamps that the deer would winter in.

The first night they set up camp in some balsams. While it had been years since the two men had trapped together, the routine of setting up for the night was ingrained and nothing needed to be said as they each did their part.

With the horses taken care of, the two men sat near the fire roasting a rabbit Rufus had shot. "You are pretty damn good with that Colt," Walter told him.

"It came from years of shooting the Kentucky pistols," Rufus said.

"I was never much good with the handgun," Walter admitted. "Now, the Hawken, that's another story. I never did teach you everything I knew about shooting the rifle."

Laughing, the mountain man replied, "With what I knew, I kept myself in whiskey for many a rendezvous."

"I remember Johnson always challenged you," Walter reminisced.

"He kept coming, but he never beat me," Rufus said. "It don't figure. Johnson was a good shot, but maybe he tried too hard."

"He never forgave you for going trapping with me that second year," his friend said.

"I was young and you were smart," Rufus told him. "It made sense going with the brains."

The two men laughed and talked late into the night about the people they'd met trapping. They reached the cedar swamps the next day. There was about 12 inches of snow and tracks were plentiful. They set up their camp about a half-mile away in some pines and got out their snow shoes.

"You think we'll have wolves to worry about?" Rufus asked.

"I remember when you faced the rabid one," Walter said. "Ain't too many wolves around here. They've been hunted pretty hard."

At daybreak the next morning the two men tramped out wearing their snow shoes. This was a ritual that had been repeated many times. Rufus headed toward the far end of the swamp and Walter the near end. Watching his friend slowly go across the snow, the mountain man wondered if the two of them should hunt together. He knew that Walter would be upset if he suggested it.

When Rufus got to the edge of the swamp, he tied the snowshoes onto his back. He was working his way through the thick cedars. Rufus had a short, leather sleeve over the end of the Hawken to keep snow out. The Colt was inside his jacket with his canteen. The mountain man found a clay slide that overlooked a stream flowing through an open area of the swamp. He removed the leather sleeve and set himself up under a gnarled, old pine tree to watch for a deer.

The sound of chickadees flitting from branch to branch was comforting. A breeze was blowing, and every so often it would dislodge a clump of snow and Rufus would hear it plop as it landed. There was the occasional snap of a branch. That alerted the mountain man that something larger was moving through the cedar.

Rufus saw something in the trees. It was too small to be a deer. Then a bobcat came into the opening, taking a few steps and then stopping to search the area. It continued along the edge of the stream and then disappeared into the cattails. It was following turkey tracks that Rufus had noticed.

Then there was a shot! Walter had had a chance at a deer. The sound of the rifle created the crashing of branches below Rufus. There were deer moving. He readied the Hawken. Three does stopped at the edge of the cedars. The mountain man figured it was a mother with two of this year's fawns. Feeling the excitement in his chest, Rufus waited. Generally, when Rufus was meat hunting he would have taken one of the does. Today was sport hunting and he'd wait for a buck.

The does went by to his left, crossing the stream after drinking. Then he heard a snort below. The mountain man watched and waited. There was the snap of a twig and then another snort. Then he saw movement. Just above the cedar branches he saw antlers move. He had a good-sized buck about to come into view.

The antlers disappeared. The mountain man fought the urge to move to get a better view of where the buck had been. Then there was another sound! It was just to his right. Slowly he turned his head and there it was. Not 20 paces away in the cedars stood the buck. Rufus would have to turn completely around to shoot.

Something spooked the deer and it turned and bounded down the hill, its white tail marking its progress. Rufus turned and brought up the rifle, watching for a shot. Then the buck was gone. Disappointed, the mountain man settled down to wait. He wondered what Walter had shot at. He might have taken a doe.

There continued to be the sound of something in the trees. It gave Rufus hope that the buck hadn't run too far. Then it was there, on the edge of the cedars. As he brought the rifle up it began to trot across the opening. Rufus whistled and the buck stopped. Putting the sights on the animal, he touched off the hair trigger.

He'd bagged an eight-point swamp buck with a large set of antlers. As Rufus gutted the animal, he figured that the rack would look good nailed on the wall of the livery. Storing the liver and heart inside the body cavity, the mountain man put the front legs between the horns and tied a rope to the deer. With the buck in tow, he climbed out of the swamp and headed for their camp.

As the mountain man approached the pines he was hungry and looking forward to some broiled liver. Then Rufus was surprised that there wasn't a fire going. The surprise was followed with concern, as he saw that the camp was vacant. "Where the hell are you, Walter?" he muttered.

Quickly he hung the buck in the pines. He began to think that Walter had missed with his shot and was waiting for another deer to go by. Glancing up into the sky, Rufus realized that it was after midday. It would be dark in another few hours.

Saddling their horses, Rufus headed out to find Walter. If his friend had a deer, Walter would be pleased that he wouldn't have to drag it back to camp. The mountain man followed the single set of snowshoe tracks. Twice Rufus saw where his friend had sat and rested.

Arriving at the cedar swamp, Rufus saw where the tracks went into the trees. Swinging off the grulla, he led the two horses into the cedars. Then he saw a place where his friend had removed his snow shoes. The mountain man tied the horses to a branch.

Rufus was wearing buckskins and wanted to make sure Walter knew he was nearby. "I'm coming in, Walter!" he called.

He got no answer. Making plenty of noise and calling Walter's name, Rufus continued into the cedars. Then he found the place where his friend had set up to hunt. That was where he must have been when he took the shot. Rufus continued along Walter's tracks and found blood where he'd hit the deer.

Spraying blood, the deer had run north toward the far side of the swamp. Rufus saw that his friend wasn't running after the deer, but was stalking the animal. Then the tracks went across the stream. Shortly after the stream, the deer had laid down. There was a large bloody spot in the snow. Walter had again startled the deer and it had continued through the trees.

The mountain man called his friend's name again. "Over here," came the reply. Rufus found Walter sitting beside the downed buck. The animal was gutted. "I shot too quick," Walter told him. "I gut-shot the damn deer. I've just been sitting here resting before I drag it out."

"You have been resting for some time," Rufus said, kidding his friend. "Let me help with the dragging."

Walter seemed exhausted by the hunt, so Rufus dragged the buck to the horses. "Damn, am I glad you brought the horses down," his friend told him.

Keeping things light, Rufus said, "I was tired from dragging my deer back, so I took the easy way and rode down instead of walking."

As the two men rode back towards their camp with the deer on a rope behind the grulla, neither man spoke. Rufus was worried. He had never seen his friend tire so easily. Walter was 10 years older than the mountain man, but that would put him in his late 40's.

Once they reached camp, the two men had to compare their kills. The rack on Rufus' was a little bigger than Walter's, so the mountain man claimed victory on the hunt. Both men had been very successful. After a supper of broiled liver, the two men filled their cups with coffee and sat having a chew.

"I'm sick," Walter said. Rufus didn't reply, hoping he'd heard wrong.

"I got the cancer," his friend said. "The doctor gave me laudanum for the pain, but the damn stuff makes me tired."

After an uncomfortable pause, Rufus spoke, fighting to control his voice. "They got a fine hospital in St. Louis. I could take you there."

"It's deep inside me," Walter said. "Doc Willis said it was the pancreas." Taking a deep breath, he added, "I don't even know what the hell that is."

Staring at his cold cup of coffee, Rufus asked, "How long?"

"Three, maybe six months," Walter told him.

The mountain man listened to his long-time friend telling him about the cancer and being so calm. There was no anger. There were no vows that he would fight it. He was just resigned to the fact he was going to die.

Then something flashed through Rufus' mind. "How long ago did he tell you this?"

"It was shortly before you got here," Walter replied.

"That's almost two months," Rufus said. "I should have come back last year. I was wrong to go to Oregon."

"You had a good trip, made some money, and damn near ended up with a wife," his friend said. "Here you would have wasted your money, stayed a month or two, and then would've had a long ride back to the mountains."

"We would have had more time," Rufus said, his voice fading.

Trying to cheer his friend up, Walter said, "It would have only been a couple of months and then you would have been here and gone before I got the news. Now we got all the time I have got left."

Mrs. Tuttle praised the deer that Walter got and promised to can much of the meat. She said little about the one Rufus got. She did scold the mountain man for taking Walter on the hunt and tiring him so much.

Rollie helped the mountain man skin his deer and boiled the heart that was in the cavity. His old friend then sliced and fried it with onions. Along with boiled potatoes, it made an excellent meal. Rufus realized that his old friend was a good cook. It was something that he hadn't taken advantage of when he'd found him.

That evening, Rufus walked up to Walter's house. Mrs. Tuttle met him at the door. "Walter is resting."

"I'd like to come in and wait for him to get up," Rufus said, his voice a bit on edge.

She looked at him and shrugged her shoulders. "I suppose you'd like some coffee."

"Very much, thank you," he said, his voice softening.

It was almost an hour before Walter stirred. Mrs. Tuttle had left and he looked surprised to see Rufus. "I figured you would be halfway through a bottle by now."

"I thought I would give your housekeeper some time off. She has your supper on the back of the stove." Then, getting up, Rufus told Walter, "Have a seat and I'll get it."

Sitting at the table, Walter growled, "I can do for myself."

Getting the venison stew from the stove, Rufus told him, "I know you can do for yourself. Just let me help a little." Changing the subject, he said, "That was a good hunt we had. Rollie cooked up the heart for me."

Poking at the stew, Walter asked, "What are you going to do with the meat?"

"Between the two deer, we got lots of meat," the mountain man replied. "I'll sell some to the butcher and the rest I'll hang in one of the out buildings."

"The hunt took a lot out of me," Walter admitted, "but I'd do it again in a minute."

After the hunt, Rufus stayed away from the Frontier House and Tillies. He spent time with Walter or helped Rollie in the livery. Walter came down to the livery less and less. The walk was too tiring and the winter cold seemed to bother him more.

At one-point Mrs. Tuttle asked Rufus to call her Rosic. She appreciated that he was there for his friend and even more so that he had given up drinking for the time being. Most nights Rufus slept in the house in case Walter needed anything.

One day Rollie asked him, "What's wrong with Walter? He isn't coming to the livery anymore."

Rufus looked at the bent little friend. While they had never spoken about Walter's illness, Rufus had thought Rollie knew that he was sick. "Walter is sick. He has cancer," the mountain man told him.

"We got to take him to the doctor," Rollie said. "The doctor will make him better."

"Not for this," Rufus told his old friend. "I'll take you up to the house tonight so you can visit with Walter."

"I will make him chicken soup," Rollie said. "That will make him feel better."

"You do that," the mountain man said. "You do that and I am sure he will feel better."

That night they walked up to the house with Rufus carrying a pot of steaming soup. Rollie's walking stick thumped on the frozen ground and the snow crunched under their feet. When they got there Rosie was about to leave and Walter was sitting up in bed.

Seeing the soup, she said, "I made him some venison broth, but he didn't eat much of it." Then, smiling at Rollie, she said, "I'm sure he'll like your soup better."

Rufus didn't know if Rollie fully understood the severity of Walter's illness, but he sat next to the bed and held a bowl of soup while Walter ate what he could. Later Rollie and Rufus sat out on the porch while Rufus shared a chew with his old friend.

"Is Walter going to get better?" he asked Rufus.

"No. No, he isn't," the mountain man told him. "You remember when your friends died? You had to bury them."

"I do," Rollie said. "Indians killed them." Then he asked, "Are Indians coming for Walter?"

"No," Rufus said. "It will be much more peaceful. Come one morning, Walter will just keep sleeping and then we will put him in the ground like you did for your friends."

"I'll dig a good hole for him so he is safe from wolves," his old friend promised.

"Walter will appreciate that," Rufus said, leaning back against the house. He had to stop talking because his throat ached too much with grief. The two men sat in the cold and Rufus prayed for his friend.

Walter made it through Christmas and was actually feeling a bit better that day. It was probably the spirit of the day that brought him up. He wanted to go to church, so Rufus bundled him up and got a buggy from the livery to bring him. Rosie and Rollie joined them.

When they got back, Rosie made them some hot cider and had some cookies for Rollie. While his old friend sat in the front room enjoying his treats, Rufus sat in the bedroom with Walter. "You should take this charm you gave me," Walter said. "I won't be needing it anymore."

"I can't take it," Rufus said. "Once given, it can't be taken back. It is bad luck."

Snickering, his friend replied, "Bad luck. It didn't protect me from the cancer."

"That's not its job," the mountain man said. "It keeps you safe. I ain't seen anyone coming in here and trying to . . . hurt you." Kill was on the tip of Rufus' tongue, but he couldn't say it.

"Well, if you won't take it," Walter said, "you got to take the rest. My will is recorded at the courthouse. It leaves everything to you. The house, my money, the livery." Then his friend smiled. "The Kentucky pistol, and Rollie."

"Anything to Rosie?" Rufus asked.

"I already took care of her," he told his friend.

The two of them sat for a long time. Rufus knew his friend was sleeping. His shallow breathing told him that he hadn't passed.

Then, in the dark, Walter spoke. His voice sounded earnest as he started. "I got two things to tell you. Every year or so, there has been men coming into town looking for Tom Wallingford. They say he had a scar on the right side of his neck. Somehow one of them put a connection between you and this Wallingford. I killed him. Then I buried him out on the prairie."

Rufus sat, his mouth open in surprise. He had never meant to bring trouble to Walter. Unsure of what to say, Rufus sat staring at his friend.

Then Walter spoke again. "The pain is always with me now with the cancer. I have made my peace with God and tomorrow I stop eating. You have to help me with this. Rosie can't know."

Dread washed over Rufus. Though he wished to, he could not deny his friend's request. "I will do this for you," the mountain man whispered.

It was a week later when Walter passed. Rufus never found out the details of the man his friend had killed, except that he had threatened Walter. It was hard to believe that they were still looking for him. It had been near twenty years since he'd killed the man cheating at faro. No one would believe the man who ran the waterfront was still after vengeance.

The undertaker kept Walter's body covered with lime and frozen in one of his buildings, waiting for the spring thaw. It was a good thing, because after leaving the house that frigid January morning, Rufus went to the Frontier House and managed to stay drunk for the next week, trying to forget the memory of pretending to feed his friend and then assuring Rosie that Walter had eaten.

The will was executed and Rufus became the owner of the livery. He never stayed in the house and as spring came Rollie had the opportunity to help dig the grave for Walter. A ceremony was held and the stone Rufus had purchased was placed on the grave.

The summer was spent taking care of loose ends. A local attorney who had rented a team and buggy from the livery several times a month offered to help with the sale of the livery. Mrs. Tuttle had a son who needed a house and Rufus sold it to her at a very reasonable price. Rollie got his choice of animals at the livery. He chose a dun to ride and a mule for his pack animal. Several trips to the bank were necessary to settle and move accounts.

Rufus was surprised to find that Walter had an old English double barrel shotgun as well as the Kentucky pistol. It was a 12-gauge flintlock. The barrels had been shortened for use in close quarters. The mountain man guessed that it had been gotten during a swap. A local gunsmith went through the workings of the smooth-bore shotgun and Rufus gave it to Rollie. The pistol went into his saddle bags.

With everything taken care of, Rufus and Rollie went through their gear in anticipation of heading west. "We are going trapping," Rollie told everyone he saw.

The two men rode away from Franklin. Rufus figured that it was doubtful that he'd ever come back. He had had plenty of time to say his goodbyes to his friend, Walter. Those who still hunted for him would find the trail ending at the Missouri River.

CHAPTER THIRTEEN

As the two men rode west, Rollie pointed everything out to Rufus, including where he had found his hat near the river years ago. Rufus had asked him if he would miss any of the teamsters he had traveled with. "No," his old friend said. "I will miss Walter and I will miss my house."

It was late August 1843 when the two men rode across the Laramie River. Rufus saw that most of Louie's trading post had been torn down. Several covered wagons were camped outside the fort, and teepees of two different tribes that had come to trade had been set up near the river.

Rollie rode proudly on the dun. Every evening he would brush the horse and mule. The time he spent talking to them gave Rufus' ears a rest. "First we will go see Louie," he told his trapping partner.

The Buffalo Hide Saloon almost looked out of place on the frontier. Louie's sister Lucy had come out to work with him. She also helped with the boarding house alongside the saloon.

The grizzled owner was behind the bar when the two men walked in. "I'm glad to see you're back," he told Rufus. "I worried that something might have happened to you when you didn't show last winter."

"I spent the winter saying goodbye to my friend, Walter Gray," Rufus told him.

"Walter was a good trapper," Louie said. "He always brought in the best pelts."

A blond woman carrying a couple of extra pounds came in from the dining room. "I see we got customers," she told Louie.

"Lucy, this is Rufus Pike," her brother told her.

"And I'm Rollie," his old friend piped up before he could be introduced.

"Rufus and Rollie," she said, smiling, "I'm pleased to meet you both."

"You'll have to stay in the boarding house," Louie told Rufus. "We are still working on it, but it is quite comfortable."

"Once you've spent a night, you won't want to leave," Lucy said. "There is one customer that has been here for a couple of months. He says he'll be organizing wagon trains going west. You should talk to him, Rufus."

"We get more and more wagons trains coming in every year," the owner said. "Mostly emigrants heading for Oregon."

"I made that trip with wagons once," Rufus told him, "and once was enough. The trail needs a lot of work before it can handle wagons."

"You'd be a good man for the job, guiding them safely over the mountains," Louie said.

Lucy insisted that the two men stay for supper. Their first meal would be her treat. After a couple of drinks, they headed out to take their animals to the livery. Rollie turned to his friend and said, "I don't feel comfortable in them fancy places. We should sleep in the livery."

Smiling, Rufus replied, "I kind of feel the same way, but it would hurt their feelings if we didn't spend the night. Tomorrow we will go to the fort and get some supplies, and then in a day or two we will continue west."

The hostler's name was Kenny. He was middle-aged, lean and missing one eye. "We'd like to put our animals up here and get them some grain," Rufus told him.

"That will be two bits for each animal with the grain," Kenny said.

They left the livery with their bedrolls slung across their backs, rifle and shotgun in their hands, and walked across the hard-packed dirt that used to be in the center of Fort William. The mountain man felt a bit of sadness with the loss of the original fort. He didn't like change.

Rufus was surprised at the number of people from the fort who came over to eat. The food was good. In the fort the fare would be greasy potatoes and burnt steak, or stew that was mostly gravy. Lucy served the meals on their fine tableware and the customers had a few different choices.

That night Louie pointed out the man who was going to set up the wagon trains. He encouraged Rufus to talk to him. Shaking his head, the mountain man told the grizzled owner, "Guiding the wagons is a lot of worry and you have a bunch of people with different ideas of how things should be done. It ain't for me."

The man was slim and sat alone at one side of the dining room. He didn't look like a man who could lead wagons across the plain, but then his job was to organize the drives, not lead them. After a couple of more drinks, Rufus and Rollie followed Louie's directions to their room.

There was the smell of fresh-cut lumber in the hall to their room, but no sign of construction. The two men's room was on the first floor, so Rufus guessed that they were still building on the second floor. The room had a double bed, a side table with a pitcher and bowl for cleaning up, and a small table with two chairs. There was a whale oil lamp on a stand near the bed.

The bedding in the room looked much too nice to be slept on by the two men. They sat at the table, looking around the room when there was a knock at the door. A man with a candle and some slim wood sticks came in and lit their lamp. After wishing them a good night, the man left.

"Too fancy for me," Rollie muttered.

"I should have bought a bottle," Rufus replied, agreeing with his partner.

As the sun went down, the lamp gave the room a soft glow. They could hear other guests walking up the halls and going to their rooms. One of the guests stopped in front of their door and then continued down the hall. Then all was quiet again.

"I ain't sleeping in that bed," Rufus said. "Let's move this table to the side, and I am going to roll my blankets out right here on the floor." Soon the two men were fast asleep on the floor, with a perfectly good bed right next to them.

The men were up before daylight and walked out of the boarding house. Rufus was feeling restless and anxious to continue west. They sat on a bench at the front of the building. Reaching into his possible bag, the mountain man fished out his tobacco.

"Have a chaw, Rollie?" he asked.

"Could use some coffee," his old friend said, accepting the tobacco.

A few minutes later, Rufus saw light at the livery. "I think I know where we can get some coffee."

Kenny had just finished brewing a pot as the two men walked in. Looking up, he smiled and said, "The smell of coffee brings in all kinds."

"Lucy wasn't up yet," Rufus said, picking up a cup and blowing the dust out of it. "I didn't want to bother her."

The three of them sat in front of the livery with their coffee, watching the sky getting lighter in the east. Rufus got to thinking about the bartender who used to be at the trading post. "Is Hube still around?"

"He got him a job at the new fort," Kenny told him. Then the hostler suddenly remembered something. "Had a man asking about you."

"Did you get his name?" Rufus asked.

"I knew his name. It's Johnson," Kenny said. "He was heading for Fort Hall with some horses."

Laughing, the mountain man replied, "No doubt I'll see him this winter if the trapping takes me that way."

"I know Johnson," Rollie said. "Saw him at the rendezvous."

When things began to stir around the fort area, Rufus turned to his partner. "You ready to get some buckskins?"

"I ain't never had buckskins," his old friend said, excitement on his face. "Let's go get some."

"There's an old gal in a teepee near the river that has the best prices," Kenny suggested.

By midmorning, the two men had their buckskins on order and had purchased supplies necessary to go trapping. The Lakota woman promised to have their buckskins the next day. Rollie had been a bit nervous when the woman was measuring him. The loss of his trapping partners was still strong in the man's mind.

With time to kill, the two men returned to the livery and got their horses. Their plan was to ride out onto the prairie and look for prong horn. They rode south along the Laramie River. Rufus had the Hawken across his saddle and Rollie had his shotgun loaded with buck in one barrel and shot in the other for small game.

Hardly out of sight of the fort, two blue grouse flew up and his old friend fired. With the wide pattern of the shortened barrels, both birds came down, one gliding and other folding and dropping. Rollie spurred his dun after the one that glided and found it tangled in the western wheatgrass, still flapping its wings.

As they continued south, his old friend rode proudly with the two grouse hanging from his saddle horn. "We will eat good today," he said.

Rufus hadn't seen his partner shoot much and was impressed at how swiftly he'd gotten the shotgun into action. It had been the mountain man's experience that what Rollie knew how to do, he did well. His old friend had told him he knew how to set traps and Rufus was beginning to think that was true.

Returning without having any luck at a prong horn, the two men stopped a few miles from the fort to roast the grouse. They tied their horses in some cottonwood along a small stream flowing into the Laramie River. Rufus build a fire while Rollie cleaned the birds.

Juices from the grouse had just started dripping into the fire when Rufus heard a horse coming from the north. The two men checked their weapons and settled back to wait for the rider. Rufus had the Colt in his waistband loaded with four chambers.

They needn't have worried as they recognized the man who hoped to organize wagon trains. He smiled and waved his hat as he rode up. Rufus got up to meet him. He was sure that the man wanted to talk to him about leading a wagon train.

He watched as the man swung off his horse. "I understand your name is Rufus Pike," the man said.

The mountain man felt the hair rise under his collar. There was something about the man's accent. "Or is it Tom Wallingford . . ."

As the man's pistol came up, Rufus tried to dive away as he felt a lead ball hit his front, knocking the wind out of him. Then came a loud roar, in his ears. The mountain man was confused and struggling to breathe. He put his hand on his stomach and felt something warm run through his fingers. He had been gut-shot! Unable to breathe, he blacked out.

It may have only been moments. Rufus didn't know, but he was lying on his back on the prairie grass and his stomach was burning and throbbing. It hurt when he breathed. His eyes were closed and memories of being shot in the stomach came back. He was going to die. It might be slow, but he was surely going to.

It was the man's voice that had first alerted Rufus. It was Cajun. New Orleans! The man had known his name was Pike. After all these years they had found him. Lying still, the mountain man decided that he wouldn't be dying alone. Slowly he brought his hand up. If he could reach the Colt, by God, he was going to kill the shooter.

A hand grabbed his! Rufus fought to get to the Colt. "Don't move, Rufus! I stopped the bleeding. Stay still."

He opened his eyes and saw Rollie kneeling over him. "Where is he?" Rufus hissed.

"He's dead," his old friend said. "I killed him."

"He shot me in the damn stomach," the mountain man said as he had trouble breathing deep.

"He shot your possible bag and hit the mold," Rollie told him. "It broke and some pieces cut your stomach."

A feeling that Rufus couldn't explain went over him. He was not going to die and . . . His throat tightened with emotion. "Can you give me a hand sitting up?"

"You might bleed some more," Rollie warned him.

"I'll take my chances," Rufus said and his friend helped him up.

Smiling, Rollie jumped up. "I think the birds are done."

Rufus looked over at the twisted body of the man from New Orleans. His bloody body was almost cut in two by what appeared to be two barrels of shot from Rollie's shotgun. The man still had a knife in one hand.

His shirt and the front of his long johns were open and Rufus looked at his wounds. His partner had ripped up a shirt and wrapped it around his waist, fashioning a bandage. His possible bag lay beside him with evidence of the ball striking it. No doubt more than just the mold was damaged.

Rollie hurried back to him and said, "Wash your hands. We can eat now. I made coffee."

Moving slowly, Rufus got up and went to the stream. He looked at his blood-covered hand. Plunging it into the stream, the water quickly became crimson from the blood. As the tainted water flowed downstream the mountain man scooped a handful and drank. Standing back up, he looked around. All three horses were tied to the cottonwoods. The shooter lay dead, from the load of buck and small game shot. Smiling, Rufus realized that when Rollie had shot that was the roar he had heard.

While the mountain man had little appetite, he complimented Rollie on his cooking. "We got to bring his body back to the fort after we eat," his friend said. "The shotgun kicked hard when I pulled both triggers."

"I appreciate your quick action after he shot me," Rufus said. "I was down and he would have cut me something awful with his knife."

"His horse was bleeding and I tried to fix it," his old friend said, tearing at the blue grouse.

With the meal finished and his stomach throbbing, Rufus looked over what had happened. When the man had brought up his pistol, the possible bag had swung in front of the mountain man when he tried to dodge the bullet. The Hawken mold had deflected the ball and shattered, spraying some iron into his stomach. He must have been coming with the knife when Rollie had fired the shotgun.

Rufus looked at his trapping partner with new respect. He would do just fine if danger came their way. His old friend must have been quite the mountain man before he was hit on the head. Loading the body onto the horse, the two men rode toward the fort. The throbbing in Rufus' stomach had become an ache.

Little explanation was needed about the dead man when they got back to the fort. The man was a stranger and he'd shot Rufus first. Doc Ward removed a couple of pieces of iron from Rufus' wound. He did compliment Rollie on doing a good job of stopping the bleeding.

As it turned out, the horse was rented from the livery. Kenny checked it over and dug a couple of small pellets from the animal, put on some salve and declared it just fine. With his stomach still giving him pain, Rufus said that he needed whiskey to lessen it. The two men left the livery and headed for the Buffalo Hide Saloon.

Walking in, the mountain man was surprised to see Hube. "What happened to your job at the fort?"

"I got a wife and a baby coming," the bartender told him. "Louie gives me some extra hours to help us out."

The whiskey did little to dull the ache of the wound, but it went a long way to helping Rufus ignore it. Rollie told Hube all about the attack. In fact, after a couple of drinks he told the story all over again. Being an experienced bartender, Hube just smiled and nodded.

The two men were still at the bar when Louie came in. "Buy the two men a drink," he called to Hube. He then waved Rufus over.

They sat at a table as Rufus heard Rollie telling the bartender about the attack for the third time. Louie placed a letter onto the table. He pointed to the address, which gave the mountain man little information.

"The man that shot you gave me this letter this morning," the grizzled owner told him. "I was to send it east with some freighters."

While he couldn't read the address, Rufus said, "It's going to New Orleans isn't it.?"

"It is," Louie replied. "Out here, when a man gives you a letter it gives you a responsibility to make sure it goes out."

Not wanting to compromise his friend, Rufus said, "Then you should send it on."

Louie motioned to Hube to bring a bottle and another glass. Filling both of their drinks, the two men drank. Placing his glass onto the table, Louie continued. "I let the man know who you were."

Then after refilling his glass, the owner continued. "What I mean is, the man asked me if I knew anyone from New Orleans. We would talk most evenings after he ate and it always seemed like general conversation. He would ask me about the mountain men that visited the fort. We got to talking about men that had been injured one way or another. I told him about Walter and about him going back to Franklin."

Picking up his glass, Louie looked at the contents and then tossed it down. "One day he tells me about a friend of his named Tom that had damn near got himself killed when a bullet had creased his neck. I seen your scar more than once and I told him that I have a friend named Rufus that had once been shot in the neck. The man just laughed and said that my friend must have been a lucky one. I told him you should be coming this way before fall and he couldn't miss your gravelly voice."

Rufus stared at his glass. His heart was pounding as he listened to Louie. "My voice got that way hawking for a brothel in New Orleans."

The whiskey was forgotten as the two men sat in silence. Louie pushed the letter over to Rufus. The mountain man picked it up and held it, wondering what was written inside. "You can have the letter," Louie said. "I am sure it tells someone where and who you are."

* * *

The next day, after a quick stop at the doc's and a visit to the Lakota woman to get their buckskins, Rufus and Rollie rode west along the North Platte River, on their way to do some trapping. It was the last of August and the weather was warm. Their pack animals carried the supplies they'd need for the fall trapping as well as traps, canvas, leather string, rope, and a few items to trade with the Indians.

Rollie had wanted to put his buckskins on right at the Lakota camp, but Rufus suggested that they wait until the coming evening. The mountain man still carried the letter Louie had given him. He wondered if there would ever come a day when the threat from New Orleans would go away.

The two men would be continuing up along the river until they came to the Red Buttes and then Rufus planned to go northwest toward the Yellowstone. It had been years since he'd trapped the area, and hoped that since trapping slowed down after 1840 that the beaver had come back some.

When they reached the river crossing at the Red Buttes, Rollie announced, "I have been here before."

"Probably many times when you went to the rendezvous," Rufus told him.

The feisty old man nodded. "We would get wet crossing the river. I don't want to get my buckskins wet."

"You will be high and dry on your horse," Rufus assured him. This time of the year the North Platte River was low and the water would only be a few feet deep, except in some holes. The mountain man knew where to avoid the holes.

They built a small fire that night. The two men were in Lakota and Shoshone territory and Rufus didn't want to attract any unnecessary attention. His old friend emptied all of his packs and inspected the gear. The mountain man sat with a chew in his cheek as Rollie inventoried every item. Truth was, Rufus figured he just liked touching them. It was unlikely that his friend had had many personal possessions since he was injured.

Once he had finished and repacked the gear, Rollie came to the fire and sat down. "We got to boil the traps." Rufus figured that was all the man had concluded from his inspection. While his old friend had taken some getting used to, the mountain man found him good company on the trail.

The next morning, Rufus was split between going back to the Wind River Range or following the

Big Horn River to the Stinking Water River, and then into the Yellowstone. The pull toward the Wind River was the shaggy, white dog. While debating the issue he suddenly realized that Rollie was trying to get his attention.

"Deer! I see some deer," his old friend told him.

Three mule deer were foraging on a hillside. They were just over a half-mile away. "They're too far to shoot from here," Rufus told his friend.

"Would the shotgun reach them?" Rollie asked.

"No, it wouldn't," the mountain man replied. "We have to save the shotgun for smaller game."

Seeing a ridge to their left, Rufus motioned his old friend to follow him. They continued just over a quarter-mile and then swung off the horses. Handing the reins to Rollie, Rufus took his Hawken and climbed up the ridge.

Removing his hat, the mountain man peered over the edge. The mule deer had climbed a little, but were now within range. Behind him he heard gravel slide. Turning, he saw his old friend climbing, carrying the shotgun. Gesturing Rollie to be quiet, Rufus moved below the top.

"You can't shoot a deer from here with that shotgun," the mountain man whispered.

"I can shoot it with the Hawken," the old friend said.

"Do you know how to shoot a rifle?" Rufus asked.

"Yes, I do," Rollie replied. "First you cock the rifle. Then you pull the front trigger and after that you pull the back trigger."

"At what point do you aim the Hawken?" Rufus asked, grinning.

"I know I have to aim the rifle," the old friend said, frowning.

The two men didn't depend on the deer for supplies, but rather for some fresh meat. With this in mind the mountain man handed the Hawken to Rollie. "Let's see what you can do, but take your hat off first."

Taking the rifle, Rollie replied, "It was your hat, but it is mine now."

Removing the tattered leather hat, the old man moved up the ridge with the rifle at the ready. Rufus peered over the edge to watch and asked, "Which one are you going to shoot?"

As his old friend took aim he said, "The one on the right."

Rollie touched off the triggers. Smoke and sparks shot out of the barrel as the Hawken recoiled against his shoulder. The mule deer on the right leaped up the hillside with the other two following. Suddenly it faltered and collapsed, sliding back down the hill.

"Good shot!" Rufus exclaimed. Looking at his old friend, the mountain man realized that there was a lot that he didn't know about the man.

"What do we do next?" the mountain man asked.

Smiling, Rollie replied, "We gut and skin the deer."

"No, it isn't," Rufus said. "Next we reload the Hawken."

Grumbling at the delay, Rollie took the necessary items from Rufus and reloaded the rifle. Once done they scrambled back down the ridge and the two men got their horses. Skirting back around the ridge, they were soon at the hillside, looking at the kill.

As they gutted and skinned the deer, Rufus told his old friend, "You shoot the Hawken well."

"I had one until the Lakota took it," Rollie replied. "I hunted buffalo for two years. I didn't like hunting buffalo. The hides stunk."

"They do at that," Rufus agreed. Looking at the skinned mule deer, he said, "We got too much deer to eat before it spoils. After we have some liver and frying pan bread, we can build racks and make some jerky."

While the mountain man got the fire going and commenced making their meal, he sent his old friend to cut poles to build the drying rack. They would save the tenderloins for their meals and the rest would be cut into strips.

That night they wrapped the meat in the hide and hung it in the trees to keep predators away. At the elevation they were at, the September nights were cool. The two men sat near a small fire drinking the last of the evening's coffee and having a chew. The lonesome sounds of the night could be heard with the wolves, coyotes, owls, and doves.

"I missed being out here," Rollie said. "I couldn't come by myself."

Looking up at the moon tracking across the sky, Rufus replied, "I spent some years alone trapping. A man gets tired of only hearing his own voice."

The next morning the two men were up early and began assembling the racks. A pile of sagebrush had been collected to smoke the meat and keep flies off. By midmorning they had the first racks filled, drying in the sun. Rollie kept feeding the sagebrush into the fire located upwind from the meat.

"Don't get too much in there," Rufus cautioned him. "We don't want to cook the meat."

"I'm putting just enough to make good smoke," the old friend replied.

As they processed the meat, the mountain man was impressed with how well Rollie cut the strips. It was evident that he'd done so before. Rufus continued to realize that his old friend knew how to do many things, but without being reminded that it needed to be done he'd just sit and wait.

Two days later they continued north with several pounds of jerky to add to their supplies. Once they hit the Bighorn River, Rufus knew of many tributaries that he wanted to check out for beaver. The Bighorn Mountains to the east had plenty of aspen for the beaver to feed on.

Following one of the streams, they found a pond with three lodges. "We got beaver," Rufus told his old friend.

"We got to boil traps," Rollie told him. "Beaver won't come unless we boil them."

Smiling at his friend's enthusiasm, Rufus replied, "First we need to set up our camp, then we can boil our traps."

Their camp was set up about a quarter-mile from the pond. That evening they were busy with the traps and cutting stakes. Rufus knew of two other streams in the area that he wanted to check out. After setting their traps in the morning, he would ride around and check them out.

As the two men crawled under the fly tarp, the sounds of beaver tails slapping on the water could be heard. There was also the sound of waterfowl. Rollie's shotgun would work fine for them. The mountain man lay in the dark, planning their fall trapping. There was a good chance that the tributaries along the Big Horn River would supply them with their trapping. After that they would build or find a cabin, or go to Fort Hall.

With the beaver meat and whatever supplies they had, they could make it through the year without resupplying. He knew that coffee and tobacco wouldn't last, but they could do without them. Then Rufus realized another thing. Since he'd started traveling with Rollie he hadn't been drinking as much. Maybe that was a good thing.

His old friend was up before daylight and had a fire going. Rufus sat up in the darkness and called out, "You can't set traps this early. We got to be able to see."

The morning was cool, so Rufus made some porridge out of cold flour and a pot of coffee for their breakfast. As soon as their dishes were cleaned, Rollie got his mule and put on the pack saddle. "We got to get the traps in the water," he said.

"You realize that we won't be checking the traps until tomorrow," Rufus reminded him.

"Maybe we will get some today," Rollie said.

"Let me correct myself," the mountain man said. "We will not be checking the traps until morning."

He could hear his old friend grumbling as he hung the traps onto his pack saddle. With the sun up, the two men led the mule toward the pond. Rollie led the way and hurried along the banks. "Here is a good spot," he called out.

Rufus agreed. It was a canal where the beaver came and went from the pond to feed at night. The two men were dressed in their buckskins. In their broad belts they carried a short axe and their knives. The mountain man also had his Colt. Their rifle and shotgun were slung on the mule.

"You can set the first one," Rufus told him. "Do you want me to tell you how?"

The old man stood with his walking stick and looked at Rufus. "I know how to do this. I taught many green youngsters how to set a trap."

Acting surprised, Rufus replied, "Why hell. I'll just let you set them all."

And that Rollie did. In just over an hour, wet above his knees, the old man had put six sets into the pond. Rufus had gotten the traps and stakes ready while watching the old trapper at work.

As they led the mule back to their camp, Rufus asked his old friend, "Why didn't you join some trappers or sign up with a company rather than hanging around St. Louis?"

Rollie looked at him, seeming confused. "I don't know," was all he said.

As they spent the afternoon making hoops for their catch, Rufus looked over at his friend. He knew why. Nobody had asked the old man. Rufus knew he'd have never asked Rollie had it not been circumstances that had thrown them together.

The next morning was exciting. They had three beavers in their traps. Rollie proudly tossed each one onto the bank as he took them out of the traps. With the traps reset, the two men brought the catch back to their camp, and prepared to skin them on a windfall.

Again, Rufus asked, "Do you want any suggestions on skinning the beaver?"

"I skinned more beaver . . ." the old man said, grumbling under his breath.

With the pelts fleshed and stretched onto hoops, Rufus suggested that they go hunting some of the birds he'd been hearing on the ponds. At the same time, they could locate some additional ponds to trap.

As they rode leading the pack animals, Rollie seemed deep in thought. Rufus guided them up into the foothills. When the two of them came alongside, his old friend asked, "Do you need me to show you how to set a trap?"

"What?" Rufus asked, his gravelly voice rising. "What kind of question is that?"

"Well," Rollie said. "I notice you didn't set any traps and I was worried that you were afraid to ask me how to do it."

Laughing at his old friend's concern, Rufus replied, "That is because we have the traps in your pond. We haven't found my pond yet."

"Then I think we should look for your pond today," Rollie told him. "We still have four traps in our packs."

Still chuckling at his friend, Rufus led them onto a rise. Below they could see for miles. The sun was reflecting off several ponds that were a short ride from their camp. They all had beaver sign around them.

"One of those is mine," the mountain man said. "Tomorrow I will set some traps."

Satisfied, Rollie's spirits rose. Rufus pointed at one of the distant ponds. "I see ducks on that one.

Let's ride down and then sneak up on them. You can show me how you shoot with that shotgun."

As they rode off the rise, the mountain man heard his friend say, "I already showed you on the Laramie."

That night the two men were roasting two ducks. His old friend kept up a constant chatter about the day's events. It had been a good day in Rollie's mind and Rufus had chosen a pond to trap in.

For the next two weeks the two men worked the ponds on the various tributaries coming out of the foothills. They had a total of 27 pelts. The leaves had gone from green to gold and many had fallen, blanketing the ground.

One frosty morning they were riding back toward camp with three beavers hanging from the pack horses. Rufus suddenly pulled up. There, on a rise ahead of them, were three braves watching them. "You see them, Rollie?"

"Yes," the old friend replied. "They are coming down. I have the shotgun loaded."

Rufus furled his brow. "Now, don't be shooting unless they attack us. We'll just keep our weapons across the saddle in front of us. Let's ride up and meet them."

The two men started toward the braves. Rufus was pretty sure they were Arapaho. He had met with some of their braves in this area on past visits. Then the mountain man saw three more braves coming around the bottom of the rise. That would make six and there could be others that they couldn't see.

Pulling up, the two men waited, leaving open ground between them and the braves. If they were Blackfoot this could mean trouble. Rollie had bird shot in the shotgun. Rufus wished that he had had one barrel loaded with buck. The mountain man had four chambers loaded in the Colt and one lethal round in the Hawken. He looked to the right and left for some cover.

"If they are hostile," he told Rollie, "leave the pack animals and we will run for the rocks on the left."

He heard his friend whisper, "Okay."

The six braves came together and continued toward the two men. Rufus searched for any sign that they might be a warring party and saw nothing. While he knew that they might not be on the warpath, their horses and mule might look like a fine prize, not to mention the Hawken.

As they got closer, Rufus made a sign of friendship. None was returned. "Get ready," he told his friend.

Then the braves stopped. He saw some discussion between them and then one of the braves rode forward alone. He carried a lance in one hand. He could suddenly ride at them and touch them with the lance, counting coup, or he might want to talk.

Feeling tension in his body, Rufus was ready for anything that might happen. He just hoped that Rollie didn't decide to do something that might get them killed. The lone brave riding towards them would make a fine target for the shotgun.

Ten paces away, the brave stopped. He began to speak. He was Arapaho and Rufus had some understanding of their language. They were on there way to the Medicine Wheel and wanted to trade for gifts they could leave there.

Suddenly the tension left Rufus' body. These braves were on a spiritual trip and would not be looking for a fight. Rufus told him that they had gifts that they would trade. The mountain man led them toward their camp.

He heard Rollie whisper, "I don't like them riding behind us."

"We have nothing to fear," Rufus told him, not as confident as his voice was.

The braves were carrying furs to trade. Rufus went to their packs and took out some items. He had knives, mirrors, bells, and ribbon. These he showed to the braves. He and Rollie had put their rifle and shotgun down, but within easy reach. The leader placed several nice furs to trade. Rufus realized that they would make the fall season very successful.

The mountain man knew that two knives, four mirrors, the bells and ribbon wouldn't buy the furs. For several minutes he and the leader discussed the trade. Then Rufus had an idea. He went to his saddle bags and got out one of the Kentucky pistols. He also took out several balls. These he brought back to the leader and placed them next to the other items.

Rollie's eyes grew large when he saw the pistol. Rufus knew that he had the leader's attention. The Arapaho brave looked at the mountain man and nodded. Using one of the lesser-valued furs, the leader wrapped up the items and went back to his horse.

Rufus and the leader raised their hands as a sign of friendship and the braves wheeled their horses and rode away.

"You gave him the pistol," Rollie said. "They will come back and kill us."

"We were lucky," Rufus told his concerned friend. "They were looking for something to offer to their gods that was more than just the furs. They won't be shooting the pistol at anyone. It will be left as a gift at the Medicine Wheel."

With the furs gotten from the Arapaho and success in the tributaries, the two men rode into Fort Hall with an impressive catch. Finn welcomed Rufus and placed a bottle and glass on the bar. "Does your friend drink?" he asked.

"I do," Rollie replied, not waiting for Rufus to answer.

Smiling, the owner said, "Then we will need another glass."

As Finn filled the glasses, Rufus told him, "Rollie here used to travel back and forth with the rendezvous caravans. If you ever got to the rendezvous you might have seen him."

"Can't say that I did," the owner replied. "He your new partner?"

"He is and he is one hell of a trapper," Rufus told him. His old friend just puffed up and took his drink.

"I take it you brought in some furs," Finn said.

"We did," Rufus replied.

"Beaver is down to $1.50 a pound," the owner told him.

"Them damn felt makers are doing all right if that's all they're paying for pelts," Rufus muttered in disgust.

"Well there's the cost of hauling them north to Montreal and shipping them overseas," Finn told him. "If a trapper could do that, you'd probably get three or four for them."

"The son-of-a-bitches just have to carry them and they get all the money," the mountain man sneered. "Men like me and Rollie freeze our arses off in the icy ponds."

Pouring the two men another drink and one for himself, Finn replied, "I'll drink to that."

While the price of beaver pelts was down, with the other furs brought in thanks to the Arapaho, the two men did all right. Rollie was very excited to have actually made money. For years he'd just worked for something to eat. Each of the men had over $150.

"What are you going to do with all that money?" Rufus asked.

"I am going to buy a rifle like you got," his old friend replied.

"You got a fine shotgun," the mountain man told him.

"I guess I will keep it," Rollie said, "but I still want a Hawken."

CHAPTER FOURTEEN

The two men were able to find quarters in a rundown cabin less than a mile from the fort. The prior owner had picked up and gone to California. After doing some roof repair and shoring up one wall, the cabin was habitable. One advantage it had was a fireplace built of stone, so the men could cook and heat the building.

Rollie had bought a Hawken rifle and spent hours just holding and looking at it. "I got this Hawken with my own money," he boasted.

The mountain man would just nod and agree with his old friend. Winter came with a fury that year, dumping feet of snow around the cabin. The two men had been in the process of making their winter wood and were left worrying about keeping warm. While they had a fine fireplace, most of the heat went up the chimney.

Several days were spent plowing through the snow, leading their horse or mule to cut trees, or find windfalls to drag back near the cabin. The men had hoped to do some hunting for elk or buffalo, but with the deep snow the trip was put off. It would be beans and rice for many of their meals.

One thing that they had done before the snow was to put in a couple of stacks of hay for the animals. When possible, they would take them to some windblown hill to graze on the brown grass, but the energy used to get to the fodder nearly offset the benefit of the grazing.

It was in the cabin, while Rufus was going through his possible bag, that Rollie saw the letter. It had become somewhat stained and worn, but the words inside were still protected. "Is that the letter Louie gave you?" he asked the mountain man.

Lifting it out of the bag, Rufus looked at it and replied, "Yes, it is. I have been meaning to burn the damn thing."

"It is a letter," his old friend said, frowning. "I ain't never got a letter. You should read it."

Rufus suddenly felt uncomfortable. Could he tell his friend that he couldn't read, or should he just toss it into the fireplace? Then he thought, "It isn't a letter to me. Louie gave me the letter to hold for someone in New Orleans."

"Then you should give it to Finn at the trading post," Rollie told him. "He will send it."

"Do you remember the man that shot me on the Laramie River?" Rufus asked.

Anger showed on his old friend's bearded face. "I do! I shot him so he couldn't cut you with his knife."

"Well, he wrote this letter," the mountain man told his friend. "I think it was about me and if it was sent, it could bring more harm to me."

"Then we should burn it," Rollie declared.

"I'll tell you what," Rufus said. "I will let you read it, but I want you to read it out loud in case it has something we should know."

The mountain man watched as his old friend pondered the suggestion. Rufus suddenly thought that maybe his friend couldn't read either. Then Rollie looked at him and said, "Okay."

Handing the letter to his friend, Rufus realized that he too had wanted to know what was in the letter, but hadn't figured out how to have it read. Moving closer to the fire, Rollie broke the seal on the letter and unfolded it. It was just one page of flowing handwriting. He began to read, tilting the paper towards the flames.

> Hahn,
> By the time you receive this letter I will be on my way back to New Orleans to collect the reward for killing Tom Wallingford. I have found him at Fort John. He had been hiding as a trapper in the west going under the name Rufus Pike. I now believe that Camille may have helped him escape from us. We must take care when dealing with her.
> Valdez

Having a little trouble with the mans writing, his old friend finished the letter and place it on his lap. He looked at Rufus with a question on his face. "Why does he want to kill you?"

"Because a relative of Hahn's tried to shoot me. I shot back and he died," Rufus told him. "Sort of like you did to him, only you were protecting me."

"He was looking for Tom . . ." Rollie had to look at the letter again. "Tom Wallingford. Why would he shoot you?"

"It is a little further in the letter. I was Tom Wallingford and had to change my name to Rufus Pike," the mountain man explained.

Pondering what Rufus had just told him, Rollie still seemed confused. The mountain man figured it wasn't important. The danger in the letter was the reference to Camille helping him. She was a voodoo queen he had befriended. Destroying this letter would protect her.

Rufus took the letter from his friend and placed it next to the flames. Slowly they curled around the page, consuming it, erasing the threat to his friend in New Orleans. He then looked at his old friend. "We can never speak of this to anyone," he cautioned Rollie.

Staring at the ash in the fireplace, his friend promised to never talk of it. Later in the evening, as they rolled their blankets out in front of the fireplace, Rollie asked, "Was Camille your girlfriend?"

Smiling at the thought, Rufus replied, "No she wasn't, but she was the mother of Gabrielle, and I did like her very much."

That night the mountain man dozed off with pleasant memories of the olive-skinned beauty he'd spent special nights with.

* * *

Spring came late in 1844 and the two men were suffering severely from cabin fever. The only bright side of the long, cold winter had been with the discovery that Rollie could read well. Rufus brought out a book about pirates that Caleb Weeks had given him. He had given it to his old friend and asked him to read it aloud so they could both enjoy it.

The flooding of the Snake River did its normal amount of damage to Fort Hall. Each year more of the dirt around the fort was washed away, weakening the footing. Men were working to fix it when the two trappers led their pack animals past it on their way to the Snake River.

Rufus and Rollie were headed for the Yellowstone area. With the fair breezes and sunshine their spirits were high. The mountain man had told him about the mountains and streams but left out the part about the geysers. He wanted his friend to feel the same surprise that he himself had felt years ago.

They continued toward Pierre's Hole, where Rufus and Walter had spent the rendezvous of '29. After days of hard riding over ridges and through seemingly impassable gorges, they reached the Pierre's Hole area. "I been here before!" Rollie said. "I was here at rendezvous with my friends."

"That would have been in 1829," Rufus replied. "They had another one that year at the Popo Agie."

"I was here," Rollie said, a smile on his face as he remembered better times.

The two men rested their horses for a couple of days at the old rendezvous site before continuing toward the Yellowstone. They were delayed for two more weeks when they found a large beaver dam across a mountain stream with a half-dozen lodges. "Damn," Rufus said. "I ain't never seen something like this."

Their moods were dampened upon leaving the large pond when a cold rain began to fall. In the high peaks above them it fell as snow. Draped in their ground cloths that were slit to poke their heads through, the two trappers continued their journey.

It was mid-June when they rode past the Teton Mountains. Rollie shot a prong horn and the two men spent a couple of days near Jackson Lake. They could see smoke in the north, which meant there were fires burning in the Yellowstone, which was quite common. No doubt lightning from the storm that they had ridden through had ignited some trees.

As they rode through the charred trees that the fire had swept through, the two men saw wolves in search of victims that hadn't been able to avoid the flames. Both men were dressed in stained buckskins and had their Hawkens across their front as they wound through the trees. Soon the fire-damaged trees were behind them and there were wide swaths of golden grass with rivers winding through. Evidence of this year's grass could be seen as their green tips sought the sunshine.

Rufus heard the rumble in the distance. It was the large geyser that he was bringing Rollie to. It would be about another hour before it would erupt again. They came to areas that were covered with white.

"There is still snow here," Rollie commented.

"It's not snow," Rufus said. "You'll see steam coming out of the ground and it leaves this white stuff."

They stopped a short distance from the big geyser and Rufus suggested they have some coffee.

"I'll get some sticks to make a fire," his old friend offered.

Making sure that the horses were tied tightly to the tree limbs, Rufus poured water from his canteen into the pot. Soon the fire was built and the water was ready. Dumping the crushed coffee beans into the pot, Rufus gave it a quick stir to stop the foaming.

"I saw some water splashing out of the ground where I was picking up sticks," Rollie said.

"You will see that a lot around here," the mountain man told him. "You'll also see some ponds that are quite hot, so watch where you wash your hands."

The large geyser began to steam and sputter. "Is that what covers the ground?" his friend asked.

"It is," Rufus said.

Then it began. First there were larger spurts of water, soon followed by a column that went over a hundred feet high. Rollie was spellbound staring at the phenomena. "My God," Rufus heard him say.

It continued for three or four minutes before it ebbed away. "Ever seen something like that before?" Rufus asked.

His old friend had no response. He just stood there, his cup dangling in his hand, the coffee spilling onto the ground. Rufus was satisfied. The surprise had been complete. While the event had left his friend speechless, for several hours after Rollie couldn't say enough about it.

Two days were spent in the area. The large geyser was seen several times and many smaller ones. They stopped at various ponds of red, yellow, or blue bottoms, some of them had multiple colors. Steaming ponds with white-crusted edges were seen several times. Towards the north there was an area that Rollie was sure was ice from the winter, but it was just crystalized minerals deposited from the water flowing down.

They also saw herds of elk and buffalo. Rollie wanted to shoot one with his Hawken in the worst way, but Rufus was able to contain that urge, telling him that they had no way to keep the meat. It was time to find some beaver ponds and get their traps wet.

After several days of searching, they found an area with several ponds just north of the Yellowstone. None of the ponds had more than two or three lodges, but there was enough to keep the two men busy for the rest of the season.

Rollie did his share of trapping and preparing the pelts. They constantly had furs drying on hoops around their camp. Most of their meals were beaver meat. His old friend did not care for the fishy-tasting beaver tails.

Three men joined them toward the end of June. They had been trapping further north and were working their way back to Fort Hall. They seemed friendly enough, but Rufus remained on alert until they left. In his and Rollie's packs they had over a hundred pelts that could be an attractive prize to less than reputable men. They tended to make sport with Rollie, but as long as his friend didn't seem hurt by it, Rufus kept quiet.

The first week of July, Rollie and Rufus headed for Fort John. While they were just over a week from Fort Hall, Rufus decided that he'd prefer to bring his furs to Fort John. It would take them a little over two weeks of steady traveling.

They spent one night near the Stinking Water River. There was plenty of complaining from his old friend. The river flowed down from the Yellowstone, washing over volcanic rocks that gave it the sulfur-like odor. Rollie continued to grumble right down to the last drop of his coffee.

The two men arrived at Fort John, which was most often referred to as Fort Laramie or the fort on the Laramie. They got $1.75 a pound for there furs. Rufus was satisfied. It would give them enough money to set up for the coming year and leave a little for entertainment at the fort.

The mountain man was on guard during their stay. There was always a chance that another man from New Orleans could show up. When he saw Louie, the grizzled owner smiled and said, "Haven't had any strangers with that southern-sounding voice."

The biggest thing the two men noticed was the number of wagons that were resupplying on the trip west. There had been a big push to get American emigrants into the northwest to establish that it was part of the United State rather than Brittan. Either way, it didn't matter to Rufus as long as he was able to hunt or trap in the mountains.

The Lakota woman was there again and the two men ordered new buckskins. This time she had a friend with her who Rufus took a shine to. A few nights, while Rollie was visiting freighters he knew, the mountain man spent time getting better acquainted with the woman.

Being responsible for his old friend had ended Rufus' staying drunk for days on end. He still drank a fair amount of whiskey, but he had to be in shape the next day to make sure Rollie was okay. Several times he was approached by leaders of wagon trains to scout for them. Some of the money offered was quite attractive, but memories of the difficult trip with the missionaries kept him from accepting any.

By early August it was time to make plans for the coming year's trapping. Rufus felt that he'd worked the north country enough and he wanted to let it recover. The mountain man's thoughts kept going back to the Mexican Territory. He and Caleb had finished trapping there one year with the Mexican Army on their heels. Rufus hadn't been back since.

He had had a shanty built up against a cliff with a large cave behind it that the Mexican army had burnt. All Rufus would have to do is build a wall to close it off and he and Rollie could winter in it. Right now there were conflicts with Mexico in Texas and California. The mountain man figured that the fighting would require soldiers to stay there, not wandering the northern territories.

It was decided in Rufus' mind. He and Rollie would trap the northern Mexican Territory. He didn't tell his old friend that, but he did tell him to start getting ready to leave. "Are we going back to the Yellowstone?" his old friend asked. "I liked the water shooting out of the ground."

"Not this year," Rufus told his friend. "How would you like to spend the winter in a cave?"

Wrinkling his face, Rollie questioned, "Like a bear?"

Laughing at his short friend, Rufus assured him that there wouldn't be any bears in the cave. Dressed in their new buckskins, the two men headed south along the Laramie River. From there they would pick up the South Platte River and take it into the mountains. The entire trip would take about two weeks.

On the way to his destination, Rufus planned to stop at Fort St. Vrain on the South Platte River. The Bent brothers were part owners of the fort, and were longtime friends of the mountain man. Rollie seemed happy to be back on the trail. Once again, he pointed out every landmark of interest. Rufus would nod and mumble in agreement with him.

His old friend like to carry his shotgun across his saddle in case something good to eat happened by. More than once, Rufus had been impressed with how fast his friend got the gun into action, bagging a rabbit or grouse.

It was a little over a week later when they arrived at the fort. It was situated on the confluence of the St. Vrain Creek and the South Platte River. It was a two-story adobe fort with a courtyard. It looked a lot like Bent's Fort. There were tree-covered foothills to the west, and grass and sagebrush to the east. The creek and river were lined with cottonwood and various types of brush and brambles.

The fort was an important trading post for trappers and various tribes. Rufus felt right at home as he and his old friend, carrying the Hawken and shotgun, stopped into a tavern for a drink. They offered whiskey and tequila. The two men got a bottle of the whiskey. They sat at one of the small tables and toasted to a successful year of trapping.

"How far are we from the cave?" Rollie asked. It was a question that had been repeated several times a day.

"We got another week before we get to the cave," Rufus told him. "We might have some bank beaver before we get there, so that could add another week."

"I smell meat cooking," his old friend said.

Smiling, Rufus had seen a steer being roasted in the courtyard. "I believe I also smell something. Maybe we can have some roast beef for our supper."

To the back corner of the tavern there were three trappers getting kind of loud. Rufus guessed they had started drinking early today or were still drunk from last night. Keeping his back to the men, he found them easy enough to ignore. This was his kind of place.

The two men were drinking trader's whiskey, which had been hauled to the fort in barrels. It was then cut with water and sold to customers. The high-proof whiskey had been known to kill an unsuspecting trapper when consumed too fast. When cut two or three to one, a man could down a bottle or two and live to see the next day, though he would be suffering from a hangover.

The bartender came over and said, "The beef should be done soon. It's from a young animal and should be good. I can get you both a plate if you want."

Rollie's eyes lit up. "I like beef!"

"We'll have two plates," Rufus said. "Put a little extra on for my friend."

There was laughter behind them from the three drunks. One of them got up and staggered to the table. "A runt like that don't need extra beef," the man slurred. "Scraps is all he needs."

"I like beef," Rollie said, objecting.

Rufus stood up and turned in one motion, planting his scarred fist in the center of the loudmouth's face, crushing his nose. As one, the other two drunks got up as their friend fell to the floor in front of them.

"You son-of . . ." the man's words were cut short as he stared down the barrel of the Colt Paterson.

"Sit back down, you bastards, or I'll gut-shoot you both and drag you out on the prairie to die!" Rufus threatened, fire in his eyes.

The bartender took it a step further and ordered the two to pick up their friend and get the hell out. Rufus looked down at his old friend and his heart almost stopped. Rollie had his shotgun leveled on the men, and only by some miracle he hadn't fired.

"You can put the shotgun down, Rollie," Rufus said as he put the Colt back into his broad belt.

The two sat back down and his old friend said, "The man didn't want me to have beef. I like beef."

Smiling as his nerves began to settle, Rufus told him, "You will have beef. All the beef you can eat."

The bartender came by with a bucket and spread some sawdust to cover the blood from the drunk's nose. He then stopped at the table. "Those three are good men when sober. The one that come over was Hank, and he tends to get stupid when he's drinking."

Rufus looked up at the bartender. "I have tended to get that way myself from time to time."

As promised, the beef was good and both men had a second plate before they were done. It was served with thick slices of bread and creamy butter. With their stomachs full and a light buzz on, the two men left the tavern. They led their horses and mule to the livery, and made arrangements for the animals and themselves to spend the night.

Being short a few items, the two men walked over to the trading post and looked around. Rufus took a deep breath, enjoying the smells of the goods for sale. Rollie had his eye on the jars of sweets near the counter.

The cave they were heading for had traps, tools, and other items toward the back that would be useful wintering in the mountains. He wondered what might be left after the burning of the front structure. It had been eight years, maybe a little longer, since he'd been there.

The mountain man picked up a sickle and another whetstone. He got some more rope and some leather string. After selecting a few additional items, he headed for the counter and found his old friend making a deal on some peppermint sticks.

Once they had all their purchases back at the livery, Rufus turned toward the tavern. Someone was playing a piano. It was dusk and there were lanterns hanging in front, lighting up the porch. "I believe I could go for some more whiskey," he told no one in particular.

"I want to stay and brush the horses," Rollie told him. Then he asked, "Are we leaving early tomorrow?"

Realizing too much whiskey would make that difficult, Rufus thought for a moment and replied, "Yes, we are leaving early."

The music was lively and the crowd seemed to be enjoying themselves. The three drunks were nowhere to be seen. Rufus sat at the same small table. The bartender came over with a bottle and two glasses. "Your friend coming?" he asked.

Smiling up at the man, the mountain man replied, "Just me."

"I'll leave the second glass in case you get company," the man said, accepting the coin Rufus handed him for the bottle.

Memories went back to his father. For most of his young life he'd been dragged from one tavern or brothel to another where his father played piano. When he closed his eyes, it was almost like he was back there listening to his father.

"The music making you sleepy?" a soft voice asked.

Looking up the mountain man saw a sweet-smelling, blond woman. She had a few years on her, but was still appealing. "Just enjoying listening to the piano," he replied.

"Mind if I sit?" she asked.

Without waiting for an answer, she moved the other chair closer to him and took a seat. Taking the extra glass, Rufus filled it for her. "What are we drinking to?" he asked.

"Later tonight," she said. "But not too late. A lady does get tired."

Most often that offer would have been taken up before the second drink was gone, but tonight there was the promise he'd made to Rollie. If he took her to the back room with a bottle there was no way he'd make it back to the livery, tonight or early tomorrow. Smiling like a love-struck fool, he looked into her eyes. For the next hour they made small talk. She flirted and hinted at pleasures to come.

They were getting toward the bottom of the bottle and Rufus knew he had to make his escape. If they started another he'd never have the will to leave.

"This has been a most enjoyable time with you," he told her.

He saw her face harden. The lady had invested a lot of time with him. Rufus had learned the value of their time years ago in New Orleans. Reaching into his possible bag, he took out a half eagle. He pressed this into her hand and saw the surprise on her face.

Fighting the urge to take her hand and head for the back, Rufus told her, "Should I every come back this way, we can do this again and I will let you show me some of the pleasures you spoke of."

With just a little stagger, Rufus left the tavern, the shocked woman watching him walk out. One might think the mountain man felt good about doing the right thing, but in truth he felt anything but. It took all his will to keep walking across the courtyard to the livery.

Climbing into the loft, Rufus found Rollie still awake. "I was afraid you wouldn't come back."

"I'll always come back," Rufus assured him, "but sometimes I might be a little late. Tonight, there was a lady that almost made me late."

"You like the ladies, don't you?" his old friend asked.

"I do," the mountain man replied. "Maybe a bit too much. Have you ever been with a woman?" As soon as he asked he was sorry. It was none of his business.

"I was married once," Rollie said. "She died in child birth. It would have been a little girl."

Now he really felt bad to have brought up those kinds of memories. Wanting to just go to sleep, Rufus replied, "I'm sorry to hear that."

"After she died, I didn't want to stay in Virginia, so I came west and started trapping," his old friend told him.

So Rollie was from Virginia, Rufus thought. Suddenly a second question came to mind. "You never mentioned your last name."

"Willis," he said. "Roland Willis."

With the night sounds of the fort filtering into the livery, the two men lay in silence and were soon sleeping.

CHAPTER FIFTEEN

Two weeks later found the partners breaking camp. They had managed to get 14 bank beaver pelts. The greener ones were hanging on hoops from the packs on the mustang and mule. The two trappers were in good spirits. It had been a good start for their fall season.

"The cave is just three, maybe four days from here," Rufus told his old friend.

"The beaver this morning must have weighed 40 pounds," Rollie told him. "I could hardly lift it out of the water."

"It was in this same area that my partner Caleb shot the bear," Rufus told him.

"He wasn't using no shotgun then," his old friend replied.

"No, he wasn't," the mountain man said. "He had a Hawken like us."

The second day away from the river, it started to rain. It was early September and the leaves were already turning, giving splashes of red and yellow in the hills. They had their ground cloths protecting them and even the weather didn't dampen the way they felt.

Rufus was going back to the cave. It was something that he never believed would happen again. Once the two men got their traps into one of the ponds, they could devote time to putting the front back on the cave, then make hay in the field. With luck the pool in the cave would still be there.

The rain had quit before they rode into the valley below the cave. Rufus sat on the grulla, looking it over. There were fewer ponds than past years. It mattered little because they would still have plenty of trapping before it snowed.

The cliff above the cave was still blackened by the fire. Very little of the charred poles were evident. Time had erased the work of the Mexican soldiers. Rufus smiled when he saw that a couple of sagging poles from their corral were still up.

He and Rollie swung off their horses. "That hole in the wall will be our home this winter," he told his old friend.

Tying the horses to the poplar, the two men stepped into the cave. The sound of dripping water welcomed the men. The afternoon sun lit the interior of the cave. It appeared that whatever would burn had been tossed onto the burning poles.

Rufus ducked as he went toward the back. In the dim light he saw some of the items they'd stored there. What condition they were in he didn't know. Rollie stood next to him, looking. "How far does it go back?"

"It goes back for quite a way, but there are big holes a man can fall into, so I wouldn't recommend going without a candle or torch," Rufus cautioned him.

The rest of September was busy. After getting their traps into the water, they cut spruce poles to close up the front. They didn't build a place for the animals, but if it got too cold they could take them into the cave. The poplar had grown and the undergrowth was thicker, which would offer protection for the animals most of the time.

Hay was cut and stacked, wood was dragged close for winter use. The rocks of the fire pit were still hidden in the grass, and after a couple of fires it was burned back. The caldron and rods to hang it were still in the back of the cave. So was the bucksaw, although it needed some repair.

By the first of October the two men had snug winter quarters and plenty of hay for the animals. They had to ride further out to set traps, but the weather remained fair and they had no difficulty doing it. Rufus stuck close to Rollie when they were out checking traps and doing any hunting. His old friend seemed to be getting a little more forgetful.

Rufus had picked up a few books and was looking forward to having Rollie read them to him. Several times his old friend got in a melancholy mood and talked of his youth and his wife. Being of short stature had always been a challenge, but from what Rufus could gather it had only made him stronger.

The ground was a foot deep in snow by the 1st of November. The two men had an elk hanging in the poplars near the cave and plenty of wood cut to start the winter. They had nearly 60 pelts dried and packed in the cave. They had a couple of blocks to sit on and spruce boughs to sleep on.

Rufus had tried to get Rollie to play cards, but while he had no trouble ciphering, he tended to have trouble creating a hand. It would not have been fair to take all of his money and furs.

Only twice did they have to bring the animals into the cave. Things were tight but they all fit. It did make living in the cave rather ripe with their urine and droppings. They had a shovel with a broken handle, but it worked for cleaning up after the horses and mule.

While the cave had been a good place to winter, both men were ready to leave when the snow melted. Rufus knew of an area to the north, and the plan was to trap their way to Fort Hall. Rollie looked back as they rode out of the valley.

"It was a good cave, but not with horses," the old friend said.

Laughing, Rufus agreed. The poles against the cliff stood out, and anyone going by would know that it was man-made. It didn't matter to the mountain man. He doubted he'd be back anytime soon.

For a week they zigzagged from stream to stream, looking for beaver, and finally found a nice-sized dam with lodges. It was in a valley surrounded with pine-covered hills. Rollie hadn't been his normal, talkative self and Rufus missed it.

Once they had the camp up, the two men scouted the ponds, finding several good spots to set traps. They put four into the pond with plans to add more tomorrow. Returning to camp, Rollie collected wood while Rufus got the fire going and started on their meal.

With a pot of beans cooking on the fire, he looked around for his old friend. Rollie hadn't come back from getting wood. Looking around the area, he spotted someone down by the pond. There was no mistaking the short-bent stature of his friend.

Heading down to the pond, Rufus called to Rollie. His friend looked up and waved. "What the hell are you doing down here?" the mountain man asked, concerned.

"Checking the traps," his old friend called back.

"We just put them in," Rufus told him. "You were getting wood."

"I know," his old friend said, looking frustrated. Then he smiled, "I wanted to look at the traps first."

The two men collected armloads of wood and went back to the camp. Rufus made light of his friend being down at the traps. Then he said, "Why don't you read some while we wait for the beans to cook?"

The pond was productive and they added four more traps the next day. Sitting in camp skinning the beavers, Rufus said, "If we find a couple more ponds like this, we will get to Fort Hall with 150 pelts."

"That's a lot," Rollie said, smiling.

Rufus and his old friend were sitting near the camp a week later, chewing the last of their tobacco and talking about making a move when Rollie pointed toward the pines. "I see something. Maybe a bear."

The mountain man looked at where he was pointing and felt a chill. It was what he always felt when he saw a grizzly. "You are right, it is a nice-looking bear."

It was about a half-mile across the valley to where the bear was eating pine cones. With the cover between the camp and the bear, it wouldn't be too difficult to get within range. That is, if the bear continued to eat. Another thing that made Rufus anxious to go after the animal was that it wasn't good

279

to have a grizzly feeding that close to the camp. It would only be a matter of time until it smelled their supplies and animals and came looking for a meal.

Both of their Hawkens were loaded. The shotgun was loaded with shot, and they wouldn't be able to fire and reload it. Just in case, Rufus added a couple of buckshot in a greased patch and tamped it into both barrels.

"If the rifles don't put it down and it's coming at us, wait until it gets close and then put both barrels into the bastard," Rufus instructed him.

Working their way through the trees, the men closed the distance between themselves and the bear. The wind was in their favor and all they had to do was make sure they made no noise. They got within a quarter-mile and couldn't see the bear due to the trees and underbrush.

They would have to move out into the valley, using whatever cover they could find. There was a wash with some brush and pools of water. It would have to do. The two men got to the wash and, crouching, they worked their way along it. Rollie stayed close, his Hawken in front of him and the shotgun slung across his back.

Suddenly, there was the sound of bark being ripped from a tree. It sounded like it was just above them! The two men froze. Rollie's face was as white as his beard. Neither dared to speak or look over the bank. Both feared they would see the bear loom up above them at any time.

Rufus worried that his plan had put them into a trap. If the bear had caught wind or sight of them it could be sneaking up for the kill right now. With his Hawken ready, Rufus knew he had to look over the side. With his hat off, he stuck his head up just enough to see the hillside. Then he froze.

The bear wasn't 100 feet away, shaking cones from a tree! The mountain man wanted Rollie to take the first shot. His old friend had never shot a grizzly. He motioned to his old friend to shoot. Removing his hat, Rollie carefully cocked the Hawken. He then pulled the set trigger. Now any jar of the rifle would fire it.

In a half-crouch, he swung the barrel over the edge of the wash. Rollie then looked up and stopped. The bear looked huge in front of him. As he sighted on the bear, Rufus started to rise. The Hawken recoiled, sending the .54 caliber ball at the animal. Rufus' Hawken cleared the bank as the behemoth roared from the ball striking it.

It turned, slashing at everything around it, searching for the cause of its pain. Rufus sighted and fired. Again, the bear reacted, clawing at the entry site of the ball. Then it turned and ran towards the two men. Both were frantically loading as the bear came, covering the short distance in just seconds. There was another shot!

Rollie had emptied both barrels into the bear. They both ducked to the side as the bear reached the wash and crashed into it, clawing its way up the other side and continued away. With his Hawken loaded, Rufus stood to take another shot.

Fifty feet beyond the wash the bear lay. It was gasping its last breaths. Rollie finished loading his rifle and the two men, covered with mud, climbed the bank of the wash. With rifles ready they walked towards the grizzly. It lay still, dead.

Rufus had shot many grizzlies in his life, but never had one come so close before dying. Rollie walked up to the animal and poked it with the barrel of his rifle. "I think it's dead," he said.

The grizzly would be an added prize to their year. After retrieving the shotgun from the mud in the wash, the two men walked up to the camp, kidding about whether they had to clean their pants or not. It was decided after they removed the hide that Rollie's shot had been a killing shot and the rest just hastened its demise.

On their way back to the fort, they found one more pond that they couldn't pass up. While both were anxious to reach Fort Hall and get coffee and tobacco, there was money to be had swimming near them. With the traps set, the two men boiled rice for their evening meal.

It would be less than a week's travel to the fort. They weather was warm and their animals were in good condition. They'd put six traps into the pond and had hopes of getting three or more beavers. Rollie was the first to get up the next morning.

"While you start breakfast, I'll go see if we got any beaver," his old friend suggested.

"You can do that," Rufus told him, "but don't be going in to get any until we're both there."

Carrying his rifle, Rollie headed for the pond. His friend was getting older and Rufus worried about him some. The rice was almost done and Rufus kept glancing in the direction of the pond. He felt a burn come on. "I bet he is in the pond pulling the traps," Rufus muttered.

Pulling the rice off the fire, the mountain man took his Hawken and headed for the pond. As he got close, he looked and did not see his friend. His frustration turned to worry. "Rollie!" he called.

No answer. Now truly worried, he started scanning the water. There was no sign of Rollie. Then he heard a shot! "What the hell?"

Rufus headed toward the sound of the rifle. His heart was pounding, not having a clue why Rollie or someone would be shooting. Then he caught a glimpse of blood on the leaves. He followed the blood trail, trying to figure out what happened. He felt some relief when he saw the deer tracks.

Stepping over a windfall, he saw the guts. The only thing he could figure was that Rollie had shot a deer and gutted it here. His friend had begun to tow the deer but it wasn't in the direction of the camp. A quarter-mile later, Rufus saw Rollie sitting on a log, catching his breath.

"You need some help with that deer?" he called to his friend.

"I didn't know you were going to hunt too," his old friend replied. "I could use some help."

"Did you find any beaver in the traps?" Rufus asked.

"Why would I be looking in the traps?" Rollie asked. "We do that after breakfast."

Ignoring the answer, the mountain man said, "I didn't expect you to get a deer."

"I told you I was going hunting," his friend said.

"Yes, you did," Rufus replied, filled with concern.

Tying a string from his possible bag onto the legs of the deer, Rufus started pulling it toward the camp. "You're going the wrong way," Rollie said.

"I think this way is easier," the mountain man replied.

"Okay," Rollie said, following behind.

Back at the camp Rufus watched his old friend skin the deer. Much of it would be wasted in this warm weather, but for now they would eat well. The mountain man was worried. Something had changed over the winter. Many times in the past month Rollie had become confused. When discovered he'd just smile and act like nothing had happened.

Two days from the fort, the two men were riding abreast on a grassy plain. Rollie asked, "Will we be seeing Walter at the fort?"

The question caught the mountain man off guard and he replied, "You know Walter died."

"Walter is dead?" his old friend asked.

Rufus looked over and saw tears in his friend's eyes. "Yes, he died in Franklin two years ago."

"I forgot," Rollie said, his head down.

Trying to bring his friend's spirits back up, the mountain man told him, "The men at the fort will be impressed with the grizzly you shot."

Suddenly smiling, Rollie replied, "I shot it with the shotgun."

"Yes, you did," Rufus said, "and also the Hawken."

"With your Hawken?" he asked.

His friend was having a bad day and seemed more confused than before, so the mountain man decided to stay with safe subjects. Rollie wasn't talking on about everything they passed, so Rufus began to do so. He got lots of smiles but not too much conversation.

The grizzly brought a good price at Fort Hall. Pelts still stayed at about $1 to $1.25 a pound. The money for the year's catch would set the two men up until the coming season. Rufus missed the days when they'd have gotten three to four times as much for beaver.

After a week of celebrating, Rufus told his old friend that it was time to head for Fort Laramie. There were wagon trains coming and going while the men visited the fort. A few were heading for California, but most were on their way to Oregon. There was land for the taking and the emigrants wanted their piece.

Rufus noticed that the normal, thick prairie grass around Fort Hall had been grazed off and the trees were being cut back. He was sure that it would only get worse as the wagons with their teams of oxen kept coming.

On their way to Fort Laramie, Rufus was able to avoid most of the wagon trains, choosing to take routes where the wagons couldn't go. He did stop at the ice slough so he and Rollie could chip some of the frozen water.

They were west of Independence Rock when Rollie suddenly pointed at a granite outcrop. "Over there! I put them over there!" he exclaimed.

His old friend led him to the graves of the friends he had buried after the fight with the Lakota. There was little evidence of the graves. He had placed a rock at the head of each one. The ground had sunk some, but in the thick prairie grass and sage it was hard to tell. Rollie then led him to a tree -lined stream bed.

"I was in there when I woke up," he said. "My head hurt and was bloody."

Then his old friend became quiet again. It was late afternoon and Rufus started collecting branches to make a fire. His old friend suddenly began to wave his arms. "No! No! We can't stay here. We might be attacked again."

Rollie was so adamant about it that Rufus had to fight back the urge to shake him and tell him that there was no danger. Kicking the sticks back toward the trees, the mountain man said, "Quiet down now. We will go and find a safer place."

They continued for another half-hour until they were at the domed rock. "Can we camp here?" Rufus asked.

"Yes," Rollie said. "Tomorrow I will show you where I buried my friends."

"Go and collect some sticks for our fire," Rufus said. "I'll get our packs off the animals."

The packs were small with the furs being gone and most of their supplies having been used. They had just purchased a few supplies at the higher prices at Fort Hall. Rufus paused, leaning against the mule and looking at Rollie collecting wood.

"What is going on in your head, my friend?" he muttered. The mountain man had a sick feeling inside.

The next morning his old friend insisted that he join him at the rock and see where he'd carved his friends' names. Rollie seemed excited to be showing him. Rufus wanted nothing more than to get away from whatever was possessing his friend.

They got to Independence Rock and Rollie took a moment searching. "Here they are," he called to the mountain man.

The crude engravings spelt John, Wil, Jim, and Tucker. "I wasn't going to put Tucker's name on the stone because it was him that caused the trouble. I won't tell you what he did, but it was him."

Standing up and brushing the dirt from the knees of his buckskin pants, his old friend smiled. "We got to go now. I know Walter is waiting for us."

"Yes, he is," Rufus said. "Do you know where Walter is?"

"You're being silly," his old friend said, laughing. "He is at the livery in Franklin. I think I got a map. I can show you."

His friend began to dig through his possible bag for the scrap of paper given to him by the caravan years ago.

"Don't worry," Rufus told him. "I know where it is."

As they arrived at Fort Laramie, Rufus noticed that several more buildings had been built around the area. It was almost taking on the look of a village. Two things still stood out: The white adobe fort and Louie's Buffalo Hide Saloon.

They took their horses to the livery. While Rufus settled up with Kenny, Rollie looked around. "You changed many things," he said.

"Yes, you're right," the hostler said. "We brought the loft out some so we could put up more hay."

As the two men left the livery, Rollie whispered, "They took off my lean-to. I didn't see Walter. He must be home resting."

"Things change," was all that Rufus said.

Even though they were dusty and dirty from the trail, Louie invited the two men in like long-lost friends. "You two were missed," he said. "Have a seat. I'll get you some whiskey."

As the owner brought the bottle and three glasses, Rufus' friend reached out a hand and said, "Hi. I'm Rollie."

Louie shook the hand and replied, "I remember you from before."

Rollie just sat down and smiled. It was a smile that Rufus has seen a lot lately.

"Have you had any guests from New Orleans?" the mountain man asked.

"None since you were here," the owner replied. "There have been a lot of wagons going through and the army sent out some soldiers to keep an eye on the tribes."

After a couple of drinks, Rufus said, "Rollie and I have to visit Doc Ward."

"Are you sick?" his old friend suddenly asked.

"Remember when the man shot me?" the mountain man asked his friend. "I got to have it checked." Rollie sat and smiled without replying.

Rufus had Rollie wait outside while he went in and explained what was happening with his friend. After doing so, the mountain man came out and told his friend the doc wanted to see him. After a little debate with Rollie claiming that he didn't need any doctor, Rufus was finally able to get him to go in.

After less than 15 minutes Rollie came back out and announced that the doctor needed help and asked him to do some things around the place. "Is it okay with you?" he asked, "And I got to let Walter know where I am."

"I'll tell Walter," Rufus told his old friend. "You just go and help the doc."

The two men spent a week at the fort. Rufus managed to get a cabin, and after a little repair it was livable. Each day he'd take Rollie to the doc's and Doctor Ward actually did put his old friend to work.

At the end of the week, Rufus sent his friend to groom the horses and he went to see the doc. Doc Ward had a stern look about him and was sitting at his roll top desk with a medical book open. He looked up when Rufus walked in and said, "Have a seat. I'll be right with you."

Sitting on an uncomfortable straight-backed chair, the mountain man waited. Then the old doc closed the book. Turning to Rufus, he said, "I agree with you. Rollie does have a problem with his memory. He can't remember things from this morning, but relives old memories like it was today. I have seen this in patients before, but it usually comes on slow and gets worse. From what you told me it happened fairly fast."

"Well, Rollie has always been kind of different," Rufus replied. "I figure it was the hit he took when attacked by the Lakota. He was almost like a kid in his mind. He'd do anything for you, but you had to tell him."

The doctor sat and listened while Rufus talked, much of it he'd already heard. Doc Ward tapped his finger on the book near him. "I've been reading up on what you said. I figure one of two things is going on. First, Rollie is not a young man, and in his advanced years his mind might be going and will continue to gradually get to the point that he forgets most everything and everyone."

"That's just getting old," Rufus said. "You and me will probably have that happen someday."

Smiling, the doc said, "I am sure, me sooner than you."

Then leaning back in his chair, Doc Ward continued. "The second one could be blood vessels in his head may have been damaged when he was attacked. He could be perfectly fine for a long time." Then the doctor paused and said, "I mean fine for Rollie, that is. After time they get weaker and put pressure on the brain. That could explain a more sudden change."

"Can you fix that?" the mountain man asked.

"No, we can't," the doc said. "At some point the vein will burst and then . . . death will come quickly."

"How long?" Rufus asked.

"Today, next week, or even several months," Doc Ward told him. "I wouldn't worry about when it might happen. His life has been good, and he told me that he killed a bear. Of course, the next day I asked him about it and he didn't remember. Flashes of memory will come and go."

Suddenly, Rufus got the feeling that he was the patient, not Rollie. The good doctor was preparing him for something that couldn't be changed. Then he asked, "Is there something I should do?"

"You can coddle him," the doc said, "make him rest and prevent any excitement around him. Or you can let him continue to live his life as he has been. The only difference it might make is how soon it will happen. Then again, it may not make any difference."

Rufus left the doctor's office, his mind on the past. He thought about his father, who had died of consumption, and Walter, who had died of cancer. Both men had lingered in pain, while those around them had waited, helpless to do anything. By what the doctor said, it would not be the case for his old friend.

The mountain man arranged to stay in the cabin over the winter. He also let it be known that he was available to scout for the army, or hunt meat, if they needed him. Thanks to Louie, Rollie was kept busy working around the livery. After explaining things to the grizzled man, he even offered to pay Rollie a stipend for his work. All Kenny had to do was remind Rollie of what he was supposed to be doing and tell him that Walter was home resting.

Kenny had been sleeping in a small room in the livery. Scouting or hunting with the army would take Rufus away for a couple of weeks at a time, so when this happened the hostler would sleep at the cabin. This went well for a few months, but by the end of December Rollie started having headaches. The doc gave Rufus some Laudanum to help with the pain.

On his good days, Rollie and Rufus would sit in front of the cabin with a chew and coffee. Rollie didn't ask about Walter anymore. Most of his conversations were about his wife and growing up in Virginia. Nothing was said about him and his friends being attacked by the Lakota.

Rollie still read to Rufus, and each time the events in the book were new to his old friend. He also asked the mountain man to get him a Bible. Rufus learned that his friend's father had been a preacher. He also learned that Rollie's father had been rather stern with him.

Spring came and went with his friend still talking about the old days, but it was like it was yesterday. Rollie had to use his walking stick to do any moving around. Rufus figured that his unsteadiness could also be from the Laudanum. Then came the stroke.

Rufus was up early and had made a quick trip to the livery to check on the horses and have a cup of coffee with Kenny. His old friend had been tending to sleep in and the mountain man didn't want to disturb him making coffee in the cabin. Rollie had been complaining about things not smelling or tasting right.

When he got back to the cabin, he added wood to the fireplace. He heard his old friend whisper his name. "Are you ready for some breakfast?" Rufus asked.

A chill went through him when he looked at his friend. One side of his face sagged like it was dead. The eye on the other side stared up at him. "Are you okay?" the mountain man asked.

The doctor had told Rufus that it could start with a stroke, and had told him what to look for. Rufus' eyes smarted as he blinked away the tears. "Old friend," he said. "Can you hear me?"

One side of Rollie's lips moved and Rufus heard, "Old friend."

Those were the last words his friend said. Rufus got Doc Ward to the cabin, and after a few minutes with Rollie the doc came away shaking his head. "It won't be long now."

That afternoon Rollie went to join his wife and child. Life around the fort continued, most folks unaware that the little man had died. Louie asked if there was anything he could do, but there was nothing that could take away the mountain man's grief. Not only was there the loss of his old friend, but Rufus was alone again. Rollie had given him purpose and companionship.

The next day, Rufus borrowed a wagon. With his friend in the back along with a shovel, he drove out beyond Independence Rock, onto the prairie to the granite outcrop. With the hole dug he laid his friend to rest dressed in his buckskins and wrapped in a blanket. Next to Rollie, Rufus put the shotgun.

After the grave was filled, Rufus stood and prayed for his friend. He also thanked God for sending the little man his way. He then drove the wagon to the domed rock and found where Rollie had shown him the names of his friends. Crouching near the names, he looked around. Several groups of wagons were camped near the domed rock.

The mountain man thought about asking someone to put his old friend's name into the stone, but changed his mind. Taking the hammer and chisel he'd brought with him, Rufus wrote his first word other than his own name. The crude letters spelt "RALE" next to his friend's.

* * *

Rufus remembered little of the next couple of days. He drank, got in a fight with buffalo hunters, and woke in the end with bruises, a headache, and a sick stomach. The routine might have continued for several more days, but Louie came pounding on the cabin door.

Staggering out of his cot and almost falling in front of the fireplace, Rufus managed to steady himself at the table. Coughing to clear the bile out of his throat, the mountain man tried to swallow. His mouth was dry and the room continued to sway.

Again came the pounding at the door. "I'm coming," Rufus said, his voice hoarse.

Grabbing the handle of the door, he lifted the latch and swung it open. The light blinded him, and instinctively he raised his arm to shield his face. "Is that you, Louie?" he asked.

"Ain't you a sight," the grizzled man said. "Hube told me he had to send you home before you tore the tavern apart."

"You come here just to tell me that?" Rufus asked, getting a little heated.

"No," Louie said. "I got an opportunity for you. Captain Edwards with his first lieutenant were in the saloon last night. They're taking a company of men west to set up temporary headquarters to protect the wagon trains. He needs a scout that can communicate with the Indians."

"There must be a half-dozen in the fort that could do that," the mountain man said.

"He asked if I knew of your whereabouts," Louie said. "I guess someone you scouted with this past year recommended you."

"I got to get ready to go trapping," Rufus told him. "I'm thinking of going up on the Yellowstone River."

Louie frowned, looking at the disheveled man. "While it ain't none of my business, Hube said you're all but broke. You'll need money for supplies."

"I got things to sell," the mountain man said. "Rollie's horse and mule along with his rifle should get me started."

Now the grizzled man knew he was treading on thin ice, but he hoped scouting for the Army would get Rufus over the loss of his friend and back on his feet financially. "I ain't said anything before because I knew what you were going through, but the bills at the livery will barely be covered by selling the animals. The Hawken will only fetch you $15, maybe $20."

Anger surged through the mountain man. Only his respect for Louie prevented the outburst he felt inside. Not once had Louie mentioned payment during Rollie's illness. Come to think of it, neither did the doc.

Then a wave of shame washed over Rufus. "Let me get cleaned up and I'll talk to Captain Edwards."

He watched from the cabin door as Louie hurried back to the Buffalo Hide Saloon. The grizzled owner was right. Rufus had built up debts caring for his old friend. Money that should have went towards them had been squandered on whiskey and cards over the past two days.

Dreading the effort it would take to clean up, Rufus looked around the cabin. He would start with cleaning . . . right after making some coffee.

CHAPTER SIXTEEN

Captain Edwards was a young officer who had come up through the ranks quickly. He had dark, wavy hair and a neatly trimmed moustache. His first lieutenant was older than him and a veteran of several campaigns against the Indians. He had straight, salt-and-pepper hair and a full beard that he kept trimmed short. They were waiting near the quartermaster's wagon. Beyond was a row of tents neatly lined up. A larger tent guarded by privates was the captain's.

Both men had sharp-looking uniforms. Around their waists they had polished belts and holsters carrying Colt Paterson No. 5 models. Both carried a small sword on the opposite hip. By comparison, when Rufus walked up to meet them he had on a stained set of buckskins, a drooping leather hat, low-heeled boots, and a broad belt that had the Colt and his Green River knife. His possible bag and powder horn were slung over his shoulder and the Hawken rifle rested in the crook of his arm. His short axe was in his packs on the mustang.

The captain smiled and said, "You look every bit of what I had envisioned a mountain man to be."

The first lieutenant's name was Harper. He just stood to the side and grinned. He'd been dealing with mountain men since he was an enlisted man. He was familiar with the name Pike and had heard stories that complimented the man and condemned him.

"Louie told me you were looking for a scout," Rufus told the captain.

"We have been assigned to search out a location so that a garrison of troops could be deployed to protect emigrants heading for Oregon. Near Fort Hall was brought up as a possible site," the captain explained. "I would like to employ you to act as our scout. You would also be expected to hunt for meat to supplement our supplies."

"Don't you think the British might have something to say about you setting up a military camp in their territory?" Rufus asked.

A hint of red showed in the captain's face, having a civilian question him in the presence of his first lieutenant. Controlling his tone and desiring to stay in charge, the captain said, "I believe the question of who has the territory will be answered soon. In the meantime, I have been asked to locate a site for the camp. If you are interested in assisting as a scout, the project will take about two months. You would be compensated $40 each month and a portion for any additional days exceeding the two months."

Not wanting to embarrass the captain again, Rufus said, "I am flattered that you asked me. The two months or more will cut into my coming season of hunting and trapping. I don't think I could do it for any less than $50 a month."

Smiling, the captain said, "You know that there are lots of mountain men around the fort that I could offer this opportunity to. Why should I pay you more than they would ask for?"

Rufus noticed that the first lieutenant was becoming restless. The mountain man wanted to tell the captain it was because you get what you pay for, but again that would have been an affront to his authority. Instead he replied, "I would be honored to scout for you, but after we're done, I have the winter to live through. I am going to get my horses, and when I come back you can let me know if I am going with you or if I am going trapping."

The mountain man walked to the livery fully aware that he was broke and had no funds to go trapping. Scouting for the army would solve many of his current problems, but for some reason he felt he had to best the young captain so each would know where they stood.

Kenny hurried over to him as he entered the livery. "So, are you going with the army?"

"That has not been decided yet," Rufus told him.

"Why you coming to get your horses?" the hostler asked.

"Sort of a bargaining chip," the mountain man told him. "I think he wants me and I got to show him that I don't need him."

"It's none of my business," Kenny replied, "but I think you do need him. That's why Louie come over and got you."

"You know it, and Louie knows it," Rufus told him, "but the captain doesn't."

Putting the packs onto the mustang, the mountain man stuffed a little hay into them so they wouldn't appear as empty. Then, swinging up onto the grulla, he ducked his head under the door header as he rode out, leading the mustang. He suddenly felt a little concern. The captain had gone back to his tent and the first lieutenant remained at the wagon. Just maybe he'd pushed it too far.

Harper watched him ride up with a wry grin on his face. "I would have left you sitting at this fort, but it appears the captain likes you. He will meet your $100 for the two months. On occasion he will ask your advice, but generally you will report to me. Your food, lead, and powder will be provided, as well as some grain for your horse. If you desire, a tent will be erected for you each evening. Your bedroll and other items can be carried in the wagons. The pack horse will not be needed. You can take it with those hay-filled bags back to the livery. If something happens to your horse, another will be provided for you. I assume this is satisfactory with you. We leave in the morning."

Without waiting for an answer, the first lieutenant turned and headed for the command tent. Rufus felt a little tight inside and would have liked to settle a few things with Harper, but he knew that they were like the company when trapping. If you get paid by them, you follow their rules. Rufus didn't like rules, but he did need the payday.

That night, the mountain man spent some time with Louie. The grizzled owner joined Rufus after supper with a bottle. "I was glad to hear you were going with the soldiers."

"They'll be a pain in my arse, especially that Harper, but I got the price I wanted," Rufus said, accepting a drink from Louie.

"Harper?" the owner asked. "Hell, he's the one that talked the captain into using you."

"Well, he sure as hell didn't sound like he wanted me," Rufus replied.

Laughing, Louie said, "It's the army. They aren't supposed to sound like they're your friend. They just want the best they can get."

"They won't let me take the pack horse," the mountain man told him.

"Leave it here at the livery," Louie said. "You're going with the army. There won't be any charge for keeping it here."

He dug into his possible bag and gave a piece of paper to Louie. "I had Kenny write this for you. It gives you Rollie's horses and rifle. We'll talk about my mustang when I get back."

For the next hour the two men talked, a partial drink in front of Rufus. Whatever the mountain man was doing, he always did his best whether working or drinking. Having work in front of him, Rufus left the Buffalo Hide Saloon after only a couple of drinks. He needed to be sharp in the morning.

The sun hadn't come up when the mountain man arrived at the army camp, leading the grulla with the gear he'd be taking piled onto the saddle. The mess sergeant was up and had the coffee ready. A pot of water was heating on the fire for the porridge that would be the men's breakfast.

"If you got a cup, I got coffee," the sergeant said. "You can toss your gear into the back of my wagon."

With their coffee, the sergeant sat with Rufus. The mountain man could hear a couple of privates working on getting the meal ready. "I ain't never been west of here," the sergeant said. "What's the country like?"

"It's good," Rufus replied. "The mountains are something to look forward to. We got some short-grass prairie to cross before we get to them."

"How about the Indians?" the man asked.

"Most are friendly, but some like to cause trouble," Rufus told him. "They will take your mules if they get a chance. The Shoshone and Bannock are trading with us. The Lakota and Crow stay away from the route west. I would worry about the Blackfoot. They tend to take offence to all the emigrants coming west."

"We ran into some Lakota east of here," the sergeant said. "It was nip and tuck for a bit, but didn't come to any fighting. Mostly they followed us too close."

"Could be they were interested in doing some trading, or they could have been looking over your mules and horses." Rufus said.

"Any Cheyenne around here?" he asked.

"Plenty of them further north," the mountain man said. "They come down here to hunt buffalo and to do some trading with other tribes."

Rufus was getting the feeling that the mess sergeant was sizing up his knowledge. After a bit the man went on to other subjects, giving the mountain man the feeling he'd passed his review. It was just getting light in the east when a bugle blew, waking the camp. Rufus had already gotten something to eat, so he just stood clear and watched the soldiers have their breakfast and tear down the camp.

It was mid-August 1845 when the mountain man left with the soldiers from Fort Laramie. There were three wagons pulled by teams of six mules, forty enlisted men and three officers. They would follow the same route as the covered wagons, which would soon be called the Oregon Trail. Several wagon trains had left from the fort in the last two months. The emigrants had to be at Independence Rock by early July to make it to Oregon before the mountain passes filled with snow.

The mountain man rode alongside the first lieutenant. "Do we follow the wagons or pass them?" Rufus asked.

"We catch up with them and the captain will talk with their leader, warning him about any trouble, and then we move on," Harper said.

When they reached Devil's Gate, Rufus cautioned the captain about the narrows and the backups he could expect on the Sweetwater River. Edwards didn't want his troops tied up behind slow-moving wagons and chose to go around the south side. This side had loose sand and their wagons sunk almost to their axles in some places. The mule teams strained against their collars as they moved the wagons forward.

They rejoined the Sweetwater River at the fifth crossing. Word came that there were two wagon trains slowly working their way through the narrows. Even with the difficulty of the loose sand, the captain was pleased that they weren't behind the covered wagons.

The platoon would travel 30 miles each day. They would stop at around 5 pm and set up their tents and post guards. Horses and mules were groomed and fed prior to the evening meal. The next morning the men were called to quarters, inspected, then the camp was struck and the platoon moved on. This was all done to bugle calls. If the platoon ended the day later than five, grooming would be done before breakfast in the morning.

Rufus just stayed out of their way until his meeting with the officers in the evening to update them on anything he'd seen scouting ahead of the platoon, and what they could expected to encounter the next day. At this meeting he'd be told whether or not to devote time to hunting for fresh meat.

Two days in a row braves on horseback had been seen watching the platoon pass. At the meeting on the second day, the captain was concerned. "I think they are calculating our strength and may have something planned."

The second lieutenant sat with a brandy and did not show the same concern. Rufus addressed the captain. "The braves we saw the past two days were Arapaho. They are hunting buffalo and simply stopped what they were doing to watch us pass. Their teepees are two miles north of the trail with their women and children."

"You may be correct, Mr. Pike," he told Rufus. Then addressing Harper, he said, "I want the watch doubled and our stock kept close to the camp."

Leaving the meeting, Harper walked next to the mountain man. "This is the captain's first command west of Missouri. We have to give him time to get comfortable out here."

Rufus was climbing the grade to the South Pass when he rode by a wagon train slowly working its way west. They had several questions for the mountain man. He was talking with the leader when the captain and the platoon caught up.

Captain Edwards took over the discussion, warning the wagon train about the Indians that had been spotted. The leader then told the captain about a wagon pulled by horses that had gone ahead of the train. Rufus heard little more and rode ahead, ranging to the north of the trail.

The mountain man had shot a mule deer and was finishing gutting it when the platoon reached him for the second time that day. The mess sergeant stopped his wagon near Rufus and said, "Toss it on the wagon. We'll eat good tonight."

Smiling, Rufus replied, "I'm keeping the liver for my own meal if you don't mind."

"Hell, I might just join you," the sergeant said, laughing.

It was close to the end of the day, so Rufus stayed with the platoon. Late that afternoon they caught sight of a covered wagon on the trail. It appeared to have no stock and a man was standing near the front wheel, waving his arms. A woman and child were looking out the back.

When the platoon got within earshot, they heard the man hollering, "They attacked us and stole the horses! They come in shooting and screaming!"

The captain ordered his lieutenant to set up a perimeter. Rufus rode around the wagon, looking for any sign. He found where the horses had been picketed and where they had been led away. While the captain interviewed the emigrant, the mountain man followed the trail. With the perimeter set up, the first lieutenant joined him.

A half-mile away, they found where the Indians had left their horses. "You think it was Arapaho?" Harper asked.

"More than likely Blackfoot or Shoshone," Rufus replied.

The captain was a little agitated when the two men returned to the wagon. "I need you to take a dozen men and go after the damn Indians. Pike can go with you and help track the bastards."

The mountain man sat listening, he jaws tight. What he'd seen and what the emigrant had said were two different things. Harper turned to Rufus and asked, "What do you think happened here?"

"Two things went wrong here," the mountain man said. "The man was in a hurry and left the wagon train. Last night he picketed his horses too far from his wagons."

"And how does that change the fact that they rode in and stole his animals?" the captain demanded.

"They didn't ride in, captain," Rufus said. "They left their horses on the bluff above and walked down and led the horses away. There were no shots fired, and other than the folks in the wagon being left without stock, they were never in danger."

"And you could tell this by what?" Captain Edwards asked.

"It's what you pay me for," Rufus replied. "I have spent a good part of my life tracking and hunting while living around the tribes."

"Lieutenant," Edwards said, "Get the men together."

"I'll go after the horses," Rufus said. "If you send soldiers in, men are going to get killed on both sides. There will be retaliation and more killings."

"We can not let them get away with stealing horses," the captain said, color coming into his cheeks.

"No, we can't," the mountain man said. "Let me see what I can do."

After getting his bedroll and a few things he'd need, Rufus rode away to follow the tracks. He had heard the lieutenant trying to calm down the captain. Edwards was young, and before he retired he'd get to see his share of battles with the Indians. If he survived the battles, he just might see it another way than to push the issue over a few horses of an impatient emigrant who should have stayed in the safety of the wagon train.

The trail was easy to follow. From the bluff he looked back and saw the soldiers prepared for a full-fledged attack. Maybe it was better to be prepared than assume there was no danger. With all the wagon trains coming west it was only a matter of time before the tribes joined together to try and stop them.

With the Colt in his broad belt and the Hawken across his saddle, Rufus followed the tracks. The braves had not galloped away once they had the horses. They had ridden easy to the north. The mountain man was beginning to think that the tribe might be Crow. The mountain man was able to speak several languages, but that one he was the weakest in.

That night he fried the liver over a small fire. He didn't bother to make coffee and drank from his canteen. Rufus was ten miles from the platoon and he figured it would be another ten before he got to where he expected to find the Crow.

The second day after leaving the stranded wagon, Rufus came upon the Crow camp near the confluence of two rivers. He could see the tribe's horses to the west. A half-dozen young braves were watching them. Rufus took a deep breath. One of two things would happen. He would be welcomed and be able to negotiate for the horses, or he would be seen as an enemy and they would take his horse.

Odds were the first, otherwise the mountain man would have been hesitant to go down and would have tried to steal the horses back. Riding down toward the teepees Rufus waited to be noticed. Suddenly there were shouts and some children ran to see the stranger.

An elder came from a teepee and stood looking at the mountain man. Rufus raised his hand in friendship. The elder returned it and the mountain man rode in. Rufus was welcomed to join the elder near the fire. Young braves surrounded the two men, leaving the mountain man rather uncomfortable.

Using sign and what few words he knew, Rufus thanked the elder for welcoming him in. It turned out that the elder spoke some Cheyenne, so the two spoke in that language. One of the women brought two bowls and dipped them into a pot steaming over the fire. One was handed to each of the men.

The bland soup was hot and Rufus was hungry. The meat in the soup was buffalo. The mountain man asked about how their hunt had been. The elder proudly talked of the many buffalo they'd killed.

Then it was time to speak of what he'd come for. He told the elder that the soldiers had sent him to get the horses that had been taken. He said the family who owned the horses were headed far to the west and needed them.

Holding his breath, Rufus waited for a response. The elder finally said that his son had been one of the braves who had taken the horses. They had done it without hurting the family. His sons had already sung around the fire about his success.

Rufus played his last card when he told the elder that if he did not come back with the horses, the soldiers would come and men would be hurt. He then asked what he could give to the elder's son in exchange for the horses. The old man looked at Rufus' rifle. Then the mountain man had an idea.

He went to his saddle bags and got out a new Green River knife and the second Kentucky pistol. He also had the mold for making the balls and a few already cast. Taking them back to the fire, Rufus placed them onto the blanket they were sitting on.

The chief picked up the pistol and looked it over. He then indicated that he wanted to see it fired. Rufus got up and took a piece of wood from near the fire. He propped it up about 30 feet away and then returned to the blanket. Taking his time, he loaded the Kentucky pistol and held it for the elder to look at. The man motioned for him to shoot.

Wishing he had just cleaned the pistol, pulling it to full cock, Rufus lined up on the wood. Smoke and sparks flew from the barrel as the pistol fired. The ball struck the wood and sent it skidding across the ground.

Looking at the elder, Rufus was relieved to see him nod. He said a few words in Crow to the braves around him and they scattered to find the horses taken from the wagon. The mountain man knew it was the threat of the soldiers coming that swayed the elder's decision, but he had to get something so others in the tribe would look at him as a good bargainer.

The mountain man rode back toward the platoon leading the six horses. He had now given both pistols to the Indians, which could someday be used against the white man in battle. One had been for his profit and the second to prevent further trouble. He was happy with both trades and would have to trust that the braves shooting the Kentucky pistols were poor shots.

The first lieutenant was thankful when Rufus got back. He had had a difficult time preventing the captain from going after the horses. The wagon train had reached the stranded wagon and the emigrant was warned about leaving the others again. With any great conflict avoided, Rufus and the platoon continued toward the west.

* * *

The two months with the army ended up being three, and snow had started falling. A site about three miles from Fort Hall was chosen to set up a military camp. The soldiers were put to work cutting trees to build winter quarters and erect a palisade around the buildings for protection from attack.

Rufus decided to winter at Fort Hall. Come spring he'd do some trapping, then use his grulla as a pack horse and lead it back to the fort and sell the furs. True to the captain's prediction, the territory around and north of Fort Hall became part of America. The Hudson Bay Company continued to run it for the time being and supplied the numerous wagon trains with supplies.

The military camp did not last long due to the difficulties of keeping it supplied, and those in the platoon were sent to Oregon. It was decided that the trail between Fort Hall and the west would be protected by those stationed in Oregon.

The mountain man continued to eke out a living trapping and hunting. On occasion he would do some scouting for the army and even led a hunting party after buffalo once. They were trophy hunters and not looking to load a hide wagon.

There were the occasional scrapes with one of the tribes, but Rufus managed to stay friendly with most of them. His Hawken and Colt worked well to turn those who attacked him. When gold was discovered in California, he was asked if he'd be going to get his share.

"I ain't never had a desire to hunt something I couldn't eat," was all he replied.

The mountain man saw the results of what gold could do to men in the summer of 1849 when he'd stopped at Fort Hall. The grass was gone as far as you could see on both sides of the trail to the fort. The trees had been cut, broken wagons and oxen carcasses littered the sides of the trail.

The Hudson Bay Company had left and some independent men had taken over the trading post and tavern. The mountain man was surprised when he learned that Johnson was buying and selling horses, mules, and oxen. He had a large area with split rail fence surrounding it near the fort, where he grazed and held the animals.

Rufus rode up with his grulla and mustang. The smoky-eyed man had a shack near the pasture that he stayed in. He was sitting in front of the building. "I see you still got your hide intact," he called to the mountain man. "You passing through on your way to California?"

"Chasing gold's not for me," Rufus replied. "Once I pick up some supplies, I am headed for Jackson Hole to hunt cats. Either that or the Big Horn Mountains. I heard there was grizzlies for the taking there."

"So, you give up on the trapping?" Johnson asked as he opened the gate to let the horses in.

The mountain man shook his head. "I still wet a trap now and then. With most folks chasing gold or hunting buffalo, the price of beaver has gone up some."

"That is if you can find beaver," Johnson replied. "You should consider buffalo hunting. We did alright back in St. Louis when we got off the steamboat."

"There are two things that I have no desire to do," Rufus said. "The first is buffalo hunting, and the second is chasing gold. Now what do I owe you?"

With his horses taken care of and his gear stowed in Johnson's shack, Rufus headed into the fort. The military camp west of the fort had been closed and some soldiers bivouacked at the fort. His first stop was at the tavern. The owner's name was Sam and he smiled when he saw the mountain man.

"Should I reserve a table for you?" the man asked.

"This is just a short stop," Rufus said. "Too many folks coming through with wagons and talking foolish about going to find gold."

For the next hour, the mountain man worked on the bottle and made small talk with the owner. He used to like visiting with Finn, but he'd left shortly after '46 and gone back to Canada when the territory line changed.

After two days at the fort, Rufus purchased his supplies, and carrying the bags he went to get his horses. Johnson was talking to some men. The mountain man took a chew and sat down in front of the shack.

The smoky-eyed man finished his discussions and came over. "You're sitting in my chair," he said.

"It's a comfortable chair," Rufus said without moving. "I'll be needing my horses."

Giving the mountain man a cold stare, Johnson went to get the animals. Getting up, Rufus got the rest of his gear from the shack. The smoky-eyed man came back with the animals. "Why the hell don't you leave them at the livery in the fort?" he asked. "It would save me the trouble of having to chase them down."

"I like the way you take care of horses," Rufus said. "Have you thought about going to California?"

Snorting, Johnson replied, "I'll make my gold right here. I got four men working for me making hay and keeping the fence up. Wagons come in with oxen that are about to drop. I take them in at a low price, feed them for a couple of weeks and resell them for a tidy profit. I don't need to go to California and ruin my back with a pan in some stream."

It was the end of August in '49 when Rufus rode away from the fort. He was glad that Johnson was doing good. Over the years they hadn't much got along and the mountain man had won money from him at the rendezvous by outshooting him, but he didn't wish the man harm.

CHAPTER SEVENTEEN

Rufus got off the wagon trail as quickly as possible and cut towards the Wind River area. He had got to thinking about trapping after talking with Johnson and decided to do that before heading to the Big Horn Mountains. There was a river that ran out of the Yellowstone where he'd had success in past years.

Riding in view of the Teton Mountains lifted his spirits. Everywhere he went things had changed, but the mountains remained the same. There had been a time when he could travel a month and not run into anyone, but now small farms and cabins were popping up everywhere. There were even some towns with folks working in shops and going to church on Sundays. The towns he could avoid unless he needed coffee or tobacco.

Arriving at the river, Rufus set up camp. He still used a fly tarp and ground cover when hunting or trapping. Picketing the horses on some mature grass, he collected wood for his fire. The mountain man had a hankering for some fish, and after bringing an arm

313

load of wood to the camp he cut an alder bush and made a pole.

Taking line and a hook from his possible bag, Rufus rigged the fishing pole and then rolled rocks and chunks of logs to find worms for bait. He had a piece of stick on the line for a bobber and sat on the riverbank enjoying the early fall sunshine. Within an hour he had two cutthroat trout and a couple of suckers lying on the bank.

Piling some sticks together and placing a couple of rocks around them, he lit his supper fire. Rufus filled his coffee pot and set it onto one of the rocks near the flames to heat. He got a very satisfying feeling being out in the wilds, cooking a meal.

His first plan had been to fry the fish, but fish broiled over the fire was always tastier. Cutting some green sticks, he put the cleaned fish onto them and shoved the end into the dirt so the fish hung over the flames. Soon the air was filled with the smell of his meal cooking.

"Hello the camp!" a voice said.

"Damn," Rufus muttered. Standing up, he looked upriver. He saw two men walking towards him with back packs and rifles slung onto their backs and some kind of fishing rods in their hands.

Realizing that there was no way to avoid them, Rufus replied, "Come in and have a seat. Looks like you folks are fishing."

The two men had the look of easterners and both had stubbly beards. One wore some kind of spectacles. "We come out with a party that are in the Yellowstone. We figured that we'd check out the fishing down here."

"It ain't healthy wandering alone," the mountain man told them. "There are three tribes that hunt this area. They may take an exception to you folks crossing their hunting grounds."

The men stopped short of the camp and looked it over. "You got a nice setup here," one of them said. "You look like a real mountain man."

"I've spent time in them," Rufus replied.

"Mind if we have some coffee?" the other man asked.

"Grab a piece of ground and have a cup," the mountain man told them. "The fish are mine, unless you hanker for suckers."

The men visited Rufus for almost an hour, talking about how it was nice that the west was opening up to folks from the east and about their plans to build lodges for people to come and enjoy the mountains.

By the time they had headed back to their camp, Rufus had eaten the fish and his coffee was gone. Inside he wasn't feeling as good about the mountains. It would only be a matter of time and he'd be bumping into folks at every turn. Come morning, he'd have to look elsewhere to set his traps.

Rufus headed back toward the Wind River region. After four days of riding, he found some ponds with lodges. It was September and the leaves were golden on the hillsides. He figured to trap for a month and then head for the Big Horn Mountains.

Just down from his camp, the mountain man had six traps set. He spent some time brushing the horses. The grulla had some years on it, and Rufus figured this would be the last year he'd take it trapping. The mustang was a few years younger and would be a good pack animal for a while yet.

That night, as Rufus sat listening to the night sounds, he wondered where all the years had gone. He could look down and see hints of white in his beard. It was seldom when he ran across men still wearing buckskins. Most of the trappers he had known at the last rendezvous had left the mountains or died. He realized that he had outlived his time.

The next morning Rufus had three beavers in his traps. Wet to his knees, he led the mustang back to camp feeling almost like his old self. He was in the mountains and catching beaver. That night he fried up some of the beaver with wild onions and stuffed himself. The only thing that was missing was a partner to share it with.

After a month in the Wind River region, the mountain man had 58 pelts. With the furs folded and packed onto the mustang, he headed for the grizzlies. He had hoped to run into one while trapping, but there had been no sign of the bears.

The leaves were gone when he reached the Big Horn Mountains. Rufus knew of a good stand of whitebark pine. The red squirrels would collect the cones and stash them. Then the bears that couldn't climb the trees to get them would raid the stashes.

The mountain man found an area with evidence of bear scat and clawed trees. Not far from the sign he set up his camp. If a bear came close, the horses would alert him, or he would smell them.

On the second night, Rufus heard a bear up in the pines. Fearing few things, the bear clawed trees and broke branches. It was to the east and south of the mountain man's camp, so the horses remained calm. He fell asleep that night, confident that he'd have a grizzly hide to take back to Fort Laramie.

On the way to the pines, Rufus had passed a dam with lodges and he figured that the beaver should be prime. Looking up into the pines, the mountain man said, "You can fatten up a little more on the cones, but I am coming after you after I catch a few more beaver."

There was another reason for catching some beaver. He could use the carcasses for bait to bring the bear in. Securing his camp, Rufus rode the grulla and led the mustang with his traps toward the dam. The fall sun warmed his back, and his stomach was full of side meat and frying pan bread. It was a good morning.

Rufus spent two hours around the pond placing the traps. The brush and trees surrounding the banks were thick, and finding good canals or entry points for the beaver took time. He managed to set four traps before heading back to his camp, which was a mile away.

The grulla began to act up as they climbed out of the valley. As they crested the rise, the mustang pulled its lead rope loose and ran. The mountain mans jaw dropped. There was a large rear end of a bear sticking out from under his fly tarp. As the grulla fought him, Rufus leaped off with the Hawken in his hand.

The horse disappeared behind him and the mountain man stood less than fifty paces from the bear. Tearing the fly tarp pegs loose, it rose up, a piece of side meat in its mouth as it shook off the tarp. Without a place to run, Rufus stood, the rifle to his shoulder, locking eyes with the grizzly.

He shouted, "Damn you, bear, eating my supplies!" as the Hawken fired, sending the .54 caliber ball at the bear's chest.

The animal dropped to all fours, losing the side meat, and roared at the mountain man like the shot in the chest wasn't even felt. Stepping behind an oak, Rufus loaded the Hawken by feel, his eyes on the bear. It was only a matter of seconds after he fired when the bear charged toward him. As he rammed the ball and wad home, the grizzly went by, close enough for the mountain man to reach out and touch.

Leaping to the opposite side of the tree, hoping to keep it between him and the bear, Rufus brought the rifle up, expecting the angry animal to turn and come for him. It did not! It continued after the grulla! The horse ran to the right, trying to escape from the bear.

Lining the sights on grizzly, Rufus fired again, shouting and swearing at the bear, hoping to get its attention. He got his wish as the bear turned and came at him. As he put the ball and wad on the end of the barrel, it slipped from his fingers and he was left with an empty rifle and a charging bear.

Pulling his knife and Colt, the mountain man waited behind the tree, fearing the worst. Then the behemoth collapsed and lay ten paces from him. Rufus remained behind the tree. Sticking the Colt into his belt and the knife into its sheath, he dug into his possible bag for another ball and greased wad. He finished loading the Hawken with shaking legs, while staring at the bear.

A poke of the rifle barrel convinced the mountain man that the bear was dead. His heart was still pounding as he went to find his horses. It was almost an hour when he got back to camp with the animals and the grizzly remained where he'd left it, its life blood on the leaves, covered with flies in the fall sunshine.

With the danger and high excitement of the grizzly gone, Rufus was singing a happy tune while he gutted the animal and hung it in a pine to be skinned. The grulla was too skittish to be use to pull the bear up into the tree, but the mustang was settled enough to do the task.

Rufus hadn't gone to investigate the damage done to his supplies, or even if the bear had gotten into his beaver packs. Whatever was done, this hide would compensate him for the loss. He had the bear liver for his supper and he would be able to make a few meals from the meat before it went bad.

The sun was low in the western sky when Rufus went to inspect the damage. He saw that the coffee pot and frying pan were still near his fire pit, so he got some wood burning and put the pot next to the fire to heat for coffee.

Then he turned to the mess the bear had made and he muttered, "See if the bastard left me any coffee."

The saliva-covered side meat lay in the dirt where the animal had dropped it. His packs were badly torn as the grizzly had ripped them open with its teeth. Bags of beans, flour, and rice were damaged. Thankfully the coffee beans were intact, but two twists of tobacco that had been lying on top of the bags were gone.

"The bastard had a hankering for tobacco," Rufus swore.

The canvas packs holding the beaver pelts had been rolled over but not opened. It was obvious that the side meat had gotten the bear's attention as it rummaged through the supply pack.

The mountain man got a handful of beans and roasted them for his coffee. It was almost dark before the packs were closed again and put under the tarp. The fly tarp would be put back up the next day. Tonight, Rufus would sleep under the stars.

He re-fought the bear that night in his dreams and the Hawken wouldn't fire. Waking, his heart was pounding and he was waving his arms. Realizing that it was just a dream, the mountain man pulled up his blanket and wondered if he was getting too old for this kind of stuff.

The ground was covered with frost the next morning. The grayish-green pile of guts lay where the grizzly had fallen. Rufus still had the task of skinning the bear. As he huddled near the fire to get warm, he enjoyed looking at the animal hanging in the tree.

He dumped some rice into the steaming pot of water. All the bags that had been ripped by the grizzly's teeth or claws had some dirt in them, but the mountain man had eaten worse food in the past. He had a small bag with salt, a tin of molasses, and a few other spices that the animal had overlooked. Rufus was pleased that he'd still be able to have sweetened rice.

After breakfast, it was time to check the traps. Riding the grulla, he led the mustang to the pond. Shedding his buckskin britches, he waded into the water. He was rewarded with two beavers. They weren't that large, but they were prime. After resetting the traps and adding castor to the bait sticks, Rufus climbed out of the pond and hung the beavers on the mustang's pack saddle.

He would have another month of trapping, if he could find some more ponds, but Rufus decided that he'd pull his traps when this pond was finished and head for Fort Laramie. When he got back to camp the mountain man had another surprise. Three men were standing admiring his bear.

"You men hungry for some bear meat?" he called to them.

The men turned and met the mountain man. "Damn fine bear you got there," the man who appeared to be their leader said.

"The damn thing put up a fight, but I come out on top," Rufus told them.

The mountain man had seen the men in the past and when they offered to help him skin the animal, he felt he could trust them. The men had beaver pelts on their pack horses and were on their way to Fort Hall. Rufus told them he'd be heading for the fort on the Laramie River.

While drinking coffee that night around the fire, one of the men said, "You may not remember, but my nose met your fist one time."

"I remember," Rufus told him. "You had said things to my partner."

Unsure if the man was thinking of retaliating, the mountain man sat ready to go at it. Then the man, whose name was Hank, replied, "I was drunk and talking foolish. I see you're not with the little guy any longer."

Lowering his guard, Rufus told him, "He died some years back. Rollie was one hell of a trapper. He killed a bear the last year out."

The men left the next morning with a couple of meals of bear meat and Rufus watched them until they were out of sight. While he felt the men where trustworthy, he wasn't taking any chances. He had planned to go down and pull the traps that morning, but instead he packed up his gear. With everything on the mustang, Rufus left the camp and headed for the pond. He'd pull his traps and skin any beaver he caught and then leave from the pond in the morning.

* * *

Fort Laramie was crowded with wagons when Rufus arrived. It was late October in '49 and most would winter there and get an early start in the spring. He passed one string of wagons that figured they could make Fort Hall before the snow flew.

Few wagons had families in them. It was mostly groups of men heading for the gold fields. Men who were walking or riding horseback would continue west until the snow stopped them. They still had 1,200 miles to the gold fields, but at 30 to 40 miles a day, they could cover a chunk of it.

The mountain man doubted anyone would make it beyond Fort Hall. They had been pushing to make Fort Laramie and would continue doing so as they went west. Most of their horses would collapse before they got to the mountains. Then Rufus smiled. "More business for Johnson," he muttered.

That night was a celebration for the mountain man. He hung the bear hide on the tavern wall for all to see. Rufus had drinks bought to congratulate him until he was at the point of staggering as he told and retold the story of the kill. Hube was bartending and took care of his friend.

While the mountain man commenced to get drunk in the fort, at the Buffalo Hide Saloon, Louie was busy serving customers as he covered the dining room as well as the bar. His sister Lucy was in the kitchen putting out tasty meals. The grizzled owner looked up several times at the young man dining across the room. His brow furled as he wondered if the man was a cause for worry.

A young, olive-skinned man with dark hair that hung in ringlets just over his ears sat eating his supper. The man was lean and medium height. He wore dark wool pants and a wool shirt.

He'd been at the boarding house for the past week. His name was Tom Lefevre and hailed from New Orleans. He was on a mission to find a man.

Tom was unaware of Louie's watching him. The young man had gotten word at Fort Hall that the man he was looking for, Rufus Pike, was planning on wintering at Fort Laramie. He'd quickly made arrangement to come here. The young man adjusted the Colt in his waist band. He wondered what Rufus would look like.

Louie came over to the table and said, "The kitchen is about to close. We got pie for dessert."

"Do you get hunters and trappers in here, or do they keep to the fort?" Tom asked the owner.

With a guarded look on his face, the grizzled owner replied, "Yes, we do. Most of them go to the fort to sell their furs before having their own little rendezvous."

Reaching into his possible bag for some coins, Tom placed them onto the table. "I think I will pass on the pie."

Picking up the coins, Louie went back to the bar and stared at the olive-skinned man. He remembered the last man who had stayed at his boarding house with the accent of the young man. It had not gone well. And Louie recalled, he'd also come from New Orleans. Tonight, a customer had told Louie that Rufus was at the fort. Come tomorrow, the grizzled man would have to go and warn his friend.

With no desire to belly up to the bar and have a few drinks, the young man headed for the boarding house. Tom had met a man named Caleb during his search for Rufus. He wished that Caleb had come with him. He had enjoyed the man's company. During the search he had panned gold with Caleb in California and, against large odds, they had gone back to Nogales and driven a herd of cattle to Sacramento for a tidy profit.

After coming over the mountains to Fort Hall, Caleb had left for Santa Fe. It was Caleb who had given him the Colt Paterson. It was the older style without the loading lever. Tom didn't even know why he carried it to supper. In New Orleans it was seldom you carried a revolver unless you were going to use it. Maybe he just wanted to be ready.

Returning to his room, Tom placed the Colt onto the small table near the window. He had been in search of this man Rufus Pike for almost two years. He hoped that Fort Laramie would be his final stop.

Tom turned the lamp up a bit and then sat on the edge of the bed. He kicked off his low-heeled boots. The room was well-done. It was much nicer than he had expected out on the frontier. The young man realized that his stay here might be quite long. If Rufus didn't show before snow, Tom would have to winter here and then hope he came in the spring.

As he lay in bed that night, the words that the owner had said came back to the young man. Most trappers went to the fort first. There had to be a place to drink in the fort where they could celebrate their catch. Tom was familiar with the rendezvous of the mountain men from stories he'd heard from men he'd met during his search.

Then the young man sat up in the bed with a thought. He should be waiting for Rufus in the fort. At Fort Hall they had learned that the man was hunting in the Big Horn Mountains. If he had had any luck, he would sell the furs in the fort. Tom now knew where to go. Come morning, he would be there early.

The young man left the boarding house shortly after sunrise. His breath created a cloud in the frigid morning air. The walk to the fort felt good, warming him as the frost crunched under his boots. Heading into an unknown area, Tom had the Colt in his waistband. He had nearly been hung once in California and wouldn't put himself in a weak position again.

The adobe walls of the fort were bright white in the morning sun. He found the main gates closed and a sleepy guard leaning against the wall with a rifle within easy reach. "You're up early," the guard told Tom. "Folks from the boarding house don't usually stir around until after breakfast."

No doubt the guard had watched his progress as he walked from the boarding house. "I have come to look for a man that might be here," Tom told him.

Noticing the Colt in the waistband, the guard asked, "Does the man have a name?"

"Yes, he does," Tom replied, getting frustrated. "I'm looking for Rufus Pike."

"Rufus you say," the man said. "There was a man here a few years ago that sounded much like you that was looking for Rufus. He got himself killed."

At the thought, Tom's hand went to the Colt. "I don't plan to get myself killed."

Laughing, the guard said, "I am just messing with you. A man gets bored standing out here." Then the guard called to a man inside and he opened one-half of the plank gate. There was a secondary closure inside that stood open. The man inside remained sitting on a stool. He also had a rifle within easy reach.

"I heard you're looking for Pike," the inside guard said. "He may still be in the tavern."

"So, he's here?" Tom asked, surprised the man outside hadn't told him.

"Is he ever," the guard laughed.

There were two buildings to the right. Tom saw that the larger one had barrels, rope, and other items on the front porch. That would be the trading post. The other had a drunk sleeping on the porch. "That would be the tavern," he said, heading for its open door. He also saw a bearskin hanging on the wall.

Walking across the courtyard, Tom could see that the fort was waking up, with men busy taking care of morning chores. Two women were visiting near the well as they got water for the morning meal. It was far from the cluttered, dilapidated look of Fort Hall. The fort had been called Fort John when built, but soon, due to the location near the river, it was changed to Fort Laramie.

Tom stepped around the man on the porch. He stopped, recognizing the man. It was the hunter Hank whom he'd come back with from Fort Hall. Shaking his head, Tom went into the tavern. The only light came from the open door and he saw a man wiping off the bar. Chairs were stacked onto the tables to make sweeping easier. The young man smelled smoke, spilt whiskey, sweat, and vomit in the enclosed building. He also caught the whiff of coffee brewing on the potbelly stove to one side.

"It will be awhile before I open. We had quite a time last night," the bartender said.

With the smells getting to him, Tom replied, "I'll wait outside."

"Hell, grab a chair off one of the tables and have yourself some coffee," the man said, coming around the bar with two cups. "I was about to have one myself."

Wanting to find out what he'd come to ask and then get out of the place, Tom asked, "Has Rufus Pike been here?"

"Been here?" the man laughed. "Hell, he's still sleeping at the corner table."

A shock went through the young man. Rufus here? "Is he . . . where . . .?" Tom stammered. After two long years, this was too easy.

"Come, I'll show you." The bartender said.

There, in the darkened corner, Tom saw a man slumped over the table. His beard spread across one side, and his hat sat on the table upside down with an empty bottle next to it. What he couldn't see in the dark was Rufus' mouth open and the drool puddling on the table.

Wanting to get out of the place, Tom said, "Let him sleep, I'll come back."

"Hell," the bartender replied, "I was about to wake him and kick him out anyway."

"Hey Rufus! You got company!" the man shouted.

The drunken mountain man's head came up a bit and bobbed for a second before his sat up. "Damn,

Hube," he growled. "That ain't no way to wake a man."

Tom stared in disbelief at the man, his beard and hair sticking out in all directions and hanging down to his shoulders, dressed in what appeared to be filthy buckskins. "My name is Tom and I come to find you," the young man said.

The hair on the back of Rufus' neck stood as he heard the Cajun accent. Tossing the table toward the young man, he shouted, "Where the hell are my guns!"

Ducking aside from the table, Tom tripped and fell. He looked up and the mountain man had drawn a knife and was coming for him. Wide-eyed with shock, Tom saw Hube swing something and strike Rufus. The mountain man collapsed onto the floor.

The young man untangled himself from the chair that had tripped him and started to get up. He looked down the barrel of a sawed-off shotgun. "Why the hell did Rufus go after you?" Hube demanded.

"Don't shoot," Tom begged. "There has to be a mistake. I wouldn't hurt Rufus. I came to give him something."

Carefully he took a small package from his possible bag. "It's an amulet made by my grandmother, Camille, for this man Rufus Pike. She had given him one years ago and had a sense that it had been lost. I mean him no harm."

Hube took the amulet and looked at it. Handing it back to Tom, he said, "Give me the revolver from your belt."

Pulling the Colt from his waistband, Tom handed it to the bartender. "You got any knives?"

"Not here," Tom replied.

"Go sit near the stove while I tend to Rufus," Hube told him.

Sitting near the potbelly stove, the young man could hear the bartender with Rufus. He was speaking earnestly, trying to convince the mountain man that Tom was no danger. Then the two men came from the back of the tavern. Tom was poised to run if Rufus came at him.

Stopping short of Tom, looking disheveled as ever, Rufus rubbed the bump on his head and asked, "Why you looking for me?"

"My name is Tom Lefevre," the young man said. "I am from New Orleans, but I have not come to hurt you."

Rufus seemed to relax. He pulled a chair off one of the tables and sat down. "I knew some LeFevre's back in New Orleans," he replied.

Hube came over, set a cup of coffee in front of Rufus and said, "Tell him about the bear."

Smiling, the mountain man began. "Did you see the hide hanging on the front wall?" he asked. "Of course you did," Rufus said, answering his own question. "She was a big bastard. I was returning from setting some traps for beaver and was coming back to my camp. There she was, tearing up my packs and eating up my supplies. Why hell, without the supplies I'd starve come snow."

Tasting his coffee, Rufus continued. "Well, there I was with just a knife and my Hawken when the bastard looked up at me. That there bear had no intentions of sharing the meal with me. It stood up ten feet-tall and roared. Its breath alone almost knocked me over. I brung the Hawken to my shoulder as the bastard dropped to all fours and come at me. There weren't a tree big enough within a mile that I could have climbed to get away from the grizzly, so I lined up on its chest and let go."

Tom's eyes were wide as he listened to the story.

"It was like the Hawken didn't hurt the damn grizzly at all," Rufus said. "It kept coming as I was slamming another ball into the rifle and hunting for a cap. It ran right on by me. I could feel its bristling hair brush me as it went after my horses. Turns out I weren't a big enough meal and it wanted a horse. With the rifle loaded, I went to chasing the bear, swearing up a storm. Then I saw the horses circling back to the camp, bringing the angry cuss right back to me."

Taking a gulp of the coffee and wiping his mouth with the back of his hand, Rufus continued the story. "Setting myself behind a sturdy oak, I took aim again and put a ball right behind the shoulder. I can only guess that I finally made the grizzly mad, because it forgot all about the horses and come for me. I stepped out from behind that oak and held my knife ready. I told the son-of-a-bitch to come and get me. Two foot, not an inch farther, it dropped dead in front of me."

"I thought you said that there were no big trees for a mile," Tom said, smiling.

"Well the oak was sturdy, but it was spreading, and not near high enough to climb away from the bear . . ." Suddenly, Rufus' face got a haunted look as he stared at Tom. "Your smile sure does remind me of someone."

"They say I look like my mother, Gabrielle," Tom replied.

Rufus' jaw dropped. Clearing his throat, he said, "I ain't heard that name in a long time."

Unable to hold the truth in any longer, Tom told him, "She says you are my father."

There wasn't a sound in the tavern as the three men sat near the stove. Rufus stared at the young man, a look of disbelief on his face.

Finally, the mountain man said in his gravelly voice, "She named you Tom."

"She told me you had to leave," the young man said, feeling his throat beginning to ache. "She told me about you having to shoot a man and then go away. When I got old enough, she took me to meet Damas."

"Damas," Rufus said. "He was my closest friend in New Orleans. He taught me to shoot."

"Did you use that old Springfield flintlock?" Tom asked. "He taught me with that."

"That, and a pistol I came by," the mountain man said.

Bewildered by the conversation, Hube got up and went back to cleaning the tavern. He looked over at the olive-skinned young man with curly, dark hair, thinking, *So the old cuss has a kid.*

Rufus asked, "How's your mother?"

"She is well," Tom replied. "She still talks of you and misses you."

While he didn't say it to the young man, Rufus thought about all the women he'd been with in his life, and the only one who stood out in his memory was Gabrielle. He was sure that her mother had put a spell on him that wouldn't allow her out of his mind.

"I've got something in my bag for you," Tom told him. "It is from grandmother Camille."

"The voodoo queen?" Rufus asked in his gravelly voice. "How is she doing?"

"She is still casting spells and helping those who are sick," Tom said.

"I always wanted to go back to New Orleans," Rufus said. "Your mother begged me to never return."

"The man, Hahn Gerber, who wanted you dead is now dead himself," Tom replied. "There are no enemies of Thomas Wallingford left alive."

"I'm an old mountain man now," Rufus said. "Too many years chasing beaver and bears. I would never fit in with town folk."

Ignoring the statement, Tom said, "A few years ago my mother intercepted a letter from a man out here that was sent to kill you. It said that he knew your name was now Rufus Pike and he was going to Fort Williams to kill you. He said he'd send another letter when it was done."

Looking away from his son, Rufus said, "He never got it done."

"That's what grandmother Camille felt," Tom replied. "Now that they knew your name, it would only be a matter of time before one of the men sent would kill you. Grandmother Camille put a spell on the whole clan of Gerbers, and one by one they died until none were left."

Slowly the fact sank in to the mountain man's aching head. His enemies were dead. Then he looked at the young man. "Damn, you're a skinny one. Are you sure you are mine?"

Tom looked at his father and replied, "Damn, you're a scruffy one. Could my mother be wrong?"

The kidding helped break the awkwardness they were feeling.

CHAPTER EIGHTEEN

With the first meeting over and Tom needing to think, he went to check on his sorrel and bay at the livery. He had a strange feeling. His search was over and now it was time to head back to New Orleans. He now knew what his father looked like and wasn't impressed, although he certainly looked like a mountain man.

They had made plans to meet at the Buffalo Hide Saloon for a midday meal, seeing that they had both missed their breakfast.

Kenny came over and told him, "Your animals looked kind of played out and I gave them both extra grain."

"I appreciate it," Tom replied. Then he asked, "If I left in the next couple of days, do you think I could make it to St. Louis before the snow?"

"A week ago, I would have told you yes, but now we're getting close to the white stuff," the hostler said. "If you were riding out there and we had a blow, you might be lucky and only lose some toes or ears, but if not it would be your life."

That was not what Tom wanted to hear. He decided after eating with Rufus that he'd go back to the fort and see if any freighters were pulling out. They'd know how to survive in a storm.

What Tom did not see while he was in the livery was Louie hurrying to the fort to warn Rufus. The grizzled owner still felt guilty about letting on that Tom Wallingford and Rufus were the same man based on the scar on their necks. It had almost got his friend killed and he wouldn't let it happen again.

A half-hour later, Louie walked back to the Buffalo Hide Saloon with a foolish grin on his face and a lilt in his step. He kept repeating, "Rufus got a kid."

Tom had left his gear at the livery. He asked Kenny to unlock the tack room. The young man went in and checked on his stuff. He was carrying gold from California in one of the packs and was pleased when he had learned that the room was kept locked to prevent intruders from stealing items from it. Even then, Tom had found a loose board and had put the bags of gold under it for safety.

It was time to go and get the meal with Rufus. Tom's stomach burned with hunger and he figured he might even have pie. When he went into the saloon, he saw Louie talking to one of the customers and he waited near the door to be seated.

The owner saw him and waved him over. Tom looked at the customer with no recognition. "Will he be joining us?" the young man asked.

"Just sit down already," the gravelly-voiced man insisted.

Tom was shocked. His father had gotten a haircut, shaved the beard, left a full moustache, and had on clean, new clothing. "Damn," the young man said as he sat down.

He couldn't believe the transformation in the man. While he looked all of his 43 years, he appeared like someone you'd see in the city. That was, except for his weathered face and scarred knuckles. They told the story of a hard, wild life of a mountain man, as did the now visible scar on his neck.

"Should we start with a drink?" Rufus asked.

"That would be fine," Tom replied. The two of them were very polite, skirting around the real issue. They were father and son.

While they had a drink and enjoyed a hardy midday meal, Rufus told Tom about meeting Caleb and about the cattle drive. Right now, knowing Caleb was one thing they had in common.

While the two ate apple pie and had coffee, Rufus asked Tom what his plans were. The young man replied, "I am hoping to join some freighters and get back to St. Louis. I know my mother is worried about me."

The mountain man toyed with his dessert and replied, "Or you could send your mother a letter and spend the winter here in the west."

A funny feeling went through the young man. That was something he'd never considered. All Tom knew about his father was that he was a hard-drinking, rough-and-tumble mountain man. The young man had already gone through a frontier winter, and he remembered the long days and cold nights.

To put off making any decision, Tom said, "I will think about it. First I have to talk to the freighters."

The mountain man nodded his agreement. The truth of what he'd suggested came from not wanting to spend the winter alone. The older Rufus got, the more difficult the long winters had become. If nothing else, there was somebody to talk to, and someone he could tell, "It's your turn to light the fire," while he was snug under his blankets.

Tom placed the small package onto the table. "I didn't get to give this to you at the tavern." The mountain man slid it closer and opened it. The amulet was green, with some kind of ragged line through it. Rufus placed the leather cord with the amulet around his neck.

"I missed the feel of the first one your grandmother made me. This feels just right," the mountain man said.

Louie came over and offered the two men another drink, but Rufus held up his hand. "None for me right now. I want to keep a clear head."

The young man also shook his head no. He needed to find the freighters. With the amulet around his father's neck, Tom suddenly felt an urgency to be on his way. Excusing himself, the young man left Rufus and Louie at the table with the bottle.

Walking by the wagons in front of the fort, Tom wondered how the men driving them survived the winter. The canvas bonnets on the wagons wouldn't hold any heat and they would freeze. Their oxen had been driven out onto the prairie to graze. A few men stood around the wagons smoking pipes or chewing while they killed time.

The main gate was wide open. In the courtyard stood four freight wagons that had been pulled by mules. The goods they'd brought in were being unloaded, much of them winter supplies that would be sold from the trading post. A man Tom didn't know was taking the bearskin down to be packed for shipping.

He saw another with some papers talking to the trading post owner, Sven. Tom guessed that he was the leader of the freighters. The young man waited until they'd finished their conversation and for the freighter to come pass him.

"Will this caravan be going back east before the snow?" Tom called to the man.

"Before or during," the man said. "As long as the snow ain't too deep, we keep hauling freight."

"I am looking for a way to get back to St. Louis," Tom told him. "I have my own horses."

"If you ain't going to need them in St. Louis, I'd recommend you sell them here and ride on one of the wagons," the man told him.

Thinking about what he carried in his packs, Tom figured that it would be better to keep them on his own horse. "I'll be needing them in St. Louis."

"No cost to ride along, unless you're needing us to carry feed for the animals. They won't get time to graze," the freighter said.

"I'll pay for you to carry feed," Tom said.

There it was. He'd made the arrangements to go back to St. Louis. From there he'd take a steamboat back to New Orleans and should be home before Christmas. He'd look up his father this evening, and if he wasn't too drunk to understand, Tom would tell him goodbye. He'd also tell him that he hoped to see him in New Orleans someday.

A feeling of loss went through the young man as he headed into the trading post to pick up some items he'd need for the trip. Tom wasn't sure what he'd expected when he met his father. Was it the look of joy and hugs that he had wanted from Rufus?

The mountain man had acknowledged that he believed Tom when he said he was his son. Maybe what he got was all he should have expected. His father had cleaned up for the meal. With winter coming on and to have removed the beard was a serious gesture.

Selecting a few things, Tom placed them onto the counter. Sven came over and began tallying them up. "I heard you ask about going east with the freighters," the owner said, making conversation.

"Yes," Tom said. "I guess they leave in the morning."

"You best be here damn early," the owner told him. "They'll be on their way by daylight and won't be waiting for any laggers."

Suddenly, Tom asked, "How long have you known Rufus?"

"Ten, no, maybe 15 years," Sven replied. "I used to trap and would see him at rendezvous."

"What kind of man is he?" the young man asked.

"He's for most part a mountain man," the owner said, finishing up the tally. "They live hard and play hard. There ain't many of them around anymore. They been replaced by buffalo hunters and emigrants heading west."

The answer that Tom was looking for wasn't forthcoming from the owner. Sven said, "$5 for the stuff." He began to put them into a grain bag while Tom dug out a coin from his possible bag.

Taking the bag, the young man thanked the owner and started out of the trading post. Then he turned back and asked, "Is Rufus a good man?"

There was a pause as Sven looked at Tom. "If you're asking if he'd be a good father, I can't tell you. All I know is that he was a good partner to those he trapped with."

The young man blushed and turned to leave. He should have known that the owner would have heard about Rufus being his father. Word of something like that would fly around the residents of the fort. As Tom walked toward the livery, he started thinking about the things he'd need to do before leaving.

Tom wanted to see Rufus one more time. The gold had to be packed onto the bay so it wouldn't be obvious to the freighters. He had purchased winter clothing while at Fort Hall and should be all set there. Then he realized he'd be best off sleeping in the livery. Time would be lost packing up at the boarding house come morning.

Kenny was cleaning stalls when he got to the livery. "Let me know what I owe you," Tom called to him. "I'll be leaving with the freighters in the morning. One other thing, I'd like to sleep here tonight."

"Rufus, your father, stopped by a bit ago to see if you were here," the hostler told him. "Said he had something for you."

"I was planning to see him tonight," Tom replied. "He can give me whatever it is then. Will you have coffee done before daylight in the morning?"

"Always do," Kenny said. "I'll have your horses fed and watered also."

The hostler unlocked the tack room and Tom spent nearly two hours going through his packs and deciding how he could pack the gold. The gold he'd received from the cattle drive would set him up quite well in New Orleans. The young man hadn't decided what type of business he was going to buy, but he planned to purchase something that would assure that his mother and grandmother could live comfortably in their declining years.

Finally, the packs were ready. It wouldn't take much time loading them onto the bay. He had a wool coat that would keep him warm, and a rabbit fur hat to protect his head and ears. The choppers and liners for his hands made gripping things a little clumsy, but Tom figured he'd only be holding his reins and the lead rope. The Colt and his canteen would be under the coat, and his rifle would be in the saddle scabbard.

The freighters were going to Westport, Missouri and the trip would take just under three weeks. Tom would have another week of travel alone to get to St. Louis. With the packs ready, the young man began to feel anxious to get started. The search for his father had been long and arduous. Now it was time to return to New Orleans.

The young man settled up with Kenny and the hostler offered to get Tom's stuff from the boarding house. The young man smiled. Things were coming together. "I have two more days paid at the boarding house. If Louie gives it back, you can keep it for helping me."

Now Tom had just one more thing to do. Find his . . . say goodbye to his father. He was about to ask Kenny where he'd guess Rufus would be when a man appeared in the open bay doorway. "I got prong horn roasting on the fire and a pot of coffee," Rufus said. "I figured you could enjoy a mountain man's meal before you go."

Looking up, a smile came to the young man's face. "I would like that very much."

Leaving Kenny to collect his things, Tom walked with his father toward a rundown cabin. In front there was a fire going and the hind quarter of a prong horn roasting over it. A coffee pot sat on a rock next to the flames, and a blackened frying pan sat warming near the fire.

There were two stools near the fire pit and the two men took a seat. Rufus said, "I stopped at the fort looking for you and was told that you signed up with the freighters to go east."

"I have," Tom replied. "Their not charging me anything except for feed for the horses."

"Son-of-a-bitches," the mountain man snorted. "You got a rifle and your own horse?" he asked.

"I do," Tom told him.

"The bastards should be paying you as a guard," Rufus said. "If some restless braves or road agents come after the mules or goods, they are going to expect you to help defend them."

Rufus continued to mutter as he mixed up some frying pan bread and sliced side meat into the hot pan. "I didn't think to offer being a guard," Tom said, watching how quickly his father put together the bread.

With the side meat snapping in the frying pan and juice from the hind quarter sizzling as it dripped onto the coals, Rufus put a couple of tin plates to heat near the fire. "The prong horn is done. All I need to do is give the bread a flip to brown the other side."

Blacken would have been a more correct word. The fire was hot and the grease from the side meat was smoking. Sliding the blackened frying pan from the fire, Rufus shook his burnt hand and cussed. Then he said, "It's time to eat."

Slabs of meat from the young prong horn were juicy and tender, and the crisp side meat and bread were tasty. The two men sat with their plates on their laps and used their knives to eat the meal, wiping their greasy fingers onto their clothes.

With a good portion of the hind quarter eaten and the frying pan empty, Rufus poured the remaining grease into the fire. "That was very good," Tom said.

"I taught Caleb how to make frying pan bread, and I assume he made some for you in your travels" his father said.

"He did," Tom replied. "It wasn't as good as yours."

"It couldn't have been too much different," Rufus told him. "Maybe the company made it taste better."

They sat drinking their coffee, the fire warming the front, while their backs felt the coolness of the early evening. Rufus continued to ask Tom about his mother and kept commenting on how his looks and movements reminded him of her.

As darkness descended around them and the fire burnt down, the chill of the late fall could be felt. "I wish we'd met sooner and gone hunting," Rufus told his son. "I would have enjoyed a few nights around the fire with you."

"We have this meal to remember," Tom said. "I best turn in. I got to be up early or they'll leave me behind."

"You might want to mention some guard pay," Rufus said. "Tell them I told you to ask."

Tom stood up and reached out to shake hands. His father had a firm grip and held on for a couple of seconds. "Have a safe trip, son," he said. Then he added, "I got something for you."

Going into the cabin, he got it and handed a heavy canvas bag to the young man. "There is something for your mother in there also. Don't look at it now. Wait for daylight."

Heading back into the dark toward the livery with the bag, Tom had the feeling that the goodbye hadn't been enough. In the same instance, he'd have hugged his mother. It didn't feel right to do so with the mountain man.

Kenny was still up when he got to the livery. He'd poured himself a drink and asked Tom if he wanted one. "Thank you," the young man said, "but just one."

While they sat in the feeble light of the lantern, Tom reached into the bag. He felt the softness of a fur. Taking it out, he saw that it was a tanned beaver pelt. Setting it beside him, the young man reached in again and took out a buckskin shirt. Feeling inside again, he found the britches.

"Rufus . . . my father got me some buckskins," Tom said

"They'll help keep you dry if you get rain or snow on the trip east," Kenny told him. "The beaver pelt must be to put on your saddle for a pillow."

"No, that would be for my . . . mother," the young man said, his voice cracking a little.

That night, in the darkness of the loft, Tom tried on the buckskins. To his surprise, they fit quite well. With his wool clothing and long johns under the buckskins, he'd be plenty warm for the trip. Not bothering to unroll his blanket, he lay on the hay. Tom's mind was going over meeting his father. There was no doubt that the young man's arrival had cut the mountain man's celebration short. It was something Tom knew that he should appreciate.

Rufus was starting a fire in cabin when he heard the shouts and cracking of the whips as the freighters pulled out of the fort. The mountain man wondered if he should have gone down to say one more goodbye. He had decided that goodbyes had been said last night after enjoying a meal. To have done so again would have added little to the parting.

With the flames licking around the wood in the fireplace, Rufus went outside to get his coffee pot. He suddenly froze. There, near the firepit, stood Tom, dressed in the buckskins. "You're missing your ride," Rufus said.

"There will be another one coming along," the young man replied. "In the meantime, I figured I could enjoy your cooking."

"The hell you will," Rufus said. "You'll do your share of cooking." Then he laughed and gave his son a hug.

CHAPTER NINETEEN

By November the snow had come and was two feet-deep. Once Tom got a good look at the cabin, the boarding house began to look like a good option. The moss and rags that caulked the logs were missing in many places, and blowing snow would cover the dirt floor as well as the bunks and table. There were no windows, and an open door or fireplace offered the only light.

On the west side in the back was the little house that provided a good view of the surroundings between the poorly fit vertical poles while sitting on the time-smoothed seat. A rope was tied from the cabin to one corner of the little house to hang wet clothing, or in the case of a white-out snow storm, one could feel their way along the cabin wall and then follow the rope to the little house.

The cabin itself was only 14 by 14, which left the two men in close quarters. One end had a crude loft for storing extra gear. Tom's packs and the gold were kept there. Most of the cooking was done at the fire pit, but when the weather was bad they had the fireplace. There were two bunks, a small sideboard, a small table and the two stools from the firepit.

Wind on the east side of the cabin was blocked by a head-high stack of wood. This was helpful because the double bunk was built on that side. Rufus had been using the lower one and Tom got the top one.

Memories came back of panning for gold in California. Tom had stayed in a slab shack on Hoss' claim. He and Caleb had helped the old man pan for gold until Caleb got the idea of driving cattle to California. The slab shack had done little to keep the wind out, and only a fair job on the rain. This cabin was only a step up from the shack.

The first winter storm found the two men eating a soup made with a few beans and some jerky. Rufus wiped his whiskered face with the sleeve of his shirt. "Have you ever played cards?" he asked Tom.

"Some," his son replied. "My mother frowned on card playing, and most of the places in New Orleans had men that were less-than-honest players."

"On long winter days, card playing can help the time pass," the mountain man explained. "We don't have to play for much money. Just enough to make the game interesting."

"With the fireplace going, we have enough light to read," Tom suggested. "I bet they have lots of books at the fort."

Rufus dipped his spoon into the broth and sipped it. The broth could have used more salt. His son did not know that the mountain man couldn't read, and Rufus was not going to make it known to him. A time would come when he'd find out, but the boy would know his father better by then.

With the meal done, Rufus leaned back against the wall on his stool. "Did you and Caleb do much shooting?"

"What was necessary for meat," Tom said.

"Ever have some men that you had to shoot at?" Rufus asked.

"We did," Tom replied. Without saying more, he picked up the bowls and brought them to the sideboard to clean them.

"It's too stormy to go out shooting and we ain't got no books, so how about a couple of hands of cards?" Rufus asked, trying to make his gravelly voice sound excited.

Tom sat opposite his father and watched him shuffle the cards. The deck had seen some wear and may have been missing a card or two. The mountain man dealt out a hand of five cards. Both men had some small coins and bet with them. Neither won or lost much.

"I see you've played poker before," Rufus said, studying his cards.

"I was a dealer for a while in New Orleans," Tom replied.

One of Rufus' eyebrows raised and he quickly re-appraised his son. "You know how to bottom deal?" he asked.

"I know how to do it and know how to spot it," Tom said, taking two. "I won't do it."

"So, you were a dealer," the mountain man said, raising.

Calling, Tom replied, "Mostly faro. Not many men played poker."

It was Rufus' turn to deal and he slapped the cards down. "Faro!" he exclaimed. "That's what almost got me killed!"

"Mother told me," Tom replied, looking at the scar on his father's neck. "She didn't want me to deal, but it was good money. I think that's why she sent me out to find you."

Rufus picked the deck back up. "I'd like to think she had other reasons."

For the next two hours, Tom enjoyed watching his father as they played. His expressions when he won or lost were funny, and the young man soon picked up several tells that exposed the strength of Rufus' hand.

After a few days of blowing snow, the wind stopped and the sun came out, making the area blindingly white. Bundling up, the two men walked to the fort. In the trading post the potbelly stove was almost cherry red and the roaring fire made the temperature inside tolerable.

"We need some side meat, tobacco, coffee, and some cards," Rufus called to the owner.

"I got some hard bread in on the last shipment," Sven said.

Looking over the blankets, the mountain man said, "We'll take some of the tooth dullers too."

Grabbing two blankets, Rufus walked up to the counter. Sven put the other items next to the blankets and told him $6.

Furling his brow, Rufus replied, "Kind of high, ain't it?"

"Blankets and side meat are in short supply," the owner said.

"How about the hard bread?" the mountain man asked.

Smiling, Sven said, "Got lots of them."

Tom dug into his possible bag and Rufus held up his hand. "You save your money. You'll need it for the poker hand I'm going to win with these new cards."

Being firm, Tom replied, "We split the cost of things. I don't want to be a burden, and when I win all your money you'll appreciate having the tooth dullers to keep from starving."

"Hell!" Rufus snorted. "Damn kid is talking foolish. Win me at cards."

Sven just shook his head, he took $3 from each one and put the supplies into a bag. The two men left the trading post and Rufus headed for the tavern with Tom following. Hube was working and came over with a bottle and three glasses.

Pouring each a drink, he held up his glass and said, "Here's to family."

Rufus tossed down his drink while Tom sipped his. The bartender refilled the mountain man's glass and then went back to whatever he'd been doing when they came in. "Drink up, son. Whiskey will keep us warm."

"I don't tend to drink too much," Tom told his father. "Grandmother Camille was kind of against it."

Looking at his son, Rufus said, "Them women were against having fun. Your mother didn't like cards, your grandmother didn't like drinking. What the hell did they do for fun?"

Realizing that his father didn't mean anything by it, Tom smiled and said, "All I can tell you is they seemed happy."

Staring at his unfinished drink, the mountain man said, "Probably happy putting spells on men that drank and played cards."

After visiting Hube for a bit, the two men headed back to the cabin with their purchases, which did not include a couple of bottles that Rufus had planned to get. The fire had burnt down and the cabin had a chill to it, so Tom worked at adding wood and stoking it up while Rufus put away the goods.

With it done, Rufus put on a pot of coffee. "We need some fresh meat," he said to Tom. "Come tomorrow, we should go hunting."

"Are you thinking a buffalo, or something like a prong horn?" Tom asked.

"Sort of in between," Rufus said. "There are mule deer in the cedar swamp north of here, or some mountain goats in the hills to the east."

"It's been a while since I cleaned my rifle," Tom told him. "I think I'll fire it and heat some water."

The thought caught the mountain man's attention. "That's a good idea. I'll set up a couple of blocks and we can shoot for a dollar."

"Two bits and you got a bet," Tom replied.

"Damn small bets," Rufus complained. "Okay, two bits."

A bucket of snow was packed full and set near the fireplace to start melting. Once melted some would be dumped into a 24-inch cauldron to heat. The two men went outside. Rufus grabbed two small blocks and walked north of the cabin, placing them out about 60 paces. Coming back, he had a sly grin on his face.

"I ain't put them too far, have I?" he asked.

"They're fine," Tom replied. "Any farther and I'd have been waiting all day for you to drag yourself back to shoot."

Ignoring the comment, Rufus said, "I just put them out two bit's worth."

Tom also had a Hawken. It had been converted to percussion caps some time before he'd used it on the cattle drive. "Youngsters first," Rufus said.

The young man pulled off his right chopper and brought the rifle to his shoulder. Sighting on the left block, Tom touched off the hair trigger. The lead ball sent the block skidding.

Rufus brought his Hawken up and asked, "Did you hit the block you were aiming at?" Without waiting for an answer, the mountain man fired, toppling the right block.

"It's a tie," Tom said. "No money was won or lost."

"The hell you say," Rufus replied. "We shoot until one of us takes the money."

A couple of men who heard the shots came over from the livery. Rufus reset the blocks and came back. "I fire first this time."

Again, both men hit the blocks. More onlookers showed up and betting between them started. For the next hour, the two men fired, moving the block farther after each round. Soon the blocks

353

were 120 paces away. They looked like two dots on the bright snow.

Rufus and Tom still had the two-bit bet going. Behind them the crowd was betting serious money. Twice the two men hit the blocks at 120 paces. Then, seeing that the two blocks lay exposed on the snow, Rufus suggested that they shoot at them where they were.

Both men were without hats or coats. Rufus didn't even have his choppers. Tom was feeling cold to his bones. He was determined not to let his father outshoot him. Rufus looked at his son. "You want to shoot first?"

"You can go first," Tom said, blowing on his hands.

The mountain man put the Hawken to his shoulder and brought the sight down onto the end of the block. The Hawken recoiled against his shoulder, sending the .54 caliber ball across the snowy expanse. The block moved as it was struck by the ball.

Tom loaded his rifle and rubbed his right hand against his shirt. "That's all I got to do is move it to tie?" he asked.

Rufus squinted at the target. "Just shoot already," he said.

Sighting on the end of the block, Tom touched off the back trigger. His Hawken fired, the smoke blowing toward his father. The young man saw the snow being furrowed as the ball went under the block. Whether the block moved or not, it was impossible to know. The match was over.

Cheers were heard behind them from those betting on Rufus. With his nearly numb fingers, Tom reached into his possible bag and fished out the two bits and handed them to his father. Taking the money, Rufus said, "That was damn fine shooting."

Thanking him, Tom hurried back to the warmth of the cabin. It took Rufus a bit longer, having to accept the congratulations from the admiring crowd. He even got a couple of swallows from a bottle being passed.

Entering the cabin, he saw that Tom had added wood to the fire and had poured the melted snow into the cauldron. "What say we clean these rifles and then go to Louie's for supper?"

"Do you want to cut the cards to see who buys?" Tom asked, half-serious, half-joking.

"I'll buy," Rufus told him. "You earned a meal today."

The holidays came and went without much notice. Tom had a birthday but didn't realize it had passed until weeks later. They continued to play cards for small bets. Rufus started to show Tom how to throw a knife. His hope was that the young man would get good enough to be talked into betting.

The two men were at the fort buying supplies at the end of February when there were shouts from the tavern. Sven grabbed the shotgun from behind the counter and ran out, followed closely by Rufus and Tom carrying their rifles.

A rider was spurring a horse as it galloped out of the main gate. A crowd had gathered in front of the tavern. "What the hell's going on?" Sven asked.

"The bastard lost at cards and stabbed Wilbert," a man replied.

Wilbert was one of the local residents of the fort who would do odd jobs and was a fair builder. He liked to play a few hands of cards and have a drink or two on the winter afternoons. Evidently someone was a poor looser and had used his knife on Wilbert.

Hube came out of the tavern with a club. "Where the hell did the bastard go?" he growled.

"He stole my horse and took off," one of the onlookers said. "Had my rifle and pack of supplies on it. He grabbed the reins and swung at me with the knife."

Rufus recognized the onlooker as a farmer who grew vegetables for the fort in the summer. He had a few milk cows and would sell buttermilk, butter, and cream.

"The tracks should be plain," someone shouted. "Let's go get him."

Rufus pulled Tom aside. "Let them go," he told his son. "We got nothing at stake here."

As the men headed for their horses, Rufus went into the tavern to check on the victim. A man was next to Wilbert, holding a rag against the chest wound. Hube came back in. "They're getting the doc," he said.

Rufus and Tom stood near the bar as Doc Ward came in. Hube set up two drinks near the men. The mountain man tossed his down. Tom looked at his father with disbelief. A man had been stabbed and his father was satisfied with standing by and having a drink.

Doc Ward stood up. "Give me a drink, Hube. Wilbert is dead."

The bartender came over with a drink and a rag for the doc to wipe his hands. "Does anyone know the man who stabbed him?" Ward asked.

A man near the door piped up. "His name is Culver. He come in with the wagon trains and has been playing cards regular. Louie kicked him out of his place because Culver tends to get mad when he loses."

Tom heard Hube say, "I wish the hell I'd known that."

The young man watched everyone standing around while Wilbert lay dead on the floor. It made no sense to him. Then Rufus tapped his arm. "Let's grab a few supplies and our horses."

Following his father out of the tavern, Tom wanted to ask him where they were going, but Rufus was walking too fast and it was all the young man could do to keep up. At the cabin, Rufus threw a few items into a sack and rolled up his blankets in a ground cloth. Tom did the same. Within the hour, the two men were riding north.

"I take it we're going after this Culver," Tom said to his father.

Rufus didn't answer, but looked steadily to the front. They were riding in the mixture of tracks that the makeshift posse had made. They were following the older tracks of the wood cutters for the fort. They all went to the north. An hour later they saw riders coming their way. It was the posse returning. They'd left without blankets and food, and the sun was now low in the western sky.

The leader pulled up and Rufus stopped to talk to him. "How far did you follow the tracks?" he asked.

"We lost them in the area that the wood cutters have been working," the man said. "It might have been earlier. How is Wilbert doing?"

"He died," Rufus said.

"We'll be going out again tomorrow," the man told Rufus.

"My son and I will be up and around looking for Culver. Just don't get trigger-happy and shoot us by mistake," the mountain man cautioned him.

Tom wasn't sure the man liked his father's request. The posse rode back toward the fort. "What's the plan?" the young man asked.

"Culver has gone too far from the fort to circle back. Even if he did, someone would spot him. He grabbed a horse with a few supplies but no blanket roll. I am betting he is lightly dressed. He will have to find shelter." Rufus told Tom.

"How about the rifle?" the young man asked.

"There is that," the mountain man replied. "I know of two cabins north of here that might be vacant. I doubt Culver will know of them, but they ain't too hard to spot going that way."

"What do we do if we find him?" Tom asked.

"We take him back," Rufus said. "He ain't going to want to come back and what we're carrying on our horses would be enough to help him escape to Fort Hall."

The young man asked no more questions. His father hadn't said that they would kill the man, but one way or the other, he would be coming back with them.

They rode in silence for a while and then he heard his father say, "Culver won't be shot in the back."

That didn't make Tom feel a hell of a lot better. He realized that there was a chance that Culver would shoot at them first, and just maybe there would only be one to shoot back. They were bad thoughts and he tried to push them from his mind.

After the wood cutting area, Rufus spent a long time cutting back and forth, looking at the sign. There were tracks of deer, wolves, and small game. There were no tracks of a man walking or a horse. Culver had either cut back shortly after heading north, or was on one of several trails breaking away that had been seen riding up to the cutting area.

"It's almost dark," Rufus said. "We'll set up a camp and start again at first light." He looked at the sky and clouds. "We could get snow tonight."

Tom envisioned them sleeping on the snow, huddling in their blankets. His father led them to a grove of spruce. He stopped in front of a tall tree with branches to the snow-covered ground. Swinging off the grulla, he tied it to another tree.

"Go find wood for the night," he told Tom. "Keep your eyes open and be as quiet as possible. Culver could be anywhere."

Doing his best to be quiet, the young man collected a large armload of wood and dragged a treetop back with the free hand. He saw his father working under the spruce. Placing the wood down, Tom knelt at the opening that had been made in the branches. "Wow," he said.

His father had cut the lower branches and woven them into the other boughs, creating a ceiling and walls that would stop blowing snow. The cleared branches beneath the tree left plenty of room for the two men to lay down.

The mountain man looked up at Tom. "It's quick but won't last too long. It will be fine for tonight."

A small fire was started to make coffee and fry some side meat. Rufus had Tom hide a distance from the fire in the dark and watch for any movement. "Do not look at the fire at any time," he warned. "It will give you night blindness."

Once the meal was done, Rufus called softly for Tom to come in. The young man sat near the dying fire for whatever heat it could give him. After the two men had eaten the side meat with hard bread, they pulled the saddles off the horses and tied them a short distance from the shelter.

Then, sitting near his son, he whispered, "I think we're having a better night than Culver."

Rufus offered his son some tobacco from his twist. The young man had taken to having a chew once in a while since he'd been with his father. The two men sat in the dark, listening to the night noises with a chew in their cheeks and the last of their coffee in their cups.

They were about two miles from the first cabin. Before they did any back tracking, Rufus wanted to check if Culver had found it. At the same time, if it didn't snow overnight, they would cut to the west looking for tracks.

Tom woke the next morning, surprised at how comfortable he'd been through the night. His father was already up and working on a fire. Looking out of the opening, he could see that all they'd had was a light dusting overnight.

While eating a breakfast of cold flour porridge he asked his father if last night's snow would make tracking difficult.

"We will still see yesterday's tracks," Rufus told him, "and any ones made today will be easily spotted."

A half-hour after sunrise, the two men were back on their horses and slowly riding toward the west to try and cut a trail. They had gone a mile and were about to cut back when Rufus stopped. He got off the grulla and followed a trail a ways. Then he got back onto the horse.

"This might be Culver's," he whispered. "They were made yesterday and the man was in a hurry. If he continued in this direction he will come close to the cabin, and unless he passes it in the dark, he should spot it."

The two men followed the tracks and saw where the rider had gotten off and led the horse for a while. When he'd remounted, he no longer rode fast. No doubt the horse was playing out. Suddenly, Rufus put up his hand to stop.

Swinging off the horse, he motioned for Tom to do the same. Coming close to his father, he heard him whisper, "Smoke."

Tom hadn't smelled anything. He began to wonder if as a mountain man his father's sense of smell had almost become animal-like. Then he caught a whiff of the smoke. Someone nearby had a fire going.

Leading the horses, their rifles cradled in their arms, the two men walked slowly along the tracks.

Chickadees and the crunch of the snow were the only sounds. Then they heard a door close. In the frigid winter air, sound could travel a long distance. The closing sounded like it was only a matter of feet away.

Without speaking they tied their horses to poplar saplings. Rufus had the Colt in the belt on the outside of his buckskins. Tom was wearing wool clothing and unbuttoned the coat, allowing him access to his revolver.

"I want you to stay with the horses," the mountain man whispered to his son.

Shaking his head, Tom replied, "I won't let you go alone."

Then there was the sound of an axe striking wood. Someone, maybe Culver, was nearby, cutting wood for the fire they had smelled. Rufus felt frustration. Putting his son into danger had not been part of his plan, and now the boy would not stay behind.

"We may be sneaking up on an innocent man just trying to keep warm," Rufus told Tom. "You stay behind me and shoot only if I do." The mountain man's gravelly voice had an earnestness the young man hadn't heard before.

Tom watched his father slowly move forward, his Hawken at the ready, each step soundless in the crusty snow. What the young man didn't realize was that he was seeing Rufus still-stalking his prey. The young man followed a few feet behind, placing his boots into those steps made by his father.

Then the shape of the cabin became visible through the trees. The cold air forced the smoke from the fireplace toward the ground, obscuring the view around the cabin. Rufus motioned for Tom to remain back. The young man ignored the request, not wanting his father to be alone against the possible killer.

The dark buckskins and whisker-covered face made the mountain man almost invisible as he stood motionless, squinting and searching for movement around the cabin. Using the smoke for cover, Tom moved closer to his father. The young man could not see the anger in his father's face as the mountain man heard him come up.

With the quarry so close, Rufus could not turn and send the young man away. He now felt his heart pulsing in his temples as he dealt with the danger ahead and the fear that Tom might be injured. He heard Tom move to his left to get a clearer view of the cabin. The two men were now only 50 feet from the side of the building.

Then a man appeared from the back of the cabin, his rifle up, taking aim. Rufus realized that the man was not lining up on him. Within a second of this realization, Rufus lunged toward his son as smoke from the pan flared and the rifle in Culver's hands fired.

The split-second delay typical of a flintlock was what prevented Tom from being struck by the ball as the two men crashed to the ground. Adrenalin coursed through Tom as he shoved himself free of his father. Culver was ramming another ball into the rifle. Their Hawkens had fallen, disappearing into the snow.

Tom pulled the Colt from his waistband and, sitting up, he fired two shots at the man. A ball struck the rifle being loaded, the other he didn't see. All the young man knew was that Culver went down, kicking and struggling to get back behind the cabin.

Turning, the young man saw that Rufus was sitting up, his Colt in his hand, wisps of smoke coming from the barrel. The young man got up, his revolver ready. "I think we hit him," Tom said. Then the young man knew that some shots had scored as he saw blood on the snow where the man had crawled away.

Looking toward his father, Tom froze. Rufus had gone down! Dropping near his father, Tom cried, "Did he hit you!"

"Keep your damn eyes on the cabin," Rufus growled. "The bastard might still be alive."

Almost in shock, Tom held his Colt with two more loaded chambers and moved to the left until he could see behind the cabin. He saw the man lying in the snow. "We . . . we got him," he said, his voice wavering.

"Go and make sure," Rufus said, sternly. "If he pulls a knife, put another ball in him."

Tom's legs were shaking as he followed his father's orders. As he approached the downed man, he contemplated just shooting him again so he could get back and check on his father. Kicking the man's boot, there was no response. There was a lot of blood on the snow. He had to be dead.

Hurrying back to his father, Tom almost tripped when his toe caught one of the Hawkens under the snow. "Where are you hit?" the young man asked.

Helping his father sit up, Tom saw the blood on the snow and more streaking down the back of the buckskins. "I'm going to get you into the cabin."

"Hell, I'll be alright," the mountain man replied.

"You have been shot," his son said, desperation in his voice. "We have to see how bad it is!"

Helping Rufus to his feet, Tom supported him as they walked toward the cabin. "You sure the bastard's dead?" his father asked.

"Yes," Tom said, tears of fear in his eyes. He didn't know and did not care. If the man wasn't dead yet, he'd soon bleed out and would be. His father felt terribly weak next to him.

A trail of blood drops marked their progress to the cabin door. Once inside, the warmth hit the two men. There was fire going and a pot of water heating in the fireplace. There was no bed of any kind in the cabin, but there was a table and a bench.

Helping his father to sit on the bench, Tom pulled up the buckskin shirt. The wool shirt underneath was soaked with blood. The young man slit the wool shirt and long johns with his knife, exposing the wound. Rufus had been hit near the right side and where the ball went from there, Tom didn't know.

While Tom wasn't aware of the extent of the injury, he could see blood coming from the entry wound. The young man looked around the inside of the cabin and saw nothing but the sack of supplies near the fireplace.

"Can you hold yourself up?" he asked his father.

"Hell yes I can," he growled. "Damn bad luck letting the bastard get a ball in me."

Shedding his coat, Tom cut the sleeve off his shirt. He then cut the sack into strips. Folding his shirt sleeve, he placed it against the wound and wrapped the strips of the sack around his father's waist. Tom was worried that the ball might have gone through the ribs and hit vital organs inside.

The strongest feeling the young man had was guilt. His father had told him to stay back and Tom had not. When the man had aimed to fire, his father had knocked Tom aside and taken the shot instead. If he had just stayed back, Rufus might have gotten a shot off before Culver.

Pulling the buckskin shirt back down over the wound, Tom wiped his hands on his pants. Then noticing a cup near the fireplace, he scooped warm water from the pot and gave it to his father. "I want you to drink this," Tom said.

"Ain't there some damn whiskey in the place?" Rufus growled.

"No, father," the young man said. "Culver didn't have time to buy any when he ran from the tavern. Now drink."

The mountain man had bled a lot less than Tom had thought. Blood in water or on snow appears to be much more than there actually is. All the young man knew was that there was damn lots of it around.

"I'll get our horses and we can head back for the fort," Tom said.

"Find Culver's horse and load him on before the damn man gets too stiff," Rufus told his son.

"Hell, with him!" Tom exclaimed. "He can rot where he lays."

"There will be folks at the wagon train he might mean something to," his father said. "It wouldn't be right leaving him here."

Tom's throat was aching and he was fighting back the tears that wanted to come. Why the hell his father wanted the body brought back made no sense to him. Leaving the cabin, he found the man's horse tied in some trees. The saddle and blanket lay in the snow nearby.

Shaking the snow from the blanket, the young man got the animal saddled and led it around the back of the cabin. Culver still lay were Tom had seen him. The last thing the young man wanted to do was handle the dead man. The saddle had a rope on it, and after loading the rapidly stiffening body over the saddle he tied Culver's hands and feet together.

The young man had noticed three wounds in the man as he dragged him to the horse: One in the right shoulder, one in the upper chest, and another in the lower left above the man's belt. Tom knew that one had to be his. He could have killed the man. At the moment, with his father wounded in the cabin, he felt no remorse.

Leading the horse to the front of the cabin, Tom looked in, fearing his father would be lying on the dirt floor. He was not. Rufus was sitting on the bench finishing the warm water. "Did you get him on his horse?" his father asked.

"I did," Tom replied. "We hit him three times."

"Damn good thing we hit him," the mountain man said. "Saved him from a hanging."

"I guess we did," Tom said, his voice weaker than he meant it to be.

"You damn right we did," Rufus said. "Now get our horses and don't forget to find our rifles."

Tom filled their canteens with the warm water and made sure their rifles barrels weren't filled with dirt or snow. After helping his father onto the grulla, he shut the cabin door. He had noticed that this cabin was in better shape than the one Rufus had. He did not mention this to his father.

It was late morning when they left the cabin and it would be dark before they got back to the fort. Tom led the dead man's horse and rode alongside his father. The mountain man was in a mood and the young man didn't dare keep asking him if he was okay.

Five miles from the fort, the two men met up with the posse returning from a second day of searching for Culver. They were quite pleased to learn that the man had been killed. One of the men took the reins of the dead man's horse from Tom. The young man watched as his father sat hunched over in the saddle.

The moon had come up, casting its muted light on the snow-covered landscape, making the view quite beautiful. This was missed by Tom as he worried about Rufus. He was numb inside as they rode until he finally saw the fort in the distance. His father was still in the saddle, but had said hardly a word since they'd left the cabin.

They rode into the fort and straight to Doc Ward's office. The doc was in his night clothes and grumbled at being disturbed. With the help of two of the men, Tom got Rufus off the horse and then they carried the complaining man into the doctor's office.

"Put him on the bed in the back," the doc said.

After placing Rufus onto the bed, the two men who helped were off to celebrate bringing the killer in. Tom sat on an uncomfortable chair across the room from the bed that the doctor used to work on his father. At one point the doctor closed a curtain in front of the bed.

The room was warm and had the smell of lye. After a bit, Tom removed his coat and hat. He looked down at his hands and saw that they were still covered with blood. He looked around the room. There was no place to wash them.

Doc Ward worked on the mountain man for an hour before sliding back the curtain. Rufus was lying on his back and covered with a clean sheet and a blanket. Tom wasn't sure if he was sleeping or not.

The doc went to his stove and added some wood. He then put on the coffee pot to heat some water. "He should be alright," the doc told Tom. "The rifle must have been loaded with ball and buck. It was a buckshot that hit Rufus. It went in and traveled under the skin and stopped just before the spine. If it had been the ball that hit him, he'd probably be crippled now."

"He shoved me over to protect me," Tom said.

"Damn good thing he did. That load would have torn you apart," the doc said.

"He told me to stay back . . ." the young man started to explain.

"How it happened doesn't matter," the doc told him. "He's your father and a father will protect his son. The coffee should be done soon and, in the meantime, I'll get us a bucket of water so we can wash the blood from our hands."

Rufus wasn't long mending and was as grouchy as ever during the process. Tom found out that Culver had gambled all his claim money away and had taken it out on Wilbert. By the sound of his friends, he wouldn't be missed. Whose shot killed the man would never be known, but the mountain man claimed he got two into the man. Maybe again he was protecting his son.

CHAPTER TWENTY

The winter dragged on, confining the men to the cabin for days at a time as wind driven storms blew through. The two men learned a lot about each other over the long winter months. Rufus found that his son was a skilled card player, and Tom learned that his father couldn't read.

Tom did learn how to make snowshoes and how to stay warm while hunting for meat. The two men made many of their meals at the fire pit in front of the cabin and Tom became quite good at putting a meal together with meager supplies. The young man learned to spit as well as his father, but couldn't hold a candle to him when it came to knife throwing.

The young man heard stories about his father's years in the mountains and Rufus enjoyed listening to books that his son read in the light of the fireplace. Every day wasn't bliss, being cooped up in the small cabin, but the two did become close during the time. Rufus liked Tom to talk about his mother and New

Orleans, yet he never once mentioned that he'd like to go back sometime.

Rufus learned that Tom wanted to hunt a buffalo, and in March the mountain man suggested they go. It turned out that several people needed meat, and after talking about the hunt around the fort and the Buffalo Hide Saloon, the hunting party ended up being comprised of twelve men and five wagons.

Southwest of the fort was a sheltered valley that ran for several miles and often had buffalo. The wagons headed in that direction in high spirits, looking forward to the hunt. The animals would be lean this time of year, but the meat was needed and the hides would be prime.

The mountain man was less than happy when he realized that two of the wagons had raised sides to carrying hides. While he grumbled to Tom about the stink of hide wagons, in the cool March weather the smell should be bearable. The remaining three wagons only intended on taking four or five buffalo, depending on their size.

Three days out from the fort the wagons cut through the spring snow and reached the valley. They were not disappointed. Several hundred animals were still in the valley after spending the winter. Rufus and Tom rode ahead of the wagons, looking for a good place to set up camp. Finding a stream with open water, the mountain man sent his son back to lead the wagons there.

The two wagons with the hide hunters continued by, waving and wishing the rest good hunting. The men with the three wagons figured that it would only take about two days to shoot and process their buffalo. The hides would be sold at the fort to offset the cost of the venture.

Tom could hardly sit still the morning of the hunt. "I'm going to look for the biggest bull in the herd for my shot," he told his father.

"Then you best have a good set of teeth to chew the tough meat that you'll get from the bull," Rufus told him. "I would recommend you keep to the younger ones."

Disappointed, the young man decided that if a big bull got in front of a tender cow, he'd have to take the one he could hit. While they got ready to hunt, in the distance the men heard the steady din of rifle fire. Mentally, Rufus kept count. "They shot near forty buffalos," he said.

"Forty," Tom said, his eyes shining. "That's a lot of meat."

"It's lots of tongues and hides," his father said. "The meat will rot where they fell."

It was decided that the men would shoot three buffalo today so they could figure how many more would be needed to fill the wagons. Tom was elected to shoot the first buffalo. The young man rode his sorrel closer to the grazing animals.

The mountain man looked over the buffalo with him. Rufus pointed to one he thought Tom should shoot. "It's kind of small," the young man said. Laughing, Rufus told him to pick the one he liked.

Tom chose a nice-sized bull. It wasn't the biggest, but it was larger than the one his father had chosen. Pulling the Hawken to full-cock, Tom pulled the set trigger. He looked to see if the others were ready. He was surprised to see that he was the only one shooting. Bringing the Hawken back to his shoulder, the young man figured the others would have to chase the running herd after he shot.

Touching off the hair trigger, the Hawken spouted smoke and fire, sending the killing ball at the buffalo. The wooly animal sidestepped and turned before sinking to the ground. "I got it!" Tom said in excitement.

Rufus slapped him on the back, "Good shot, son."

Then a look of surprise passed over the young man's face. "Why didn't the others run?"

"They're a big animal with few natural enemies," the mountain man explained. "They don't fear the sound of a rifle. Some day they might, but right now as long as good shots are taken, the herd will continue grazing, unconcerned."

Two more shots were taken, bringing a total of three buffalo down. One of them was surrounded by others from the herd and the men had to wait until they moved off before heading down to do the skinning.

The buffalo was the largest animal Tom had ever skinned and it was an exhausting task. The wagons were driven down and the meat was loaded onto canvas placed on the bottom of the wagon boxes. After the butchering was done, Tom went to the stream and attempted to wash the fat and blood from his hands. That night some tongue and liver were made for their supper.

He asked his father, "How many days will it take for the hide hunters to skin all the buffalos they shot?"

"Most of the day, I suppose," Rufus told him.

"They'll skin them all today?" Tom asked in surprise.

"Each morning they kill as many as they can skin," his father told him. "The rest of the day is skinning and fleshing."

The next day, two more were shot and by early afternoon the wagons were loaded and ready to head back to the fort. Rufus asked Tom to stay back with him. The two men rode west out of the valley. The day was cool, but sunny, and the air was fresh.

The young man pointed ahead of them. "Lots of piles of snow ahead of us."

"Those are buffalo that have been skinned," Rufus told him.

Looking at all the carcasses, Tom asked, "Don't they use any of the meat?"

"The money is in the hides," his father said. "I been told there are more buffalo than hunters can kill in this country."

The two men rode past dozens of skinned buffalo on their way out of the valley. Tom could not grasp why the meat wasn't being used, until the thought about the cattle drive in California when Caleb had talked about the hide sheds in San Diego. At least with the cattle they rendered the carcass for the fat as well as taking the hide.

An end-of-winter celebration was organized by the fort with roast buffalo, vegetables from the root cellars and desserts made by women residing at the fort and from the wagon train encampments. Louie provided whiskey along with the tavern at the fort.

Rufus commented that the cut for both was well over two to one.

As the sun went down, the celebration was declared over and most of the attendees headed back to their homes. Rufus and Tom remained with some former trappers who reminisced about the rendezvous and how much tamer the celebration had been. The young man looked at two men who lay passed out in the mud near where the temporary bar had been.

"It looks like some men drank like it was a rendezvous," he said.

"Some men you can give sugar water and they will drink their selves stupid," Rufus snorted.

As the father and son headed for the cabin in the dark, Tom noticed that his father was staggering just a bit. *Good thing they weren't serving sugar water*, he thought.

With the snow melting and grass beginning to sprout on the hillsides, the wagon trains pulled out on their way to riches in California. Rufus shook his head. "They're a month too early. They're climbing in elevation and there ain't enough grass for the animals."

Enough grass or not, the wagons kept coming from the east, staying only long enough to resupply and then they were off, leaving an endless, muddy trail as the frozen prairie thawed. The first of many freight caravans arrived at the fort with blankets, beans, rice, coffee, tobacco, and other necessary items for those going west.

Spring rains began to fall, washing away any sign of winter. The two men were sitting in the cabin with the door wide-open, watching the inclement weather. "Three days of rain ain't slowed the stream of wagons one bit," Rufus noted.

"I saw the freighters come in," Tom told him. "They'll be heading back tomorrow, and I plan to be with them."

"If you wait another month, we can go hunting and maybe wet a few traps for beaver," the mountain man suggested.

"Another month, or even two, would make little difference," Tom said. "I can't stay out here with you, and it's time I headed for New Orleans."

Rufus didn't reply as he looked down at his worn boots. The mountain man had nothing to offer his son that would keep him in the west. The two men were too different. Rufus could survive just fine away from folks most of the year. One or two trips that offered whiskey and the comfort of a willing woman was all he needed.

Looking at his son, the mountain man realized that the young man was just starting out and life in the mountains offered no future. Any years spent would be years wasted. It would be hard to say whether having his father around during those years would've made up for the loss of being with family in New Orleans that he'd miss.

The mountain man made his decision. It would cause him to miss the early trapping season, but it would give him a few more weeks with his son. "The trip back east has its dangers, and I want to go with you to make sure you get to St. Louis safely," Rufus told Tom.

Without hesitation, his son replied, "I would like that."

Like one, the two men got up and headed through the rain towards the fort. "I hope the freighters let us go with them," Tom said.

"Let us go with them, hell," Rufus replied. "I figure we can get paid as guards to make sure they get back to Independence."

Grinning, the young man saw the determination on his father's face as the rain dripped off his beard. The two men walked into the fort and saw the freighters' leader in an earnest discussion with Sven.

The two men stepped up onto the porch out of the rain and listened. As it turned out the freighter had lost some men once he'd gotten to the fort. They heard him say, "The damn bastards barely stopped their teams when they jumped off the wagon and joined up with wagons going west."

Sven said, "I understand your problem, but I don't know of anyone that would drive a team back for you. I have enough damn trouble keeping wood cutters for the fort."

Pulling Tom aside, Rufus asked, "Have you ever driven a mule team?"

"I've driven horses," the young man replied. "It can't be too much different."

With that, the mountain man butted into the men's conversation. "Tom and I can handle mules. If the price is right, we'll drive two wagons back for you."

The leader, whose name was Gunther, looked at Rufus and then Tom. "You say the kid can handle mules?"

"Handle them, hell," Rufus replied. "He can handle them better than me."

The young man stood back while his father made the deal. Their food, plus grain for their horses, would be included. The pay offered was $2 a day, but by the time the dickering was done, the two men would get $3 a day.

"Hey, kid," Gunther said, "Turn that team around and drive it out of the fort. Then bring the next one in."

The young man looked at the leader and said, "The name's Tom." Climbing up onto the seat, the young man grabbed the reins of the eight mules and released the brake of the wagon. Rufus watched as his son swung the team around and drove the wagon out. A short time later, Tom drove the second, heavily laden wagon into the fort.

Hopping down, Tom walked over to his father as local men began unloading the wagon. "Damn glad he didn't ask me to do that," Rufus said. "It's been 25 years since I drove a mule team."

Then Rufus walked over to the leader. "Our pay starts today."

There were two things that made Rufus regret signing on. One was that three of the wagons were carrying buffalo hides. Second, part of a teamster pay was caring for his mules. They had to be unhitched, fed, and watered every evening. Come morning it was repeated again as they were hitched to the wagon. Rufus hadn't thought it through, and wasn't happy taking care of his team and having the smell of hides around. The animals were put on a picket line between the wagons in an attempt to prevent theft. Five wagons comprised the caravan and Gunther always led the way.

Each day they passed wagons heading west. The men driving the oxen would shout questions to the freighters, asking about the trail ahead. On the second day they saw Chimney Rock to the south. It was a popular stopping place for wagon trains, but the freight wagons continued by. The freighters reached Ash Hollow early on the fifth day. Both Rufus and Tom had come this way by horse, but now, looking at the 300 feet-long climb seemed an insurmountable obstacle.

Gunther addressed the drivers, saying, "We rest the mules most of the day. Then using a double team, we'll take the first wagon up before dark. We'll bring them back down and spend tomorrow bringing the rest of the wagons up."

Throughout the day, while resting the mules, Rufus and Tom watched the wagons being lowered down the hill using ropes. One wagon broke loose and careened to the bottom, sending the load and parts of the wagon flying. Gunther said that when traveling west he would take an alternate route to avoid the hill. It added four to five days onto the trip and had dry stretches, but when going east he'd found that double teaming the wagons on the hill worked.

Late afternoon, 16 mules were hitched to a wagon and it was hauled to the top of the plateau that ran between the North and South Platte Rivers. The next day the remaining wagons were hauled to the top and the caravan continued east.

The only other challenge the trip gave the caravan was crossing the South Platte River once they descended from the plateau. Gunther had done this several times and even though the river bottom would change after each spring flood, he had found a manageable crossing.

After 17 exhausting days of travel, the wagons pulled into Westport, Missouri. Rufus wasted little time getting his and Tom's pay. The young man had already gotten his packs off the freight wagon and onto his bay. With his saddle on the sorrel, he led the animals away from the freight wagons.

A man came by and asked him if he was joining a wagon train west. "I just come from there," Tom told him. "I'll be leaving for St. Louis tomorrow."

"You wouldn't be willing to sell your horses?" the man asked. "I can get you good money for them and a ride to St. Louis."

The man was persistent and finally Rufus came with his horses and ran the fellow off. "Horse flesh is in short supply," Rufus said. "We best keep ours close."

"I figure it will be about a week and a half to St. Louis," Tom said. "The freighters will be going back to Fort Laramie in three days. I may as well head for St. Louis, and you can make some money on the way back."

"Not so fast, son," the mountain man said. "I got someplace that I want to show you before you go back to New Orleans. It's a place a good friend of mine is buried."

"I really don't want to drag these goodbyes out," Tom replied. "I know you want to spend time with me and I do appreciate it, but I got to get back home."

Rufus felt a pang go through him at the words. He wished that his son's home was wherever he was. Feeling a bit desperate, the mountain man said, "It ain't but a couple of miles off the route. Three days later you would be in St. Louis along the Salt Lick Trail."

"You'll miss going back with the freighters," Tom said, feeling awkward seeing his father almost . . . begging.

"There's always a freight train going west," Rufus said. "Maybe I'll lead a wagon train."

Forcing a smile, Tom replied, "I'd like to see your friend's grave. Would that be Walter?"

He saw his father's eyes light up. "Yes, it would. Never was there a better friend."

The two men rode east toward Franklin leading their packhorses. It was little enough to do for his father, Tom figured.

Four days later the two men rode into Franklin. They had just crossed the Missouri River and Rufus had pointed out where Walter's house was. They rode to the livery that Walter had owned. It had not changed much. The new owner, Charlie, was living in the lean-to on the side. He was sitting in front of the bay doors when the two came up.

Standing, the owner asked, "Will you be needing a place to put up your horses?"

"We will," Rufus said in his gravelly voice. "The animals have come a way and need grain and grooming."

"Rufus! Dang if it ain't you," Charlie said. "I would recognize your voice anywhere."

The mountain man swung off the grulla. "This here is my son, Tom."

The hostler looked up at the young man and hesitated for a minute. "It's a pleasure to meet you."

While they were putting the horses in stalls, Charlie asked Rufus, "Did you leave his mother back west?"

"His mother is Cajun and does voodoo in New Orleans," Rufus replied. "He got the knack from her and could put a spell on you that would make what's left of your teeth fall out overnight."

The hostler covered his mouth and said, "Oh my."

Laughing, the mountain man went over to Tom. He saw that the young man was carrying some of his packs. "You can just leave them here," his father said. "Nobody will bother them."

Hanging onto his packs, Tom led the way out of the livery. "I can't leave them," he said.

"What do you mean you can't?" Rufus replied. "You mean you won't."

Smiling, Tom told him, "I can't and won't because I have eight pounds of gold in them."

A look of surprise came over the mountain man. "Hell, I was just about to offer you some money to get home on."

Looking around, Tom saw that they were alone on the street. Still keeping his voice low, he told his father about receiving the gold from the cattle drive.

"We better take that stuff to the bank," Rufus told his son. "They got a decent safe and are holding my money."

"You keep your supply money here in Franklin?" Tom asked, familiar with others holding his father's money.

"Some is mine that Walter made me save. The rest is his," the mountain man said. "He had no kin around here and left it to me."

There was a sad look on Rufus' face as his thoughts went to his deceased partner. Noticing this, Tom realized that money didn't replace the feeling of loss in his father. The bank was owned and run by Talbert Wallace. He was a robust man with thinning hair. His face lit up when he saw Rufus.

"I am glad to see you back in Franklin," the banker said. "Did you want to add to your account?"

Shaking his head, no, Rufus replied, "This is my son, Tom. He'll be in town a few days and needs to keep some gold in your safe."

"Always happy to have a new customer," Talbert said. "I'll need some information."

"It will only be for a day or two," Tom said. "I hope that won't be a problem."

Obviously disappointed, the banker forced a smile and said, "None at all."

With the gold safely in the bank, the two men headed for a café for a midday meal. While they ate the special of the day, Rufus said, "I was hoping you would stick around a little longer."

Moving his spoon through his stew, looking for another piece of meat, Tom avoided Rufus' eyes. "I've been gone from New Orleans for a long time." Tom said, then he looked at his father. "I have enjoyed our time together and I will never forget it, but it's time for me to go."

Leaving the café, Rufus took Tom to see Walter's grave. It had an impressive stone with his name and the date he died. It also had 'A Mountain Man and Friend' carved below the name. Both men stood for some time, hats in hand with their own thoughts. Before leaving Tom was moved to say a few words over the grave. It appeared to be appreciated by his misty-eyed father.

At the mountain man's suggestion, each man got a room at the hotel. Tom figured that his father wanted time alone to think about his old partner. Plus, as it turned out, they both had plenty of money.

Sitting in the room alone, Rufus could hear the tinny sound of the piano calling to him from the hotel across the street. The Frontier House had been his second favorite place in Franklin. The first was Tillies. Knowing that his son would be gone in the next day or so, the mountain man was getting that familiar feeling of loss that he'd had too many times before. Whiskey didn't fill the loss, but it dulled it until he sobered up. Getting up, Rufus headed down the stairs following the music.

Tom got up the next morning and washed up. He thought he looked older in the mirror. The young man needed a shave and haircut. Running his fingers through his shoulder-length hair, he figured that he'd do that on the steamboat.

Putting the rest of his gear and his rifle under the bed, Tom stepped into the hall and knocked on his father's door. There was no answer. Waiting a moment, he knocked again. Giving up, the young man headed down the stairs. Now he knew why his father had suggested two rooms. He'd no doubt gone out for a few drinks.

Reaching the bottom, the young man stopped. Sitting in the lobby was his father, a broad smile on his face. "They've got a fine breakfast here at the hotel," Rufus said. "I've been waiting for you to get up and join me."

By all appearances, the mountain man looked clear-eyed and far from hungover. "I knocked on your door, and when you didn't answer I thought you might have gone out last night."

Looking a bit sheepish for a moment, Rufus replied, "I got to the bottom of the stairs and the piano was calling me. Then I realized something."

A young girl came to the table with coffee and sweet breads, stopping the conversation. "We have eggs this morning if you'd like them."

"We'll take the works," the mountain man said, smiling at the girl.

"What is it you realized?" Tom asked as the young girl headed for the kitchen.

"It's that letter you sent to your mother," his father replied.

Tasting the sweet bread, Tom then sipped the coffee. Wiping his mouth with the cloth napkin, he said, "The letter."

His father had a mouthful and the young man sat waiting for an explanation. Swallowing, Rufus replied, "She got a letter saying that you found me and you gave me this amulet. Now if you don't get back to

New Orleans she will blame me for not watching over you."

The food forgotten, Tom said, "I don't think she would blame you. Besides, what difference would it make if she did?"

"What if when I get a little older and decide to come out of the mountains, and I go back to New Orleans?" he asked. "I'd be coming into a hornet's nest, and she'd put such a spell on me that I'd never get over it."

"You don't believe in spells," his son told him.

"I sure as hell would then," Rufus replied matter-of-factly. "To make sure that I am free to come and go from New Orleans whenever I want, I am going to make sure you get all the way there safely."

"Nothing could happen between here and there," his son told him.

The eggs and ham arrived and the men watched the young girl place them onto the table. "I'll get you some more coffee," she said, leaving them alone again.

Picking up his knife and fork, the mountain man hushed his voice. "I ain't ever told you this, but I was attacked right on the pier in St. Louis and had to kill the man."

"Really?" Tom said, questioning the revelation. Then he asked, "Did you know if it was one of the men sent to kill you?"

Waving the hand holding the knife, Rufus replied, "It don't matter. It still happened."

The two men ate in silence for a bit, Tom pondering what had just been said. Then he realized that his father coming to New Orleans was a big step for the mountain man. Looking at his father's whisker-covered face, he said, "I want to thank you for coming with me. I will feel a lot safer."

"There you go," Rufus said, shoving the last of his eggs into his mouth.

* * *

Leaving Franklin along the Boones Lick Road, the mood was light between the two men. Much to Talbert's dismay both had closed their accounts at the bank. Rufus told his son that he planned to put the money into an account in New Orleans. The young man was shocked at how much money his father had considering what a meager lifestyle he lived in the west.

Three days later, Rufus once again saw St. Louis. After years of growth, little of the city looked familiar to the mountain man. They rode by the docks, which were still stacked with goods coming and going.

Tom was excited and looked forward to being back on a steamboat. Dressed in the dirty buckskins and wool clothing wouldn't do on the boat. After they arranged for berths and the horses on a morning boat, it was time to scrub the frontier off and shop for new clothing.

Early the next morning, the two men arrived at the waterfront, leading their horses. Rufus watched the activity of loading and unloading the steamboats. Bails of buffalo hides were swung onto the boats using a boom. While much of the heavy work was done with winches and hoists, there was still a steady stream of men carrying cargo on and off the boats.

A man came and got their horses while Rufus and Tom were directed to a forward gangplank. Memories of his hasty trip away from New Orleans came to mind. He had boarded that vessel with only a sea bag containing a few necessary items and a pistol. His quarters had been aft of the boilers, with a hammock for his bed. Rufus had shoveled coal into the boilers to earn a few dollars on his way upriver.

Now, after boarding, he and Tom were directed to a stateroom with a comfortable bed and several amenities to make the trip more enjoyable. They were told that the captain was holding a get-together on the upper deck, with food and drink prior to the boat's departure.

After a four-day trip living in luxury on a steamboat paddling down the river to New Orleans, the two men stepped onto the wharf. It had been 25 years since Rufus had left to escape those who wanted to kill him. The smell and feel remained the same, but the look had changed as the city had grown.

Rufus and Tom looked good in their store-bought suits. They had visited the barber for a shave and haircut while on the steamboat. They looked much more like gentlemen than mountain men. It surprised Tom that Rufus hadn't had a drink on the boat. They had both spent hours watching the shore and other boats passing. Tom continued to asked his father about the mountains, and Rufus got genuine pleasure from telling his son stories about his years living in them.

The rifles, possible bags, and knives were the only things out of place as Rufus followed Tom through the narrow streets of New Orleans. As they got closer to the home Tom had grown up in, the area began to look more familiar to the mountain man.

The cabin was gone, and a larger house had replaced it. The house where Camille lived looked much the same and had been kept in good repair. Tom led his father to the new house. The young man hesitated and wondered if he should knock after being gone so long. Deciding not to, he opened the door and they walked into the sitting room, where he called to his mother.

Hearing her son's voice, Gabrielle rushed from one of the back rooms and froze in mid-step when she saw a man with her son. Tom's mother was still a beautiful woman. The shock on her face quickly turned to wonder as she asked, "Is that you, Rufus? Have you come back?"

"It is," the mountain man replied. "I am back."

The words brought a smile to Gabrielle's face. It was a smile and face that Rufus had dreamt of many times in the mountains on cold and lonely nights. Unsure of what to do next, the mountain man stood watching as Gabrielle slowly walked over to him, offering her hand. Memories of proper etiquette that had been abandoned in the mountains came back to Rufus. He took her hand, feeling a shiver as he touched the soft skin, and he kissed it.

The urge to grab her and give her a big hug was strong, but Rufus knew that the ways of the saloons would not be tolerated by a woman like Gabrielle. What he did not know was that inside Gabrielle wished he had done so. It was all she could do to refrain from throwing her arms around the man she had longed for these many years.

Then Gabrielle turned to Tom and gave him a hug, holding him close as tears filled her eyes. She had sent him on a mission to bring the amulet to Rufus. It had been as much to have him meet his father as to provide protection for the man she loved. It had been two years since Tom had left, receiving only a letter from him. She had begun to fear that he would not return.

Wiping her eyes with a kerchief, she told her son, "Go and get grandmother Camille, and bring her over here. She must not worry a moment longer."

The young man quickly left the house to get his grandmother. Rufus and Gabrielle were left standing alone in the sitting room. She motioned to him and said, "Please have a seat. I will put on some tea."

The mountain man brushed lightly against her as he headed for the chair. What happened next could not have been stopped as primal desires raced through them as they grabbed each other, holding on for dear life.

Gabrielle broke into tears as Rufus held her, fighting back his own tears. "I thought I would never see you again," she whispered. "Mother said she saw you back in my life but it had been too many years. She made the amulet and I sent our son to find you. I was sure you were both lost to me."

The sound of someone entering the room finally forced them to let go of each other. Again, Gabrielle dabbed her eyes with the kerchief. Rufus looked at the voodoo queen and saw little difference from when he had left. She walked up to him and put her hands on his shoulders.

"You have grown into a fine-looking man," Camille said, smiling. "Several times in the past years you gave me cause for worry, but each time the danger passed."

Thinking of all the times he had felt that the original amulet had saved him, Rufus said, "It was a comfort to know that you were watching over me."

"Then you gave it away," she said, her brow furled. "Another had it and was near death."

"My friend Walter was injured during an attack," Rufus explained. "His leg was broken and he had been scalped."

With a look that she appreciated the explanation, Camille added, "This man has since died. His death was peaceful."

Feeling somewhat uncomfortable in front of this voodoo queen, Rufus replied, "Yes. He died in his sleep just three years ago."

How Camille knew all of this made little sense. It was almost like she had an eye watching the wearer of the amulet. Gabrielle broke in and said, "I was about to make some tea. Would you like some, mother?"

Camille nodded, a look of satisfaction on her face as she observed Rufus.

The three of them sat while Gabrielle went to make the tea. Tom began to tell his grandmother all about his trip west. There was a look of pride as she listened to his account of the search. This continued until Gabrielle brought in the tea.

It was served from a fine tea set, along with a plate of small, shortbread cookies. For years Rufus had drunk out of a pannikin with a large-looped handle. He found it difficult to hold the small tea cup. The tea was served English-style, with milk and sugar. The mountain man sat and enjoyed being surrounded by the two ladies and his son.

With their tea finished, Camille turned again to the mountain man. "Has the name Rufus Pike served you well?"

"It has," he told her. "It has the respect of many a brave, and even the grizzly fear it."

"Now you are just bragging," Camille scolded him gently. "It is a fine name. Do you plan to keep it or will you go back to being called Thomas Wallingford?"

"To be truthful, it is easier to spell and I was figuring on keeping it," Rufus said.

"I am sure that Tom told you that those that were after you are all gone," she said.

"He did," the mountain man replied. "You didn't have something to do with that, did you?" he asked, kiddingly.

Ignoring his question, Camille looked at her daughter. "I have things to do before it gets too late. I would like you and Rufus to come to dinner at my house tonight. It will be something special to welcome the men's return."

"I look forward to it," Gabrielle said.

Standing up, Camille said, "Come with me, Tom. I will need your help."

"Should I change?" he asked his grandmother.

Looking him up and down, she said, "You are dressed just fine."

Bidding Rufus goodbye, they headed out of the house.

As the door closed, Rufus and Gabrielle sat back down. Rufus was too nervous to remain still. He was blaming the feeling on the tea he had drank. "I should take care of the horses and gear. I also have to find a place to stay."

"I have plenty of room here," Gabrielle told him. "Mother has already had someone take care of the animals. Your gear is on the back step. I will help you carry it in."

Rufus helped her bring the dishes and remaining cookies into the kitchen. There, on the back step, was his gear. They collected the items and carried them to one of the bedrooms.

"Will this be satisfactory?" Gabrielle asked him.

Looking around the room, Rufus replied, "This will be fine."

The room was actually very nice. He noticed that it had a double bed that was tastefully made up: Crisp curtains on the window, a lamp next to the bed offering light in the evening, and a delicate wash stand with a pitcher, bowl, mirror and its own candles to provide light. On the wall there was another full-length mirror, and Rufus saw himself for the first time since he had cleaned up. The man he saw had a striking appearance.

He saw Gabrielle come up behind him in the mirror. She put her arms around his middle and breathed softly on his neck as she kissed him. Turning to her, Rufus held her close and kissed her soft, inviting lips.

Suddenly he felt concerned about the desires that were coursing through his body. "Tom or you mother might return," Rufus cautioned the desirable woman in his arms.

"Why do you think mother asked Tom to come and help her?" Gabrielle whispered into his ear.

Over the next hours, Rufus experienced something he hadn't felt since leaving New Orleans. It wasn't two people lusting after each other. He lay with Gabrielle and they experienced love, true love.

That night at dinner, Rufus looked around the table and saw a family. It was a family that he was part of. Tom told his mother, "Rufus . . . my father, was kind enough to make sure I was safe during the trip back. Once he leaves, he promised to come back again."

The conversation at the table halted. After and awkward pause, Camille asked the mountain man, "How long will you be staying before you go back west?"

The mountain man knew that whatever he said, only one answer would prevent pain. It would also end his life as he'd known it for the past 25 years. It had been a life that for most part he had enjoyed. Realizing that everyone at the table was waiting for his reply, Rufus cleared his throat.

"If it is acceptable, I would like to stay here in New Orleans," the mountain man said. A great sigh of relief was felt around the table. "I will have to find a place to stay and hope I will be welcome to visit often."

"Don't be silly," Camille told him. "You can stay right here. I am sure nothing unacceptable will happen."

Over the next few weeks Rufus and Gabrielle spent time getting reacquainted, and soon were planning their wedding, which was blessed by Camille.

Another thing that Rufus learned more about was that those who'd been after him had slowly gone mad before dying. Rumor had it that Camille had cast a spell on them, which Rufus did not doubt.

The mountain man went to find his father's grave. When leaving New Orleans, he would have been in danger had he visited it. The graveyard was in an old part of town. The church that had once stood among the graves was gone. The wooden cross that had once marked the grave was also gone, but Rufus knew its location well enough to stop in the general area. He sat on a large stone that had some scripture chiseled into it and prayed for his father. He prayed that his father had found his mother in heaven.

Another day, while looking for familiar places, he went back to the street where Damas' livery had been located. The man who now owned it remembered Damas. He and Rufus talked about the good old days when the La Maison was still open and Rufus had spent his days in charge of the front porch, hawking customers in.

On the way back he walked to the waterfront and stood in front of his last place of employment in New Orleans. It was still a place to drink and gamble, but it was run-down and seedy-looking. Maybe nothing had really changed in the place, but his memories had it looking bigger and a bit nicer.

Money wouldn't be a problem for Rufus or Tom, and both knew something would come up that they could invest in. In the meantime, it was in a safe place until needed. Rufus offered the amulet back to Camille, telling her that he wouldn't need it to keep him safe any longer.

"It never was to keep you safe," she said. "It was to bring you back to my daughter if you still loved her. Keep it around your neck. It will lead you away if that should ever change."

While Rufus still liked rye whiskey, the days-long drunks were a thing of the past. Cards could still be a problem, so the mountain man suggested that Gabrielle hold onto their money. Reluctantly she did, and she also let it be known that she would put a spell on anyone who cheated her man.

Sitting on the porch listening to the evening sounds, Rufus took Gabrielle's hand and said, "I regret the 25 lost years we could have had together."

"One should not lament on the past, but rather look forward to the years we will have in our future," Gabrielle told him, kissing Rufus softly.

THE WHITE DOG

The white dog in this story was based on the Pyrenean Mountain Dog. It is believed that settlers from France brought them to Canada. They were used to protect livestock from wolves and other predators. While guarding a farmer's stock, it also brought the family members within this shield of protection.

In the case of the shaggy white dog in this story, its master died while traveling the Rocky Mountains. Its devotion to the departed master was so strong that it could not leave the area and was destined to live its life out waiting for its master to return.

www.ingramcontent.com/pod-product-compliance
Lightning Source LLC
Chambersburg PA
CBHW051440260626
47162CB00001B/176